EAST

STUART ROSSON

Published by Stuart Rosson, 2018
stuartrosson@gmail.com

 A catalogue record for this
book is available from the
National Library of Australia

9780648413905 : Paperback

9780648413912 : ebook - mobi

Cover design and execution by Brendan Downs and
Catherine Larsen

Editing, text design and layout by Nan McNab

Printed and distributed by IngramSpark

ACKNOWLEDGEMENTS

Thanks to my amazing boys Sam, Luke and Harry, for their enthusiasm, encouragement and ideas; for their steadfast support and love through thick and thin and for always knowing when to drag me off to go surfing. To my sister, Judy for her unswerving support and belief, and to Nan for thoughtfully and patiently plying the magic of her invisible repairs, of which so many were needed, whilst putting up with my tantrums. Endless appreciation to Fran for all her help, encouragement and expertise throughout and to Fiona for her insightful counsel and always being there to listen and advise. Thanks to Suzanne for banishing me for my own good, so I could get on with it, and to Joanne for her early encouragement and Bruce for his interest and early feedback; to Deanne for getting me out of the house to breathe the sea air; and to Mark for showing me the pelicans. Lastly and with utmost sadness to Bill (RIP) for his generous advice, which provided the last vital piece of the puzzle.

For my mother, Nanette

PROLOGUE

Now he always slept light. A legacy of his nights alone in the desert. Or maybe it was the training camps ... the pre-dawn starts.

The slightest sound would stir him, but this was no possum on the roof. It sounded like the door was off its hinges, boots stomping in the hall, and he heard his mother's thin wail of protest.

After so long away, everything in his mother's house had seemed unaccountably small, but he could still get through the window and drop to the ground in moments. He slid off the sill, landing with a soft crunch on a mound of mulch. Only then did he think about shoes. He scuttled barefoot across the yard and through the wire fence, pausing in the shadow of the lilly pilly.

Up the lane, he could see the manic orange pulse of a military patrol parked in the road. Keeping to the shadows, he bolted down the lane, heading for the scrub, his heart bounding in his chest.

But he didn't even reach full stride before his legs went from under him, lead weights cracking at his ankles, cords binding his shins. He crash-landed in a muddy puddle from last night's rain.

Hauling himself up to his hands and knees he found his legs were locked together by the weighted lariat that had felled him and soon he felt the cold hard tip of a sword or crossbow bolt pricking the nape of his neck.

A jaundiced moon danced murkily in the puddle.

'Elias Arrowsmith?' The voice was low, hoarse, almost solicitous.

'You just missed him.'

A boot stomped between his shoulder blades and his face was in the puddle again. He bucked and twisted to take a breath, the mankiness of the mud filling his nostrils. When he blinked away the muck, he saw a thicket of military jackboots all around him. A lone cricket chirruped in the quiet of the night.

'Try again.' The same harsh voice, challenging and loud.

'Who wants to know?' He coughed and spat.

A dark shape swooped down on him, extinguishing what little light there was.

CHAPTER 1

BARRAK SHOULD'VE KNOWN SOMETHING wasn't quite right.

Was that crisp spring morning a little too perfect? The bay too calm and pristine?

Perhaps.

Even though the day had dawned balmy, there *had* been an electric quality to the air, a barely perceptible threat of calamitous change. Maybe he should've consulted the oracle of the heavens and there he would have seen, plain as day, transiting Uranus – that ruthless harbinger of disruption and upset – lurking on the cusp of his fourth house.

But he hadn't consulted the oracle. He rarely did anymore.

As he watched the sun rising over the bay, he gave himself to the routine of herbal extraction, draining the dark glistening fluid from the spent herbs then adding it to a fresh batch of dried herbs to extract even more of the healing principles.

He walked out onto the small back verandah and up a flight of stairs to the rooftop garden and his beloved chooks. His morning routine: collecting the eggs. At the top of the stairs, did he pause for a few slow, mindful breaths as he gazed out at the sea? Could he have smelled the winds of change in those breaths? Indeed, though he may not have noticed the absence right there and then, he would assert strongly in years to come that there'd been not a single peep from any bird that morning, as he stood on his rooftop surveying the mirrored bay.

And so what should have been an ordinary and forgettable morning was indelibly etched in Barrak's memory, because nothing was ever the same after that day. And yet, strangely, the image that would persist was the shattered remains of Hilary and Hildergard's contribution to his never-to-be-eaten breakfast, gooily leaking on the kitchen floor as his front door burst open to reveal a mud-spattered and barefoot Gracie Arrowsmith, struggling to catch her breath and explain her presence to a startled Barrak Brethrenhope – physician and village delegate to the High Council of Tamouer on Eyre.

Fresh tears welled up, and her plump face, normally so vibrant and rosy, was alarmingly pale in the bright morning light of Barrak's kitchen.

'Councillor, they've taken him—' she croaked, her voice deserting her at the very moment she needed it most. She swallowed forcefully, willing her voice to return.

'They've taken Elias!' she blurted out, her voice now morphed into an unearthly, throaty wail, so unlike Gracie's natural voice it sent a chill through Barrak.

Words tumbled out of her. 'They came just before dawn, Councillor. My boy, he's gone! Gods be merciful, what am I to do?' She sank to her knees as if the stream of words had deflated her. Barrak took her arm and eased her into a nearby chair. A violent shiver ran through her, and he took a blanket from a pile of folded laundry and wrapped it around her.

'Who? Who's taken him, Grace?'

She looked up at him, one hand ensnared in a tangle of hair. 'The Keepers,' she breathed, as if confiding a dark secret. '*They* took him. They broke in. He tried to run, but … Why would they take him?' She stamped a muddied foot under the table. 'What's he done?'

Gracie stared past Barrak's shoulder. 'We thought we'd lost him once before you know, when he ran away as a youngster,' she confided. 'Gone those three long years. Given up hope, we had. But then he came back and it was like a miracle. You remember, don't you, sir? Orlan's grace, he was so grateful for that job you gave him.' Gracie smiled briefly. 'But then he went again … Gods, it near broke my heart! Gone *again* he was for close on two more years.' She looked desperate, confused.

'He'd only just come home, just last Sunday. Turned up out of the blue, all growed up and manly, with a beard and all, and full of all kinds of stories as usual ... But he seemed different somehow ... older; older than his years.' She blinked. 'And then *they* came ... the Keepers!' She eyed Barrak fiercely and sobbed. 'They beat him senseless, Councillor, those swine! And they took him away ... What are they going to do to him?'

Barrak rested a big hand on her shoulder as she sobbed, while he struggled with the implications of the news. The Keepers coming and taking someone away? Surely this was the stuff of legend and myth, the sort of scary story a cruel parent might tell a wayward child. It had never actually happened, not to his knowledge, not in his lifetime. The Keepers of the Light of Orlan were certainly a strange mob, a secret society whose origins went back at least three hundred years to the time of the Great Transformation.

But surely today they were now nothing more than a bunch of old men with funny handshakes and secret meetings. Barrak himself had been approached to join, more than once, but it just wasn't his style.

'What makes you so sure they were Keepers, Gracie?'

'It's what they said, Councillor. And they were military types – had a military patrol parked out the front and all – but when I asked them, "What do you want with him, what's he done?", they didn't say. The nasty-looking one, the leader, he just said, "We are the Keepers of the Light of Orlan."'

There was a long pause, during which they both stared at Barrak's old kitchen table, as if its greasy knots might offer some answers. When Gracie spoke again, her voice was touched with a great weariness. 'Why would they take my boy, Councillor? Why?'

'I don't know Grace, but we're going to find out.'

Abruptly, Gracie's demeanour changed and a wave of relief, almost excitement, passed over her face. 'Oh thank you, sir. My Dan said you'd know what to do, being on the High Council and acquainted with the Lord High Councillor himself. Surely it's all a mistake, don't you think Councillor? A horrible mistake, and once they know Elias has done nothing wrong ...'

Barrak only half listened as he cleaned up the broken eggs and then made Gracie a tea of chamomile and hops to calm her nerves. He gave her a flask of concentrated tinctures to take home – chamomile, oats and vervain to help her sleep, and a drop of attenuated aconite to treat the shock.

As he dispensed the medicines and listened to Gracie, he thought about Elias. In particular, he thought about the many conversations he'd had with him years ago, when he was a young man. And the more he thought about those conversations, the more uneasy he became.

When Barrak had begun to build his house by the bay, the village folk thought he'd gone mad. *A physician building his own house ... What must he be thinking?* But he had been hell-bent on the great endeavour. No point asking why. The idea had burrowed into his marrow and he was bloody well doing it, come hell or high water.

No one questioned him on it, because everyone knew poor Brethrenhope needed the distraction. Not three weeks had passed since he'd lost his wife and son before he launched himself into the project. It was a pure manifestation of denial: that which could not be faced would not be faced, at least not yet. He'd gone directly from funeral arrangements to drawing up plans. Another two months and he had started construction, thus occupying himself so intently that he had given himself no time to think, to grieve, or in any other way process the incalculable catastrophe that had obliterated his family.

It was to be, after all, Persephone's dream house. She had loved the spot, and whenever Barrak stood on the site and looked out across the bay, she stood right there beside him, her voice in his ear, quiet and sure; *This is it Barrak, I love this spot.*

She spoke to him often as he worked on the foundations, encouraging him, advising him, making suggestions. And he talked to her in turn about his latest ideas for the house, musing about how it would look when completed. The clinician in him may have been alarmed, had he been assessing the condition of one of his patients; Barrak seemed to be happily teetering on the brink of madness brought on by irreconcilable grief. Free as a bird and content in his cocoon of denial, he gave himself with abandon to this obsessive pursuit.

He had set about excavating the site and digging post holes furiously for hours without a break until his hands bled and his back was wrenched with spasms, his face and shirt muddied with sweat and dust. He pushed himself on and on like a crazed ascetic seeking enlightenment through suffering. But it was not enlightenment he sought, it was absolution. He threw himself into the task with disgruntled passion and doggedness, almost as if his sweat and pain would combine in some kind of vital alchemy to expunge his guilt and helplessness.

He went on for days, until finally Persephone put a stop to it. *Easy now Barrak, you'll do yourself a mischief,* she chided him gently. *Tamouer wasn't built in a day, you know.*

Gradually, with Persephone's help, he managed to regulate his efforts, and over the weeks and months that followed he began to fit himself more comfortably into his worker's skin. His blisters were replaced with calluses, his back and limbs recovered from the original assault and began to feel strong and taut, and he began to tan.

Thank the gods he had Persephone's level-headed advice to keep him on track. He cherished their conversations, which sometimes seemed to last all day, like the murmuring of waves on the shoreline in the background to his work.

Absorbed by both the task of building his house and the conversations with his dead wife, Barrak could hardly have been expected to notice he was being watched. Especially when the surveillance was being carried out by a wraith of a lad of no fixed abode or profession whose unconventional talent, amongst many others, was to make himself practically invisible, even in broad daylight.

Checking a post he had just braced in position, Barrak was squatting down and sighting up the hill toward his reference post when he noticed the boy, sitting on a tussock in the paddock across the road. Barrak straightened up, squinting, and raised a hand to shade his eyes from the afternoon sun. But already the lad was on his feet, scampering up the hill and away.

The fleeting impression was of a youth with dark, unruly hair and angular features. His clothes seemed out of place – some kind of long coat unsuitable for the early spring weather. As he took off up the hill, he seemed to have a slight limp. It put Barrak in mind of an archetypal villain, swirling his black cloak as he left the stage at the village playhouse.

Barrak stood for some time looking at the crest of the hill over which the boy had vanished and scratched his stubbled chin thoughtfully before returning to his post.

The second time he saw the boy, he was taking a break after setting one of the bigger posts into a deep hole where the land fell away. Staring sightlessly into the middle distance of the shoreline, his eyes had been drawn to a strange shape by the water's edge. He squinted a little and realised it was the dark-haired lad in his peculiar garb, sitting on a rock near the shore.

His first instinct was to throw down his crowbar and strike out down the hill to confront his inquisitive visitor and demand an explanation. But something about the boy's demeanour stopped him. He was like an awkward bird, and Barrak sensed a kind of fragility in him.

A moment later, the boy turned, realised he'd been spotted and froze, holding Barak's gaze for a moment. Barrak lifted a hand and waved casually as if acknowledging the arrival of an unexpected guest. The lad stayed completely still for a moment, then gave the slightest of nods in acknowledgment of Barrak's salute. But a moment later he was away, swooping across the sand for fifty yards in the open before disappearing around a small rocky point just north of what Barrak regarded as his little stretch of beach.

'Bugger me,' Barrak muttered, shaking his head as he loosened his crowbar from the clay.

'You can judge the character of a civilisation by the buildings it erects.'

Absorbed in the task of plumbing the final post, Barrak had been taken completely by surprise. He swung around, cracking his head against a piece of bracing timber. Stifling a curse he staggered on the uneven ground and fell to one knee, his hammer now a stumpy crutch. To make matters worse, his visitor was standing in line with the mid-afternoon sun, its glaring halo casting the figure into silhouette.

His head starting to throb, Barrak could only be sure of two things – one, it was the young man he had seen watching him before and, two, he was laughing.

With a surge of indignation Barrak pushed himself up, looking to spring lithely to his feet and save face. He'd demand an explanation from this young interloper. But he lost his footing in the loose tailings and went down on his backside. All at once, Barrak's anger subsided and he found himself laughing too.

'You look like you could use some help,' said the boy as he stepped forward, securing a foothold and reaching down to help Barrak to his feet. With a grunt of exertion and the boy's help, Barrak was quickly up, brushing off clay dust as he fixed the boy with a sceptical eye.

'What did you say?'

'Looks like you could use some help ... '

'No, before that. Something about building ... '

'Oh. You can judge the character of a civilisation by the buildings it erects. Just a quote from one of the first settlers.'

Barrak gingerly touched his injured head to check for blood and, finding none, gave it a tentative rub, all the while keeping a wary eye on the boy.

'You've been spying on me.'

'Guilty as charged, your honour. Spying is my weakness, I confess.' The boy gave an apologetic shrug. 'But let me tell you, sir, what I have gleaned from my spying. I've ascertained you're a man of great determination, if I might say, in pursuit of the grandest of enterprises, no less than building your own abode—'

'But what are you doing here?'

Barrak immediately rued his interruption because the boy's face sagged at the rebuff. Clearly he was just trying to impress. He fixed

Barrak with a critical stare. 'As I said, sir, it appears you could do with some help.'

'Are you asking me for a job?' Barrak straightened and put his hands to his hips. 'Is that what this is about?'

'Elias Arrowsmith, at your service.' The boy's face broke into a broad grin and, to Barrak's bemusement, he bowed, an elaborate gesture of supplication that was so out of place on Barrak's ramshackle work site, it made Barrak laugh again, in spite of himself.

CHAPTER 2

JASMYN OPENED ONE EYE, her face still comfortably cocooned in the downy softness of her favourite pillow. Moonlight filtered through the oak tree outside her bedroom window, giving a curious, luminous glow to the satin throw cushions aligned along the window seat.

There it was again! Jarringly loud in the stillness of the night, *crack*, against the window pane, then a clatter as the pebble came to rest on the balcony. She threw back the covers and crept toward the window, bobbing and weaving to get a clear view through the shadows of the oak leaves.

Orlan's ghost! Her heart skipped as his big blond head shot up over the balustrade, flashing his trademark grin. He vaulted onto the verandah with a theatrical flourish and too much damn noise. Jasmyn was already out the French doors and had him by the shirt sleeve like a schoolboy, dragging him inside.

'You idiot!' she whispered. 'What are you ... sixteen?' She flung him away. 'What the hell are you doing here?'

'I had to come, Jazz. I can't stand it. I had to see you.' One hand was stretched toward her, palm up. Rufus had his puppy-dog face on.

'And did you bring your wife?' Jasmyn made a show of peering out over the balcony to see if anyone was climbing up the tree after him, then flashed him a withering glare. It had little effect. He was on her again, grabbing her arms and pulling her toward him.

'Don't be like that, Jazz. I can't sleep, can't think.'

'Quest's sake, keep your voice down!' She shoved him across

15

the room. Her petite stature belied the strength and coordination conferred on her by long years of martial arts training, insisted upon by her father. And when she was aroused, as she was beginning to be now, she could centre herself with such alacrity and precision that her power intensified to giddying heights. She knew he loved that in her. They all did.

As their eyes met, his look of indignation was replaced with a grin. He licked his lips and came at her again. She rolled her shoulder and batted him aside. She hadn't finished with him yet.

'Why would you come here? Gods! My father's downstairs. Do you know what he'd do if he found you here?'

'I don't care.'

'He'd string your guts out along the city walls.'

'Jasmyn ... '

'And all the better, he'd say, for you being a senator.'

'But Jazz ... '

The pantomime had run its course and done its job. The delicate dance of disdain honed her desire and heightened her senses. And it drove him crazy, putting a delicious edge to his infatuation.

Now she let him take her.

She tensed in his arms and pushed against him for a moment, one last struggle. His hot breath was on her neck and she caught a faint nutty smell. She mused for a moment that he might have been snacking on acorns on his way up the tree and the image helped her to hold on for one last moment.

She'd let him sleep for a while, but now she was determined to have him back down the tree and away before first light. The milkman came at some ungodly hour, and wouldn't that be a memorable sight for the old coot as he juggled his bottles – the honourable gentleman clambering down from a window of the Lord High Councillor's grand manor.

She dug her elbow into his ribs one more time, not quite as gently as the last.

Now he stirred.

'Is the senator entirely satisfied with my submission?' Jasmyn enquired delicately, as she propelled a series of perfectly formed smoke rings through a shaft of moonlight falling over the foot of the bed.

Rousing himself and sitting up, Senator Rufus Seaworthy gave an appreciative grin and nodded emphatically.

'Where do you get those bloody things? You do know how illegal they are, don't you?'

'I'm giving up,' Jasmyn declared, gazing fondly at the thin cheroot as she rolled it between her thumb and index finger, before sending another ring rolling and wobbling to ruin itself on Rufus's ear. 'It's getting early. You'd best be off.'

It was the most delicious hour, a wrinkle in time, where all transgressions could be forgiven. The morning sunlight ignited the leaves of the oak and bathed her entire bedroom in a green and golden glow. Jasmyn luxuriated between the silk sheets, arching her back and swishing her legs as she relived the sensation of Rufus's hot rush of vitality inside her. She smiled at the thought of him clambering up the old oak to reach her and then laughed out loud.

Fully awake now she began to feel the first pangs of remorse about yet another impetuous liaison which, she had to admit, was not likely to end any better than the others. *How the hell does it happen?* Jasmyn flung back the sheets and got up. She stepped toward the glass doors of the balcony and looked out across the bay. It was calm and shimmering. The morning was so clear, it looked as if she could reach out and touch the old city across the bay. A cargo ship was docking at one of the wharves and she could even make out the big elms lining the town square in front of the parliament.

Did she mean to do it? It had happened in an instant – she knew that much. One glance and he was gone. She had been giving a submission to the senate planning committee, right over there in the great hall of the parliament, not two months ago. He was a new senator from Silvendale. They had locked eyes somewhere between current trends and progressions, and that was it.

It wasn't her fault, surely. Perhaps the planets were partially to blame. After all, as assistant to the High Council's Chief Astrologer, who could invoke celestial fate if she couldn't? And transiting Pluto was conjunct her Black Moon after all. All that intensity plumbing the murky depths of her moon in Scorpio … *yikes*. Lilith, the Black Moon, primordial earth goddess, temptress, succubus, purveyor of dark sexual energy. Lilith, who thought it might be a good idea for Eve to tempt Adam with the apple. But was that really Jasmyn? Perhaps; especially just recently, with that inscrutable god of the underworld and power-monger of all the gods locked in unholy communion with her Black Moon.

Surely, then, Jasmyn was not to blame if some of that energy was projected onto an unsuspecting and naive senator from the sticks, who had never before encountered such a heady mixture of feminine power nor stared into eyes so bright with mischief, so dark with sensuality and as hypnotic as black opal.

Though the morning was warm, Jasmyn suddenly felt a chill. Goosebumps. She snatched her robe from the bedpost and wrapped it around herself tightly, hugging the soft fleece to her naked body. She really should shower and put on her make-up, but she was in no hurry. It was her habit to breakfast late, preferring to be quite sure her father had left the house before going downstairs. And Alissa always made sure to keep her something nice.

Instead she snuggled herself into the window seat, surrounded by cushions. The view across the bay filled her with such a mixture of feelings. Since early childhood it had been a place of refuge and daydreams, but nostalgia for the place had lately given way to regret and dissatisfaction.

There were times she felt like a caged animal, smelling the jungle through gilded bars. Twenty-seven years old, her biological clock was pounding away more loudly with each passing year. Here she was, still living at home with her father and mother – the dark lord of procrastination and his doleful consort – living a life, let's not forget, of shameless luxury and privilege, in blatant contravention of at least half a dozen of Orlan's Principles.

She'd made her choices, although it had sometimes seemed there were none to make: astrologer, the most respected of all professions, theoretically one that all could aspire to. In reality, only a few of the most well-connected and moneyed were ever accepted into the degree of esoteric studies at the University of Natural Sciences. Her place, of course, had been assured. And now she was being groomed for the top job in the business, Chief Astrologer to the High Council. Her apprenticeship probably only had another twenty years to go.

At least she had had her way in one important respect. From the earliest age she had bridled at being treated as breeding stock for some well-connected family. By sixteen she had become expert at dispatching the suitors her father sent her way, and she'd done so with such ruthless efficiency the memories still made her wince. She would flirt with them shamelessly, inflaming their desires, doing them over with her eyes, making them sweat like stallions and sometimes, if it suited her, she might even have sex with them just to spice the pot before cutting them off at the knees and crushing their hearts.

Once the eligible suitors dried up and her father, Enoch, had given up on her, Jasmyn had replaced them with a continuous supply of bad boys and miscreants. Some she actually liked. Some lasted a while. But ultimately they all went the same way. It was like an itch that just had to be scratched, but once it had been, her passion dissolved and she was compelled to move on.

She realised that her plans had backfired somewhat, leaving her at almost thirty stranded like a maiden in the tower of the family castle. Perhaps she was too attached to her life of privilege and independence. Perhaps the idea of striking out in search of the new life she craved so much scared her more than she liked to admit.

Was she the hypocrite? Could be a family trait.

Strangely enough, her senator was probably the closest she had come to someone who could meet her father's criteria, apart from his inconvenient wife. All the more reason to keep him a secret. Besides, she'd sensed that familiar detachment creeping in as they made love just hours before. Poor old Rufus had run his race. *Prophet's mercy ...*

She wondered if one day she would start biting their heads off when she'd finished with them.

Feeling a bit peckish, Jasmyn headed for the shower and a new day.

Barrak slammed his front door and checked the latch, before slinging his carryall over his shoulder and making his way up the garden path. Outside the gate he paused and checked his watch, rolling his wrist back and forth a few times, absently testing the winding mechanism. Since Gracie's startling appearance the previous morning, Barrak had become increasingly concerned. By day's end, his unease had increased to the point where he had booked his passage on the next day's mid-morning ferry to Tamouer.

He'd been neglecting his duties as a councillor for some time. He might have been forgiven his truancy at first, given his tragic circumstances, but finally his friend and mentor, Enoch, the Lord High Councillor himself, had given him a quiet warning. There'd been rumblings around the council about his absence. At first Barrak thought it a little ironic. As one of the youngest members of the High Council, he'd often noticed that some of his esteemed colleagues seemed to view the council chamber as a nice quiet place for a nap. It was a wonder they'd even noticed his absence.

But now was the time to make amends. It was the spring equinox, the Festival of Orlan on Sunday, followed by the opening of the spring session of parliament on Monday, the ceremonial start to the political year, with a joint sitting of the Senate and the High Council: he'd better be there, attend the opening session at least, maybe even go to the festival.

Gracie's visit had decided him. He would go up a few days early and make some discreet enquiries about Elias, make some sort of attempt to reconnect with his network of colleagues and friends in the city.

He had not slept well. In the early hours he'd awoken, cold and clammy, his heart pounding with stark images still flaring in his mind's eye. A classic nightmare, all darkness and stormy weather, clattering hooves and sweating beasts. He'd been transported back in time, to the days of the Transformation, with the Keepers abroad in the land. Running scared through his inner landscape, he'd been fleeing and hiding, harrowed by spectres with ill intent, but not toward himself it seemed, rather towards someone he was trying to protect, someone he held dear, but couldn't quite identify.

Later, as he lay panting and staring wide-eyed at the ceiling, caught somewhere between consciousness and sleep, it had hit him like a punch, he'd been trying to protect his son, a grown-up version of his son, Noah. Little Noah, forever five years old in his memory, but resurrected and somehow grown to maturity in the lurid confusion of his rambling nightmare. No wonder he had been frantic to protect him from the marauding Keepers of yesteryear. Barrak's tears had flowed then, in the small desperate hours, until his pillow was as drenched as his sweat-soaked bedsheet.

Standing on the grassy verge outside his house he shuddered at the recollection of his nightmare and scanned the esplanade for his ride. Most of the houses in his street hadn't been there five years earlier, when he'd started his house. It was a brand-new housing sector then, set out along part of the shoreline reclaimed from the margin of the wetlands extending to the west. Rarely did land become available this close to the water; it had all been snapped up quickly, and now the only vacant ground was the wedge of land planted with fruit and nut trees, directly opposite his house. The wedge of orchard doubled as a corridor, allowing access to the obligatory ten-acre village comfarm plot, which was the main urban production unit for his sector. Similar corridors radiated in all directions, most planted with food-bearing trees, bushes or vines.

Looking east along the esplanade, Barrak could see where the new estate finished and the older part of the town began. At the far end of the esplanade, nestled in the lee of the headland, was the old township, some of it dating back to ancient times when Rylanswood was a health spa for the earliest inhabitants of the capital, Tamouer, 160 miles to the north.

The oldest part consisted of a cluster of manor houses, inns and villas near the river mouth and along the western side of the headland. While most of the old town had been given over to upscale eateries, expensive B and Bs and trendy coffee houses, the village square still had its original cobblestones, and the old spa resort and one of the old taverns had been preserved and restored.

The original old town had been a tiny fishing village, at the south-western extreme of the Eyrean Sea. It was the most distant coastal settlement from the capital, a good eight hours by ferry. Gradually over time it had grown, in layers, like a tree. At its heart, the ancient spa gave it a unique character, then, as farming spread to the south, the population expanded and changed. Later, mining booms sparked by the discovery of useful minerals in the mountains to the west and south-east, made it the commercial hub of the south. Eventually the old spa town around Point Prudence grew to become the key provincial town of the southern region, the third largest town in all of Eyre, named Rylanswood after one of the founding fathers.

'Who've we got 'ere then? You'd be the one ordered a convec, sir?'

Barak hadn't noticed the quietly humming convec pull up behind him, with something of a miracle too, a polite connie. Instead of just blasting his horn he was out of his vehicle and stowing Barrak's bag in the back of the black four-seater, a classic model with tinted windows, leather upholstery and polished timber trim inside.

His driver's name was Mylo, a master of interrogation. Before they had even reached the outskirts of Rylanswood, he had extracted from Barrak more information than he would normally have disclosed to any but his closest friends. Mylo had established his intended destination, the Sol Ferry terminal at Westhaven, the length of his intended absence, and where he would be staying in Tamouer.

As Mylo eyed him discreetly in the rear-view mirror, it occurred to Barrak there was something in the inquisitive driver's gentle brown eyes that helped to make him such an artful interrogator. There was a depth of understanding in those eyes that bore witness to his experience of human striving and suffering. These were eyes that could be trusted with secrets and with matters of the heart. In addition, there was something in Mylo's posture at the wheel – erect and alert yet relaxed at the same time, with a slight tilt of the head – that somehow inspired confidence, expressed empathy, and an openness to shared experience.

Before they were more than a few miles along the coastal highway, Mylo had a synopsis of Barrak's life's story, expressed his great admiration for Barrak's profession and position, learned of his terrible bereavement and expressed his heartfelt condolences, marvelled at Barrak's resilience and his adaptability in constructing his own dwelling. And, for the record, Mylo had wished him a well-deserved turn-for-the-better in his fortunes, which he calculated would be pretty much guaranteed according to the laws of karma as he understood them. To balance the ledger and keep the conversation rolling, Mylo had divulged to Barrak a little of his own story and had even asked for Barrak's professional opinion on a nagging medical condition.

But Mylo's greatest gift as a driver (and interrogator) was divining the exact point in the course of a journey at which to shut up. Depending on circumstances and passengers, this could be the very moment the customer's backside hit the leather, or the conversation might roll on, amiably waxing and waning, ricocheting from topic to topic until the final destination had been reached. More often, he and his passenger realised at some point, that sufficient intimacies had been shared to create a sense of travelling solidarity, so that a comfortable and amiable silence would sustain the remainder of the journey.

And so, as he and his driver fell silent, Barrak allowed himself to relax into the cushioned comfort of the convec's back seat. A willing captive of Mylo's speeding fishbowl, he gazed out at the midday-bright rural landscape as it flashed past. At one point, the passing pylons of a wind farm created a slow rhythmic strobe effect in the convec, lulling him into a dozy state of detachment. At the end of the wind farm, a road sign flashed by: *Rubyvale Power Station.*

As Barrak dozed, a childhood memory bubbled to the surface of his consciousness, of the obligatory school trip to the tidal ramparts at Rubyvale. He remembered being herded into the underground chambers with his schoolmates and how oppressive it had felt. As they descended into the bowels of the beast, the air was filled with roaring and whooshing sounds echoing through the acoustically peculiar rocky chambers. They were shown a massive turbine ensconced within one of the mighty ramparts, of which there were seven spaced evenly across the gorge. He remembered seeing incomprehensible diagrams of the great shell-like inlets built into the outer walls of the ramparts and the networks of tunnels and ducts that captured and focused the force of each surge, to drive the turbines.

How the ancients had conceived such a grand apparatus was impossible to imagine. Built by the first settlers some six hundred years earlier, it was a marvel of ancient engineering. Perched on a low cliff, it overlooked Edwyn's Gorge, where the Eyrean Sea narrowed to just half a mile across, and converged with the Southern Passage to create powerful tidal surges known as The Rip – dangerously unpredictable and the bane of local fishermen.

But the ancients had seen the potential in harnessing the surges through the gorge to generate power for their fledgling settlements. Building the ramparts and the power station was a huge undertaking. Barrak remembered one craggy history teacher trying to impress his charges with the scale of the enterprise, which had taken thirty years.

A bump in the road brought Barrak back into the present and he cracked open the window to get some air. But before long he was dozing again.

Now images from the previous night's dream returned. Another face crystallised before him. This one was a real person, someone he knew all too well, who had been masquerading in his dream all along, as one of the ancient and malevolent Keepers. He realised with a jolt that it was Manson Meldrick, the High Council's Head of Security.

Meldrick was urbane but intense. Persephone had disliked him with an intensity that was foreign to her, a woman who normally found good in everybody. His dark, brooding intensity, which she said some women found attractive, was downright sinister and disturbing to her.

24

'He's like a snake,' Persephone had once observed. This was the man Barrak might ultimately have to confront to get to the bottom of the disappearance of Elias. His inner voice, which more often than not still manifested itself as Persephone's delicate whispering, was growing louder and more persistent by the moment.

Be careful Barrak. Watch your step.

A drop of blood detached itself from the tip of Elias's nose and seemed to hang suspended before splashing into a pool of sundry bodily fluids. Elias stared at the familiar pattern of the linoleum floor. He recognised it, he knew it well; it was his mother's kitchen floor and seeing it filled him with a child-like euphoria. Safe and sound, he could smell his favourite meal cooking and thought he could hear his mother humming a tune he almost knew . . .

But Elias was puzzled. No, no . . . it was not his mother's kitchen. He was face down on a padded table, his eyes peering at the floor through the face hole. *Had he dozed off? And what sort of massage makes a mess like that on the floor?*

His head was spinning, aching and throbbing as if it were bound too tightly. He tried to lift his head out of the face hole, only to find there *was* a tight band around it, pushing his face hard into the opening, making his head pound. Next, he noticed his hands and feet were fastened to the table somehow. And he was cold and wet. Shivering.

The facts of his painful reality gradually became clear. Panic seized him. He bucked on the table, arching his back and pulling at the restraints, but only for a moment because the pain of it knocked the air from his lungs and he collapsed, deflated and prostrate, lashed to the table like prey. He tried to relax, tried to stare down the panic, tried to take long slow breaths. But even as he tried, more details of his predicament were coming back to him. All this had happened before and would happen again.

Had he fainted, passed out, fallen asleep?

He knew sleep was unlikely. He was stuck here, and had been forever. He now knew why he was wet and cold.

The next one was coming.

You could never tell when it would fall but it would fall, as relentless and inexorable as night. And that was another thing, there was no longer any night; that had been taken from him too. The harsh and hateful glare of the cold fluorescent light had been with him, seemingly forever.

It had become unbearable, but that was a lifetime ago. He began to moan and sob all over again. The drops had, little by little, laid his brain bare, shattered and dissolved his skull. Surely the next one would pierce his brain and finally end his suffering. But no, it wasn't true, he was delirious, they were just drops of water, each one worse than the last.

That was the point.

At first he thought it was a joke. Water torture? Is that what this is supposed to be? Then he became irritated, angry. Then the drops began to jar and hurt. Inevitably, unbelievably, each drop fell harder than the last.

Gravity and physics were no longer playing by the rules and neither was time.

Sometimes they felt like a hammer, sometimes like a nail or spike being driven into his head, but that wasn't the worst of it, the worst part was the waiting, the anticipation. Time had lost its composure, bending and twisting, stopping and starting … it could no longer be trusted. Sometimes, what might have been only minutes could stretch on and on, seemingly for hours. Elias thought he could sense the next drop forming, hear it falling, but still it wouldn't come. He would bellow and screech, raging uncontrollably, using the weight of his body to try to wrench the table from its moorings, swearing and cursing with words he was surprised he even knew.

Alternately he sobbed and begged and cried like a baby, drooling and dribbling into his own personal puddle.

'Turn it off.'

Was this the voice inside his head, repeating its constant refrain? *Turn it off. Please, please … turn it off.*

No. Wait. This was a voice outside his head, and the only voice that existed outside his head in this, his abysmally altered reality, was that of his inquisitor, Brown Shoes. There were footsteps, more than one set, and a chair scraping across the floor. Elias tensed, waiting for the blows, but none came. Brown Shoes had positioned himself beside Elias's head, his stylish brogues just clear of Elias's puddle. Elias recoiled at the sensation of hot breath on his ear as the man spoke, his syrupy smooth tone belying the malicious intent he'd already amply demonstrated.

'Enjoying your stay with us so far, Elias?'

Elias bucked and strained, grunting his response.

'You know, Toby tells me water restrictions have been lifted, isn't that right Toby?' There was no reply. 'Above average spring rains. Dams full. Unlimited supplies, use as much as you like, say the water authorities.'

Brown Shoes' tone changed to a low conspiratorial whisper and, disconcertingly, came even closer to Elias's ear. 'I'm a patient man, Elias. We can go on like this as long as you like, it's neither here nor there to me. But is there really any need for more of this unpleasantness?'

Elias saw no reason to change his strategy. It was the same strategy that he'd started with when his head was a lot clearer, and he assumed it was still the best one. *If I tell them truth, they will thank me very much and kill me. If I tell them a pack of lies and they believe me, they will express their gratitude likewise. If I tell them a pack of lies and they don't believe me that will only anger them ... Better, therefore, to just play dumb.*

'You know I have a right to ask you these questions and it is your obligation to provide us with answers. Your travel documents are a mess. Great slabs of time outside the inner boundaries unaccounted for ... unauthorised border crossings ... suspected travel into the forbidden zones, apparently for quite lengthy periods, on at least one occasion. These are serious charges, Elias, but they can be mitigated if you provide us with some of the details we seek.

'You see, we already know what you've been doing, the gist of it anyway. And we have a pretty fair idea why and with whom, as well. We have our own very good sources you know. In the end it comes down to tidying up the paperwork, dotting some i's and crossing some t's, not such a big deal, really. Give us some of those details and I promise you it will improve your situation.'

Brown Shoes' voice was gradually acquiring a brittle edge as if the strain of civility was taking its toll. But Elias was concentrating on a blood clot that seemed to be working its way down the back of his throat from his sinuses.

'Ultimately you will tell us what we want to know, Elias. It's up to you how much of a meal you want to make of it . . . '

At that moment, Elias hawked the blood clot with a largely involuntary gagging cough, and with a deft flick of the lower jaw, sent the blob of bloody mucous spinning onto the toe of Brown Shoes' left foot.

There was a moment of deafening silence.

The screech of the chair across the floor was ear-splitting but abbreviated before Elias heard it smash and clatter against the far wall at the same time as Brown Shoes stifled a howl of exasperation.

'Fool! Gods damn you. Let it be on your own head then. Toby, take him downstairs. Clearly he requires a more robust means of persuasion. We'll let Angus have a crack at him, see if he can do any better than your feeble efforts here.' With that, Brown Shoes was out the door, awkwardly trying to scrape his shoe on the door jamb as he went and leaving Toby and Elias to work out between themselves the details of Elias's escalating interrogation.

CHAPTER 3

BARRAK STOOD ON THE ferry's upper deck as it approached the harbour. The sea was a sapphire mirror, incongruously dark under the vivid blaze of colour engulfing the western sky. He watched the low headland of Cape Byron slip by as the ferry turned for the breakwater, and his attention was drawn to Tamouer's stately manors nestled along its edge, enjoying views of the bay and the distant western ranges beyond.

As the ferry chugged against the tide, the manicured lawns glowed fluorescent green in the last rays of the sun, which flashed gaudy orange across large windows, all aligned for the spectacular scenery and tinted to ameliorate exposure to the westering sun. The sky was infused with fingers of orange and red and washed with a soft palette that graduated imperceptibly from yellows through greens, pale blues and violets to a deep slaty blue above the headland.

As the sky darkened, the lights of the city created their own galaxy in the still, dark waters of the harbour. But what had drawn Barrak out onto the chilly deck was not the twinkling lights of the city, nor the sunset itself, but another natural spectacle playing out in the western sky. The saw-toothed silhouette of the western ranges was marked by an eerily enlarged crescent moon hanging directly above the highest point, Angel's Peak. Nearby was beautifully bright Venus, and smouldering Mars, setting in close conjunction.

Barrak was mesmerised. The many possible astrological implications of the convergence were lost on him because the sight of it was so striking. It evoked a vague sense of foreboding, too, because somewhere beyond the grasp of his conscious mind lurked a memory of a similar dusk, which preceded a calamity worse than he could have ever imagined.

These days when he travelled alone to Tamouer for council business, he preferred to take the late evening ferry, which allowed him to sleep through most of the trip and arrive at dawn. This allowed him time for a leisurely breakfast before starting on whatever had brought him to the city. And to be honest, it suited his frugal nature, saving him the expense of a hotel for one night.

When Persephone had travelled with him it was different. She had always preferred the early-morning ferry that got them in around mid-afternoon. 'Welcome to the Sapphire City!' Barrak remembered her yelling with playful glee, as they sailed into the sparkling harbour on a clear, blue summer day, seemingly aeons ago.

How different the city looked to Barrak this day, as the ferry edged toward the ancient sea-worn dock in the grubby gloaming.

Jasmyn liked to work late. She often arrived at the academy just before or even after lunch. Her afternoons were soon gobbled up answering mail, dealing with students and all the other intrusions that kept her from her research. When the academy had emptied itself she would sometimes go down to the café strip opposite the university for some food and good coffee to sustain her through her night-time travail. There she would blend in with the mishmash of students and other young people gathering to socialise, eat and drink in the cafes and pubs. Along Jeserary Way, on the river side of the university campus, the atmosphere was always boisterous and vibrant. It made her feel like a student again, and it did her ego good to know she could still pass for an undergraduate and attract interested looks from the male students frequenting the alfresco eateries with their young girlfriends.

On this occasion, Jasmyn was a little more focused: she had a lot to do. She'd already eaten and by seven o'clock she was back in her office, on the second floor of the main academy building. Seemingly palatial when she first moved into it, her office had over the years taken on an ambience of cluttered homeliness with a mix of furniture and exotic bric-a-brac, and her personal effects interspersed with a chaotic peppering of files, charts and student papers. In truth it was her second home.

A large picture window gave a view of the academy's eastern gardens and the towers of the old city wall. Beyond that were the cafes and pubs nestled along the river at the back of the university. Her large, leather-topped desk was positioned so her back was to the window, to stop her becoming distracted by the view. In reality, she spent a lot of time with her back to her desk, as she was now, pondering the best way to sum up her spring equinox presentation to the High Council.

'Good evening, Jasmyn.'

She didn't exactly jump, but her heart skipped a beat or two and she let out a small and embarrassingly girlish gasp before swinging her chair around to face her visitor, whose voice she had already recognised. Manson Meldrick, Head of the Combined Security Forces, was effectively the man in charge of the entire region's armed forces. Meldrick, Jasmyn knew, had romantic designs on her and had done for a very long time. It made her skin crawl.

'Gods, Commissar, you nearly frightened the life out of me.'

Meldrick had positioned himself midway between Jasmyn's desk and the doorway, as if to block her exit should she feel an urge to bolt. He held his black leather officer's cap at his side, the gold and blood-red insignia gleaming as it caught the low light of her desk lamp; his other hand was on his hip, just above the ornate silver guard of his sword. She supposed he was trying to affect a casual but authoritative pose, but all he managed, in her judgement, was to look weird and effeminate. He was a few inches taller than Jasmyn, but still slightly below average. His pale complexion seemed almost jaundiced in the subdued light and his dark hair looked oily. He gave her a crooked smile, which took quite some effort to arrange on a face more used to showing disdain.

Immaculately turned out as always, in his black leather uniform with red epaulets and insignia, Meldrick no doubt fancied himself a dashing figure. A good friend had once confided that she was attracted to him,

31

but maybe she just had a thing for men in uniform. Jasmyn didn't. In her profession and in her personal life, she was more concerned about the inner man. She had learnt to trust her intuition when it came to divining the deeper urges that ruled the hearts of men. In the case of Meldrick, he had always failed muster completely.

'You're out late tonight Commissar. Is there something I can do for you?' Her tone was professional, polite, with a warm, friendly inflection.

Meldrick tilted his head slightly and raised one eyebrow, his smile widening into something akin to a lascivious leer. 'Well, there's a leading question if ever I heard one. Do you really want me to answer that, Jasmyn?'

Jasmyn was hard-pressed not to roll her eyes at his thinly veiled innuendo, the kind a schoolboy might find clever. She tried a polite smile but it felt like a sneer. Meldrick gave a brief humourless chuckle before his smile abruptly vanished.

'But surely it's late to be still working, Jasmyn?'

'Well, I like the peace and quiet. You'd be amazed how much you can get done when there's no one around to interrupt you. I'm not breaking any by-laws am I, Manson?' she added cheekily. Few would dare address Meldrick by his first name, but Jasmyn used the licence conferred by her father's position with careless abandon.

Meldrick seemed to brighten at her use of his name. 'Purely concerned for your safety, Jasmyn. You know, the lights all on … front door unlocked … no security at all, really.' His voice took on a condescending tone. 'You know things are not what they once were in the city. It's becoming less and less safe to walk the streets at night. And if you're still in the habit of walking home along the Beach Road promenade … '

'If it's late, I usually take a convec.' Jasmyn's tone was appeasing, but inwardly she was more than a little annoyed that her personal habits were known to Meldrick.

'Good, good. You see, I'd be concerned … personally, if anything should happen to you.' He held her gaze a little too long until Jasmyn looked away.

'We've increased our patrols in the city at night, but still. It's the insurgents, you know, troublemakers and criminals all of them … anarchists,' he added, with a peculiar, distracted expression that came and went. 'We'll be taking steps to put them out of business very soon, but in the meantime … '

'Well, don't worry, I'm always very careful,' she said emphatically, trying to wind up the conversation.

'Excellent.' He nodded several times, but stood his ground, fixing Jasmyn with a cryptic stare. Instead of taking his leave, he stepped forward and put a hand on the desk, craning his neck slightly to look down at the charts she had spread across it. 'So what *are* you working on so late?'

'I'm quite busy actually. Zaira is away, so that means I'll be delivering the spring equinox address to the council. Big responsibility and, to be frank, I'm on a pretty tight deadline.'

He ignored her unsubtle hint, reached over and turned one of the hand-drawn charts toward him, examining it with mock interest. 'So what's going on with the planets right now? Anything I should know about?'

Jasmyn was getting annoyed. Bad enough that he had invaded her privacy and spoiled the sanctity and solitude of her late-night work ritual; worse that he'd clearly had his henchmen spying on her; and now he was in her personal space and even had his grubby little hands on her charts. Only a slow deep breath stopped her from making the kind of acerbic remark that would've let Meldrick know just how much she despised him. Instead, she leaned forward over the desk and spun the chart back to face her. 'Hmm, let me see, well, there's a Uranus–Saturn opposition … Could be some unrest,' she said, glancing up at Meldrick.

'Well, we've certainly had some of that already,' he agreed, easing his buttock onto the edge of her desk, his sword clunking against the polished blackwood. 'Tell me more.'

Jasmyn knew he had little interest in the planets, but she humoured him anyway. 'This,' she gestured at the chart, 'represents an archetypal urge for change within the collective consciousness, likely to be at odds with conservative forces and traditional structures. This particular aspect has been around for a while, waxing and waning for the last few months, so it probably corresponds with an upswing in all these protests and so on.'

Meldrick didn't really seem to be listening to what Jasmyn said, but instead stared disconcertingly at her lips as she spoke. 'Amazing. You know, that's precisely what's been happening. How extraordinarily clever.'

He was off her desk now and had started to move around to the side of it. Jasmyn pushed her chair back and spun it around, moving back and away from him as he rounded the desk. She began to feel a little panicked. Any moment she could imagine the situation degenerating into a theatrical farce, with Meldrick chasing her around and around the desk.

'You know, Jasmyn, there's something I've been meaning to ask you.' He was advancing toward her as she backed toward the door of her ensuite bathroom. *Orlan's breath, here it comes.*

'Commissar ... excuse me, sir. I'm sorry to interrupt.' A young trooper had materialised in the doorway, unnerved by the terrifying duty of interrupting his supreme commander. 'Urgent message from Colonel Motlov,' he blurted. 'They've made an arrest, sir, downtown, sir ... the colonel insisted we fetch you right away.'

Jasmyn's sigh of relief was audible to both Meldrick and the young trooper, who stood twitching like a frightened chicken in the doorway. Meldrick scowled at his underling then glanced back at Jasmyn with a look of frustration tinged with resentment at her all-too-obvious relief. The cowering trooper didn't know where to look as Meldrick strode toward him and snatched the note from his hand.

'I'm terribly sorry, Ms Mooney. Urgent business, I'm afraid. Perhaps we should continue our discussion at a later date. Next week over lunch, perhaps?' He didn't even pause for a reply. 'I'll ask my secretary to schedule a time.' Meldrick attempted a casual smile. 'I'm leaving a man down in the foyer until you're ready to leave. He'll arrange transportation home whenever you require. Goodnight, Ms Mooney.'

Meldrick strode past his trembling subordinate as if he might just as easily have walked straight through him, leaving Jasmyn to sink into her office chair, hands clasped over her mouth. 'Orlan's blood,' she breathed with a long sigh.

The night was balmy and still. It was only two city blocks, more or less, from the dock to the Plaza Hotel where Barrak had booked a room. He worked his way up the wide pedestrian mall on time-worn cobbles, under the dim illumination of a row of street lamps alternating with large palms in planter boxes. Working his way past the dour edifice of the Port Authority he found himself keeping pace awkwardly with a lone ruran weighed down by an over-stuffed animal hide sack and a wicker cage housing a live chicken. He wondered where all the other ferry passengers had gone.

At Station Street the city came alive with pedestrians spilling out of the railway station and merging with the remnants of peak-hour traffic on the main street running east–west along the bottom of Tamouer's central business district. This had once been the heart of the ancient city known as Orlan's Keep. Large sections of the old town's ancient fortifications, lovingly restored by the City Trust, could still be found in the parks and gardens in quiet corners of the modern city.

Over the centuries, city planners had tried to impose an orderly structure on the jumbled plazas and narrow laneways of the old town. Their success or otherwise was hard to gauge, but the overall effect was an unexpectedly happy marriage of order and chaos. Large established trees along the major thoroughfares and public spaces, together with sensitive development to accommodate and complement the ancient architecture, gave the old town precinct a rustic, utilitarian charm.

Running right through the centre of it all was Orlan's Boulevard, a wide tree-lined thoroughfare starting modestly enough by the customs houses at the western end of the city and extending to the grand Providence Arch at the north-eastern edge of the old city limits. Beyond the arch, the boulevard swept south, past the sports stadium on one side and the hospital on the other before crossing the Clare River near the university and eventually running into Beach Road and on down to the salubrious suburbs of Cape Byron.

His hotel was on Orlan's Boulevard. To get there, Barrak had simply to cut through the town square and the temple gardens and up to the boulevard. Marching through the square, he threaded through knots of folk out enjoying the mild spring evening. He saw a young couple throwing coins into the Prophet's fountain as he passed, and a young boy on the other side trying to fish them out with a stick. A young couple were oblivious to Barrak's passing as they embraced under the sightless gaze of Orlan the Resolute, twelve feet high and frozen in bronze.

From the square, Barrak cut across into the temple gardens, making for an old landmark, like a pilgrim intent on observing the stations of his faith. It was an old gingko tree down in the southern corner of the temple grounds. The tree was as old as Tamouer itself and it was where he and Persephone had first kissed. Barrak eased his bag off his shoulder and let it fall to the ground. He leaned a hand against the great gnarled trunk and imagined he could feel the ancient life force of the old tree coursing through him. Time vanished and he closed his eyes. He could almost feel Persephone's lips lightly brushing his skin and her breath at his ear, as if she were about to whisper something to him ...

A clang of weapons and amour, and sudden raucous shouting ripped Barrak from his reverie.

Soldiers! In the temple grounds?

Crunching down the path, they were advancing on a group of civilians standing under a street lamp.

The gaggle of men milled around, seemingly unsure whether to flee or stand their ground against the approaching soldiers. Much of their attention seemed to be focused on one man at the centre of the group. He was slim with longish hair and a loose-fitting red shirt. A couple of them were pulling at him, as if encouraging him to run.

As the soldiers surged forward, their black armour glinted in the lamplight. Barrak realised his position in the shadows made him virtually invisible. By contrast, the men and soldiers were lit like actors on a stage.

The leader, whose uniform and sword marked him as an officer, loosed his blade with an ominous shriek of metal. The group tensed and a couple of them took up a protective stance about the central figure, shoulders squared, chests out.

An older man, tall and grey with long hair protruding from a scholar's cap, seemed oblivious to the approaching soldiers. He stood toe-to-toe with the red-shirted central figure. They may have been talking or arguing, Barrak couldn't tell amongst the cacophony of clanking armour and competing voices.

Abruptly, the white-haired scholar grabbed Red Shirt by both shoulders, pulled him in and kissed him on the cheek, before pushing him roughly away and spitting theatrically on the ground.

As if this was a sign, the officer gestured with the pommel of his sword. 'Arrest this man!'

Bravely, one of the protectors stepped forward and put himself between the officer and his friend. In a blink, the point of the officer's sword was at his throat. He used it like a pointer to back the would-be rescuer away until he tripped and fell into a nearby garden bed. Another soldier, a huge and ugly beast of a man, swung his crossbow off his back and pointed it one-handed at another of Red Shirt's protectors – the only one remaining who had not yet fled or backed away into the shadows. He lunged at the terrified man, grunting loudly and then bellowing with laughter as the man turned and ran.

It left only the red-shirted figure and the soldiers facing off in the circle of light.

Red Shirt stood erect, defiant in the face of the soldiers' aggression. The officer circled him, glaring. Red Shirt glared back, his shoulders back and chin set, returning the officer's stare with steely defiance.

Barrak felt a surge of empathy and respect for the young man and wondered who he was and what he was supposed to have done.

Out of the blue, the bear-like soldier lunged, crashing the butt of his crossbow into the side of the man's head with a sickening crack.

Red Shirt crumpled like a rag doll. Somehow he managed to raise himself to his hands and knees. The soldier took a step and swung a boot into the man's ribs with such force it lifted him off the ground and flipped him onto his back. He measured his stride again and came in for another go, but the officer raised an impatient hand.

'Enough!' he snapped.. 'Idiot. Do *you* want to carry him back to the Uvec yourself? Shackles! Hands only … and you better hope he can still walk.'

Two soldiers got Red Shirt to his knees, binding his hands behind his back before hauling him to his feet. He cried out in pain as they pulled him up and Barrak thought he would surely have broken ribs, and gods only knew what kind of head injury. As they set off, the brutish one pushed Red Shirt hard in the small of the back, causing him to stumble and fall to his knees. He bawled at him and pulled him up violently by his hair. Every few steps he pushed him again, needlessly, making him stumble and cry out in pain.

When Barrak reached for his bag his hand was shaking, from fear, shock, anger, he hardly knew. He felt suddenly incensed at the treatment meted out to the stranger, who appeared innocuous enough and was clearly unarmed and not resisting. A wave of shame broke over him and he admonished himself: *Why hadn't he done something?* He supposed it had all been over in a matter seconds. He'd been transfixed by the drama and there was little he could have done, although, had he announced his presence, it might have curtailed the brutality of the soldiers. Perhaps.

He strode up the path that angled through the gardens, making for the crowds and the brighter lights of the boulevard. He barely even noticed the spectacle of the grand old temple as he hurried past. The Temple of the Blood of Orlan was magnificent at night, its two massive spires and façade lit up from below – bright white for the massive rose window above the entry, soft pink for the twin spires, and all around the temple, rows of yellow spots firing up into the branches of giant elm trees. It gave the building a beautiful but eerie majesty at night, a must-see for first-time visitors to the city.

Not only did Barrak hardly notice the temple, but he barely even remembered checking into the hotel. He hoped he hadn't been rude to the receptionist. As he stood, subdued and troubled, waiting in the elevator alcove, a fresh-faced young porter came to attention beside him, reverently holding Barrak's tatty old tote. The young lad reminded him uncannily of Elias.

More memories came back to him, as they had been ever since Gracie's early-morning visit. The flashbacks were more vivid now, of the seven months Elias had spent labouring with Barrak on the house. Barrak really hadn't thought much about Elias in the two years since then, he'd had no real reason to, but he realised more clearly than ever, standing there in the hotel foyer, that there was a bond between him and Elias, a bond born of their shared experience. And he was surprised how fond the memories were as they came flooding back to him.

During that first week when Elias came to work for Barrak they were both figuring each other out. Elias quickly realised, to his alarm and amusement, that Barrak didn't have much of an idea about how to build a house. At the same time Barrak was finding out that there was more to Elias than a cocky kid with a penchant for spying on people.

At least he looks the part, he thought, when Elias turned up for his first day on the job. Gone was the black tee and oversized jacket, in fact, Elias looked like a genuine craftsmith, or at least an apprentice to one – shorts, work shirt, flannel-lined jacket, he even had his own tool belt and hammer.

By the end of the first week, Barrak realised the kid had a lot of nous, a good steady hand, and was a whole lot stronger than his wiry physique suggested. And pretty soon Elias realised that while Barrak might've lacked building experience, he understood the bigger picture. He seemed to comprehend the plans he kept poring over and, in the end, it became apparent Barrak did know how this particular house was supposed to fit together.

By the second week they were working like a team. Elias was the saw man, his steady hand cutting straight and true with the power saw. Barrak would measure and mark and drill bolt holes. As each of the large bearers went into position, checked in on either side of the foundation posts, they gradually found they needed to say less about what they were doing, and so started to talk to each other about their lives.

Elias never asked about Barrak's family. He seemed to know not to go there. Barrak asked him why he couldn't ever remember seeing Elias around Rylanswood, and Elias embarrassed him by telling Barrak he had treated him for chickenpox when he was a child and a broken wrist when he was a bit older.

Elias had left home early, at sixteen. *Exiled into oblivion*, was how Elias put it. *Irreconcilable philosophical differences with his stepfather.* Barrak appreciated the young lad's sense of humour. He had a wry and quirky world view and a talent for making light of even the most dire situations with an intelligence and wit that belied his tender age. He entertained Barrak as they worked with stories of his adventures, all told with an eye for the ironic or farcical. For a kid of only nineteen, he was wise beyond his years, a street-smart wisdom born of the extraordinary life he'd led to date.

Barely sixteen, Elias had found a job as a farmhand out in the wheat belt between Tamouer and Silvendale. Then he had roamed the southern regions of the Eyrean Sea, working on the fishing boats out of Lilbetown and Seamist. Later he had ventured east looking for better wages and worked for a time in the mines around Mount Olympus, well outside the inner boundary, in the lawless border zones. Barrak sometimes lost track of the stories because Elias's tales came out in a confusion of anecdotes, which sprang from the kid as the mood took him, or sometimes when a house-building task reminded him of an unusual experience in some wild, far-flung part of the world.

Before long the two of them had all the bearers and joists on, the entire raised floor section complete. This part of the house, supported by cypress posts, would be the main living area, with large windows all along the northern side. Not only would this allow for a panoramic view over Duck Bay toward Westhaven, but with the changing elevation of the sun through the seasons, the carefully designed roofline and eaves would allow passive heating and cooling of the entire house. Barrak was proud of his design and Elias showed a respectful appreciation of the concept whenever Barrak took the opportunity to educate Elias on the finer points of it, as he quite often did.

The morning they finished putting on the joists they stood on them for a time, congratulating themselves and admiring the view out over the bay from where the floor would soon be, then they broke for lunch. Sitting on a half-buried length of joist, their backs against a pile of excavated earth that gave them shelter from a stiff breeze coming off the bay, they talked, and Elias began to tell Barrak a story. This wasn't one of his colourful anecdotes, but a longer narrative, and as he began to tell it Barrak realised Elias was telling him the real story of his travels.

'I was away from Eyre for almost three years altogether. Can you imagine what it was like for a kid of sixteen?

'It was quite a thing at that age to work as a farmhand or as a deckhand on the trawlers. It toughens you up pretty quick you know. I had to do some growing up ... fast. Lilbetown's such a hole – a harbour town with a few fish factories and farms. Not like Rylanswood. Rylanswood is positively cultured compared with that place.

'By Orlan they know how to drink, those farm boys. The boat crews were even worse. We'd stay out at sea for anything up to a week. When we got back half of them would drink for days in the old Seafarers Inn at the harbour. Wouldn't even go home to their families some of them. I had no family, so I was one of the worst offenders, and I wasn't even legal drinking age.

'I had to get out of there. It was no good. I haven't touched a drink since my eighteenth birthday.'

Barrak was glad to hear it, nodding and making approving noises as he munched on his bacon sandwich.

'Out west, in the stone quarries, it got even weirder. You know the sandstone quarries on the other side of the western ranges? Pretty bizarre. Past the farmlands on the flats it's all bush and then thick forest that turns into proper rainforest higher up in the mountains. But once you go down the other side it gets really dry and by the time you reach the plains on the western side, it's just desert. Bam, just like that. Like being on the moon or something and hot as hell.

'There's this little town you come to on the other side. It's called Paris. A one-horse town, but it has this casino in it. It's the only town on the western side of the ranges for hundreds of miles until you get to the opal mines, way out west near the outer markers. But there's all these workers. Workers from the quarries and from the mines and the geothermal plant down at Copper Mountain, and they all live in Paris, except the ones who live in the camps. And there's nothing to do in town but go to the casino – Waldo's Jupiter Emporium. And Waldo, he buys the opals from the miners who come in from the west and gold from the local prospectors and he takes all the miners' money off them in the casino ... ' Elias paused with a far-away look in his eyes and a puzzled frown, as if he himself could scarcely believe it.

'The tables were all rigged, for sure. But there was nothing else to do in town but gamble and try to get rich so you could get the hell out of Paris. And this guy Waldo, who was completely nuts, he had a zoo. It's what he did with all the money, like a hobby, and it was free to get in, but nobody went except the occasional misguided tourist from the city.

'Man, it really was a weird place. I lasted almost a year there, trying to break the bank at Waldo's. After that ... well, gambling's another thing I'll never do again.'

'Good for you.' Barrak had heard of the casino and the zoo, of course, but he'd never been there himself and he hadn't heard any of it described the way Elias was telling it.

'But let me tell you Barrak, none of this was a patch on the places I worked, out past the border zones. Do you know the solar array complex out in the Stony Desert?'

Barrak shook his head and kept munching.

'It's due north of Tamouer. Out that way, the boundary crossing is only about twenty miles past the last of the settlements. I guess it's because there's nothing out there but desert, but then it's another sixty miles dead straight further out into the desert. The road's as straight as a pin. A good road too. Runs along next to the transmission lines. *Just follow the transmission lines.* That's what the border guards tell you. *Don't go anywhere off the road or out of sight of the lines.* Ha! Who would want to? There's just nothing out there.

'Eventually you get to the array. It's all brand new, very high-tech and fully automated. There's not a lot to do but run routine checks and wait for something to go wrong, and that almost never happens. There's a crew of eight, mainly technicians. I was the crew cook, because cooking was what I ended up doing on the trawlers and I was also the dogsbody. *Miscellaneous labouring duties* they called it. In other words, anything the techs didn't want to do.

'The accommodation was pure luxury – like a hotel. Everyone had their own room *and* their own bathroom. I had this huge kitchen to cook in and a massive coolroom that was restocked every month by the company truck. The same one that took us out there.

'But man it was boring. We were stranded. It's totally isolated and it feels like you're the last person alive. And it could get blisteringly hot. You could fry an egg on a rock, and all around are these collectors made of shiny mirrors. You couldn't even step outside without sunglasses. You'd go blind.

'I swear I never saw a cloud in the sky. And at night it was amazing. You've never seen the stars so bright. And the starlight would reflect in the collectors. It was kind of weird. Eerie but beautiful in a way too. It's the sort of place that can start to make you go a bit loopy. And this one time, one of the techs actually did go nuts. He went all paranoid and peculiar and eventually he started telling us there were spacemen from the stars watching us and that he'd seen their spaceships landing at night. Eventually we had to call the company and they came and took him away and brought up a replacement.'

Barrak looked at Elias with dubious admiration and shook his head. 'Sounds like an interesting place.'

'Yeah, I suppose you could call it that, in a weird, scary kind of way.'

Barrak lobbed the balled-up paper of his lunch bag into the rubbish skip and looked quizzically at Elias over the top of his sunglasses in a way that invited elaboration.

'I mean, it's just, I was never so sure that tech *had* gone mad. I saw some pretty weird things out there myself. Things I couldn't explain.'

'Like what?' Barrak raised his brows and looked intently at the boy. He had his glasses off now and was cleaning them on his shirt.

'I dunno ... trucks coming up there, but not to deliver supplies. And soldiers who had nothing to do with the array company. And once I reckon I saw something up in the sky at night too ... something very bloody strange.' Elias tilted his head slightly as he watched Barrak's reaction to what he was saying.

'And, you know, there was this road that continued on to the north. There wasn't supposed to be anything out there but desert, but that's where the soldiers would go, further north.' Elias's eyes were intent. 'The solar array is supposed to be the northern outer marker. So where do you reckon they were going?'

Barrak stood up and wiped his hands on his trousers and shrugged.

'Well, you're not paying me to crap on about the crazy times of my misspent youth,' Elias conceded, following Barrak's cue that it was time to get back to work. But then he fixed Barrak with a quizzical look and asked him: 'Haven't you ever wondered what's out there?'

'Past the outer markers? North of the arrays?' Barrak gathered up his tool belt and rummaged around for the marking pencil that always seemed to elude him.

'No. No. Not just to the north. All over the place. South, west ... east. I mean, the outer markers ... Gods! What does that even mean, Barrak? And the forbidden zones beyond the outer markers ... forbidden to who ... and why?'

Barrak frowned and opened his hands, showing he had no answers. 'Beyond the outer markers lies only desolation and despair,' he said, flippantly quoting the ancient texts.

'You don't really believe that do you Barrak? I can tell you, I've seen some sights. Met some pretty interesting people, particularly in the eastern border zones, and the further east you go the more interesting it gets.'

'So how far east have you been?' Barrak asked, narrowing an eye at his young friend and glancing from side to side as if checking, only half-jokingly, for eavesdroppers.

'Prophets' mercy, Barrak, if I told you that, then I'd have to kill you, wouldn't I?'

Barrak frowned. Elias's faced cracked into the broadest of cheeky grins and he winked at Barrak and threw something in a long curving arc toward him.

It was his marking pencil.

CHAPTER 4

BARRAK EMERGED FROM HIS room at the Plaza Hotel bleary-eyed and famished. Between a strange bed and his increasing concerns for Elias, his sleep had been fitful at best, so his first priority was a good strong pot of the Plaza's rare blend of real coffee.

After finding a table and downing a cup of the aromatic brew, he set about trawling the buffet. Distracted by a kid in a chef's hat constructing an omelette to his specifications, he was taken by surprise when a young woman, striding past on her way to the exit, stopped. 'Councillor Brethrenhope ... Barrak?'

Elegant and attractive, she stared intently at him and after a heartbeat he recognised her. She was already giving him a look of mock outrage. 'Don't tell me you don't recognise me, Barrak?'

'Jasmyn. Yes, of course. Gods! How are you?' Barrak put out an awkward hand. Jasmyn looked down at it with a quizzical expression and a cheeky smile, before taking it in hers and planting a kiss squarely on his cheek.

'It's good to see you. It seems like an age.' Aware she'd hardly seen Barrak in the past few years, her tone dropped slightly. In a more compassionate tone she added, 'How've you been?'

Barrak assured her he was fine and asked after her mother as he took delivery of his omelette from the baby chef. 'Have you eaten? Why don't you join me? I'm just over here.'

Jasmyn protested that she didn't want to impose, even as she trailed Barrak back to his table, pulled out a spare seat, poured herself a cup of coffee from his pot and topped up his. She proceeded to give him a brief synopsis of the latest events at the Mooney residence.

Her father, Enoch, had been a mentor to Barrak, grooming him for a place on the High Council. Enoch was fifteen years Barrak's senior and so their relationship had always been somewhat distant and respectful. Jasmyn's mother had become good friends with Persephone and so their families had bonded. Since Persephone's death, around the same time Enoch was invested as Lord High Councillor, Barrak had drifted out of touch. His only recent contact with Enoch had been over council business.

Barrak picked at his omelette while Jasmyn sipped her coffee and surveyed him over the top of her cup. She was staring at him frankly and affectionately, noticing the extra lines on his brow, the crow's feet around his eyes and the weather-beaten skin. 'I hear you've been building houses. Looks like it agrees with you. You're a man of many talents, aren't you?'

'Well just one house actually – and that was a couple of years ago. But, you know, the country air … it puts a spring in your step.' Barrak had pretty much given up on his omelette. Even though Jasmyn was an old friend, having her watch him eat was making him nervous.

She put her coffee down and reached across, taking his hand. 'I'm so sorry about Persephone and Noah. It must have been so hard for you these last few years.' She gazed into his eyes, her own dark eyes soft with compassion. Barrak felt a small shudder go through him, a catch in his chest, the same sensation that, as a child, let him know tears were on the way. He managed to confine it to a barely perceptible quiver of the lip and returned Jasmyn's look sheepishly, before dropping his gaze.

'Thanks,' was all the reply he could manage.

'I still don't really know what to say, Barrak. None of us knew what to say, what to do. It's been so long now. I feel terrible. It's been years and I've barely seen you … not since the service … We sent a card, flowers. How awful … What could be more inadequate.'

'Jasmyn. It's all right. You know people rarely say anything to me

47

about Pers and Noah. They can't bring themselves to, I suppose. But it would be better if they did … you know, just to mention them, acknowledge what happened, that's all. It does help. So, thank you for that.'

Jasmyn gave his hand a small squeeze and then released it, smiling a distant, sweet smile and blinking back a tear herself, before returning to her coffee. She remembered thinking of Barrak as a grown-up brother, a swashbuckling adventurer who would appear from time to time to rescue her from the boredom of her life at home with her embarrassingly dull parents. By age twelve this had morphed into an overwhelming infatuation. She remembered, fondly now, how devastated she had been a year or two later when he had become engaged to Persephone. Thirteen years old and her whole world had collapsed – at least for a week or so.

'You've heard about all the unrest, the protests? There was a march last week … five thousand people right down Orlan's Boulevard from the Arch to the steps of Parliament. Turned ugly in the end, when Meldrick's goons tried to break it up. Lots of people hurt and this time three protestors were killed. The word is some of Meldrick's troops were masquerading as protestors and deliberately started the trouble, just to give them an excuse.'

Jasmyn paused for a sip of coffee and Barrak described what he had seen in the temple gardens the night before and told her about Elias, and the men who arrested him referring to themselves as Keepers. 'It's one of the reasons I came up to Tamouer a few days early. I need to see Enoch and ask for a bit of advice. What does he say about all this … trouble?'

Jasmyn leaned forward and lowered her voice. 'You could ask just about anyone in Tamouer. We've all heard stories about disappearances, just like your friend's. Just last week a woman in the canteen at the academy, one of my pro-bono clients, told me her boy had vanished … didn't come home from university. She was beside herself … hadn't heard from him for a couple of days.

'As for Father, I'm not sure how much help he'll be to you. Honestly, sometimes I think he's got his head in the sand. You know, ever since that blasted Meldrick combined the city police with the provincial security forces he's been acting more and more like a law unto himself.' Jasmyn leaned forward and dropped her voice to a whisper. 'For my money, it's Meldrick behind these disappearances.'

She examined her coffee grounds then looked up at Barrak with a quizzical half smile that morphed into a frown. 'I'm just not sure father has the backbone to take him on. Anyway, I can't talk to him anymore. Maybe you can talk some sense into him. He trusts your judgement more than anyone's you know, Barrak. But good luck getting a meeting with him.'

'What about Meldrick?' asked Barrak. 'He'd be KLO, wouldn't he? Have you heard anything about his troopers passing themselves off as Keepers?'

'The Keepers of the Light of Orlan,' intoned Jasmyn and followed it with a derisive puff of breath. 'There's been some talk, rumours, you know – as if they're gonna fling off their aprons and start banging heads … take on the rebels. But really, aren't they just a bunch of doddery old men with secret handshakes and the like? Gods, my father's a member, isn't he?' Jasmyn rolled her eyes before fixing Barrak with a serious expression. 'But if Meldrick's involved … '

Suddenly Jasmyn's eyes widened. 'Didn't you go to school with him? You weren't friends, were you?'

Barrak gave a crooked smile. 'Nah … he was a couple of years ahead of me. Maybe he was the one holding my head down the toilet in junior school.'

Jasmyn gave a whoop of laughter, enough to turn heads in the restaurant, then quickly clamped a hand over her mouth.

'Maybe I should just go and see Meldrick and ask him what the hell is going on. Ultimately that's going to be the best way to get information about Elias.'

'I'm not so sure. Be careful with Meldrick. It might not be a good idea to show your hand. Maybe talk to my father first … work your contacts on the council, see what else you can find out … Uh-oh.'

Jasmyn looked at her watch. She'd been running slightly late, now she was very late. Telling Barrak about her encounter with Meldrick the previous night would have to wait.

'Got to go,' she got up, dabbing her lips with a napkin. 'There's plenty more I could tell you. If you've got a few days in town we should have lunch or something. Maybe tomorrow? I'll get you up to speed on all the latest.'

'Yeah, great ... ' Barrak was nodding and getting to his feet too.

'You know where my office is, don't you?'

Barrak wasn't sure he did, but Jasmyn was already sliding her card onto the table. She looked into his eyes for a moment, and Barrak could feel the warmth and affection. 'It's been too long,' she said and planted another kiss on his cheek, turned to go then turned back, her face lit up with an idea. 'Hey, you like football don't you? It's the season final on Saturday. Enoch and his cronies have the council section in the members all locked down, but I think I know where I can find a couple of tickets. It would be the perfect place to corner him for a chat. He won't be able to get away and he'll be more relaxed. What do you say?'

'Perfect,' said Barrak.

Jasmyn strode off, leaving Barrak a little stunned and remembering it was Jasmyn's trademark verve and vitality that had always made her a pleasure to be around. Returning to the last of his coffee, he recalled another time, when things had become a bit awkward between the two of them.

Barrak had been teaching a subject at the university – History and Philosophy of Natural Medicine – a foundation unit for both medical and astrology students, and it was Barrak's first semester teaching it. Jasmyn was taking the subject in her first year. She was just eighteen.

Naturally they spent time together, with Barrak buying her a coffee here, a meal there. He would tell her she needed fattening up. He considered himself to be her surrogate father, after all. He was careful not to embarrass her in front of her friends, or appear to favour her.

Jasmyn's issues with her emotionally absent father had flared up during adolescence, and by the time she was at university, she was behaving in ways that Barrak guessed had their origin in her father's emotional neglect. There seemed to be legions of boys and men orbiting Jasmyn, while she flirted with some, and indulged in brief relationships with others. Barrak quickly became her confidant, and she would divulge, sometimes to his embarrassment, quite intimate details of her liaisons.

At some point this shared intimacy crossed an impossibly fragile line and to Barrak's surprise and shock, Jasmyn was flirting with him. Somehow it had slipped under his guard. He had always been so careful about proper boundaries in his practice, but he had been brought undone by his role as a mentor to Jasmyn, and he castigated himself for letting it happen.

Suddenly the flirting and the relationships with other men seemed like a device to attract Barrak's attention, for she and Barrak were soul mates, she was sure. And she had become bored with her immature friends, preferring his more adult company.

On one occasion, Jasmyn had made quite a production of telling him about an encounter with a friend's parents. She had met the girl's father for the first time and was surprised by how much older he was than the girl's mother – his sixty to her forty-six – and how they had enjoyed thirty years of blissful matrimony. She left Barrak to calculate for himself that their age difference exactly matched hers and Barrak's.

It was as if the ground itself had moved and thrown him off balance. He didn't know how to handle the situation. The worst of it was – and he would barely admit it even to himself – that he had felt flattered and drawn by Jasmyn's magnetism and vitality. She had blossomed into a beautiful and charming young woman with a sensuality and warmth that attracted men to her in droves. It had made him doubt the quality and meaning of his own tender feelings for Jasmyn, and with Persephone heavily pregnant with Noah, the situation left him feeling guilt-ridden and confused.

In the end, the university semester finished and Barrak declined to renew his contract. His experiment with teaching was over almost

51

before it had begun, which he calculated was no great loss to himself or his students. He had found the teaching itself somewhat onerous. He went back to his practice full time, devoting his attention to Persephone and their new son and, for the most part, stayed well away from the city, and from Jasmyn.

So much time had passed and so much had happened since then. The Jasmyn he'd just breakfasted with was all grown up – so mature and self-assured and completely at ease with herself. Gone was the insecure and precocious girl of a few years ago. In her place was a sophisticated and intelligent woman. He felt a curious sense of relief – almost euphoria. It was as if he'd regained a lost piece of his past – and an old friend.

Elias woke to the stench of urine and the creeping cold of his windowless cell. A single bare light bulb eyed him with its unblinking electric glare and the ever-present noises, often strange and unidentifiable, seeped through the walls and into his head. Sometimes there were screams, not his own, which let him know his suffering was shared by others and reminded him that any reprieve would be short-lived. He wondered if Toby and Angus had a torture roster.

His injuries and the chains on his wrists made it difficult to raise his arms, but he had managed to make an inventory of his wounds by touch. He was missing at least one tooth on the left side, and the remaining upper teeth on that side were numb. His head generally felt all wrong and there was a clicking noise whenever he opened and closed his mouth. His left eye was swollen shut and he was pretty sure his left arm was broken. Compared to his left side, which felt like he'd run flat out into a speeding truck, his right side was relatively unharmed. Angus was the hitter, and a right-hander. Elias thought Angus should change hands occasionally, to lessen the risk of repetitive strain injury, and he had suggested this to him ... once.

His body was mottled with innumerable bruises and Elias looked like some kind of pale sea creature camouflaged to fade into the sea bed.

Time had lost all meaning and real sleep was little more than a fading wish. Whenever he did lose consciousness, for brief periods, he was beset by troubling images and dreams. Just lately a recurring image had started to unnerve him. He was back east, before his return to Eyre, sitting in a training class and his instructor was commanding him to pay attention. His fevered mind had recreated the character perfectly – a steely-eyed military doyen with a rapier tongue and wit and the imposing physique of a mountain bear – except for his name, which was lost to Elias.

Now listen up, this is important. It could save your lives one day. If you are captured, you will be interrogated, and how you conduct yourself under interrogation will determine two things. One: will you or will you not have the intestinal fortitude to refrain from betraying your brave fighting comrades and selling them into the hands of the enemy to be slaughtered like dogs just to save your own miserable, cowardly skins? And two: will you make it out of that interrogation alive? Now, pay attention ... ELIAS! Wake up for the gods' sake!

He did wake up, back in his cell, to the sound of the metal latch grating on the cell door. Elias's gut lurched as if looking for a way out of his abdomen and a wave of fear swept over him. *Prophet's mercy, no! Not again, not already.* Elias struggled to his feet and moved over to where his chains joined the wall. He thought this would give him enough slack to throw a punch, if he was lucky. He dragged the thin, ragged mattress off the bed and threw it down between him and the door – an obstacle to distract them.

They were used to Elias by now – he was a fighter. He sometimes wondered whether they enjoyed it, just a little. Maybe it broke up the monotony of their daily grind. He guessed many prisoners wouldn't resist, fearing the consequences. Elias reckoned he didn't really have much to lose so he'd damned well make them work for it, and who knew, one day if they dropped their guard ... maybe he would take one of the bastards with him. He sensed a faint respect from them for at least trying, but it evaporated pretty quickly the one time he landed a punch on Angus, splitting his brow and straightening up his boxer's nose for him. Retribution had been savage and swift.

They were wary of him now and usually came well-armed. On this occasion, seeing Elias's combative stance, Toby carefully pulled the mattress toward himself and flicked it out of the way, eyes fixed on Elias all the while. He and Angus then quartered him at forty-five degrees left and right, and while Toby feinted, Angus rushed in, baton swinging. Having read the feint, Elias flung both arms up and pulled his hands apart to extend the chains, catching the baton and pulling it in. Angus had made a fundamental error, swinging too hard and leaning into it too much, so he was off balance. Elias pulled him in and down and simultaneously swung his elbow hard into the side of his head. Angus was on his knees, stunned and wobbling. Toby panicked and backed up, but went the wrong way, toward the corner instead of back to the door, and Elias could still reach him. He lunged and ducked Toby's wild swing then jabbed hard into his exposed rib-cage and looped the chains around his neck. He would crush his windpipe in seconds ...

Whatever happened next never made it into Elias's long-term memory after his scalp was split by a baton-wielding, woozy but nonetheless extremely pissed-off Angus.

He slowly regained consciousness, finding himself no longer in his cell but strapped to the old wooden office chair in the interrogation room. His shirt was red with fresh blood and he could feel the congealing tightness on his scalp. Angus prowled up and down like a sulking panther, slapping his truncheon into the palm of his hand and occasionally glaring at Elias with undisguised malice. Meanwhile, Toby had his back turned, busying himself with something on a portable table set up a few feet away.

No longer able to contain his displeasure, Angus jammed the truncheon into Elias's ribs. 'There's only one thing worse than a lippy damned zoner in an interrogation ... ' He brought the baton up and pressed it under his chin now, making him look up, 'and that's a lippy zoner smart-arse who punches like a girl.' With that he whipped the baton down, smacking it hard across the fingers of Elias's right hand, with a crack that sounded a bit too much like bones breaking.

'Now, Toby here has himself a new toy. Made it himself, he did. He was going to give you a play with it, just for chuckles, as your reward for being such a clever dick. You know, we don't even have any questions for you today and besides, we've had a fair gutful of your tough-guy routine. So … don't feel like answering our questions? Fine, we're not asking any. But we did think to ourselves, who deserves a trial run with Tobe's new toy more than Elias? No one, that's who … damn sure. First prize goes to you, zone-head.' Angus had begun circling the chair and, as he did, Elias glanced down and noticed he was positioned in the centre of what looked like a large thick rubber mat. 'But after this morning's little hissy fit … well now, that deserves more than just a trial run, don't you think Tobe? I think we can put the damn thing through its paces.'

Angus was behind him now, the truncheon across his throat pinning him against the chair back. Through gritted teeth, he continued. 'But Elias can take it. In fact he'll lap it up, won't you zone-boy? Because Elias is a gods-bane tough guy, aren't you?' Angus emphasised his clearly rhetorical question by pulling his baton back even harder against Elias's throat.

As Toby turned from his work bench Elias finally saw what he'd been tinkering with. He was holding it up in front of his smug face, rotating it back and forth for all to admire. But it wasn't much to look at, just a metal rod, insulated at one end by a red plastic handle. At the other end there seemed to be two fine filaments or spikes poking out. From the back end of the handle, two thin black cables extended to what looked like a transformer on the table. As Toby moved, he winced slightly. And as he advanced on Elias his scowl seemed to say, *My sore ribs are spoiling my fun, so you're gonna pay.*

Abruptly, Angus had him in a head-lock from behind and was roughly stuffing something, a rubber mouth guard, into his mouth and telling him to stop struggling and not to spit it out or he'd be damn-well sorry.

The first jab of Toby's homemade cattle prod was like nothing he could have imagined – as if every muscle in his body was pounded with sledge hammers and simultaneously stabbed with a hundred fiery needles. His skull would soon explode and his eyes would pop out of his head and fly across the room in cartoon formation. He screamed inside his head but no sound came from his paralysed body, apart from the visceral grunts of a dying animal. Then there was nothing ... but only for a few heartbeats. The blessed blackness was short-lived and he was jolted back to consciousness as the convulsions and seizures took hold and shook his body and flailed his mind. As they subsided, his tormentors came dimly into focus, hovering around him in a fog. They seemed excited, animated, dancing about as if at a sporting event and talking big. He saw their mouths forming words, but no sound reached him.

When Toby came at him again with his infernal prod he caught his breathe and involuntarily tensed ... BANG ... Elias's heart stopped. He was floating, distracted ... there seemed to be sun shining on his face and distant voices making no sense at all ... but something demanded his attention ...

Are you daydreaming again Arrowsmith? Sergeant Riggs was glaring at him from an oddly undersized podium, which looked as if Riggs might pick it up at any time and casually crush it with one huge hand, just to emphasise a point. His old instructor had been reunited with his name, and he was clearly annoyed.

You damn-well need to pay attention to this stuff Elias. It may be important to you one day if you're ever captured ... now ... If there has been coercion, and by that I mean torture, then what you don't want are interrogators who let you see their faces ... Interrogators who happily pass the time of day calling each other by their real names ... 'How's the missus, Joe, and regards to Auntie Beatrix,' et cetera. Because if that's what they're doing, then you can be one hundred per cent sure they have no intention of ever letting you see the light of day. Whatever you tell them – the location of the crown jewels, latest orders from high command, or that you just flew in from Jupiter and your Uncle Buck is a jack rabbit – doesn't matter. When they are finished with you they will *kill you, so again, your only option and your primary objective has to be escape.*

He became aware he was drifting back into real time and tried to resist. He could hear the familiar, hated voices of his tormentors and he had no desire to return to their company. The voices were a garbled babble. Little by little he realised the voices were raised; they seemed to be arguing. 'No, just put the damn thing away Toby, for quest's sake, I thought you'd killed him ... Well, you had it up too high, obviously. Not now ... let's just get him back in his cell.'

One of them was untying him from the chair and reattaching his shackles. Elias remained limp. If feigning unconsciousness was a ticket back to his cell, that suited him fine.

Down the corridor to the cell they dragged him, then dumped him unceremoniously on his rack. As the door slammed shut, Elias realised Sergeant Riggs was still with him, whispering in his mind's ear, imparting his sage words of military wisdom, curiously giving comfort to Elias as he floated in and out of consciousness ...

The only way you might *survive your interrogation is to have a rock solid, iron clad, one hundred per cent leak-proof, water-tight cover story. This, of course, will be provided for you. Now, if you are captured, the first thing you must do is forget who you are, what you know, where you've been and who you have associated with. You expunge this all from the very fibre of your being ... and then, you* become *your cover story. Because, of course, long before you were ever captured you learned it backward and inside out. It is your alter ego. And now that you have been captured it is* you. *You must take the real you, the old you, the you that can never be revealed, and kill it. It no longer exists. You strangle it in the darkest corner of the dingy pit they've put you in and then flush it down the drain, along with the blood and sweat and shit they've been beating out of you ...*

Of course the real trick is to know exactly when and how to reveal the wonderful truth of your alter ego. The timing has to be right. Too soon and they probably won't believe you. Too late and, frankly, you're probably already dead. They've got to think that you have, in fact, been coerced ... that whatever they have been doing to you, tickling your tootsies or flambéing your nuts with a blow torch, has brought you undone; that you are at your wits' end ... you are broken, and you will do anything to make them stop ... you will tell them what they want to know: the truth. Except it won't be, will it? It will be a perfectly crafted replica of the truth. A story so close to the truth in many ways, so confusingly similar to the real you, that you almost believe it yourself – even though it is unmitigated bullshit, designed to send the enemy straight up the garden path. And this is what you will tell them. Remember, if you can't escape you are probably already dead, whatever you tell them.

Elias was unable or unwilling to anchor himself in the reality of his foetid cell for longer than a few minutes here and there. Otherwise he journeyed through the dreamy inner landscapes of his past lives, with Riggs providing the incongruous soundtrack, vivid and loud, complete with the thickly accented eastern dialect Elias had learned, with difficulty, to understand. He struggled, in his semi-delirious and fragile state, to make sense of Riggs's musings. Was Riggs trying to tell him something ... was it time to talk?

CHAPTER 5

THE MASSIVE CANISTER OF polished brass and tinted glass emitted a weary sigh before depositing Barrak inside Tamouer's police headquarters. He stood for a moment in the cavernous foyer and marvelled, not for the first time, at the architectural extravagance of the place. The administrative heart of the Combined Security Forces was one of the city's most impressive buildings. People had taken to calling it the Citadel. It took up an entire city block along Landen Way, directly opposite the west side of the parliamentary precinct, flanked by the Port Authority on one side and the law courts on the other. Parts of the old building, preserved inside the new, dated back to the first settlers, when it was the garrison housing Orlan's Guard.

Meldrick's new headquarters was the administrative centre for the entire military network, including border control, provincial security and metro police. Meldrick's greatest political feat had been to combine the three services into a single entity. Barrak knew his ambition had caused some ructions in the higher echelons of government at the time, some fearing the consolidation would put too much power into Meldrick's hands. He reckoned it was a combination of Meldrick's political savvy, cunning manipulation and bloody-minded coercion that had allowed him to pull it off.

Meldrick's second great work was the recently completed renovation, in which police headquarters and the old garrison buildings were literally brought under one roof. They had been joined by a massive new façade of stone and glass, which gave entry to a vast reception area with a highly polished stone floor, where Barrak stood now, considering his options.

Towering tinted plate-glass panels alternated with portraits around the curved walls and statues of significant military figures stood amongst a veritable forest of potted palms. At the centre of the atrium, giving access to the three upper floors, was a sweeping circular staircase of brass and polished blackwood. It was lit by a dome of glass and refracting crystal panels, which captured and magnified the rays of the sun as it tracked across the sky. Below the dome was an elaborate and fanciful sculpture spiralling down and around the upper reaches of the stairwell. It was composed of light-sensitive absorption panels, supplying power to the entire building and more – a perfect combination of form and function.

Barrak knew it was the most advanced application of crystalline solar power generation in the city. His hotel had something similar, but it was much older and nowhere near as pretty. Staring up at it, Barrak gave a low whistle. Only in Eyre would security headquarters be the most impressive and extravagant public building.

The staircase was busy with scurrying personnel – some uniformed, some not – largely oblivious to the marvels of the staircase and totally oblivious to Barrak as he made for the public enquiries counter, which was away to the left, and notable only for its lack of activity.

The young trooper at the reception counter had been gone for only a few minutes. He re-emerged holding a clipboard and closed the frosted glass door behind him with a meticulous click. 'Now, Councillor Brethrenhope, you say the young man was arrested in Rylanswood?' The trooper's manner was polite and deferential, but his body language and stony glare told another story.

'No, sir, we have no record of an Arrowsmith at all. Not in the last month at least. Couldn't be under another name, could it, Councillor? Might've given us a false name, perhaps. Sometimes they do … ' The officious youngster looked up from the clipboard and narrowed his eyes. 'Don't happen to know why he was detained by any chance, do we sir?'

'No, I don't. Are you sure there's nothing? It was only a few days ago.'

'Yes, quite sure, Councillor. All CSF activity is logged right here, centrally, sir. Every provincial station, border outpost, mobile unit ... whatever; they are all required to lodge a daily report. We're really rather strict about that you see, sir. I'm sorry, Councillor, perhaps there's been some mistake?'

Some mistake. Barrak was not surprised. The sergeant at Rylanswood Police had given him the same response at the front counter of the old ramshackle country station the morning Gracie had raised the alarm ... no record of any arrest.

He stood his ground for a moment longer, countering the young trooper's condescending gaze with his own look of smouldering dissatisfaction. But even as he stood there, a sense of dark foreboding crept over him. There seemed to be little doubt of it now – Elias had joined the ranks of the disappeared.

And as the crisply dressed young defender of military procedure dared him to enquire further, Barrak wondered what lay beneath the surface of the new security headquarters. Were its bowels riddled with ancient dungeons and cells, still dank and foetid with centuries-old suffering? Could Elias be right below his feet, even now, chained and abused, blind in the darkness, ears straining for the sounds of rescue?

Barrak wandered distractedly from the Citadel across the road to the parliamentary complex, through the gardens and up the wide front steps into the council buildings. Being the Friday before the spring opening, the chambers were gradually waking from their winter slumber. Most of the permanent staff were back at work and some of the councillors were drifting around, gossiping, summoning staff, fussing over details.

Barrak sat in his office and drummed his fingers on his desk for a few moments, opened some drawers, and shut them again. He stood at his window and stared sightlessly out at the gardens for a time, before leaving his office for the inner concourse of the council chamber. Finding himself at the main entrance, he opened one of the heavy oak doors and peered in. It looked forlorn and empty, but for a team of cleaners quietly going about their business.

Eventually he found himself in the council library. It was where he liked to go to gather his thoughts during council recesses. There was something about the atmosphere, the smell – musty books and leather upholstery – and the low light from the green glass desk lamps. He found the hush comforting. It was almost as if the very proximity of all those weighty tomes, the sheer extent and concentration of knowledge, held out a promise that answers could be found.

'Looking for inspiration, Brethrenhope?' The soft croak came from behind him.

Absorbed in a modern translation of a volume of Orlan's *Principles*, Barrak had not noticed the old councilman peering over his shoulder. Icabod Varco, council archivist and the oldest and most revered of delegates to the High Council. No one knew his age but he had served on the council for as long as anyone could remember. Iggy, as he was affectionately known around the halls of the High Council, was a living relic.

'Ah ... Orlan's *Principia Cardinale*, eh?'

Iggy's time-battered face wore a benign smile as he peered at the tome over the top of a pair of gold-rimmed spectacles.

'Responsibilities and duties of the Guard? Unusual reading material for a young physician, isn't it Barrak?' Iggy observed thoughtfully.

'True, Councillor. I was just browsing, really.' Barrak stood up and pulled another seat around, offering it to the ancient councillor.

Barrak had gravitated toward the familiar volumes, the distillation of the founding fathers' philosophies, and he had, almost absently, selected volume five, *Guarding of the Keep*. He didn't really know what he expected to find in it. Maybe some insight into the founders' thoughts on keeping the peace.

'We live in fearful times,' Iggy said as he settled himself with a soft groan. 'Why do you think people are so afraid?'

Barrak was puzzled at first by the question. 'Well, personally, I fear for the safety of a friend who's gone missing.'

'Oh ... I'm sorry to hear that, Barrak. "Disappeared?"'

'I'm afraid so.'

'Afraid ... yes ... ' Iggy trailed off and gently nodded his head as he surveyed Barrak, his eyes soft with kindness and understanding, but not without a lively twinkle.

He always reminded Barrak of a mischievous and benevolent old wizard. Some of the younger councillors thought him senile and superfluous, but Barrak knew better. On a few occasions he had benefitted from Iggy's pearls of wisdom and sharp insights.

'Why do you think the first settlers constructed such a great wall around the old keep, Barrak? What do you think they feared?'

'I don't know. I suppose those were fearful times. They'd come here fleeing the retribution of the gods, the flood and the great pestilence. They were the chosen ones.'

'Yes. The chosen ones, indeed. So they were. But why so fearful do you think?' Iggy demanded gently, raising one eyebrow.

'The ancient texts talk of darkness and chaos. Perhaps that's what they feared.'

'Darkness and chaos you say, Barrak? Yes, yes, I think perhaps you're right. Darkness and chaos,' Iggy nodded several times and his eyes seemed to close. For a moment Barrak thought he might have drifted off, but when he looked up his eyes were clear and focused.

'It's in the hearts of men, of course. That's the problem. That's why we fear it so.'

'I'm sorry ... ?' Barrak thought he'd missed the point.

'The chaos and darkness. It lurks in the hearts of men, you see. That's why we fear it so, don't you think? Problem is, we take it with us wherever we go, don't we? Yes, yes, well ... ' Icabod gave a snort and a kind of ambiguous harrumph and began to hoist himself out of the low chair with some effort. 'But, you know, there's something that troubles me even more, young Brethrenhope ... ignorance and complacency. That's what we should be afraid of.'

Once he was more or less upright, he leaned in slightly toward Barrak and lowered his voice. 'Was he taken by the Keepers, your friend?'

The directness of Iggy's question shocked Barrak. He looked intently at the old councillor. Iggy held his eye, and in that moment, in the quiet library, an unspoken understanding seemed to pass between them.

'Well, the boy's mother seems to think so, but surely that's not possible. They don't have that kind of authority … ' Barrak faltered.

'Don't be naïve, Barrak, the Keepers of the Light of Orlan is a secret organisation. Why? Why does their little club operate in the dark, unseen and unchecked by the wider society? Think, Barrak … secrecy and power always make such fine bedfellows and the spawn of their debauchery is so often corruption, is it not, my friend?'

Iggy must have noticed Barrak's guarded expression and he shuffled a bit closer before continuing. 'It's happened before and it's happening again. But we've not seen one as malignant or as hungry for power as our current tyrant.'

Barrak frowned. He knew Iggy wasn't talking about Enoch, the democratically elected Lord High Councillor. He knitted his brow and tilted his head. 'You mean Meldrick?'

'Meldrick. Of course Meldrick, who else?'

'You know he's had himself installed as flame-keeper? It seems lording it over all three of the security services wasn't enough for him.' Iggy squinted at Barrak as if he thought him slow. 'You know there was a time, long ago, when the Keepers of the Light of Orlan did perform a useful function, moderating government, behind the scenes checks and balances, you know. It was liberal, altruistic, properly dedicated to Orlan's true principles.'

Iggy was staring past Barrak as if surveying a distant view. 'But now that he's got the KLO in his pocket and has installed his cronies as office bearers … and his bloody secret police, scaring the living Prophet out of everybody … it's just like the bad old days.'

Barrak looked around uneasily, wondering how many different types of sedition the old-timer might have committed in just one passionate tirade.

'You're not one of them, by the way, are you Barrak?' Iggy inquired of him suddenly, narrowing his eyes and tilting his fuzzy white head slightly.

'No, of course not!' Barrak protested.

'No, no, of course, yes … thank the gods.' Icabod had decided to sit back down, and paused to catch his breath, dabbing the corner of his mouth with a handkerchief before continuing. 'Once you have a secret society – constituted as a religious order being run by the military, well, things can become very murky indeed. Like a cancer, likely as not to pop up in any organ. As a physician you'll appreciate a medical analogy.'

Iggy peered searchingly at Barrak, gauging his reaction, then he began to haul himself to his feet once again, grunting and puffing even more with the effort. 'Yes, that's it; a damned cancer.'

Barrak was up and helping Icabod to his feet.

'You're a good man, Brethrenhope, with a stout heart.' He had Barrak's shoulder in his spindly grasp now. 'And a physician to boot. Maybe you're the one to cut the bloody cancer out.' He chuckled and coughed, then patted Barrak's shoulder a couple of times before shuffling away into the hush of the reading room.

Barrak had never met the cardinal's youngest wife, but here she was, serving him tea and cake in the temple vestry and apologising for the absence of her revered spouse who, she assured him, would be along shortly. Her name was Madeleine. She seemed much too young for the cardinal, fresh-faced and eager, her cheeks rosy in the blaze of late-afternoon sunlight brightening the stained-glass window above the table.

Cardinal Jasper Selwood – Chief Prelate of the Church of Orlan and the Prophets – had two other wives, Camdyn and Audrey, whom Barrak had met several times on his annual visits. But Madeleine was different. Barrak took a shine to her as they chatted over the tea, but he couldn't help wondering how the relationships worked and how the three women felt about each other.

Barrak and Madeleine were on their second pot of tea and starting to get quite chummy when the cardinal finally arrived, apologising profusely for his tardiness and pumping Barrak's hand like an early settler priming an irrigation pump.

'How are you, my old friend? Has it been a whole year? Sorry to keep you waiting so long … something completely unexpected. You know how it is, leading up to the festival. Where are you? At the Plaza? Taking good care of you, I trust? And Maddy's been looking after you for tea and so on … yes?'

Barrak and the cardinal went through the pleasantries, with Barrak asking after the girls, as Jasper liked to refer to his wives. He got a bit lost trying to retrieve the names of the many children and, frankly, he wasn't even sure of the number anymore, but the cardinal let him off the hook diplomatically and before long they were getting down to business.

'How many neophytes do you think you'll have this year, your eminence?' Barrak asked as he stood up from the table and smiled his thanks to young Madeleine.

'We think almost two hundred. Well up again from last year.' The cardinal glanced at his youngest wife and tipped his head toward the vestry door. 'Councillor Brethrenhope and I will be in the temple for a short while.'

Barrak followed him, and as they approached the altar Jasper glanced over his shoulder and said, 'It's almost getting unmanageable, Barrak. We might have to tighten up the criteria again.'

Behind the altar and below the elaborate stained-glass depiction of Orlan's quest was the ancient carved stone coffer, the mysterious contents of which were known only to the leaders of the church. Most believed it to contain holy relics of Orlan, perhaps even the remains of the Prophet himself. Above it were the reliquary and staff of Orlan – the most potent symbols of the church – and these, Barrak knew, were the genuine articles, seven hundred years old and once held by the hand of Orlan himself.

Off to the side, Jasper was busying himself within the inner sanctum – a closeted corner hidden from the view of the congregation, his conjurer's lair, as he sometimes liked to call it, containing all the paraphernalia of temple ritual. Laid out in meticulous order on starched linen was an assortment of items of religious service; incense burners, cymbals, chalices and, hanging in an alcove behind the table, the cardinal's vestments in all their ceremonial variations.

The cardinal unlocked a small timber cabinet built into the alcove, its doors inlaid with a coloured glass mosaic of Orlan's crest. He took out a small chest inlaid with crystal and placed it on the table next to Barrak, flipped it open and took a glass phial from the blue interior. Holding it up to his eye and for Barrak's perusal, he glanced questioningly at Barrak. 'What do you think?'

Barrak played along with Jasper's little pantomime. 'I best give you a fresh one of those I think, Cardinal.' This, of course, was why he was here. He reached into his jacket pocket and took out a small case containing an identical phial, this one filled to the top with liquid and sealed with wax. It had a small white label inscribed by Barrak: 'Ors 50 M'. They swapped phials and the cardinal held the new one up to the light, giving it a shake and squinting at it, as if to check the purity. 'Very good. Excellent. Thank you, Councillor.'

Barrak nodded and smiled as the cardinal carefully locked the new phial away and dropped the key into the large side pocket of his cloak.

The preparation of Orlan's remedy of spirit – or the holy tincture, as many churchmen called it – and the maintenance of supplies to the city temple, were Barrak's responsibility as the High Council's Chief Physician. The giving of Orlan's spirit was the most sacred and fundamental ritual of the church and central to the spiritual life of all Eyreans, but to Barrak's mind it was where religion and medicine collided, and not without causing some discomfort to his sceptical scientific brain. The blurring of this particular boundary seemed inevitable to Barrak, given that Orlan himself had been a healer.

Even though it was part of every physician's dispensary, questions about the holy tincture nagged at Barrak. What was the source of the medicine? Potentised remedies were usually sourced from a plant, mineral or animal, the consumption of which, in its raw state, might cause quite severe symptoms. This was the basic medicinal law of similars: like cures like. But what was the source of Orlan's remedy of spirit? No one knew except perhaps Orlan, and he certainly wasn't telling. There was nothing in the ancient texts, spiritual or medical, to give a clue as to the original source material. And the action of the remedy? Well it was said that Orlan's Remedy of Spirit acted at the highest levels of the vital force, promoting spiritual attunement, and was therefore greatly beneficial for the whole person … the ultimate constitutional remedy. But this, too, troubled Barrak's strict medical mind. The concept that a single constitutional remedy was suitable for an entire diverse population was counter-intuitive.

'Done,' said the cardinal, turning back toward Barrak and gently rubbing his hands together. 'All set for the invasion of the barbarian hordes on Sunday. Now, I'd say the sun is well and truly over the yardarm, Barrak. I think we've earned a drink.'

The invasion the cardinal referred to was the procession of the neophytes, which would take place at the temple on the Sunday of Orlan's Festival. The 'barbarians' were those adolescents whose well-connected families could afford the tribute, who'd turned thirteen during the intervening year. They would line up at the culmination of services to be administered the holy tinture, by the cardinal himself, as part of their rite of ascendancy.

For most, the remedy of spirit was administered at their local temple, usually around the time of the festival, or any time during their fourteenth year. It was customary to receive the holy tincture at naming, at ascendancy, and as part of the marriage ceremony. For many Eyreans, receiving it was a significant spiritual moment in their lives. Indeed, Orlan himself, in his teachings, emphasised the importance of this, above all other religious observances.

So Barrak kept to himself his suspicion that the whole thing might be based on superstition. Barrak certainly wasn't the only unbeliever, in fact, the younger generations seemed to be turning away from the church in droves. But so entrenched in Eyrean culture was the practice of taking the remedy of spirit that physicians routinely gave the remedy to patients who didn't even attend temple, but still wanted the remedy, as a tonic or perhaps as insurance.

'Would you like some ice with that, Councillor?'

Barrak nodded, and the cardinal's valet spirited a measure of cracked ice into his glass with a discreet tinkle.

A fire was already crackling in the large brick hearth, to ward off the chill of the early spring night. All this was part of the ritual that had grown up around Barrak's annual visit to restock the temple's supply of tincture – the obligatory whisky in the drawing room of the Selwoods' grand residence.

'Interesting times, eh, Barrak? I worry that the young ones just don't get it. Do you know what I mean?'

Barrak gave a considered nod.

'I mean, there's a natural order. Always has been … All these protests and whatnot. Becoming quite violent too. Equal rights indeed. What do they even mean by that? Do they want the common folk to be able to vote in the senate elections? I'm not one for politics, as you know, but what rubbish. And land rights. Of all things! Have you heard what they're saying Barrak?'

'Yes, your eminence, I've heard snippets.'

'Can you imagine if everyone were allowed to own property? Chaos! And freedom to travel outside the boundaries. Where do they think they would go?'

Assuming the cardinal's last volley of questions to be rhetorical, Barrak just nodded and examined his whisky. 'Well, it certainly has been a turbulent year,' he offered, without much conviction.

'Indeed. Indeed it has.' A pensive frown troubled the cardinal's brow for a moment. 'Oh well. Festival on Sunday, New Year just around the corner; perhaps we can hope for a better year to come … In fact, let's drink to that, shall we? To a peaceful and happy New Year.' The cardinal leaned forward in his chair and inclined his glass toward Barrak, who did the same, and the two tumblers chimed their agreement.

'To an uneventful seven-oh-eight,' Barrak ventured with a hopeful grin.

In the long quiet hours before dawn, sleep eluded him and Barrak found himself again assailed by images and memories he thought long forgotten: recollections of the days and weeks he had spent with Elias, working on his house. In his rambling half-conscious state, some of them seemed as vivid as if they had happened last week ...

Elias climbed with the casual agility of a tree monkey while Barrak could only look on nervously from below and steady the ladder. He'd been dreading this job. It was the highest part of the entire house and he didn't know whether to feel relieved or culpable that Elias had volunteered to check out the top of the post. They were working high above the sloping rear part of the block on the verandah, which ran the length of the living area at the back of the house. Two anchor posts extended from below ground, right up through what would be the verandah decking, and continued up to the height of the roofline. Their mission was to bolt the outermost corner post to the support beam, which would then hold the roof trusses.

A nice shady verandah at the back, with a view out over the bay, had seemed like a good idea on paper, but the logistics of building it were giving him second thoughts.

The deck was still just open joists, to which they had lashed planks to form a temporary floor. To access the outside of the corner post, Elias had suggested they cantilever the planks, creating an overhanging platform extending six feet out beyond the verandah, at a height of some fifteen feet above the ground. After testing the platform for strength, Elias had positioned a stepladder on the overhang, hard up against the post for some meagre support. Seeing Barrak shaking his head in disbelief, the boy had grinned and told Barrak not to worry.

Elias was now standing astride the top of the perilous ladder, leaning his hip into the post for support. Unhooking the saw, he tested its weight, adjusted his stance slightly and pulled the trigger a couple of times to test the power.

Barrak clenched his teeth and fought the urge to look away.

'Hey Barrak,' Elias shouted.

'What?' Barrak yelled back, alarmed.

'I think I can see my mother's house from up here.'

'Orlan's mercy! Just be careful will you? Concentrate!'

In a matter of minutes it was all over. Elias had made the cuts, about six in all, and chiselled out the chunks of timber, showering Barrak with woodchips. He lowered the saw to Barrak and climbed down onto the relatively stable makeshift deck with a triumphant told-you-I-could-do-it grin.

'Bloody nerves of steel,' Barrak conceded, shaking his head and smiling appreciatively.

Over lunch Elias was very talkative, a little over-excited, which wasn't surprising, following his death-defying feat up the ladder. The conversation had ricocheted from one topic to another, with Elias waxing lyrical and Barrak making the odd observation as they munched on their sandwiches.

Eventually Elias quietened and even seemed to become a little pensive for a moment or two. Then he asked Barrak, 'Why are you building the house this way?'

'What do you mean, the verandah? I don't know. I'm beginning to wish I hadn't. We still have to get that beam up there.'

'No, no, I mean the whole thing – the solar panels, the insulation criteria, passive solar design principles, recycled waste water, all that stuff.'

'It's the building code. You know everyone has to comply.'

'Yeah I know, but why? Where did all this regulation come from? And the technology? Y'know, like solar panels, liquid crystal technology. Don't you ever wonder where all that came from? Holy quest. I mean, how did the first settlers come up with something like Rubyvale? And crystal arrays, and solar towers? Haven't you ever wondered where it all started? Originally, I mean.'

Barrak looked gravely at his young helper and gave him a wry smile.

'And what about us? Where did we come from? You know, before Eyre … The time before this. Don't you ever wonder?' Elias looked at him with a hint of exasperation.

Barrak just made his eyes go wide and shrugged his shoulders, which he knew would annoy the kid, even as he did it.

'I'm serious Barrak. And what about the forbidden zones, for quest's sake? Haven't you ever wondered what's really out there? I mean, why all the restrictions? Desolation and pestilence? Really?' Elias pulled a face, doing an imitation of someone pompous and stupid. 'You don't really believe that mumbo jumbo do you, Barrak? Don't you want to know what it's really like out there, beyond the outer markers?'

Barrak ran a hand through his hair, squinting at Elias. 'Not especially. And besides, talk like that anywhere but here could get a person in all kinds of trouble.'

'Phah!' Elias fixed Barrak with an intense, almost haunted expression for a moment or two. 'I've seen some things out in the border zones, Barrak. Things I can't un-see. And I've heard things. Things I can't un-know.' Elias smiled then, and his fierce eyes softened a little. 'I'm just not sure I can live in a bloody fishbowl the rest of my life.

'One day I'm gonna find out. One day I'm gonna see for myself.'

CHAPTER 6

JASMYN SLID TWO TICKETS across the linen tablecloth and winked. 'Liberated from father's personal assistant. I could've had her undies, too, and she'd have been none the wiser, the old dear.' She gave Barrak a mischievous grin.

It was Jasmyn's idea to meet for lunch near the stadium, then walk to the arena. The Providence Room was one of Tamouer's swankiest restaurant, just around the corner from the city's premier shopping strip at the eastern end of Orlan's Boulevard. It occupied the ground floor of one of the high-rent office buildings that ran along Bank Street, most of them occupied by lawyers, bankers, mining companies and the like. Just a stone's throw from the Providence Arch, the restaurant was opposite the Grand Hotel – the city's most expensive.

'Impressive skills.' Barrak picked up the tickets. 'Does Enoch know we're coming?'

'Well, not exactly – I thought we'd surprise him … I told him you're in town and you wanted to talk, but I didn't mention I'd appropriated a couple of his balcony passes.' Jasmyn accepted the tickets back from Barrak and slipped them into her jacket pocket. 'Any progress yesterday?'

Barrak told her about his fruitless visit to security headquarters and meeting the cardinal's new wife. He related a little of what Iggy had said to him in the council chambers and Jasmyn laughed. 'He's a radical old bugger, isn't he? If he wasn't a bona fide living antiquity, I reckon they'd have to lock him up for sedition.'

Barrak chuckled.

Jasmyn was radiant, with the morning light spilling in through the tinted window. Subtly made-up with a hint of eye-liner accentuating her blue-grey eyes, she was dressed impeccably in a white halter neck top, under a fitted silk jacket, highlighted with gold embroidery. At her throat was a simple diamond and silver pendant on a delicate silver chain.

Over her shoulder Barrak spied the tall maître d' gliding towards them, solemnly bearing a blue bottle of mineral water. They were seated at a window table in the front corner of the restaurant, at what he had called *Ms Mooney's preferred table*. When Barrak had arrived – early and casually attired – the same supercilious head waiter had examined him like something the kitchen cat had dragged onto the doorstep, until he mentioned the booking was in Jasmyn's name, at which point there'd been a celestial brightening of his demeanour and Barrak had instantly become his most revered customer.

'Would sir and madam care to order?' he enquired as he poured the sparkling water. 'Yes? Very good.' With a barely perceptible flick of an eyebrow he summoned a young waiter who appeared, pad and pencil poised almost before the maître d' had finished dispensing the water.

'OK, wait – I haven't really looked yet.' Barrak retreated behind the oversized menu.

'Well, I know what I'm having.' Jasmyn engaged the waiter with a polite smile – no need for her to even consult the menu. 'I'll have the duck – but no shaved potato – and can I get some of that special wild lime and desert-raisin relish please.'

Barrak settled on a rib-eye fillet with a thyme and pepper crust, but was still puzzling over his choice of salad. He was looking at the young waiter for inspiration when the world, quite unexpectedly, stopped. Then it started again – but in slow motion.

The waiter's face seemed to light up – orange at first, then with surprise. His order pad hovered and his eyes screwed shut as his teeth clenched and he lurched backwards, away from the table. Jasmyn seemed to have found something on the floor that required urgent attention and she had dived headlong off her seat.

Where the restaurant window had been, a blizzard of crystal gems billowed like a sail across the table top, sweeping everything before it. A maelstrom of shattered glass caught Barrak across the side of his head as he twisted and dropped. As he hit the floor the breath was knocked out of him, an exhalation which may have turned to an expletive, but his voice was lost in the thunderous boom that followed, so loud, it shook the foundations of the building and the internal organs of the cowering souls inside it. It came in unison with a shock wave, which invaded the restaurant like a brutal entity, buffeting diners and bursting eardrums.

Then, silence. A small waterfall of glass sounded, then another, and overhead a chandelier swung sickeningly, as if the room had been cast adrift on a wild sea. As if to support that absurdity, a brief squall – an ungodly back-draft – sucked napkins and other flimsy debris out into the street, before it too subsided.

The silence gradually changed to a low humming inside Barrak's head and then a high-pitched ringing. He got unsteadily to his feet and saw Jasmyn was standing too, brushing glass from her hair and looking around her, searching the floor for something: her bag. Then he had her by the arm but he wasn't sure who was holding whom. Her lips were moving and he was shouting – but all he heard was a distorted echo of his own voice inside his head. *We have to get out of here!* All around were upturned tables and crumpled bodies; diners turned to hapless typhoon survivors floundered amongst the debris of the shattered dining room, the scene made all the more surreal by the eerie silence of Barrak's ringing deafness.

He pulled Jasmyn deeper into the restaurant – away from the window and the alien landscape beyond – which moments ago had been the porte-cochère of the Orlan Grand on the opposite side of the road. His mind struggled to make sense of the image before his eyes – twisted metal and large irregular black lumps of debris strewn over the street. An ominous cloud of black smoke wafted up into the clear blue sky and wisps of white smoke hung closer to the ground. A vehicle was on fire, yellow tongues of flame flickering from its vacant windows. As he and Jasmyn edged toward the back of the restaurant his mind grappled with a half-formed question: *Had he seen anyone … were there any people there – in the driveway, at the front of the hotel, before the blast?* He didn't know. He was angry with himself for not knowing, for not being more observant, for having no answer to that vital question.

He stopped and started moving towards the front door. Jasmyn grabbed his arm and pulled hard. 'What are you doing?' she mouthed at him – Barrak wasn't sure whether he had heard her, read her lips or just guessed. 'I have to go and help – people may be hurt,' he shouted back, gesturing towards the front.

'No! Barrak, no! It's dangerous … We have to go!'

Barrak was sure he was hearing actual words now, or parts of them, phasing in and out with the ringing. That earnest look reminded him of the Jasmyn he knew as a little girl and quite suddenly, ensuring Jasmyn's safety overwhelmed his impulse to help others. In the street, there was already a patrol of city troopers, shepherding people away. Pretty soon the area would be cordoned off and emergency services would arrive, fully equipped, as he was not, to handle any casualties.

He let her pull him towards the swinging service door into the kitchen. Picking their way between the stainless steel benches, crates of produce and confused kitchen staff, they made their way to the back entrance and out into the laneway beyond.

'You're bleeding,' she said, dabbing a handkerchief at the side of Barrak's head.

'I'm fine. Thanks.' He took the handkerchief and pressed it gingerly to his head. 'How about you – are you hurt?' Barrak touched her arm gently.

'No. I'm all right. I'm just … Shit!' Jasmyn stifled a sob and drew in a series of short sharp breaths. 'I'm just … Gods! … ' Her face seemed to drop and her lower lip quivered; Barrak could see tears welling in her eyes. She dropped her bag and flung an upturned palm in the direction of the kitchen door. 'What was that? … What the hell? Bastards! What are they *doing*? … Orlan's mercy!' Jasmyn was starting to tremble and

Barrak grabbed her by both shoulders. She put a hand to his chest as if to push him away – but she didn't. She slapped his chest softly with one hand then both, slapped him harder and then harder still. Tears streamed down her face as she dragged in two big breaths. 'Why? What's … going on?'

Barrak pulled her to him and put his arms around her. She clung to him now and he felt the sobs shake her body.

After a moment or two she pulled away from him and quickly composed herself, punctuating sobs with expletives and sniffles. 'Sorry … Gods!' She looked sheepishly at Barrak. 'What the hell is going on in this city?'

'Rebels, I'm guessing.' Feeling lost for words, he offered Jasmyn her handkerchief to wipe away her tears. She took it and looked at it – dirty, crinkled and spotted with Barrak's blood. 'Thanks,' she snorted, holding the little rag with mock disdain.

Looking past Jasmyn up the narrow laneway to where it opened onto Orlan's Boulevard, he saw first one, then two city patrols flash past, lights blazing and sirens wailing, and heard the distinctive lament of a Medivec in the distance, drawing closer.

By the time they got back to the restaurant corner, police were already erecting barricades and moving people along. A panicky young trooper blocked their path and pointed across the boulevard, directing them to the opposite side.

Barrak craned his head to see down Bank Street. There was already a Medivec and three patrols in front of the hotel. People spilled out of the restaurant and the hotel lobby, dazed and disoriented – only to be further confused by the dissonant flashing of hazard lights, as they stumbled into the street, and were pointed to the barricades.

'Was anyone hurt?' he asked the trooper directing traffic.

'Move along sir – there's nothing to see here.' The young lad's voice was shrill, his eyes wild and distracted.

They crossed the boulevard with a throng of survivors and spectators and, looking back at the scene unfolding in front of the Grand, it seemed every emergency vehicle in the city was in on the act.

'What are we going to do now?' Barrak mused, half to himself as he watched the crowd flow past them.

Jasmyn raised one eyebrow, then reached into her jacket pocket, extracting the tickets with a flourish. 'Well, I suppose the show must go on.'

Maybe Barrak was looking at her strangely, because she began to justify herself: 'The game's almost starting, the stadium'll be full. They can't exactly call it off ... What else are we going to do, Barrak? Besides – when father hears about this he'll be worried. Better to give him the news in person.'

Down towards the Providence Arch, the boulevard was crowded. Shocked survivors of the blast merged with a crowd of blithe football supporters on their way to the game. Barrak thought he could pick out some in the crowd, like themselves, dishevelled and pale-faced, still trying to process what had happened. But the majority were high-spirited and rowdy, decked out in their team colours and paraphernalia, intent on fun and apparently oblivious to what had just happened nearby.

As the path beside the Arch opened onto parkland beyond, the numbers seemed to increase. He and Jasmyn had entered an alternate reality, where all was well, the sun was shining on grand-final day and rebels didn't blow up five-star hotels in front of your eyes while you ordered lunch. They both felt that peculiar lightness of spirit that comes after a brush with mortal danger – the simple euphoria of being alive.

Orlan's Boulevard widened to become one of the city's main arterial routes. A wide swathe of parkland ran parallel to it, marking out the mile or so from the Arch to the sports stadium. Stands of well-established maples and birches, together with towering eucalypts and cedars, were threaded with well-manicured paths and contrived waterways. The whole area, which acted as a green belt between the highway and Tamouer's expensive inner eastern suburbs, was filled with thousands of spectators, like a human vine, snaking its way to the stadium.

Swept up by the collective will of the crowd, Barrak and Jasmyn walked on, almost automatically, heading towards the stadium precinct. But Barrak's relief was starting to give way to anxiety. He glanced back at the city, but there was no indication now that anything was amiss. Closer to the stadium, along the near side of the boulevard, was a line of troop carriers, the type normally used by the provincial police and border control. Barrak began to count. There were eighteen in all, and troopers too, lots of them, standing around the vehicles, surly and bored, watching the crowd as it flowed past.

'What do reckon that's about?' Barrak gestured with a nod in the direction of the highway.

'Maybe they're expecting trouble at the football – it is the West Tamouer Eagles versus the Silvendale Panthers after all.'

'Yes– but not *that* much trouble,' Barrak observed drily.

The sound of sixty thousand cheering fans was reduced to a muted rumble within the upholstered interior of the members lounge. The thunder of applause came in waves, marking the changing fortunes of the game, and in between he could hear the rhythmic chants of the hard-nosed supporters duelling around the stands.

When they arrived at the stadium, Enoch, the other councillors, senators and their guests were on dessert and coffee, and the game had yet to begin. News of the explosion had reached Enoch just moments before, and as Barrak and Jasmyn walked into the dining room he was standing up at his table, locked in earnest conversation with two young officers, who were no doubt briefing him. When Enoch saw them, the old man brushed past the troopers and rushed to Jasmyn, as if to embrace her, but stopped short and instead just touched her lightly on the forearm. 'Thank gods you're safe. Were you in the city? Did you hear what happened?'

Jasmyn glossed over the closeness of their near miss to avoid concerning the old man more than necessary.

Barrak laboured through the pleasantries for an hour or so, with some of the other members in the bar. The main topic of conversation was his and Jasmyn's close encounter with the rebel attack, and more generally, the worrying escalation of trouble in the city. Once the game was well underway and most were distracted with the play, he managed to coax Enoch to a secluded table on the mezzanine above the main dining area.

'Thank the gods you were with Jasmyn this afternoon, Barrak.' Enoch left the statement hanging with the most subtle of inflections, making Barrak wonder if he was really thinking, *What were you and Jasmyn doing there, Councillor?*

'Disturbing times. I've seen a bit about the protests in the local papers down south, but I had no idea it was getting so serious. What's going on?'

'Indeed, indeed Barrak – what *is* going on? In all my years on the council there's rarely been a time when there wasn't some sort of dissent. But this is different – more radical … and the violence, like today. It's getting out of hand. Clearly it's got to do with this new rebel leader everyone's talking about – holed up somewhere out there in the eastern ranges, apparently. They call him *Gitan*. We don't even know his real name.'

Enoch paused and stared vacantly past Barrak for a few moments, then, as Barrak began to speak, shifted his gaze sideways to meet his eye.

'Do you think these so-called rebels have ever even read the Prophet? In any sort of detail, I mean.

'I've spent a lifetime studying Orlan's teachings, the Principles, the quest diaries, even most of the dissertations, and all the other prophets as well. There's a recurring theme throughout the lot, you know, the weakness of the human condition. That's what does us in, Barrak.

'Even if they have read, do you think these bloody dissidents have the faintest idea what Orlan had experienced? He'd seen it all, the flood, the chaos, the reckoning of the gods. He knew that civilisation was flawed, at risk from those same human impulses, carrying the seed of its own destruction … ' Enoch trailed off and shook his head slightly, then examined Barrak over his glasses. 'And there you have it, humankind – ultimately bound to be corrupted by its own venality.' His pained expression seemed to entreat Barrak's support. But Barrak just nodded.

'You don't get this from just reading the *Principia Cardinale*, you have to go deeper – a lot deeper … I suspect he was a tortured soul, our poor old Orlan. I don't think we can even imagine the things he would have seen in his time.'

'Do they think his political philosophy just sprang out of the blue?' Enoch demanded, indignant. 'Do they not understand the subtlety of his Sustainable Political and Economic Dynamic, malleable autocracy and democracy, working together in harmony, imperfect obviously, but self-correcting. No, no. It seems it's lost on them.'

Barrak made some non-committal sounds.

'Are we really doomed to repeat our mistakes over and over? It was the same in the past: dissent, calls for freedom. It happened back in ancient times when they overthrew Orlan's son Rylan and again during the Transformation. Both times a total disaster, and in both cases the only solution was to return to the teachings, to Orlan's Principles and the dynamic laws. Will we ever learn, do you think, Barrak?'

'Perhaps not.' Barrak looked away pointedly, staring down at the game, wondering how to distract Enoch from his political diatribe and steer him towards the issue he wanted to discuss. *Best just out with it.*

'So, tell me Enoch, what have you heard of these disappearances?'

Enoch stiffened slightly and there was a small, awkward pause. 'Disappearances?'

'Yes – apparently there've been dozens. Even Jasmyn knows someone whose son went missing, a woman at the academy. Surely you—'

'Rumours, Barrak.' Enoch cut him off a little bluntly. 'Rumours and exaggeration. Scare tactics, probably invented by the rebels themselves. Meldrick tells me there have been no confirmed cases, all just runaways … or misunderstandings. He's made some arrests obviously, in connection with the rioting and property damage, but all routine. No one has *disappeared.*'

'But Enoch, a patient came to my house, she said her son had been taken away that very morning, this Wednesday, just gone. She said men had come – she thought they were troopers but they weren't in uniform – and one of them identified himself as KLO.'

Enoch narrowed his eyes and, taking up his drink, settled back into his chair, looking down at the football pitch. Barrak followed his gaze and they both watched as the ball sailed high, wobbling on the breeze and through the goal posts into the great shimmering net behind. A deep roar broke over the stands, louder than ever, rumbling towards them from the far goal and crashing like a wave over the members wing.

'That puts the Panthers ahead,' said Enoch. 'They'll get a couple in a row now, run right over them, that's what they do – have done all season and always in the third quarter, *the slaughter quarter* – that's what the Silvendale fans call it.'

'Enoch, I asked about this woman's son at the Citadel yesterday. The security forces have no record of his arrest.'

Enoch seemed to drag his gaze wearily from the game and back to Barrak. He looked bleakly at his old friend, his eyes glassy and devitalised. 'I'm afraid that's just not possible Barrak. Meldrick reports to me directly, and he says he has the situation well in hand; it's all routine.'

'But Enoch, he's gone and ... '

'No!' The old ruler underlined his protest by banging his glass down a little too hard on the glass table, the sharp crack drawing some concerned glances from the members gathered below in the bar. 'Now listen to me, Barrak. I've been a member of the Keepers of the Light of Orlan for almost forty years. It is an organisation devoted to preserving and refining the Prophet's social and political philosophies – that's all. We *do not* go around kidnapping people. Now you yourself have been asked to join, many times I believe, but you have always declined. I don't know why. We're not devil worshipers and maybe if you acquainted yourself more with the organisation and its goals, you would be less inclined to listen to scurrilous rumours.'

Barrak drew a breath, but Enoch wasn't finished. Still looking out over the playing field, he went on, raising a hand towards the window, as if he were ministering to the players as well as Barrak. 'We're living in dangerous times. There are sensitive political issues involved in maintaining the council's independence and autonomy, while still trying to modernise the political system. It hasn't been easy trying to navigate between the council factions, appease the Senate and still try to keep the general population from boiling over.

'Look, since I took office our population has nearly doubled. According to the last census there are over 720,000 souls in greater Eyre. Incredible. This winter there've been grain shortages – at one stage people couldn't buy bread in the western provinces. Infrastructure is crumbling everywhere you look, the education system is bursting at the seams, the church is struggling to attract young people. Youth culture is becoming disrespectful, rebellious, self-destructive, and to make matters worse the security services are struggling to maintain our increasingly porous borders, especially to the east, where the latest intelligence suggests there could be a full-blown rebellion brewing.

'I've had my hands full, Barrak. It's not been easy. And most of this time, you've been down there in your bloody spa town tinkering with your carpentry and sulking …'

Enoch reigned himself in and turned to face Barrak squarely, giving him a rueful smile over the top of his spectacles. Barrak returned his stare evenly, trying not to show just how much he'd been stung by Enoch's jibe.

'I'm sorry – that was harsh. It was devastating, such a terrible loss. But how long has it been now? Four years? I can tell you, Barrak, this last year, allies have been thin on the ground in the council. I could have used a bit more support.

'You know how I feel about you Barrak – you really are like a son to me. You know that. But it's been getting harder and harder to excuse your absences from council. You've let yourself get out of touch. A lot has happened in the last few years, and you haven't really been a part of it, you've barely even made it to the mandatory sittings.'

'I know, you're right Enoch.' It took Barrak some effort to quell a surge of prideful ire, born of self-pity. He held Enoch's eye for a long moment. 'But I'm back now, and you know you can always rely on my support in the council.' Barrak paused pointedly. 'But I also have a duty to my patients and I do intend to find out what has happened to Gracie's son – whatever it takes.'

Enoch sighed, shaking his head. He'd always said it was Barrak's integrity and steely resolve that had attracted him in the first place. Some would call it stubbornness. He knew Barrak would not give up.

'What's the boy's name, Barrak?'

'Elias Arrowsmith.'

'Arrowsmith? I'll make enquiries with Meldrick myself, that's the best I can do. But don't expect too much. He'll be preoccupied with security for the festival, which is a nightmare given the recent unrest, and after today's incident, God knows what he's going to do.'

'Well – I think he may be already doing it. Did you see the troops along the highway this afternoon? It looks like he's gearing up for a full-scale riot. Are we sure he's not over-reacting?'

'Never forget, Barrak, one of the High Council's obligations is to protect the people. It's a heavy responsibility. If it were easy, maybe I'd still have my hair. Meldrick and his people are the council's instrument to provide that protection. Truth is, there always has to be a Meldrick. So let's just let him do his job.' Enoch's tone indicated he had no more to say on the topic. It was Barrak's turn to shrug, conceding Enoch's point.

The two of them settled back into their leather couches and directed their attention to the game. After all these years, even if they were at odds on an issue, he and Enoch were comfortable in each other's company. It seemed they could say whatever needed to be said to each other, without fear of offence. As if on cue, a waiter delivered a pot of coffee to their table and poured them each a cup.

The Silvendale players were running amok. West Tamouer had struggled and grafted to get the ball halfway down to its forward line but then a wayward pass was all it took and the Panthers pounced. In a blistering surge they ran the ball straight up the middle of the ground, running, weaving and passing with precision and pace, leaving the opposition flat-footed and frustrated. Before the Eagles players could regain position, the Panthers had scored again, the fourth goal in ten minutes. A cheer went up, with a subtly different timbre to it – less expectant, more triumphant. Enoch was right, the game was as good as over; the Eagles players were demoralised and lead-footed, their fans hushed and dispirited in their strongholds around the grandstands.

Looking down from their perch on the mezzanine, Barrak noticed Jasmyn standing with her back to one of the large windows at the front of the lounge, leaning against the heavy brass rail, oblivious to the game. She had a glass of wine in her hand and was engaged in animated conversation with a young man – possibly an intern at the academy, Barrak guessed, maybe even a footballer. He felt a wave of contentment and relief seeing her happy and safe, chatting with some handsome young fellow.

Enoch followed his gaze, and smiled the smile of a doting father. Jasmyn turned to look up at them, a daughter's ready smile for Enoch and a cheeky wink for Barrak, before seamlessly returning to the conversation.

'She's always had a soft spot for you, Barrak. Dayana once told me she had a crush on you, when she was a teen. You were like her champion, her protector.

'Do you remember the party at our house for Dayana's birthday? I hadn't known you for very long. I think you and Pers had only just met … Do you remember? Jasmyn was about seven and she disappeared and no one could find her. Dayana was beside herself, the nanny just about had kittens. It turned out she was playing down at the bottom of the yard, near the cliffs, and she'd climbed down and got stuck on that ledge – been there for hours – and remember you climbed down and got her.'

'Yeah, funny – I'd forgotten all about that.' Barrak felt a wave of nostalgia and noticed Enoch looking a bit glassy-eyed too, as he stared into space and went on with his story.

'Later that night Dayana and I asked her if she had been scared, and do you know what she said? She said, "I wasn't scared – I knew Barrak would rescue me."'

Both of them felt the poignancy of Enoch's story and sat and sipped their coffee in silence for a moment or two.

'Barrak, whatever happens, you'll always look after her, won't you?' Enoch demanded, his eyes intent, earnest.

'Of course I will Enoch.' Barrak was a little flustered. 'But lighten up for quest's sake … nothing's going to happen, and besides, it looks like your team's won.'

'What? No … I'm an old Westy from way back, I thought you knew that, Barrak. Damn it.' Enoch poured more coffee and fixed Barrak with a penetrating stare. 'I'm serious, I want you to promise me.'

'You know I will,' said Barrak, looking uncertainly at the old man and then down at Jasmyn. He thought he felt a chill as the stadium grumbled and sighed one last time before the final siren.

CHAPTER 7

ELIAS RESTED HIS HANDS on the laminated tabletop, a shiny new pair of manacles at his wrists. Toby had put him on a simple office chair, where he sat studying his reflection with great interest. At first he barely credited that it was his reflection – perhaps this was another lost soul, staring vacantly at him through the glass. But he blinked and twitched when Elias blinked and twitched, and so he concluded the lost soul was indeed his own, gaunt and bruised with matted hair and a crooked nose, but undeniably himself.

He wondered if there were people – interrogators, torturers, long-lost rescuers – observing him from the other side of the glass. A single door to the left of the mirrored wall was the only other feature in the small room. He watched the door and waited.

Eventually the door opened and Toby entered, placing a pitcher of water and a glass on the table and glaring warily at Elias. Elias was surprised to see he was wearing the khaki and black uniform of the Provincial Security Service with lieutenant's bars on his shoulders and a standard issue short combat sword at his hip. The man who followed him into the room was in civvies – black pants and shirt and a leather jacket. No weapon. He sat down opposite Elias, and placed a brown folder on the table neatly in front of him.

'Drink, please – go ahead.' He reached for the pitcher and poured some water into Elias's glass.

'My name is Bartell. Colonel Bartell, if you like. I'm with military intelligence … Yes I know, an oxymoron if ever there was one – but there you are.'

Elias reached for the glass with his manacled hands and gulped down the water, his eyes darting between Bartell and Toby. Clumsily he refilled the glass, spilling a good measure on the table, then drank some more.

'Commissar Meldrick himself has asked me to have a word with you, Elias. Seems he is quite keen for us to chat. And yours is such an interesting file.' Bartell fished a pair of reading glasses from inside his jacket and opened the folder. 'Comprehensive too – makes me wonder why Meldrick hasn't shared you with us sooner.' He glanced up and smiled.

'Please,' he said, refilling the glass while his free hand sent a signal to Toby to *refill the pitcher and get a bloody rag to clean up this mess.* 'Would you like anything else? Coffee, cigarette?'

Elias dead-eyed the colonel and sipped his water.

As Toby left the room with the jug, Elias considered vaulting the table and strangling the colonel with his manacles, but Bartell seemed to know his thoughts. Elias knew he was probably too weak to do much damage and the colonel radiated urbane malevolence, letting him know, without a single word, that he wouldn't stand for any shenanigans and would happily snap his neck, if need be.

'Now then, down to business. They tell me you have seen the light and stand ready to repent and cleanse your weary soul – am I right?'

Elias said nothing.

'But just let me say this, whatever Meldrick's clowns may have done to persuade you is not condoned, not one iota of it, by my people ... not at all. In fact, we have only just been brought in on this. And besides, when need dictates, we have our own methods of persuasion, which I assure you are nowhere near as crude as the CSF's, although much more effective. But that's beside the point, isn't it? Co-operation. Respect. Pursuing a mutually beneficial outcome – that's what we're about today, is it not? So, where should we start?' Bartell shuffled some papers in his file and Toby returned with the pitcher and quietly mopped up the spill before seating himself in the corner.

'What say, first of all, *I* tell *you* what we already know? After that, you can just fill in the blanks … sound all right to you?'

Elias bit his upper lip, gave the colonel a dubious sideways look and allowed himself a faint nod. 'Elias William Arrowsmith … Born, 14 February 685, Rylanswood Hospital. Mother, Grace Arrowsmith. Father … unknown. Educated, Point Prudence Primary and then Rylanswood Technical Institute.'

Bartell went on and on, laying bare the particulars of Elias's young life in so much detail that he found himself again imagining his irons around the colonel's neck. *Damn you, you supercilious son-of-a-sow*, was what Elias would say as he strangled the life out of him.

'Now this is where it gets interesting: after crossing the border at Lomond's Gate on 23 March 702, Elias Arrowsmith worked in the silica mines at Benbonny, and later in the Mount Olympus silver mines. We have you accommodated at the camp at Hell's Gate, and again, living in town at one of the hostels at Bowman's Rest.

'Let's see, employment records, identity checks, even tax payments. All very good, right up until August 703 … then *poof*, no more Elias. Elias vanishes into thin air and no one's any the wiser, until … let's see … about six months later.' Bartell paused for effect. 'That's six months – unaccounted for.' He took off his glasses and looked pointedly at Elias. 'Six months is a long time to be away with the fairies.'

Elias shifted in his chair and drew a breath, but before he could speak, Bartell went on. 'Never mind, let's not worry about that right now. We'll mark that down as query number one.' The colonel exaggerated the pains of making a note in Elias's file.

'So then, March 704 – young Elias reappears, back from oblivion, blessed by the fairy king and back in the land of the living – crossing the border at the same point, Lomond's Gate, on … let me see, Tuesday 2 March. From there it's straight back to Mum's in Rylanswood. Hugs and kisses, return of the prodigal son, all that … marvellous. So then, you've barely even dusted off your boots when you're in the employ of one Councillor Barrak Brethrenhope, well-known physician, libertarian and delegate to the High Council of Tamouer.'

89

Bartell looked up and caught Elias's eye, holding it for a just a fraction longer than was comfortable. 'Now that, I would say, *is* interesting, very interesting indeed. If you don't mind, I think we'll mark that down as query number two.' Bartell made an even bigger show of marking the file, 'Councillor ... Brethren ... hope.'

Elias shifted uneasily but didn't speak, sensing that Bartell would soon arrive at *query number three*. He didn't like the way this was going at all, and he was quietly horrified that Barrak's name had been mentioned. He never expected that anyone would make a connection between his travels and Barrak ... there was no connection. Once he was home in Rylanswood, he had simply needed a job. It worried him that he might have inadvertently implicated the councillor.

The colonel pressed on. 'Now, this next part really is perplexing. No sooner had you finished working for Brethrenhope – and if my margin note here is correct, it was before the poor councillor's house was even completed – than you got itchy feet again and off you went. September 705 ... across the border again, Lomond's Gate again ... Off into the zones for another spot of working in the mines perhaps.' The colonel stared pointedly at Elias. A dead quiet filled the room. Even Toby seemed to be holding his breath.

'Problem is – there are no records of you working in the border zones after that crossing ... not this time. No employment contracts, no tax records, no health checks ... nothing.' Bartell's face was a picture of mock befuddlement.

Elias registered that Bartell's eyes were a cold blue, with an intensity that was strangely at odds with his otherwise tranquil deportment. 'Not for *two years,*' he whispered emphatically, watching Elias across the table.

Elias was determined not to flinch or shift in his chair. He met Bartell's gaze gamely. Inwardly he rejoiced that Riggs' psychic visitations had helped him hone his cover story to razor sharpness. It was perfect. And it would be his gift to Bartell.

But Bartell hadn't finished just yet.

'After two long years, everyone had given Elias up for dead,' the colonel confided delicately. 'And yet here you are, July 708, popping up at Clay Pot Hill border crossing, way out near the solar arrays, one of your old stamping grounds.

'Let me see … you worked at the arrays back in … the last half of 701. But this time you didn't go there to work, did you? Not by the look of it. Still had some contacts out there I'm guessing – put you up, did they? Helped you cover your tracks? But what were you actually *doing* out there in the middle of the gods-blasted desert?'

Bartell didn't expect an answer. He forged ahead. 'I know I don't need to tell you about the forbidden zones north of the arrays, do I? I think we both know they are a little *more* forbidden than some others, aren't they?' Bartell smiled conspiratorially, but then his blue eyes iced over and his face suddenly stiffened.

'The whole damn area is a military exclusion zone – strictly no go, absolutely no exceptions.' He paused, took a breath, and went on in his usual civil tone. 'So there we have it, two years – two long years unaccounted for – and then, back into Eyre and you make straight for the arrays.'

Bartell tortured his eyebrows until one rose higher than the other. 'I think we can agree – that's query number three,' he said, making the annotation and folding his hands on the open file.

'I must say, I do count myself fortunate to be the one to hear your explanation for all of this … should you be so kind as to share it with me.' He gave Elias an expectant smile.

Outside the stadium, Barrak felt a chill wind. Not the mild, cool breeze that, in the summer months, swept in off the sea to quell the afternoon heat, this was blowing out of the west, cold and heavy with impending rain. A desert storm. The air already tasted of the bitter change that would sweep in from the south-west, dragging in cold, moist air, mixing it with the dust and sand of the desert. The sun was all but vanquished by dark clouds brewing over the western ranges and advancing on Tamouer. It peeped valiantly between the mountains and the glowering sky, creating an eerie interface – an underbelly of smouldering cumulonimbus, fired with a crimson hue.

Barrak zipped his jacket and hunched his shoulders against the cold, calculating he could just about make it back to the hotel before the rain hit. He had stayed after the game to catch up with a few council cronies and long-lost acquaintances – probably for one drink too many. Jasmyn had left soon after the game and Enoch not long after that. He was relieved to have shared the burden of Elias's absence with someone who might actually come up with an answer. But he knew realistically that nothing could be done until after tomorrow's festival and Monday's opening session.

As he tacked into the wind, making his way back through the park towards the city, the crowd thinned to just a few stragglers. Even the troopers, whose cordon had surrounded the entire stadium to prevent trouble at the end of the game, were starting to move away. By the time he made it back to the city, the wind was whipping down the boulevard and a premature dusk had enveloped the city, with leaden clouds blotting out the sky, leaving only a distant dome of radiant light, far away to the east.

The streets were strangely quiet, except for the odd burst of rowdy merriment spilling from a bar in amongst the elegant stores, all now deserted for the weekend. But there were still troop carriers, like the ones he'd seen by the stadium, positioned at regular intervals along the grand thoroughfare, parked and abandoned or, in some cases, with groups of troopers gathered nearby. Barrak couldn't remember ever seeing such a concentrated police presence in the city, not even around festival time. *Things are changing*, he thought as he mooched along the street, hunched against the cold.

As his hotel came into view, the heavens opened. Barrak made a run for it but was soaked as he splashed the last few steps to the awning. He noticed a patrol parked near the hotel entrance, and saw troopers amongst the crowd sheltering from the rain. He made for the door, but a deep young voice boomed, 'Councillor Brethrenhope?'

He turned. Two troopers hemmed him in to left and right, both equipped with wet-weather capes and caps. One was idly tapping the hilt of his short sword, while the other had what might have been a clipboard sheltering under his cape, which he was checking.

'Councillor Barrak Brethrenhope?' he repeated.

'Yes,' said Barrak, attempting a note of affront but probably only managing surprise. 'Is there a problem?'

'No sir. No problem at all. But you will need to come with us.'

'Oh, really? Where and why?' Barrak was blunt. He was now genuinely annoyed and intended to pull rank on the two young troopers, who had clearly overstepped their authority.

'CSF headquarters, if you don't mind, sir. It is rather important.'

'I have no intention of going down to the Citadel or anywhere else at seven o'clock on a Saturday evening. Whatever this is about, go back to your superior officer and tell him to contact my office at the High Council next week and I will consider … '

'I'm afraid we are going to have to insist, Councillor.' The second trooper stepped forward, putting a hand lightly on Barrak's arm. 'We have rather strict orders.'

Barrak looked at the hand on his arm and then at the trooper. 'Are you arresting me?' he demanded indignantly, glaring at the lad.

'Only if we have to, sir. Commissar Meldrick would like to see you in his office down at security headquarters, right away. He apologises for the inconvenience.'

'Meldrick? Why didn't you say so? I have a few questions for the commissar myself. Now … ' Barrak glanced at the trooper's hand on his sleeve, then looked pointedly at the tall youngster. The lad removed his hand and seemed briefly at a loss to know where to put it.

'Now,' Barrak continued, 'first I'm going to my room to change into dry clothes. One of you can come with me or you can both wait in the lobby – as you choose. I will be twenty minutes. Then we will go down town and see what the commissar has to say for himself.'

'Councillor. So good of you to come.' Meldrick swung around to face Barrak and the troopers backed out of the office. In his hand were two tumblers – liquor, no ice – one of which Meldrick held out as he rounded the massive oak desk and approached Barrak. 'Drink?'

'Good to see you, Commissar,' Barrak countered. He would not acknowledge that he'd been brought against his will like a common criminal. 'I was hoping to get a chance to speak with you.' He took the drink and sniffed it, advisedly, then put it on the sideboard near the door.

Meldrick frowned fleetingly, then turned it into a smile; he would let Barrak's impertinence pass. 'Please, have a seat.' He indicated an armchair beside a low, polished timber table in front of a vast bookcase. As Barrak took his seat he discreetly surveyed his surroundings – he had not been in Meldrick's new office. It was palatial, and furnished with an impressive collection of antiques, many of which appeared, to Barrak's untrained eye, to be pre-Transformation. An elaborate tapestry with an historical theme hung from the wall behind the large desk and on the adjacent wall, a gilt-framed portrait of Meldrick in full dress uniform and ceremonial weaponry.

'Well now, why all the urgency, Manson?' Barrak eased himself back into the soft leather. 'I've had a tough day – already had rebels try to blow me up once and my team just got done over in the final, so I hope you'll excuse me if I ask you to get straight to the point.'

'I heard about your near miss – you and Jasmyn Mooney, I believe. Lunching at the Providence Room, no less ... how lovely.' Meldrick sat in the seat opposite and placed his untouched drink on a coaster. 'Nasty. Such a rude interruption to your little ... tryst.' He gave Barrak a look of mock concern, tut-tutting as he did.

'And that's not the half of it,' said Barrak, determined not to be unsettled by Meldrick, 'we hadn't even ordered.'

Meldrick brooded for a moment, shrugged and then gave a dismissive grunt. 'Well, let's get down to it shall we?' He crossed his legs, tilting his head back and literally looking down his nose at Barrak. 'You've been making enquiries about a young lad called Elias Arrowsmith. What is your interest in this person, if you don't mind me asking, Councillor?'

Barrak sat forward. 'My interest is that I have a patient – the boy's mother – beside herself with worry for her son, who seems to have been abducted. And yes, I did ask about Elias right here – at the front desk,' Barrak, jerked a thumb over his shoulder, 'just yesterday – and

I was told you have no record of his arrest. Are you now telling me you have him in custody?' Barrak could not mask his incredulity.

'I didn't say that,' Meldrick countered, annoyed that Barrak had him on the defensive. 'But we do have a legitimate interest. The boy has made some serious transgressions – illegal border crossings and so on. We think he may be involved with the rebel movement. Some say he could even be a serious player, so I need to know what you know, Councillor.'

It was Barrak's turn to push himself back into the plush comfort of Meldrick's armchair and look down his nose at his adversary. He folded his arms across his chest and shook his head sceptically. 'This is ridiculous. I've known Elias for years. He even worked for me once. He's just a kid – a good kid. He may have been a bit wild as a teenager, but what kid isn't? I'd vouch for him any time. Do you have evidence of any wrongdoings?'

Even as Barrak defended Elias, details of past conversations on the building site flashed through his mind. He re-examined those memories now, and felt a vague sinking sensation in his gut. *Could Elias have got himself into some sort of trouble?*

Meldrick continued, banging on about deteriorating law and order and the increasing boldness of the rebels and how they threatened the way of life cherished by all Eyreans. Gradually he made his way back to his need to learn from Barrak what he knew about Elias.

'I've told you all I know about the boy. As far as I'm concerned, he is a law-abiding citizen. He once worked for me as a labourer. He and his mother are my patients – have been for many years. That's it. That's all I know.'

'Councillor—' Meldrick blurted this out, caught himself and then adjusted his tone. 'You do know it's a crime to withhold information in relation to rebel activities don't you?' He stared flint-eyed at Barrak, as a hectic wave of anger threatened to erupt, then subsided. 'It's a serious crime – punishable by imprisonment. I cannot overstate the threat these rebels pose to the security of Eyre. Strong action is required. You *must* tell me what you know about Arrowsmith.'

Must, thought Barrak. He gave the commissar, a hot, inflammatory glare. If he could have bored a couple of smoking holes through the security chief's skull, he wouldn't have been displeased. Meldrick returned his stare and neither blinked. Somewhere a clock ticked loudly.

'You have him, don't you Meldrick? You have him in custody.'

'That's none of your concern, Councillor.' There was thinly veiled malevolence in Meldrick's reply.

'If he has been arrested without charge,' Barrak spoke very quietly, 'if he is being detained without representation or counsel,' he felt the resonance in his voice building, '*if* he is being held in secret and questioned under duress,' Barrak leant across the table, his voice ramping up ruinously with each accusation, 'then by Orlan's blood, it damn-well is my concern and the concern of the High Council, and every last citizen of Eyre to boot!'

Meldrick seemed to be holding his breath. He slammed his hands onto the arms of the chair and shot to his feet with a sharp exhalation that didn't quite form itself into any intelligible words. His hands clenched into fists and he drew a deliberate deep breath and exhaled slowly. He turned away from Barrak towards his desk then spun back around to face him.

'You really need to be more cautious, Councillor.' Meldrick enunciated the words meticulously. 'You are not above the law, and it would be a serious mistake to think yourself so. Your position on the High Council does not give you immunity, not when rebellion and sedition are in the air. You and your ilk sit in your chambers deliberating, procrastinating, passing judgement, but to what end? Our world will crumble and fall before the High Council takes any effective action.' Meldrick jutted his chin at Barrak. 'And you have the impudence to come in here accusing *me* of wrongdoing, barking at me like some kind of rabid scrub dog.'

'I don't have to listen to this bullshit.' Barrak was on his feet and heading for the door.

'But you probably should listen, Brethrenhope, because it's not looking good for you. A delegate to the High Council, consorting with a rebel spy, refusing to co-operate with an investigation ... '

Barrak rounded on him loosing off a burst of hostile intent, pleased to use his larger stature to intimidate, and gratified to see Meldrick flinch. 'I don't know what you're talking about, Manson, but I'll tell you this. You've crossed the line. I promise you I will find out what you've done to that boy and you will be held to account for it – *and* for all the other disappearances. At the next session of the parliament I intend to put an urgent motion to the council, and mark my words, one way or another, this will end in a full senate enquiry. So I dare say you're the one who should be cautious, my friend'. With that, Barrak fixed the security chief with a stony stare and then turned towards the door.

'You're wrong! There is more at stake than you know. You're a fool Brethrenhope.'

Barrak stopped and he let out a sigh of exasperation. He turned and gave Meldrick a quizzical look, as if to say, *Why you are such an ass?*

'Gods curse you, Meldrick,' he said evenly, then reached for the door.

Meldrick called after him. 'Goodbye Councillor. Be sure to give my very best regards to young Ms Mooney, when you see her next.'

Barrak took a long slow breath, fighting the urge to march back into Meldrick's office and snap him in half. Then he chastised himself for allowing the man to get under his skin so easily. He'd lost his composure and said way too much, probably not doing himself or Elias any favours. He cursed his lack of restraint. Meldrick had also guessed Jasmyn was special to him, but he didn't want him to know how special, so he held his tongue and kept on walking.

CHAPTER 8

A FITFUL SOUTH-WESTERLY buffeted the city on the Sunday of Orlan's Festival. The streets of Tamouer were scoured with frigid gusts of wind, alternating with patches of calm which – when the sun broke through – gave an impression of spring. The storm front had passed overnight and by morning the rafts of low grey cloud were starting to break up. With luck, by midday the gale would ease enough to allow people to enjoy the celebrations.

But Barrak's mood was far from festive as he lingered over the last of his coffee. From his vantage point in one of the breakfast nooks on the first floor of the hotel's atrium, he could see up and down the boulevard, and despite the double glazing, he could hear the lines of prayer flags strung across the thoroughfare chattering furiously in the wind. The decorations, so carefully arranged over the last few days, had not fared well in the storm and some formed drifts of flotsam swirling at the whim of erratic gusts in the street below. Vendors had begun to set up their stalls and a few hardy souls, rugged up against the morning chill, were staking claims to the best vantage points, hours before the procession would make its way down Orlan's Boulevard.

He had woken too early, feeling anxious and unrefreshed. His run-in with Meldrick the night before had left him agitated and the day seemed to match his mood. Looking distractedly at the street below he was transported back to a festival long ago, another wind-swept spring day of his childhood, watching the parade from his father's office on the first floor of the Museum building. He remembered his father's stern demeanour as he stood beside him lecturing him on the floats as they passed, instructing him on their meaning and historical context. He recalled trying so hard to understand what his father was telling him, but it must have been beyond him at such an early age, slipping away no matter how hard he tried to grasp it. And he remembered feeling anxious that his father would be angry about his lack of understanding. The feeling of unease he had woken with that morning was strangely reminiscent of that childhood anxiety.

Then a warmer recollection swept away his disquiet: his mother arriving to rescue him from his father's strict tutorial, gathering him up in her arms and holding him while he sat on the window sill and pointed and laughed and chattered excitedly as the spectacle passed below. Later they would go down into the crowded street, where all he could see were glimpses of the procession between the legs of the spectators. But he didn't care, his mother had him by one hand and in the other he held a special treat, reserved for festival day. Frustratingly, Barrak could not remember just what the treat was; its true nature was locked in a bubble of young Barrak's sensory memory, the taste tantalisingly familiar and yet unknown to his adult self. It was as if the wonderful little morsels, ensconced in a crinkly paper bag, had existed only in that moment in time, a magical treat conjured by his mother, but not of this world, just as she too, was soon to be no longer of this world.

It was the happiest and saddest memory he had – pretty much the only clear memory he had of his mother, who had died from an infection when Barrak was not yet five. Barrak always assumed she had died not long after the festival and this was why Orlan's Day left him overwhelmed with nostalgia. In the past it had bothered him that he didn't know the date of her death. His father refused to mark the occasion or speak of it, and Barrak had never found any written record. Her gravestone only recorded the year, *In loving memory of Evelyn Brethrenhope 625–666*. It must have been his father's way of coping; the only way he could move on was to try and forget her awful end.

It is remarkable how resilient children can be. He had taken it in his stride and kept a shrine to his mother: a small framed photograph of her smiling happily, young, beautiful and carefree, her hair blowing in the wind. Barrak could tell just from her smile that she was on holiday. This he kept with a polished stone she'd given him – his *touch stone*, she had said, because he'd grown so attached to it as a child. It was a smooth translucent green with a creamy mottled pattern shot through with flecks of gold. The other relic in his shrine was one of her business cards: *Evelyn Sage: Crystal healer and practitioner of Orlan's Touch*. It was in flowing calligraphy and surrounded by strange and fascinating symbols. Barrak still had those three items to this day.

Children seem to be able to accept the impermanence of human existence so much better than adults. He didn't remember feeling bereft as a child, not as his father had done, not until history repeated itself and he lost Persephone and Noah. Then he coped as his father had – he supposed that's what people do, learn by absorption. He put up a wall, nay, he built a whole dam to hold back the sorrow, and he distracted himself by building that house – obsessively, diligently, belligerently building it – hammering flat and bricking up any hint of the reality of what had occurred. He had no choice, because the avalanche of grief when it finally came, when he finally stood alone in Persephone's dream home, bereft of her and their son, surrounded by the empty, cold and futile structure – was overwhelming. He had never truly felt the loss of his mother until then, and the grief of her loss became one with the unbearable pain of losing his wife and child; it engulfed him, like a dark fathomless ocean.

He sank in it like a stone.

With the house finished and the life-raft of his industry suddenly gone, he was powerless to halt his descent, and in a way, he didn't want to. He consigned himself to the depths and waited to drown; but he wouldn't be allowed that mercy. In the depths, the gods of that dire underworld assaulted him further. Sadness turned to self-pity and indignation. Guilt assailed him from every angle and there was resentment, and petulant anger.

And so it was that months later he emerged from his sea of loss weighed down by a yoke of bitter umbrage, hardly recognisable to friends and family. He could barely contain the hatred and bile he felt towards the world, the universe at large, for doing this to him. Why him? What sort of karmic contradiction had led him to this? Had he not dedicated his life to good works, to trying to help others?

If it had not been for his oldest friend, Thomas, he would have completely unravelled. Barrak had reopened his practice after moving into the house, despite the awful state he was in – anything to keep himself busy. It was Thomas, the gnarly old sea-dog and eschewer of bullshit who spoke the unvarnished truth to him one clear cold day, over coffee at the shack that passed for a café at the end of the fishermen's wharf. 'You're gonna kill one o' them patients of yours, Barrak,' Thomas had said to him. 'You're in no fit state. You need to shut up shop for a while. Strip y'self back to the bare timbers, and take a good hard look at whatever it is that's still holding you together, and do some much-needed repairs'.

Only Thomas, fisherman and childhood friend, could have got away with telling Barrak he was unseaworthy and needed to go into dry dock. It was Thomas who had driven him into the mountains a few days later, and it was Thomas who had come and picked him up nine months after that, when the monks had finished with him and pronounced him fit to return to the world.

By the time Barrak made it outside, Orlan's Boulevard was awash with a multihued assortment of Eyrean humanity. Streaming up the streets either side of the temple from the ferry terminal and the railway station were families and groups from every corner of the land, laden with picnics, umbrellas and every imaginable accessory for a day out. The heart of the city was transformed into an outdoor theatre packed with revellers and once-a-year visitors.

Making his way the short distance from the hotel to the main square, Barrak was accosted by street vendors, fortune tellers and trinket sellers and singed by a fire-eater belching huge fireballs into the air above the milling mob in front of the temple. City police and patrols of provincial troopers seemed to be everywhere, manning the barricades separating the central thoroughfare from the crowd and threading their way through the masses of revellers.

The chaotic throng, together with a seemingly disproportionate military presence, did little to alleviate his anxiety. As he rounded the corner into the square he saw that the first of the rural exhibits was trundling down the central part of the boulevard to ironical and good-natured cheers from the crowd. He made for the raised marquee bearing the colours of the High Council – it was set back from the boulevard and flanked by two smaller marquees. Barrak usually avoided the official set-up in the square, preferring the anonymity of the crowd, or a spot away from the noise where he could observe and enjoy the atmosphere in peace. But now he was committed – he'd given Enoch his promise and Enoch was keeping him to it – he'd even had a grandstand pass delivered to his hotel early that very morning with a note attached to remind him.

Jasmyn squirmed on the rickety stool and pulled her woollen jacket together at the front to insulate her from the chill air in the marquee. They seemed to have erected the damn thing in a wind tunnel. She had a passionate disdain for the annual festival, but seeing Barrak and her father all chummy the previous day had left her with an unaccountable urge to be more social. She'd firmly declined a seat along the front of the stand overlooking the parade route – she couldn't think of anything worse than being on display with Tamouer's crusty political and business elite. Instead she'd found the bar near the exit at the back of the marquee and she was in the process of negotiating some kind of acceptable cocktail with the barman. She caught a glimpse of Barrak coming up the stairs, put the barman on hold with a raised finger and deftly grabbed Barrak's sleeve and guided him towards the bar.

'What a relief. I thought I was going to have to drink alone. He thinks he might know how to make a Desert Storm. Probably the best we'll do, under the circumstances.' She put up an extra finger and mouthed the word *two* to the barman. Barrak settled himself next to Jasmyn at the bar, shaking his head in mock dismay. Jasmyn's irreverent approach to life always made him smile and he found his mood lifting already.

'I see you've got yourself a good view of the parade,' he observed wryly.

'Trust me, these are the best seats in the house, and you'll need this, if you want to thaw out,' she said, handing him his drink and holding hers aloft for a toast. 'Vitas!' They clinked glasses and sipped their strange cocktails, chatting about this and that. Jasmyn listened with horrified delight as Barrak told her about his run-in with Meldrick the previous evening. After a while they drifted over to the front of the marquee to watch some of the parade. The sky had cleared and the wind had suddenly dropped, so the midday sun spilling into the front of the tent brought some welcome warmth.

Leaning against the massive corner post, Jasmyn felt relaxed and a little sleepy, unaccustomed to strong drink in the middle of the day. She was half watching the parade and half watching Barrak. The military exhibits had started to come past and frankly she was bored. Barrak seemed distracted too, but there was something else, something in the set of his jaw and his furrowed brow. She followed his gaze and soon saw what had caught his attention. At the edge of the square was a man about Barrak's age or maybe a few years younger – a fit outdoorsy-looking man in boots and moleskins with a hide jacket. On his shoulders was a little boy no older than three or four, one hand around his father's brow and the other pointing at the parade. It could have been Barrak and his little boy, Noah, a few years earlier.

All at once Jasmyn understood Barrak's long absences and felt the pain of his loss deep in her own heart. A powerful surge of compassion welled up in her. Barrak felt her gaze on him and gave her a sidelong glance that was boyish and vulnerable. Jasmyn reached out and squeezed his arm but, feeling that wasn't enough, she put her arm right around his shoulders in a friendly hug. She felt him take a deep breath and hold it, before exhaling slowly.

This was the real reason he avoided events like this. For Barrak, any of the recurring events throughout the year could evoke memories, and the Festival of Orlan – an obvious favourite for families with young children – was probably the worst of them all. Barrak closed his eyes momentarily and dipped his head to Jasmyn's whispered query, her lips close to his ear.

'Yes I'm fine. Thanks. It's OK ... really.'

His attention was drawn back to the parade by the noise of the spectators along the route, cheering but also booing and jeering, above the general hubbub of the mob.

'Orlan's blood!' breathed Barrak. It was Meldrick riding at the head of the next contingent in the procession: the Parliamentary Guard, parading in traditional dress uniform and ceremonial arms.

Barrak thought it interesting and instructive that Meldrick had chosen this role in the parade. There he was, riding tall and proud in the saddle of a sleek black stallion, wearing the full dress uniform of a colonel in the elite Parliamentary Guard, complete with polished black armour, ornate helmet with flowing horse-hair plume and ceremonial weaponry.

Barrak noted the jeering with interest. Meldrick was shamelessly promoting himself as head of the Guard.

Under Meldrick, the elite Parliamentary Guard and the Keepers of the Light of Orlan had begun to align themselves. Some said the Guard was beginning to act as if it were the Keepers' military arm. Clearly some, from the anonymity of the crowd, were expressing their views on the Guard's recent heavy-handed tactics. As he scanned the faces of the horsemen he wondered if some of those very men had had a hand in the abduction of Elias ... and the other disappearances.

As they drew level Meldrick spotted him and Jasmyn in the marquee just as Jasmyn, following Barrak's gaze, saw Meldrick in the parade.

Meldrick's stony stare communicated volumes to Barrak, none of it friendly. It told him he had made himself an enemy – a powerful one – and it said Barrak was now a marked man. As the phalanx drew level the horsemen all turned to face the official marquee, as if following their leader's cue. As one they snapped a salute to the assembled councillors and then, after a heartbeat and once again in unison, they turned their eyes forward – all except Meldrick. He kept his eyes on Barrak – like a hunter on prey, and his stare seemed to intensify. Barrak wondered how much of Meldrick's animosity was historical and how much was due to the previous evening. And then of course, there was Jasmyn.

Barrak glanced at her, and she widened her eyes and contorted her mouth in a comical look of mock consternation, then mouthed the words *Holy shit* to him and laughed out loud. He turned back in time to see Meldrick's eyes flare with rage before he snapped his attention back to the front of the column.

Barrak frowned at Jasmyn but she just smiled impishly and shrugged her shoulders and wagged her head towards the exit: time to go.

Barrak suggested they could watch the festivities more comfortably back in the warmth and comfort of the upstairs lobby at his hotel. They wandered back along the busy boulevard, catching glimpses of the passing parade and taking in some of the street performances as they ate the ice creams Jasmyn had insisted on buying. Some teenagers tried to beat the impossible odds at a side show, and after watching them for a time, they passed by the temple and skirted groups of prim, proud parents fussing and photographing their adolescent children, surly and awkward in the ascendancy vestments they would only ever wear once. Barrak wondered how the cardinal had weathered his *invasion* and thought briefly of Noah and all the rites of passage he would never experience.

As they approached the hotel, a ripple of disquiet pulsed through the crowd and a brief shout rose above the clamour. In that same instant a man bumped hard into Barrak's shoulder and threw him off balance. He caught a glimpse of hard-set features, but the man didn't stop or even look at Barrak, let alone apologise. He pushed ahead, almost knocking down an old woman, and bolted towards the hotel.

A rush of sound went through the crowd like a loud whisper, or an off-key cheer but with an edge of alarm. Barrak heard a couple of distinct screams.

The crowd nearby surged, opening up a view to the centre of the boulevard. Through the gap he glimpsed a puzzling scene. The parade had dissolved into a shambles. People were fanning out, fleeing the area.

A uniformed man was on the ground, face down. He looked contorted. Unnatural. Several people were around him, on their knees. Another had the man by the arm as if trying to help him up.

'He's been shot!' someone shouted. The news galvanised the mob and set off more screaming and confusion as people surged away from the scene.

It seemed to be happening slowly, but had probably only taken an instant. Jasmyn gave Barrak a concerned look and said something he didn't quite catch. He caught a glimpse of the man who'd bumped him, dodging a clutch of spectators and breaking into a run. Barrak broke through the crowd and onto the pavement in front of the hotel. He could see the man clearly now, pushing his way through another bunch of people milling around the entrance.

Jasmyn had Barrak by the arm. 'What is it?'

'Wait here – wait in the hotel!'

Barrak took off after him; he didn't really know why – instinct perhaps.. He could see the man up ahead, running hard, then he braked and skidded, the loose debris on the pavement underfoot almost bringing him down, before he darted into the laneway beside the hotel.

He looked up as Barrak came sliding to a halt at the top of the lane. There was panic and fear in the man's eyes. He was thirtyish, with an athletic build, dark hair and skin and the garments of a ruran. He scrambled along to the next doorway and disappeared.

Barrak ran to the door and threw it open – he could hear footfalls echoing in the fire-escape stairs, maybe two flights up. He legged it up the first flight, pausing at the landing long enough to ask himself what the hell he thought he was doing. This wasn't like him.

At the next landing Barrak sensed something just in time to flatten himself against the wall of the stairwell as a huge missile crashed onto the metal handrail, its top bursting open as it bounced off into the void, spinning and spewing garbage over the stairs and down into the well. Barrak's heart pounded and his throat tightened. He sucked lungfuls of air and exhaled hard two or three times before sneaking a peak up into the stairwell.

It seemed clear.

Clammy fear mingled with the sweat of sudden, unnatural exertion. He took the next two flights two or three steps at a time and stopped on a landing where there was a door with a large sign. *Roof – No Admittance.* He was gasping like a marathon runner and felt sure anyone on the other side of the door or for a mile around would hear him panting. And he was terrified. But surging adrenaline cleared his mind enough to make him wary. Carefully he reached for the door handle and slapped it down – simultaneously jumping two steps to the side. Sure enough, the door flew open with a mighty boom, kicked with such fierce force that the door handle smashed chips from the brick wall, the sound of it reverberating in the stairwell like rising thunder. It would have knocked him backwards, maybe right over the balustrade and into the void. He felt faint, and for a moment thought he would vomit. He tried to control his breathing but couldn't curb his need for air. Beads of cold sweat prickled his brow, and he was unsure whether to flee down the stairs or rush out the door with a blood-curdling scream. Instead he just froze. After a moment he heard footsteps. Running. The man was out on the roof. One deep breath and he bolted through the doorway.

Ahead was a low parapet and beyond that, who knew, maybe a drop to the street below. To his left was a large water tank. He went right and as he cleared the corner of the fire escape, he almost tripped on something. A crossbow. He stopped and looked at the thing for a moment, but then his attention was caught by a figure clambering over a parapet some thirty yards ahead of him.

'Hey! Stop!' The words came out of him for no sensible reason … *Why would he stop now?* The man glanced back briefly then leapt over the low wall. Barrak picked up the crossbow, even though he had little knowledge of weapons – perhaps it would make him feel less vulnerable. He charged towards the parapet only to find a drop of four or five feet on the other side. Besides that, what he saw ahead of him stopped him in his tracks.

The ruran was standing at the far corner of the rooftop with two other men. He had his hands on his thighs, his chest heaving as he tried to catch his breath. The other men were both military. One was an officer, Barrak thought a lieutenant by the insignia at his collar and the sword at his hip. The other soldier wore a plain coreman's uniform – an ordinary provincial trooper. They both had crossbows slung at their shoulders, sleek and smaller than any weapons Barrak had seen before. He wondered if they were the new automatic rapid-fire combat bows he'd heard about.

An animated conversation was going on between the three men, but the soldiers made no move to arrest the fugitive. The runner straightened and pointed at Barrak and seemed to be pressing some kind of point with the two soldiers.

Confused and struggling for breath, Barrak yelled, 'Hey!' between gasps. They looked at him, but more with uncertainty and annoyance than any real concern.

'Arrest that man. He's a suspect,' Barrak blurted out.

The officer and the ruran looked at each other then back at Barrak, but made no reply.

'I'm Councillor Brethrenhope, delegate to the High Council, and I'm telling you, detain that man.' He climbed down onto their level and slowly approaching the group.

The officer unslung his bow and very deliberately raised it and pointed it at Barrak. Barrak stopped walking.

'Put that weapon down on the ground,' the lieutenant said.

Barrak looked at him askance and then at the crossbow he held in his own hand – as if noticing it for the first time. He carefully put the crossbow down on the asphalt, without taking his eyes off the lieutenant. 'What do you think you're doing, Lieutenant? Do you understand what I'm telling you? This man may have been involved in an assassination attempt. Now, you need to take him into custody.'

Barrak kept his patience, trying to resolve the misunderstanding.

The lieutenant exchanged a furtive look with the young trooper. He then nodded deliberately at the trooper and inclined his head towards the ruran. The trooper looked uncertain and frightened, his eyes darting back and forth between his lieutenant and the fugitive. There seemed to be some unspoken understanding between them, but the young soldier looked like he wanted to run away.

'Do it!' the lieutenant shouted with unexpected violence. The trooper unslung his own bow and rounded on the man in ruran garb. Barrak noticed there was something out of place about his ruran attire – he was wearing gloves.

The young trooper waved the bow at him, gesturing him to move back toward the edge of the building. The man looked perplexed, darting questioning looks at the two soldiers. The trooper advanced on him and forced him to back away, closer to the edge. Barrak saw the man's expression turn from confusion to realisation and then quickly to panic. 'No,' he said in disbelief and then repeated it more stridently. 'No. No. What the hell are you doing?' He looked to Barrak now, as if imploring him to intervene. The man's eyes were wide with fear but even as he locked eyes with Barrak, his expression changed to something else ... was it acceptance? Resignation?

At that moment the trooper fired, almost at point blank range, a volley of three or four arrows, all in the blink of an eye. Barrak saw the poor soul look down at the shafts protruding from his chest, then at Barrak, his expression a mixture of bewilderment and disappointment. He stumbled backwards and then, quite suddenly, as if by some dire magician's sleight of hand, he vanished.

Barrak's mind refused to accept what he had just seen. The ruran he had chased onto the roof was gone, killed. The trooper standing by the roof's edge dropped his hands to his side, still holding the crossbow slackly. His shoulders slumped and he bowed his head – he looked deflated. Perhaps he too was bewildered.

The officer still had Barrak squarely in his sights. Barrak looked at the discarded crossbow at his feet and thought about picking it up. He was no longer scared – in fact a strange clarity had come over him. It was as if, all at once, he could see and hear everything in detail. The clouds above his adversary's head were vivid and majestic; melodic bird song erupted from the treetops just beyond the edge of the roof and the afternoon sunshine had an exquisite warmth to it, which he felt he had never quite experienced before. From below, the sounds on the street reached him clearly – as if he could distinguish every single voice in the crowd, every panicked cry and every barked order. He smelled doughnuts and horse dung.

He realised he was about to die.

He thought this altered state of consciousness must be what happens in the moment before death, and yet it did not diminish the wonder of it. He looked into the eyes of his killer and knew his thoughts, which was how he saw the lieutenant change his mind, even as it happened. The officer looked down at the assassin's bow at Barrak's feet and then back at Barrak. He smiled and lowered his weapon. 'We're getting out of here. Right now!' He gestured to his subordinate. 'Come on, move! And bring his bag.'

The youngster seemed dazed and confused, no doubt still in shock himself.

Barrak saw the young trooper bending over the backpack that had belonged to the murdered ruran. He could see tears running down his face as he crammed the spilled contents back inside. A trooper's uniform! Even from a distance Barrak could see the distinctive colours. The shooter had been carrying a military uniform.

'Take the bow too,' he said, nodding at the weapon near Barrak's feet.

'You won't get away with this,' Barrak ventured.

'Get away with what, Councillor?'

'You've murdered him. He wasn't even armed. You executed him!'

'Are you sure, Councillor? Because I think maybe you killed him – with that crossbow.' The lieutenant indicated the bow on the ground as the trooper stooped to pick it up. 'Careful not to touch it son, wrap it in something – it could have the killer's prints on it.

'You might be interested to know he was a sergeant in the Special Metro Response Unit, the man you killed – he was working undercover,' the lieutenant elaborated. 'I think maybe *you* shot the general, right in the middle of the damned parade, and then you shot this undercover officer when he tried to arrest you. And maybe you were careless and left your prints all over the murder weapon too, Councillor, so don't tell me who's getting away with what.'

The lieutenant was smug as he watched the implications of his words break over Barrak like waves. Images flashed across his mind: the assassin's gloved hands, picking up the crossbow, the uniform in the bag, the conspiratorial manner of the three men on the roof, before the cold-blooded execution.

'That's right, Councillor. Now, let me give you some advice: you were never here and you saw nothing. I'd be keeping my head well down and my nose right out of CSF business, if I were you.' He said all this in an offhand manner, as he busied himself, checking his equipment, scanning the roof area and giving his young subordinate a once-over before clapping him on the back. 'Well done, son, suck it up lad, we're out of here.'

'Good luck, Councillor,' he said sardonically. Without a backward glance, the two soldiers ran to the parapet, vaulted over it and made for the fire-escape door, leaving Barrak to ponder his plight alone, under a cavernous sky.

He checked his messages at the reception desk then sought out the concierge, trying to control the quaver in his voice and the panic rising in his chest. There was no sign of Jasmyn – he'd checked all of the public spaces inside the hotel and even checked his room.

He sensed a brittle tension inside the hotel lobby, almost as if patrons and staff were unsure whether to retreat to safety or carry on regardless and assume the mayhem erupting outside their plate-glass refuge didn't concern them. Out on the boulevard, the remains of Orlan's Festival had disintegrated into chaos. By the time Barrak had made it down from the roof, the situation out in the street had completely unravelled.

As he paced anxiously in front of the concierge's desk he glanced out at the surging crowd. He could only guess what had happened after the shooting. The area directly in front of the hotel was cordoned off and surrounded by troops. People seemed to be running in all directions, some carrying children, some helping the elderly, teens avid with the excitement of it, craning necks to watch the action, unsure where they should be. Across the road, near Parliament Square, he could see what looked like a focal point of dissent, an unruly mob waving sticks and flinging missiles. The group was surrounded on three sides by provincial MVs and there were troops on horseback, looking like they had come straight out of the procession. As he watched, a blister of flame erupted over one of the MVs then morphed into a mushroom of black smoke. A mighty cheer rose from the mob and another volley of missiles was launched at the soldiers. A heavily armoured vehicle rumbled across the boulevard towards the trouble spot with something mounted on the back – probably a water cannon, Barrak thought.

The mob scattered in all directions.

Finally the concierge returned and said no one had seen Jasmyn and Barrak insisted he check again for messages. There were none. Barrak's hand was shaking as he took his key. He knew Jasmyn could look after herself but he was still worried, and not only for her. The menacing words of the murderous lieutenant still rang in his ears.

Unsure of his next move, he stood for a moment and stared sightlessly at the front window of the hotel. At that very moment the window shook as a body slammed against it. A trooper had forced a young protestor right into the plate glass and had him pinned with a baton across his throat. A gasp went through the lobby as a second soldier appeared, swinging his baton with sickening force over and over again until the man slumped, his blood smearing down the window as he slid to the ground.

Barrak made for the corridor that would take him to the back exit and into the service lane. From there he could cross into Market Lane and walk down to the railway station. If there was no train he'd take a convec down to Cape Byron to check that Jasmyn had made it home. With any luck Enoch would be there too and he'd alert him to the afternoon's horrific events and his own bizarre involvement in them.

CHAPTER 9

MELDRICK PACED THE LENGTH of the drawing room and back again. He paused at the huge bay window and frowned, as if he disapproved of the luminous trail thrown across the water by the setting moon. Turning back to his guest, his eyes were alight with unconcealed fury.

'So, what *are* you telling me exactly, Colonel – that you don't believe him? He tells you he's in cahoots with the rebels, been doing a spot of spying for them *and* he's been positively identified at one of their camps in the mountains, but you think – what? Actually, I don't know what the hell you think, so please enlighten me. You think he's making it all up, just to have some fun with us? See if he can get himself the death penalty, just for laughs?'

It annoyed Meldrick immensely that Colonel Bartell had his back to him, poking the fire with one of his antique pokers, which were purely ornamental and never meant to be used. He knew Bartell was listening intently, but it still annoyed him, and it irritated him all the more because he was just making the damned fire smoke.

'It's never simple validating intelligence from a hostile source like this.' Bartell had replaced the poker and straightened up, turning to face Meldrick and rubbing his hands together, inspecting them for traces of soot.

'My assessment – he's very intelligent. He may even have had some training in counter-interrogation techniques.' Bartell leaned an elbow on the mantel and put his other hand on his hip and shrugged. 'You see, he made us work for it. Wouldn't say a word at first. It took some serious punishment to get him to open up. But that's what you'd do – if you knew something about interrogation, if you knew the ropes. You're more likely to be believed if your interrogators think they've broken you.

'And his story was good – almost too good – and it all hung together very nicely. Problem is … to some extent it was exactly what we wanted to hear. Nothing new. No names we didn't already have. No camps we didn't already know about. Essentially he gave us nothing.

'So you think he's hiding something, still? Meldrick offered.

'Impossible to say,' said Bartell. 'Our man in the camp says this Arrowsmith character walked straight out of the desert, with some sort of cock-and-bull story about being lost in the outlands. Says he was only there in the camp for a short time, not involved in any real training, but he did get friendly with the rebel leadership … apparently.

'Trouble is, this still leaves almost two years that the kid was off the reservation, completely unaccounted for. He claims he *was* lost – rescued by wild tribesmen and lived rough with them, until he could find his way back.'

'But you don't believe him?' Meldrick came closer to Bartell and put his hands on the back of a large armchair and held his gaze with a potent, questioning stare.

'Well, it's not a matter of believing him or not, the story itself is quite plausible … '

'But?' A blood vessel had begun to pulse in Meldrick's temple.

'Well, something just doesn't quite gel,' Bartell said as if pointing out the obvious to a slow learner.

Meldrick gritted his teeth. 'Orlan's blood! You *know* what I want to know. You know what we're trying to establish here, did he or did he not go anywhere near Skeleton Creek? Has he seen the damned mines? That's what we need to know. Quest's end!'

Bartell sucked a sharp breath through his teeth and bit his lip, assessing Meldrick and his theatrics with a blend of suspicion and regret.

Meldrick sighed, and continued with strained patience: 'All right, so what about this trip out to the solar arrays? What was that all about?

Surely that's suspicious. Hell, it's only forty miles from the restricted site. What was he doing out there?'

'He says the rebels gave him the job to reconnoitre the site. Says he was the ideal choice because of his prior knowledge of the area and he still had a friend who worked there at the arrays.'

'And have we talked to this friend?'

'Gone I'm afraid. No trace. We think he may have joined the rebels.'

'Holy spirit of Orlan!' Meldrick cupped his forehead in one hand. 'So, let me see if I can summarise the intelligence we've garnered to date.' Meldrick deadpanned Bartell and gave the word *intelligence* a swipe of sardonic emphasis. 'We really just don't know,' he intoned drearily. 'No idea,' he asserted, wide-eyed.

'As far as we know the kid has made a god-damned photographic survey of our most secret facility. Someone *was* seen up there, you know. Security went after him, tracked him through the desert for half a day, but he got away. The description could well fit your boy. But we just don't know, do we? Fine. Great. Don't know. Maybe he did, maybe he didn't. You were interrogating him weren't you? What with? Did you give him the feather duster treatment?'

Bartell pointedly gave no reply. He made little further effort to hide his disdain. He was fed up with Meldrick's inane sarcasm. He had long considered him a witless sycophant who'd clawed his way up through the ranks with a combination of guile, rampant ambition and opportunistic thuggery. If it were not for the nepotism inherent in the military establishment he wouldn't have had a chance. Bartell still found it hard to believe he had reached the top job. And he knew Meldrick sensed his scorn. He fairly bristled at Bartell's air of superiority.

'Gods, man! We need to know just how much he knows. Quest's sake – the kid's got all chummy with a council member, that damn Brethrenhope. Maybe he's blabbed the whole story to him. Maybe they're in it together. Maybe the damn rebels have infiltrated the High Council itself and Brethrenhope is their inside man.'

Meldrick's hyperbole got little or no reaction from the colonel and so he pressed on.

'Did we at least find out what the deal is between Arrowsmith and Brethrenhope? Tell me you got something out of him about that.'

Bartell took off his reading glasses and set about polishing them. 'Only that he knew Brethrenhope. He insisted that their only connection was Arrowsmith's employment as a labourer for a short time. Says he went looking for a job when he arrived back in Eyre after his … first escapade in the bush. But that was it. He was firm and clear on that point – Brethrenhope was a coincidental contact.'

'And you believed him?' Meldrick's question carried a note of incredulity.

'I did,' said Bartell. 'On that point if no other – I think he was telling the truth.'

Meldrick returned to scowling at the bay – his back turned to Bartell, his figure silhouetted in the bay window.

After a moment or two Bartell assumed their meeting was concluded. He gathered up the file, which he hadn't even opened, and returned it to his briefcase. 'Well, if that's all, I'll be on my way.'

'Yes, yes, quite,' said Meldrick, seemingly distracted by a cloud bank that had stolen the moon.

Bartell made for the door.

'You're wrong you know,' Meldrick said quietly.

'About what?'

'About Brethrenhope,' Meldrick said. 'He's gone bad. He's in this up to his neck.'

Bartell paused in the doorway and shrugged. 'You have my report.' He turned to go then said, 'What about the boy?'

'He's of no further use to us,' Meldrick said absently.

'Perhaps not. You can't hold him without charge indefinitely,' Bartell ventured.

Meldrick turned slowly and stared at Bartell with frank disdain. 'Don't worry – I'll take care of Arrowsmith.'

Jasmyn saw the colonel catch her primping in the mirror, an overly ornate, antique thing, hanging in the corner of the grand entry hall.

She saw him come smartly around the corner as if he had somewhere he needed to be. As he moved past the grandiose curved staircase that dominated the atrium of Meldrick's mansion, he slowed and their eyes met in the mirror momentarily. She thought she saw a glint of recognition and offered a reserved nod, noting his precise, self-assured movements, which said *military*, and the smart but understated civilian attire. It sparked her curiosity.

He nodded politely but barely paused before heading for the entrance. He knew well enough who Jasmyn was, daughter of the Lord High Councillor: an academy intern with a reputation for rebelliousness. They had never met. In his line of work he knew all the players, but it served him better to avoid overt social networking.

Nonetheless, it was his habit to observe and assess and he wondered what Enoch's daughter was doing at Meldrick's house at this time of night. She had an air about her as she lingered there in Meldrick's anteroom … curiosity … misgiving? Or was it something else? Fear perhaps. No, it was more like annoyance or impatience … perhaps anticipation. And he noticed the two troopers loitering in the atrium – but for what purpose? Guarding her? Perhaps. The atmosphere was certainly not friendly. They seemed to be keeping their distance, respectful but alert.

Quietly heading out into the blustery night, Bartell made a note in his mental files under *Incongruous acquaintances*: Jasmyn Mooney and Manson Meldrick.

'Ms Mooney here to see you, sir.' Sergeant Mackie was stating the obvious for the record, as was his wont. Jasmyn didn't wait to be asked but swept past Meldrick like an exasperated monarch, trailing a mixture of sandalwood and ill-will, and took up a position in the middle of the room, her arms crossed, glaring at the two troopers who'd been her escort.

Meldrick started to fuss – 'I'm so sorry to have kept you waiting, Jasmyn, please, please come in,' – then noticed her staring darkly at the two troopers. He was about to shoo them off when something about the sergeant caught his eye. Mackie was old school, a soldier's soldier –

forty give or take, and fit as a Tamouer bull. Formerly a sergeant-major in the provincial forces and now the head of Meldrick's elite bodyguard regiment within the Parliamentary Guard, Mackie wasn't at his best in civilian company. In fact, if you couldn't shoot it, shout at it, or throw a security cordon around it, it was of little interest to Mackie.

Meldrick's close scrutiny made the sergeant's skin prickle and he clenched his big fists with nervous disdain, willing his commander to hurry-the-hell-up and dismiss him.

But Sergeant Mackie was bleeding.

'What on earth is the matter with your nose, Sergeant?'

'Uhh.' Mackie swiped the back of his hand across his nose and examined it. 'Sorry, sir. I thought that had stopped.'

Meldrick waited.

'Um,' Mackie said again, and stole a tell-tale glance at Jasmyn. She glared back, indifferent, defiant. At that moment, the guard next to Mackie stifled what, for Meldrick's money, sounded like a guffaw. Meldrick and Mackie both turned on him – the commissar's eyes simmering with impatience, Mackie's with rebuke.

'Well, what?' demanded Meldrick impatiently, barely keeping his temper.

'It was Ms Mooney sir, she aah … she hit the sergeant, sir.' The trooper's words were strained and clipped with the great effort of keeping a straight face.

Mackie looked crestfallen and muttered something under his breath to his subordinate. Meldrick looked at the sergeant, then the trooper. An awkward silence took hold. The two guardsmen had never witnessed their commander struck dumb before. Mackie seemed to shrink slightly, which was no mean feat for a 180-pound sergeant-major. Meldrick glanced at Jasmyn but she simply smiled at him demurely, with exaggerated sweetness and glacial eyes.

His men were already backing away, sensing Meldrick's ire.

'Get out!'

But the guards were already gone, their hushed remonstrations still audible as they retreated down the hall.

'Gods, Jasmyn, I don't know what to say. Really, I'm mortified.' Meldrick touched Jasmyn's arm and shepherded her further into the drawing room, steering her towards the fireplace. 'Can I get you something?'

'Yes, as a matter of fact, a convec back into the city, if you don't mind. And, oh yes, I'd quite like an *explanation* ... because I'm wondering why on earth you had me abducted and brought out here in the first place.' Jasmyn kept her tone light as if there was a possibility she might be joking, but her eyes made it quite clear she wasn't.

She discreetly but firmly shrugged off Meldrick's unwanted hand and faced him, her back to the mantel. She'd already noticed the antique fire set the colonel had been playing with, and humoured herself with the notion of its possible usefulness as a weapon – if needed. The look she gave Meldrick was frankly loaded with indignation, and she set her chin at a defiant angle to emphasise her displeasure.

Meldrick was excited by the dark and alluring energy Jasmyn exuded when riled – her anger just made her all the more bewitching. In the subdued light, her smooth dark skin and smouldering eyes were lit by the flickering firelight and her hair was slightly dishevelled, wisps of it had escaped the bun she had speared with chopsticks, and trailed over her face and neck – giving her an air of sassy indifference. Here, in the privacy of his house by the lake, on a faintly moonlit night, by a crackling fire, there was no doubt, she was Meldrick's dark angel.

'Come now, Jasmyn, please don't be angry. Rest assured, those men will be severely reprimanded if they have offended you in any way.'

'Actually your sergeant's a pussycat, Commissar – a perfect gentlemen. He just didn't realise that sergeants don't put their hands on the Lord High Councillor's daughter unless they're asked. 'But let's not blame *him*. I assume he was following your orders, so maybe you should tell me what in quest's name this is all about.'

'There *is* something important I needed to discuss with you Jasmyn. I'm sorry about the unorthodox invitation, but this truly couldn't wait. And it's been such a trying day. I assume you heard about the assassination? Shocking business. Poor old General Hawkins – he was a good man, my tutor at military school, you know.

'Anyway what I've got to say to you is of a sensitive nature and highly confidential. That's why I took the liberty of inviting you here, so we can talk in private. I've also arranged supper.' Meldrick had shimmied past Jasmyn, one hand out in a welcoming gesture toward the bay window where Jasmyn noticed for the first time there was a table set for dinner. *Orlan's ghost! What is this?* Jasmyn was impressed anew by the perversity of the man – *one of my generals has been assassinated, so let's party.*

'Look, Manson, I've already eaten and I have a big day tomorrow—'

Meldrick cut her off. 'Yes, we all do,' he said, with a peculiar grin. 'But please, join me for a glass of wine at least.' He waved a hand in the direction of what was presumably the kitchen and a servant appeared from the shadows with a bottle and proceeded to pour two glasses at the table.

'Come.' Meldrick took Jasmyn's hand. She noticed that it felt cool and reptilian, oddly just as she had imagined it would. She shuddered but let herself be led to the table, unsure of the best way out of the situation.

Meldrick waved the waiter away and picked up the glasses, handing one to Jasmyn.

'A toast,' he offered. 'To kindred spirits.'

Jasmyn gave a crooked smile and allowed her glass to clink against Meldrick's. Cold fingers of panic crept over her and her mind began to race. 'Look, Manson … I really don't want to be impolite, but—'

'Please Jasmyn, there's something you should know.' Meldrick sat down and she followed suit. *Buy some time – think of a diplomatic way out of this.* There was starched linen and polished silver, flowers on the table and candles, already lit. Faint moonlight spilled through the bay window and across the water. Far away on the other side of Lillian Bay she could see lights winking on the headland. One of them would be her father's house.

'This may come as a shock to you, but we have discovered that

Councillor Brethrenhope is a traitor.' He paused just for moment to let this sink in, watching for her reaction before continuing, but Jasmyn kept her face impassive. 'He's been working with the rebels to destabilise the government from within,' Meldrick elaborated, to fill the awkward silence.

Jasmyn made a noise that was neither gasp nor giggle, but a bastard hybrid, and her first sip of wine caught in her throat. Her hand went to her mouth to try to stem the eruption, but she laughed and coughed and almost gagged, looking incredulously at Meldrick. 'That's ... ah, very amusing Manson, I'm sure.' Her benign expression ran contrary to what she really thought of him. *You are bat-shit barking mad, Meldrick.*

'Jasmyn, this situation couldn't be more serious. I'm telling you this to protect you. There are some who question *your* relationship with Brethrenhope, some who would tar you with the same brush ... But I won't allow that to happen.'

Jasmyn treated Meldrick to a disagreeable scowl, angry now at the impudent effrontery of the man. 'You're actually serious aren't you? Barrak? For God's sake ... that's insane. And besides, my relationship with Barrak is neither your business nor the business of any of your nosy bloody minions.'

Meldrick's eye's flared with anger for a brief moment before he calmed himself and said evenly, 'Please Jasmyn, I really am trying to protect *your* interests. We're living in dangerous times right now. You know this, you academy people, custodians of the secret knowledge ... You must know that change is coming, surely it must be written large in the stars?

'There's going to be a great upheaval – and sooner rather than later, I'd say. In your business you understand the dynamics of change, old structures are swept away in order that a better, more enlightened reality can take shape. When such things happen, it's important to be on the right side of it.'

Jasmyn rolled her eyes and shot Meldrick a perplexed grimace. Some of what he said made sense, but she couldn't get past his accusation against Barrak.

'Our destinies are intertwined – yours and mine,' Meldrick went on, his tone becoming more imploring. 'Have you seen this in your charts? What do you astrologers call it? Synastry – isn't that it? Yours and mine … it must be remarkable.' He gave her a manic, confused smile.

Jasmyn tried to form a response, but for once she was speechless.

'You have to trust me, Jasmyn. Brethrenhope is no good. You must have no more to do with him. He's finished! Your future is with me Jasmyn.'

'No! No! Are you completely insane?' Jasmyn's temper flared and suddenly there was no shortage of words. She blurted out more than she ought in a sudden lapse of control. 'How dare you accuse Barrak?' She was on her feet, her chair screeching on the floorboards before it tipped and crashed to the floor. 'Barrak? You've got a damn nerve – he's the finest man I know. One hundred times the man you'll ever be!'

Meldrick rose like a bedevilled dancer, one arm describing an arc across the table, sweeping away an entire setting in a sickening cacophony of shattered crystal and china.

Jasmyn froze.

'SIT DOWN!' he bellowed, his eyes ablaze.

Jasmyn felt her heart begin to pound in her throat. A hot flush reached her face and for an instant she thought her voice had failed her completely, but then a rush of words came unbidden, beyond her control.

'What right do you think you have to shout at me like a common house wench?' Jasmyn hissed at him, hot with indignation. 'You forget yourself Meldrick, *and* you forget who I am!' She squared her shoulders now and gave him a withering look of condemnation. 'By Orlan, you drag me out here, against my will, for your mindless amusement, as though I was one of your bloody whores! How dare you!?'

She held her breath. Meldrick didn't move or even blink for the longest time and Jasmyn fancied her diatribe may have turned him to stone.

No such luck. As he glared at her, her righteous indignation drained away, to be replaced by chill trepidation. Meldrick closed his eyes and exhaled slowly, his palms flat on the table as if channelling his anger out of his body into the timber. Through gritted teeth he said, 'Please don't do this, Jasmyn. I'm going to pretend I didn't hear any of that.' He sighed heavily. 'If only you could understand that what I'm offering you here is an opportunity. A great opportunity …'

'No, no, no! I'd sooner die a thousand hideous deaths.' She took a step backwards, but foundered on the fallen chair. Meldrick lunged as she tried to negotiate the chair awkwardly, looking wildly for a way out.

'Let me go!' She wrenched her hand from his grasp. 'Stay away from me!' she screamed, hoarse and high-pitched, half crying, half shouting, backing towards the door and stamping a foot for emphasis.

'Jasmyn. We have to be together. You don't understand. I'm the only one who can protect you. I need you.' His tone had changed so completely it frightened her even more. He was beseeching her now, like a spurned lover – grovelling and obsequious – but then he lunged again and caught her by the arm, pulling her to him.

Her calm centre – cultivated through years of martial arts practice – was faltering and she could feel herself being sucked into a vortex of hysteria and clamorous fear. Why had she come so unstuck now? Normally, under duress, her training took over, bringing clarity and calm and allowing her to use her skills to extricate herself from danger. Why not now? What was it about Meldrick's mad eyes, his creepy coercion that brought such panic?

Gathering herself, she willed herself to be calm and concentrated energy into her core. Wrenching her arm free again, she glared at Meldrick. 'I refuse to be treated this way Manson. Now, I am leaving and I would like you to arrange transport for me, right now.' Meldrick's eye's blazed with furious reproach and his nostrils flared. Jasmyn turned haughtily for the door, and it was this oversight, this woeful neglect of the fundamentals of her training, that was her undoing.

She didn't see the blow coming. The violent backhand spun her off her feet and stunned her brain to buzzing whiteness.

The next thing she knew, her head was pillowed on a soft woolly surface – it was the sheepskin she'd noticed in front of the fireplace.

As the dullness cleared and she brought herself back into the room, she found Meldrick on top of her, one hand on her breast and a knee prying her legs apart. His eyes were wild and his teeth clenched. She could smell the sweet foetid odour of wine and sweat. She struggled and turned her head away, straining to avoid his thrusting lips. She felt the warmth of the fire on her face and in her peripheral vision she could see the flickering flames and the poker stand, its three implements hanging like charms ... almost within reach.

She twisted and strained under Meldrick's weight as he writhed and struggled to control her. His grunting and puffing appalled her and his hot breath seemed to be all around her like a noxious fog. Even though the room still spun, she had her clarity back and with a calmness her old qui gung master would have applauded, her mind was fixed on just one thing – the poker hanging to the right, the one with the nicely curved spike ...

Persephone looked at Barrak with laughter sparkling in her clear blue eyes and her long hair blew about her face in the breeze, strands catching across her mouth and eyes. She brushed it back with an easy sweep of her hand and mouthed a few words to Barrak through the sliding glass door to the verandah. Behind her he could see the expanse of the bay, dark grey and brooding with the approach of a storm. But the sun was still bright and Persephone kept mouthing the same words to him. *Why couldn't he hear her through the glass? What was she trying to say?*

Suddenly Noah appeared and ran to his mother, throwing himself into her arms. She lifted him up to her eye level and kissed him on the forehead. But Barrak had been mistaken – it wasn't Noah in her arms, instead it was a large bird, an eagle. Persephone held her arm high out over the balustrade and the bird gathered itself and sprang off her arm into the space beyond the deck.

All at once the storm was upon them and the sky had darkened. Large black clouds rolled in off the bay and a vivid blue sea boiled with white caps. Persephone turned back to face Barrak through the glass, her eyes no longer laughing but suddenly filled with fear. The word she mouthed at him was clear now: *Barrak!*

Barrak tried to go towards the door to let her in, but he couldn't move. He looked down at his feet and saw that they were stuck, trapped between the floorboards as if the floor had been built around him. He started to panic and saw that the clouds rolling in were not clouds at all – there was thick black smoke and he could see flames leaping and flaring all along the verandah rail behind his wife.

Persephone's voice reached him now and she was banging on the glass with her hands. 'Barrak!' Her eyes were filled with panic but also with a deep sadness, as if she knew Barrak could never reach the door to save her.

He heard her clearly now: 'Barrak! Let me in! Barrak!'

Barrak's body shuddered as if hit by a jolt of electricity and his head came off the pillow. His eyes made little sense of the colourless shapes in the dimly lit space until the banging placed the door for him and the space solidified into a ghostly room. Someone was knocking on the door. This was his room. Plaza Hotel. Tamouer ... Jasmyn!

'Barrak! Let me in ... Gods, please. BARRAK!' Jasmyn's voice was plaintive and clear, outside the door.

By the time he flung it open she wore an expression of exasperated despair. *Barrak's not here.* This changed instantly to relief and a smile broke across her face but didn't take hold, dissolving instead into teary distress. These were not the first tears – she was smudged and dishevelled and what looked like blood, a spray of tiny drops like surgery gone wrong, speckled the side of her face and collar.

Jasmyn teetered on the threshold before collapsing into his arms. He half carried her to the two-seater by the window and she crumpled into it. He wrapped her in his hotel duvet against the midnight chill.

It took some time before he was able to patch together her story, between shuddering sobs and unpredictable bouts of tears. Now and then her upset turned to outrage and she launched into fiery tirades, raining down punishing blows on the upholstered arm of the sofa.

Once Barrak had the gist of it, he held Jasmyn on the couch when she needed to be held and let himself be pushed away when she needed space. He satisfied himself that the blood was not hers and set about sponging it all away – the last thing he supposed she would need was to wake up with Meldrick's blood on her. After a while she settled, nestled in the crook of his arm, warm inside the duvet, and Barrak continued to mop her face with the warm washer. It seemed to soothe her, and in the end that's how she fell asleep. Barrak sat quietly until she was deeply asleep, hardly daring to breathe himself, for fear of waking her. It reminded him so much of putting little Noah to bed as a toddler, he felt a great rush of poignant tenderness which made his concern for Jasmyn seem all the more impelling.

Eventually he carried her to the bed. She stirred and tensed as he tried to lay her down without waking her, but hearing his voice was enough to settle her and she snuggled between the duvet and Barrak's big fluffy hotel pillows.

Barrak found a spare blanket in a cupboard and bedded himself down on the two-seater.

If he slept at all it was a sleep indistinguishable from anxious speculation. As he watched the night gradually turn to tepid dawn through the flimsy bamboo-print curtain, he was assailed by apprehension and uncertainty about the coming day, interspersed with vengeful thoughts and imagined reprisals against that miserable wretch, Meldrick. At times he seemed lost on a fitful ocean of fears and contingencies, and when he entered half-sleep, it became a terrifying bardos of mindless confusion, filled with images of murderous rooftop lieutenants or Meldrick lying in a pool of blood, killed by Jasmyn's passionate rejection. At times he lay listening to Jasmyn's heavy, even breathing and felt calmed by her presence. Somewhere between first light and sunrise he finally found the mercy of a morsel of rejuvenating sleep.

He woke with a new clarity and a sense of urgency. He must find Enoch, as he'd failed to the previous evening, and alert him to the troubling events of the last twenty-four hours. There would need to be an investigation, maybe in due course even a parliamentary commission. Meldrick had gone too far with his heavy-handed use of the security forces. Now Barrak himself had witnessed the cold-blooded murder of an unarmed suspect by his men. Meldrick's despicable behaviour towards Enoch's own daughter would seal the deal. If Barrak had anything to do with it, with Enoch's help this would be the end of Meldrick as head of the CSF.

CHAPTER 10

BARRAK KNEW HE WAS too late, once he saw Enoch in his robes at the top of the steps, ready to enter the Great Hall, with his aide at his side holding the caisson of the Scrolls of Decree aloft like a sacrificial offering.

It had been a calculated risk. He'd raced the five miles down to Cape Byron to catch Enoch before he left home, but his trip had been wasted – again. Enoch had departed early, leaving Barrak with little choice but to bolt back with just enough time to get to his hotel and change into his own ceremonial garb.

There was little point trying to capture Enoch's attention now. In a few minutes he would proceed along the Great Hall to the massive double oak doors of the council chambers and pound on them three times with the ceremonial opal rod. The doors would open for him to walk, at a funereal pace, into the chamber. Some of the senators and councillors with more sense of occasion than others, would chant a particular verse from Orlan's Proclamation of Sanctuary as Enoch approached the chair of the Guardian of Council. There he would hand the scroll to the Guardian and ask him to read from it – the ancient words originally spoken by Orlan himself – instituting the articles of parliament for another year.

Senators and councillors were bustling past Barrak, up the wide stone steps into the Great Hall, robes billowing, intent on a good seat before the chamber was closed, in preparation for the ceremonial door-knocking.

The opening session was a joint sitting, councillors and senators all together once a year, packed like hamsters into the ancient High Council chamber. To the chagrin of many councillors, their counterparts from the *other place* generally showed little respect for the customary seating arrangements and Barrak guessed his chances of a decent seat would already be slim.

Standing at the foot of the parliamentary steps Barrak took a moment to look around. The morning had dawned crisp and still – gone was the biting wind of the previous day – but the desert heat that would envelope the city by mid-afternoon was yet only a hint on the balmy south-easterly breeze.

Standing on the familiar time-worn stone steps, he felt a strange sense of peril in Tamouer today. A small crowd had gathered, festival tourists gawking at the odd-looking parliamentarians in their ancient attire, city workers pausing to take in a slice of ceremony as they hurried to their work, a school group on excursion … some were taking pictures of the striding parliamentarians as they funnelled up the steps to the Great Hall. A queue was already forming at the side entrance on the eastern side of the parliament where invited guests would be allowed into the viewing gallery on the mezzanine above the main chamber.

Barrak felt strangely disconnected from the unfolding tableau, almost as though he were viewing the scene through glass. None of this normality could be reconciled with the horror of his rooftop experience the previous day and the insidious threats of the deadly lieutenant. But he felt an even greater concern for Jasmyn and the implications of her late-night altercation with Meldrick.

Not far off on the side of the boulevard was the burnt-out shell of the troop carrier that had fallen victim to yesterday's rioters, its blackened skeleton like a carcass in the desert sun, a chilling reminder of how bad things had been the day before. Military vehicles still lined the boulevard and were even stationed along the sides of the parliamentary buildings.

Why so many troops? Surely most of the excitement was over.

It was no longer possible for him to distinguish between his unease and paranoia. He watched a nearby group of soldiers watching him. The eyes of the tall angular officer seemed to bore a hole right through him. *What the hell was he staring at?* A week ago, Barrak would've taken him on, returned his arrogant stare and perhaps walked over to question him on his orders. Instead Barrak turned tail and took the steps two at a time – just another councillor hurrying to find his seat.

Inside the Great Hall, he saw that the chamber doors were already shut, and turned towards the library. He would have been too late to claim a seat in the council chamber in any case, and besides, he had a better option. Unknown to some of the visiting senators, one of the best vantage points could be gained from the library. On the top level was the Councillor's Reading Gallery, a mezzanine balcony overlooking the council chamber itself, allowing studious councillors to keep a weather eye on proceedings. It was directly opposite two similar balconies which made up the public galleries.

Although all councillors were expected to be in the chamber proper for the opening, Barrak was happy to flout the rules in favour of this uncrowded perch.

Enoch worked the chamber like a seasoned performer, resplendent in his ochre robes finished with snakeskin and lined with shining black leopard pelt. A natural orator, he was in his element as he gave the traditional preamble to Orlan's blessing.

This involved retelling the story of Tamouer's founding as an allegorical invocation, which each year, by tradition, was told differently … an imagined and exotic tale, interwoven with historical fact. The more fanciful or ironic it was, the better, and the greater the applause when the final rabbit was produced from the orator's hat. And Enoch was the best there was, holding the chamber in his thrall, before drawing gasps of admiration as he implausibly turned his tale at the very last minute to arrive at the obligatory finale.

He gathered himself for the conclusion of his part in the opening ceremony, his final summation and update. Then the cardinal – who

Barrak could see on the sidelines, his young aide firing up an ornate incense burner – would give the formal blessing and the bells would be rung, declaring the parliament open.

Surveying the scene from his eyrie, and keeping an eye on the public gallery for Jasmyn, Barrak noticed a ripple of murmurs go through the benches; the mood of the assembly changed. A figure had entered the chamber from one of the four side doors: Meldrick.

What was he doing here?

Enoch was begging the chamber's indulgence in a sanguine tone, explaining the change of agenda. 'Commissar Meldrick has requested special leave to address the council to update members on the current security situation, which I'm sure is a matter of grave concern to us all. He has been granted leave to give his address now, before the blessing by the cardinal.' Enoch went on to explain that his own customary update on the state of the region would be curtailed somewhat because news of increased rebel activity and related security issues would be covered more expertly and in greater detail by Meldrick.

'Commissar ...' Enoch backed away to the front bench where his ministers sat, offering the security chief the speaker's podium with a genuflecting hand.

Uneasy murmurs, nervous coughs and shuffling feet troubled the chamber for a few moments before an expectant hush fell. Stepping up to the box, Meldrick took some time to gaze around the chamber, as if taking the measure of the assembled members.

Barrak glanced across the chamber. With uncanny timing, Jasmyn appeared in the public gallery opposite, peering down intently at Meldrick. As her head came up their eyes met, and bewilderment, incredulous annoyance and fear were all part of the troubled expression she telegraphed across the vaulted space between them. She mouthed a few words which Barrak half guessed and half lip-read. *What the hell is going on?* Barrak shrugged.

Meldrick began his address. 'Thank you Councillor Mooney, your eminence, councillors and senators. I come before you today at a time of great consequence to our beloved land. It is also a time of considerable danger ... a time when we will be challenged to hold our nerve and defend the values of our great land against a dire and insidious threat ... a threat that has grown like a cancer amongst our own people and now turns against us.

'Let us not be mistaken, this menace threatens the very fabric of our society and seeks to destroy and debase the values and principles that were enshrined by our great founder, under our constitution in this very place many centuries ago.'

Meldrick paused to let the gravity of his assessment sink in. There were murmurs and grumblings and a small outbreak of foot tapping and *Hear hears* ricocheted around the chamber, signalling a consensus of concern amongst the gathered representatives.

'We must stand firm against this rebel alliance. Make no mistake, their intention is to destroy all of the institutions we hold dear, do away with the rule of law and ruin the prosperity of Tamouer.' Meldrick paused for effect and took care to make eye contact with a few of the councillors and senators he knew enjoyed vast amounts of Tamouer's wealth.

'Even more disconcerting than this, honourable members, is the rebels' intention, if they ever have their way, to open our borders, threatening the very purity and sanctity of our great Eyrean culture with an influx of savages and miscreants from every corner of the badlands beyond the outer boundaries.'

A low hostile murmur swept over the chamber.

'What's going on Barrak?' Jasmyn hissed under her breath. He turned, surprised to see her beside him, and noted her look of anger and mistrust. He had been so engrossed he hadn't noticed her leaving the public gallery and crossing over to his side of the gallery. 'Why is *he* here? Does the man have no decency at all? This is the High Council for quest's sake.'

Just at that moment, Meldrick turned and looked up at Barrak and Jasmyn, allowing himself a faint, smug smile.

Barrak glanced at Jasmyn and raised a cautious finger to his lips.

'During this last winter we have seen the insurgents growing in boldness and depravity. The most worrying development has been the appearance of fire-burst weapons, weapons of mass terror, which have traumatised all who have witnessed their terrible destruction. The latest – just two days ago – was employed right here in the city.

'The rebels' use of such terrible weapons – weapons explicitly prohibited by one of Orlan's twelve parameters of civilisation – is a crime against the entire Eyrean nation, a crime of such magnitude, that it forces us to take strong and decisive action.'

The assembly hall was utterly silent now as Meldrick engineered another dramatic pause.

'Accordingly, several months ago, I instructed the CSF Weapons Research Group to begin work on similar weapons, using fire-burst technology – for use by our security forces.'

A muted roar of disbelief and protest erupted. Barrak himself was not sure he had heard right and looked incredulously at Jasmyn.

'This decision was not taken lightly!' Meldrick was forced to raise his voice over the hubbub, which subsided abruptly, councillors and senators avid to hear just how Meldrick could possibly justify such sacrilege. 'We simply have no choice, given the rebels' dire and terrifying threat to the security of our land.' Meldrick strained to be heard over a new round of rumblings in the chamber. 'We must fight fire with fire!'

The disquiet subsided somewhat as if the chamber were uncertain now, perhaps willing to be convinced. But no one had ever suggested that one of Orlan's cardinal laws should be overturned. Surely it was inconceivable. *No weapon large or small, impelled by burst of fire …*

'The first of these military weapons will be available to CSF forces in the coming weeks and we expect that this will give our security forces a decisive edge and allow us to finally end this dangerous and destructive rebellion,' Meldrick continued, trying to calm the audience.

'In addition, thanks to new technology, we have another device that will significantly increase your security forces' effectiveness against the rebels. It is a portable and wireless communication device, already in use in some CSF units.' Meldrick produced a small, square black object about the size of his palm with a coiled wire extending into his jacket. He held it up to the crowd, before putting it to his mouth and speaking into it quietly.

A roar went up around the chamber. Members were on their feet, protesting and stamping. There were jeers and boos and shouted protests: *Shame! Disgraceful! How dare you!* To overturn not one but two of Orlan's precious principles was too much. This they could not stand. *Communication shall be by voice or printed word only – and not be transmitted by energetic means.*

Meldrick bided his time and waited for the uproar to subside.

'I would remind the honourable members …' he interjected over the din, his voice loud and solemn, 'I would remind the honourable members, that as of yesterday, the rebels' crimes have reached new levels of wickedness and audacity, with the assassination of one of the CSF's finest officers, General Hawkins, during the annual parade. Furthermore, I can now reveal to you that yesterday evening *I myself* was subject to an assassination attempt!'

With that, Meldrick removed his officer's cap to reveal a bandaged head wound, with a small patch of blood. There was a moment of heavy silence. Barrak felt a sudden claw-like grip on his arm and looked at Jasmyn. The blood seemed to have drained from her face, her mouth was open and disbelief mingled with panic in her dark eyes. He put his hand on hers, a reassuring gesture, and gently pried loose her fingers.

As the implications of Meldrick's deception dawned on her, disbelief turned to indignation and then hot contempt. 'Bastard!' she whispered. 'Cursed snake.'

Barrak shook his head and swore under his breath, not sure which was more disturbing – that Jasmyn had done so much damage to Meldrick or the ominous implications of his passing it off as an attempted assassination.

'It is also my unhappy duty to inform this joint sitting of the parliament that military intelligence has recently uncovered irrefutable evidence that several members of this very council have been colluding with the rebel forces to destabilise the government. One of these betrayers of the peoples' trust has further been implicated in yesterday's murder of General Hawkins.' He paused, glaring around the room as if daring anyone to gainsay him. 'These criminals will, in due course, be arrested to answer charges of high treason, sedition and murder,' Meldrick proclaimed.

Barrak felt someone walk across his grave. *Meldrick intended to frame him for the general's murder!* Staring down into the chamber he could see Enoch glaring at Meldrick with undisguised malice. Cardinal Selwood sat beside him, baffled, his incense burner long since extinguished. An eerie hush fell over the chamber, broken only by a few isolated exclamations.

Meldrick went on, building towards a climax. 'For this reason, in due consideration of the continued threat to the security of the realm, it is incumbent on me as Head of the Combined Security Forces to hereby invoke Section 21A of the Eyrean Constitution specifically requiring security forces to take over administration of the city of Tamouer on Eyre and all surrounding provinces until such time as the security of the land can be fully restored.'

The hushed chamber seemed to tremble.

'All of the conditions laid down under Section 21A, Subsection 3, have been met, including the presence of violent attacks from an enemy outside the borders of the land of a kind likely to threaten the continued safety of Tamouer and surrounding settlements ...'

Meldrick's voice was lost as the assembly erupted. Barrak saw Enoch on his feet in animated debate with several of his cabinet members. Others from the front bench were yelling and shaking their fists at Meldrick. Jasmyn had Barrak by the arm again, her face ashen, her eyes full of disbelief and dread.

'In accordance with the constitution, both houses of parliament will be suspended until further notice.'

A roar of protest drowned out whatever Meldrick had to say next. One of Enoch's ministers grabbed Meldrick, but he wrenched his arm free. A soldier appeared from nowhere and dragged the offending minister away. Dozens of soldiers had entered the chamber and positioned themselves throughout the benches. Barrak noticed they were wearing the uniform of the Parliamentary Guard.

He watched aghast as Milburn the elder was flanked by two soldiers and marched towards the exit. Barrak had served alongside the councillor on several committees and knew him to be an unswerving libertarian and defender of the prophet's laws. A pair of guards was stationed at each exit, effectively sealing the chamber, and a cordon of troopers had entered through the front doors, with the High Council's sergeant at arms in their custody.

Meldrick tried in vain to make himself heard over the pandemonium: 'A military administration will take over government from today and warrants will be issued for the arrest of all enemies of the state believed to be working in conjunction with the rebel alliance.'

After that, Barrak only heard fragments ... *a curfew from nine pm until dawn ... identity papers ... arrest and detention ...*

Meldrick spoke to one of his lieutenants and gestured towards Enoch who was in urgent consultation with a huddle of his ministers. The lieutenant took Enoch by the arm and pulled him firmly away from the conversation and marched him towards the front entrance. Enoch resisted and struggled, but he was no match for the burly guardsmen.

'*No!*' Jasmyn's voice rang out across the chamber from the balcony. Her body was rigid and her eyes were filled with anger and fear as she watched her father being led away.

Meldrick looked up, his mad eyes avid with the thrill of power. He summoned an officer and tilted his head at Barrak and Jasmyn, issuing a terse order. The guardsman looked up, locking eyes with Barrak.

Barrak's scalp tingled. His mouth was dry and he felt a pulse begin to pound in his temple. At the same time, an icy calm gripped him as he realised with sickening clarity the full implications of what was unfolding before him. He reached out and grabbed Jasmyn by the wrist. She resisted, her eyes on her father, but Barrak tugged, spinning her around to face him.

'We have to go. Now!'

'No! Barrak ... no. My father. We can't leave him ... That bastard!' Jasmyn's voice croaky with emotion. 'Please ...'

'Jasmyn.' Barrak took her by the shoulders to steady her. 'Jasmyn – we can't help him if we're arrested too. We have to go. Now.' He saw the tears welling up, saw her bite her bottom lip. She understood.

Barrak froze, his heart pounding. He heard Jasmyn exhale tremulously, then hold her breath. Troopers were in the front reading room, crunching across the polished stone floor. A shouted order elicited an improbably loud *shush!* from the librarian, no doubt – surprised and annoyed by the sudden intrusion.

Barrak and Jasmyn were almost down the spiral staircase at the core of the library, where the oldest of the library's collection was stored. Loud voices approached, and only a bank of bookshelves protected them from the soldiers' view. There was no way out. They were trapped.

Cat-like, Jasmyn crept to the next landing and gestured urgently to Barrak to follow her. There was a click and a small timber panel opened up on the landing. Jasmyn slipped through it and pulled Barrak after her, before closing the door and carefully clicking the latch back into place.

They were in a storeroom of sorts, perched on a small mezzanine platform with bookshelves on two sides. Jasmyn hurried down a ladder to the floor below, beckoning Barrak to follow. A door was open a crack, and through it they could see the bottom of the spiral staircase they had just left, and the main atrium of the library. Troopers flashed past, pounding up the steps to the gallery.

Barrak didn't dare breathe.

Jasmyn tugged at his sleeve, wordlessly indicating that he should follow. At the far end of the storeroom was a cluttered desk, and in the corner nearby was an open trapdoor. How did Jasmyn know her way around, Barrak wondered. She was halfway down the stone steps and mouthing the words *Come on* to a bewildered Barrak. As he descended into the darkness Jasmyn whispered urgently to him. 'Shut the door. Pull it shut, there's a rope.'

He carefully lowered the trapdoor and felt his way down the last few steps to the cellar floor. As his eyes began to adjust he realised there was a faint light coming from somewhere ahead.

'What … How did you …?'

'Summer job … in my student days,' Jasmyn volunteered. 'The council archives are kept down here.'

'You're incredible,' Barrak breathed. 'We were gone!'

Jasmyn allowed herself a satisfied grin.

Nonetheless Barrak was uneasy, his mind racing through contingencies as he caught his breath. *It wouldn't take the troopers long to find the storeroom and then the trapdoor.*

'Who's there?' The croaky query from the shadows startled them both.

A figure emerged from the dimness at the end of the cellar.

'Iggy?' Jasmyn whispered. 'Is that you?'

'Jasmyn? Well, as I live and breathe … Jasmyn, my dear.'

Icabod Varcoe, whom he'd spoken to only two days previously, enfolded Jasmyn in an embrace. Barrak remembered the old councillor was the curator of the council archive. His craggy features arranged themselves into a blissful smile in Jasmyn's embrace.

'It's been too long, my girl.' He chuckled and patted Jasmyn's hand.

'And who's this?' he demanded, turning his attention to Barrak and not troubling to hide his irritation that he didn't have Jasmyn to himself. 'Brethrenhope, is that you?' He released Jasmyn's hand and squinted. 'Well, perhaps someone better tell me what's going on.'

'Trouble, Iggy,' said Jasmyn. 'Big trouble. 'Meldrick's gone too far. He just marched his troops into the council chambers and suspended the parliament. Announced the military is running the government from now on, and he's arrested Father, Iggy …' Jasmyn's voice broke and she put a hand to her mouth.

Varcoe took her hand in his again, rubbing it like a small pet and looking enquiringly at Barrak.

'He says he's invoking some bloody arcane section under the constitution. Because of the rebel attacks. Claims it allows him to take over, to maintain security,' Barrak continued.

'Section 21A?'

Barrak nodded. 'How did you know?'

'Oh, it's always been a weak point . . . badly worded, open to misuse in a dozen different ways. It was only a matter of time. Meldrick, eh? I wasn't sure he had the mettle,' Iggy mused.

'But Iggy, it's worse still.' Jasmyn grasped the old man's hands. 'He implied Barrak was involved with the rebels *and* the assassination of General Hawkins . . . and he's got me in his sights as well because I, um . . . he . . .' Jasmyn frowned darkly.

'He tried to have his way with Jasmyn,' Barrak interrupted, 'and Jasmyn rearranged his hairdo with a poker for his trouble.'

Iggy looked shocked and impressed in equal measure, then offended. He hugged Jasmyn again. 'We must get you out of here.'

As if on cue, footsteps sounded on the floor overhead.

'There's nowhere to go,' Jasmyn whispered. 'We're trapped down here.'

'Quickly now, this way.' Iggy shepherded them deeper into the archives, past several banks of shelves that stretched away into darkness. 'You young folk sometimes think you know it all,' Varcoe muttered with a small chuckle, 'but old Iggy might have a trick or two up his sleeve yet.'

At the far end of the archives, Icabod busied himself with something in the shelves lining the back wall.

The trapdoor at the other end of the archive creaked.

Jasmyn looked at Barrak, alarmed. The old councillor didn't seem to notice the sound. Torchlight flickered through the open trapdoor, lighting the cellar with a dust-filled beam.

Finally, they heard a faint click, then a strange rumbling noise. It took a moment in the deep gloom for Barrak to realise the bookcase had rolled to one side, leaving a gaping hole in its place.

'You better take this.' Iggy held out a headlamp to Barrak. Barrak took it limply in his hand, looking at the old man doubtfully.

'The tunnels, Barrak, you know about the tunnels under the old city, don't you?'

140

Barrak thought they were just a myth, or long gone. He wasn't sure he was pleased to know they still existed. Jasmyn looked panicky.

'Go,' said Iggy. 'Turn left just down there a bit, then go straight ahead. You'll be right under the boulevard. Take the third tunnel off to the right, and it'll bring you up under the museum.'

They looked at each other and then back at Iggy. There was no alternative. They heard orders barked above. Jasmyn took Barrak's hand and planted a kiss on Iggy's cheek, then stepped through the opening, pulling Barrak into the darkness.

Once the bookshelf had bumped back into place they found themselves in utter blackness, dense and impenetrable. The lamp wasn't working.

Barrak forced himself to breathe; the air in the tunnel reeked of earth and time. He felt Jasmyn come up behind and press herself against him. It was a comfort.

Her hand found his elbow in the darkness.' Come on, we should go,' she whispered.

He took a tentative step and then two more, hands out before him. The floor of the tunnel sloped, but in the darkness it felt like a precipice. He stopped and fumbled with the lamp, which he'd hurriedly fitted to his head. The light came on but its feeble beam reached only a yard or two ahead. Suddenly Barrak was in an abyss, free-falling. His head swam and he found himself on the ground, propped on one knee and a hand, disoriented, palms sweating.

'What's the matter?' Jasmyn demanded, squatting beside him.

'I'm not good in tight spaces, especially in the dark,' he said, embarrassed. 'This thing is useless!' Barrak snatched the headlamp from his head.

'Give it to me.' Taking the lamp from him, Jasmyn held it up and out to the side, where it lit the rock wall dimly, but well enough. She helped Barrak up and they inched along, Barrak feeling sheepish now that his eyes and his mind had begun to adjust to the darkness. As they felt their way Jasmyn murmured to herself. 'Left ... Iggy said go left ...'

The opening in the wall came sooner than they expected. Jasmyn faltered as her outstretched hand fell into thin air and they both stumbled to the left through a large opening into what seemed like a great cavern but was in fact another tunnel, much larger and running at a slight angle to the small tributary from which they'd entered.

The tunnel, obviously the main trunk, was wide enough for a small lorry. A breeze wafted along the passageway and Barrak realised there was light. Ten feet above, were a series of small bluish white lights, spaced every ten yards or so.

They went straight on, just as the old archivist had told them, their way lit by the pallid blue lights above. They were grey ghosts, wafting along on a subterranean breeze. Barrak's eyes strained to make out any detail on the tunnel wall and he veered right to get a better look. *Third exit right will bring you to the museum.*

Lachlan Enright had made first lieutenant before he turned twenty-three. He was ambitious and smart. By the time he was fifteen he knew a career in the military was his way out of the soul-crushing monotony of farm life in the tiny rural settlement of Rockbairn. His father, brothers, uncle and grandfather were all farmers through and through, from their matted hat-hair to the soles of their dung-covered boots.

But Lachie was different and had been from an early age. As a child, his fascination with military matters had bordered on obsessive. Even just the sight of small patrols moving back and forth between Lilbetown on the coast and the western border post at Lomond's Gate was enough to fire his imagination. The soldiers rarely even stopped in his town. *Blink and you'll miss it.* But Lachie would watch them from the rocky escarpment that marked the farm's southern boundary. His surveillance was meticulous and surreptitious, a perfectly camouflaged ten-year-old lookout, with a mail-order telescope and a head full of romantic dreams of the adventurous life of a military man.

By the time he was a teenager his father and brothers had given up trying to turn him to rural pursuits. The local farm girls with their ample breasts and lusty appetites had given up on him as well, because Lachie was different in other ways, too.

He even looked different, taller and slimmer, with aquiline features and much paler skin than his sun-baked, beer-soaked brothers. His dark hair and eyes and good bone structure meant he would grow into a handsome man. When he scrutinised himself in the mirror he would puff out his chest and align his chin, imagining himself in ceremonial dress uniform, like the soldiers he had seen in the parade his mother had once taken him to see in the big city.

When he looked around at his family and friends, he sometimes wondered if he'd been left on the doorstep in a basket.

He had insisted on finishing his studies even though it had meant taking the bus down to the high school in Lilbetown every weekday for three years. In his final year, he scored so highly that he gained a scholarship to the military academy in Tamouer, just as he always knew he would, and then he proceeded to break his mother's heart by turning his back on rural Rockbairn forever, without so much as a tear or a backward glance.

He had topped his graduate year at the academy and excelled in every assignment since then, but the crowning glory in Lachie's short and meteoric career was his recent promotion to the Parliamentary Guard, an appointment that was all the sweeter because it came with an automatic invitation to join the Keepers of the Light of Orlan. He would be one of the youngest-ever members of that august society, assuring further rapid progress in his military career.

And that's what had brought him to this moment, which, whether he realised it or not, was one of those pivotal moments in life. Commissar Meldrick had given the order himself, speaking directly to him, if not actually by name, in the Great Hall outside the council chambers: *Lieutenant, find Councillor Brethrenhope and Ms Mooney and bring them to me.*

Nothing, therefore, was going to stand in the way of him carrying out this particular mission, least of all a senile and decrepit old man in a cellar.

'Old man, I said show me your hands,' Lachie repeated.

'There's nothing interesting about my hands,' declared Icabod Varcoe, holding them out in front of him as he shuffled forward. 'Look.'

'Move this way, slowly.'

'How fast do you think an old fossil like me can go, lad? I'd say this is about top speed.' Iggy shambled toward the two soldiers standing at the bottom of the steps. The officer was edgy and impatient, the non-commissioned trooper was nervously sweeping his torch beam back and forth and peering into the murky archive.

'What are you doing down here? Is there anyone with you?'

'Well now, I was down here practising a few songs with the Tamouer and Districts Boys Choir, but blow me down if they didn't all just vanish … *poof* … in a cloud of smoke.' Iggy performed a sorcerer's gesture with his arms and grinned at the young lieutenant.

Lachie smiled indulgently. 'Who are you, old man?'

'Icabod Varcoe, councilman and archivist, at your service, sir.'

'Sergeant!' Lachie Enright shouted up the stairs, 'please come down here and place Councillor Varcoe under arrest.'

'Corporal, I want you to search every inch of this cellar or archive or whatever it is and don't stop until you find something, preferably a way out.'

Lachie Enright made his way up the stairs issuing orders as he went: 'Sergeant, put together two squads and get them down to the ferry terminal and the railway station, quick as you can. No one leaves town without a full and rigorous identity check.'

At the top of the cellar stairs he assembled his troops. He knew the old councillor was up to something but there was little point trying to make him talk; he wasn't about to make a name for himself as the lieutenant who sweated an octogenarian councillor. He knew about the tunnels under the city and he suspected that his quarry may have escaped that way, but whether they were underground or gone to ground in the city streets, the councillor and the girl would have to surface sometime.

'Corporal, get Lieutenant Hunt on that contraption of yours, tell him our orders are to establish a perimeter around the entire southern sector of the old city, everything east of the Citadel and south of Broadway.'

'The rest of you come with me, I want a regulation grid search, house to house or bar or office or whatever, every dark corner and bolthole from here to the Providence Arch.'

Barrak had never felt more conspicuous or vulnerable in his ceremonial councillor's robes – cream silk with gold embroidery and the distinctive bright scarlet satin lining – and Jasmyn was no better, dressed to the nines for the opening-day formalities.

They made their way furtively along Pendlebury Way, which ran parallel to Orlan's Boulevard, behind the museum and the Plaza hotel. Pendlebury formed a T-intersection with Marine Drive, which in turn ran down to Station Street, where the railway station and the Sol ferry terminal were situated.

Iggy's instructions had brought them to the surface in one of the museum's basement storerooms. Barrak found he had a deep instinctive memory of the layout of the basement level, no doubt acquired in a childhood spent exploring treasure troves and hidden spaces in the bowels of the building where his father had worked.

He remembered enough to get them to an exit beside the loading dock at the rear of the building. Relieved to be out of the tunnels, they had paused amongst the crates and pallets to get their bearings, anxiously running scenarios by each other and trying to assess contingencies and dangers. It was a surreal situation and for the second time that morning Barrak had felt disconnected, like an observer of his own mutated reality.

Finally, they decided against making their way to Jasmyn's place out on the cape, it was too obvious. It made more sense to get right out of town, and so they agreed to head for Barrak's house. If they could travel quickly, maybe get the mid-morning ferry, and make it all the way down to Rylanswood, while Meldrick and his troops were preoccupied securing the city, it might buy them some time, time in which to consider their next move. The mid-morning sun was high and bright as they hurried along, sticking to the east side of the street, which at least afforded some shade and an illusion of cover. They had been forced to take refuge in a produce market when they heard a patrol approaching, the merchants bamboozled to see two august citizens in formal attire hiding behind a stack of fruit boxes until the police had passed.

As they rounded the corner into Marine Drive, Barrak scanned the station at the bottom of the street and saw two patrols parked outside, with troopers surrounding the building. There was a decent crowd coming and going from the station, but still, in their attire, they would be spotted long before they could get anywhere near the station or mingle with the crowd.

In a moment of panic, Barrak pulled Jasmyn through a doorway into a gloomy space that seemed at first, after the bright morning light, almost as dark as the tunnels.

A bell on a spring announced their presence, not that anyone could have missed them, back lit in their finery by a burst of daylight. They stood there in the doorway for a small eternity before their eyes adjusted to the semi-darkness of the bar. It was a seedy establishment, maybe one of the city's seediest, being just up the road from the railway station and opposite the docks and warehouses.

Rows of ancient bottles were lit by sickly yellow down lights. Dingy walls adorned with faded posters and a weird assortment of dockers' paraphernalia contrasted with a garish neon beer advertisement, flickering at the far end of the bar. As their eyes adjusted to the gloom, the first thing Barrak noticed was that all eyes were on them – four sets in all – those of the barman, a man and a boy sitting up at the bar, and a woman with a polka-dot scarf on her head and a mop in her hand.

The barman stopped polishing a glass mid-squeak and the woman plopped her mop onto the floor at her side. Barrak wondered why anyone would be drinking in a bar at ten o'clock in the morning, but the old man and the boy had foam-streaked glasses in front of them. The old man looked deeply offended, the boy as if he'd seen a pair of well-turned-out ghosts.

The old man, who was not really all that old, just badly weathered, pushed his glass away as if it had lost its charm and turned his attention to the barman, giving him an unpleasant scowl and an ambiguous nod.

He straightened on the bar stool and Barrak realised that he was taller than Barrak and built like the proverbial masonry outbuilding. He had the leathery skin that comes from too much sun and drink and was wearing denims and a filthy black singlet. On the stool beside him was a full-length hooded oilskin cape, of the sort favoured by sailors and outdoor workers.

The boy was a teen or young adult, his face smudged with dirt and freckles, dressed in a flannel shirt and muddy moleskins, his own oilskin flung over the empty stool at his side. He was smiling broadly, not at Barrak, but at Jasmyn, showing her a wide gap where two front teeth may have once been and, Jasmyn later claimed, painstakingly undressing her with his eyes.

The older man cracked his knuckles and then, alarmingly, did the same thing with his neck, cupping his mighty jaw in both hands and rotating his head to release a sickening crunch, before fixing his eyes on Barrak once again, with double the hostility.

Barrak looked uncertainly at Jasmyn, but she was smiling intently and sweetly at the teen, who returned her gaze, licking his lips. Jasmyn had produced a red leather purse, one with a drawstring and a braided trim, old-fashioned, in a fashionable way, and from it she was shaking gold coins into her hand. Barrak was puzzled. *Surely this was not a good time to buy a drink*. But she seemed to have enough coins in her hand to buy the whole bar ...

Lieutenant Lachie Enright had taken his own squad and backtracked along Broadway as far as the opera house. Saddner's Place ran north from its intersection with Broadway along the side of the opera and old theatre complex. The cobbled mall was wide and long with stage entrances and offices along one side and restaurants and cafes dotted all around the square, together with specialty shops and an old stone pub, a favourite with both actors and scribes. Taking up most of the western side of the mall was the old bluestone edifice of the offices of the *Tamouer Morning Chronicle* and the *Eyrean Times*. This was where he found Meldrick's personal protection unit, seven men in all, standing guard of the oversize revolving door that gave entry to the headquarters of Tamouer's two daily newspapers.

Sergeant Mackie gave him a nod of recognition as he approached, just a terse lift of the head and a deadpan stare. Mackie was, for all intents and purposes, the commander of Meldrick's personal guard, which was handpicked from the ranks of the Parliamentary Guard.

'You lucky prick,' was Mackie's bland pronouncement as Lachie and his men approached. 'If you fell on your face in a field of shit, you'd come up with a rose between your teeth; you would, Lieutenant, no question about it.' Mackie flicked a cautioning glance at one of his men who ventured a snigger, letting him know only he had licence to rib the lieutenant.

To say there was no love lost between Lieutenant Enright and Sergeant Mackie was an understatement. Mackie detested the effeminate officer's manner and appearance and resented his accelerated rise through the ranks and favoured treatment by Meldrick. Lachie in turn considered Mackie a ham-fisted psychopath who'd found favour with Meldrick only because his brutality frightened the wits out of all and sundry and gave Meldrick's bodyguard unit an appropriately fearsome reputation.

'Did you tell him?' Lachie demanded as he and his men came to a halt in front of the entrance.

'Yeah, look the Commissar was a little preoccupied. Right now he's talking to some editors and the owner of this little rag. Wouldn't mind being a fly on the wall in that meeting.'

'Sergeant, you told him didn't you? That I had Brethrenhope and the girl?'

Mackie's eye's narrowed and his lip curled. 'Yeah, I told him all right, but I don't see any councillor, or his little girlfriend. Are you quite sure you've got 'em? Maybe the girl was too much for your men … I hear she's quite a handful.'

'Don't you worry about that, Sergeant. Stokes's squad picked them up down by the marina a few minutes ago and notified me right away by transmitted message. They'll be here any minute.'

'Well then, that'll be quite the feather in your cap, won't it, Lieutenant?' Mackie managed to inject the subtlest note of effeminate sarcasm into the comment, just enough to make it sting.

Minutes passed in awkward silence, men shuffled and muttered amongst themselves, keeping to their respective squads. Lachie paced from the newspaper office entrance to the corner and back, on tenterhooks. *Where the hell was Stokes?*

Finally the patrol rounded the corner into the square at double time, the two prisoners at the rear, hands tied, struggling to keep up with the troopers.

Even as Enright took the first few steps to meet Corporal Stokes, something made him hesitate. Something was awry, off kilter: the councillor's gait was all wrong, as if he had a gammy hip . . . perhaps he did. And the girl, learned astrologer and aristocratic daughter of the Lord High Councillor, seemed to be cowering under the hood of her fine satin cloak, not haughty and indignant as he would've expected.

As Stokes and his squad came to a halt, the smile was wiped off the corporal's face by the lieutenant's disapproving glare, tinged with rising panic. He brushed past Stokes and approached the prisoners, hemmed in left and right by troopers, heads bowed, shoulders hunched.

As he reached for the hood of the councillor's ceremonial robe, he already knew he was in deep trouble. He flung the hood back, revealing a half-bald nut-brown head, with unkempt tufts of greying hair around the temples. A pair of bloodshot eyes glared at him out of the ragged unshaven face of a sun-bronzed labourer, who bared what remained of his rotten teeth with an unpleasant grunt.

Enright stifled a gasp and pushed the man. He hauled the woman roughly towards him and snatched the hood away from her head. Now it was Lachie's turn to grunt. The teen's toothless grin and vacant stare seemed to mock him as he took in the scrawny young lad, filthy and smelling of sweat and beer, dressed head to foot in a trendy but tastefully understated ensemble from one of Tamouer's high-end boutiques.

He turned on Stokes, who was already backing away, slack jawed and pale, the implications of his mistake slamming into him like a volley of arrows. Lachie's mind swam and the hot morning sun seemed suddenly offensively bright. Sergeant Mackie had come up next to Stokes to see the fun, and in the middle distance, Lachie saw Meldrick come out through the revolving door and down the front steps of the newspaper office, looking expectantly in his direction.

Lachie Enright's illustrious future career flashed before his eyes, on its way to oblivion.

Mackie walked slowly towards Lachie and his mouth formed an exaggerated *Ooh*. He winced in mock sympathy for Lachie's pain, and as more and more blood drained from Lachie Enright's face, the sergeant's grin grew broader. Shoulder to shoulder with him, as if they were about to dance, Mackie's lips came close to Lachie's ear. 'You are right royally stuffed now, boy-oh!' he said softly.

Chapter 11

THERE COMES A POINT in any sea voyage when the last landmark is lost and the ocean stretches away to the horizon in all directions. At that point, every mariner knows, there is a need for faith, faith in your captain and your vessel, faith in your compass and in the sun or the wind, that it will continue to impel your vessel towards its destination.

Sailing south from Tamouer, this doesn't happen until well into the journey – more than half way – when Tamouer's western ranges finally dissolve into the sea mist, but before the headland of the southern port city of Westhaven appears on the starboard bow, or the towering pyramid of St Mary's Peak, far off to the south, emerges from the shrouded horizon.

Barrak peered out over the shining water. It was mirror calm, its untroubled surface more silver than blue. His own faith had been deeply shaken and a part of him wondered whether the Rylanswood he knew, his childhood home and refuge, would be where he'd left it when they reached the southern shore. He fancied himself adrift on a sea of uncertainty, as if he and Jasmyn were stepping across a watery threshold to a new reality that was itself shrouded in mists of uncertainty and ambiguity.

The ferry's motor whirred away steadily, powered by a full set of solar sails unfurled on both masts.

Shunning the crowded mid-section of the ferry, they had made for the open deck at the rear of the vessel, and now that the sun was high and bright, they were alone amongst the sun-bleached benches and tables bolted to the deck. Barrak was forced to use the old docker's smelly cape to shelter from the sun, which only exacerbated his discomfort.

Jasmyn had discarded hers, declaring she would burn to a crisp rather than continue to wear the putrid rag, for which she'd paid a prince's ransom.

She had said very little since they'd run the gauntlet of troopers checking papers at the ferry terminal. It was out of character for Jasmyn to be quiet for long, but Barrak allowed her solitude and space; there had been a lot to digest. She sat on the slatted timber bench opposite Barrak, her forearms resting on the gunwale of the ferry, staring out to sea, her chin propped on the back of her hands. When she did finally speak, her voice was distant and tinged with sadness.

'We're in a lot of trouble, aren't we Barrak?'

'Jasmyn, *we've* done nothing wrong. Meldrick can't be allowed to get away with this.' He hesitated. There was something about the look in Jasmyn's eyes that scared him, a deep sadness and a dullness, like resignation.

'It's not legal. He can't just take over ...' For a moment Barrak wondered who he was trying to convince. 'Look, there's a man in my town, a retired councillor, a friend. In his day he was an expert in constitutional law. This, this ... coup can't be allowed to continue.' Barrak struggled for words, puzzled and upset by his own hesitancy and all the more fazed when he noticed a tear rolling down Jasmyn's cheek.

'I've been an absolute pig to my father lately,' she said quietly. 'I don't even know why. I've been like a teenager, hating him and letting him know it. What's the matter with me, Barrak? I don't know why I would behave like that.' She tilted her head and looked enquiringly at Barrak. 'I'm twenty-seven, by Orlan, and I've been behaving like a child.'

She blinked and another couple of tears escaped. 'And now ... did you see the look on his face when he was arrested? Now, I might never get the chance to tell him ...' Her voice faltered and more tears tumbled down. She looked away, out over the water.

Barrak leaned across and put a tentative hand on her shoulder. He could feel the sobs shaking her body as she wept quietly, adding her tears to the shimmering ocean. 'Enoch will be all right. We'll put this thing right I promise.' But Barrak sounded uncertain, even to himself.

Barrak snatched items from the pantry and crammed them into a carry bag. If you asked him what he'd included he couldn't have said, some obscure instinct was in charge of packing, while his mind raced, trying to put together a plan.

The comforting familiarity of his home collided paradoxically with his battered sense of reality and he felt unhinged as he trawled the rooms, randomly stuffing things into a bag with more madness than method.

There was a fuzzy memory just beyond his grasp, of a place far away, a refuge of sorts, where he'd stayed with his friend Thomas long ago, when they were young. It had been a hunting trip, not that Barrak had any real aptitude for killing things. It was Thomas's father's lodge, just a tiny cabin really, away in the hills to the west of Lilbetown. They'd spent a long weekend there. For some reason it was important to Barrak to form a clear mental picture of the place, but it kept slipping from his mind's grasp and it annoyed him as he went about his manic packing.

Jasmyn found him, wild-eyed and sweating, casting about in the kitchen, which did her no good at all, and it did little for his mental state to have Jasmyn suddenly appear in Persephone's favourite anorak over an old shirt. The shock of it momentarily stopped him in his tracks.

'What are we doing, Barrak? she asked him gently. 'Where are we supposed to go?'

Barrak looked lost. 'I don't know … there's a place up in the mountains, it belongs to a friend, a good friend. He'll let us stay there. He'd probably take us there if I asked.'

Jasmyn put down the carry bag Barrak had asked her to fill and sat on it. She gave him a dubious look.

'We certainly can't stay here. This will be the next place they look, right after your place. It won't take them long. We have to find somewhere to lie low for a while … and we need to go now,' he urged.

'But how?' Jasmyn was sceptical, a deep frown crinkling her forehead. 'I have nothing.' She held out her hands as if to prove it. 'I mean, I appreciate you offering me Persephone's things but …' she stared past Barrak for a moment. 'I just think, Barrak, I think maybe I should just go home and …' She trailed off.

Barrak found himself staring at her with a troubled frown of his own.

'I mean, maybe we're overreacting.'

They both turned to stone at the sound of heavy, hurried footfalls on the deck outside the kitchen door. The sound was unmistakable, but stopped almost at once.

In the short silence that followed Barrak felt his neck hair bristle. Staring into Jasmyn's wide, round eyes he saw his own fear reflected there. The brief, anxious silence seemed to amplify all the creaks and groans of the house, normally only audible in the dead of night. He held his breath and fancied his heart had stopped to listen too.

But not for long.

The back door exploded from its latch, splintering the stopper and crashing against the inside wall of the kitchen. Two troopers were framed in the bright doorway, one recovering his balance from the massive kick, the other, an officer, glaring over his subordinate's shoulder directly at Barrak as he stood granite-still on the far side of the kitchen.

Lachie Enright nodded to his corporal to go left and he himself took two nonchalant steps through the broken doorway, before settling himself against the door frame, as if he were at a friend's house.

Barrak felt a rush of fury rising from his gut to his throat. 'How dare you!' This he bellowed with such intensity, it took everyone by surprise. The corporal tensed and raised his crossbow. His eyes flicked between Barrak and Jasmyn and darted back to his lieutenant, who had one hand on the haft of his sword, his own crossbow holstered at his side.

'Uh-uh, Councillor.' Enright's tone was genial but his eyes flashed a warning. 'Let's not get excited. You'll have to excuse us *bursting* in unexpectedly,' he said with a sour grin, 'but it seems we missed you this morning in Tamouer and there're a few small matters that need to be cleared up.'

The lieutenant glanced down at Jasmyn, still perched on the bag, her back hard up against the wall as though she might try to push herself through it into the other room. Between dishevelled locks of hair, she stared darkly at the two intruders.

'Not the least of which is the matter of treason and sedition.' The lieutenant spat the words contemptuously as he switched his gaze back to Barrak. '*And* the murder of General Hawkins.' Enright's voice broke slightly with this last accusation and it occurred to Barrak the young lieutenant was on edge and strangely aggrieved, as though there was a personal score to settle.

Barrak had no way of knowing what his and Jasmyn's successful ruse had cost Lachie Enright. He had no way of knowing the ambitious lieutenant had been humiliated in front of his men, dressed down for his incompetence and failure and berated by Meldrick in front of not only his own squad, but also Mackie's.

Enright had been crestfallen and quietly furious that Meldrick had lambasted him in front of his subordinates. He may as well have ripped the lieutenant's bars from his shoulders and dispatched him to the Citadel dungeons.

Barrak was also oblivious to the risk the lieutenant was taking, after Meldrick had assigned him to processing detainees back at headquarters. He had ignored Meldrick's orders and elected to play his hunch instead. Now, Enright was past the outer markers, insubordinate and mutinous, a rogue agent.

He'd taken an all-terrain MV *and* Corporal Stokes and headed south on the coast road. Stokes had been horrified, but somehow he knew he was fated to sink or swim with his lieutenant; it was his penance for his part in the debacle. Enright had driven the MV himself, driven it hard, like a man possessed and with little or no regard for speed limits or safety. He was sure their quarry had taken the ferry, headed for the councillor's home in far off Rylanswood. He would have done exactly the same.

It was a gamble. But only this would redeem him in the eyes of his commander, delivering Brethrenhope and the girl to Meldrick, as ordered. It would expunge his sins and save his career.

So, Barrak really had no idea what was at stake for the young lieutenant as they glared at each other across his kitchen.

Lachie Enright was fascinated as he held the councillor's eye, trying to assess his mettle and fathom the soul of the inscrutable and infamous Brethrenhope.

The stand-off finally ended when Enright nodded emphatically to Corporal Stokes. 'Take them into custody, Corporal.'

Time slowed.

Barrak saw the steel in the lieutenant's eyes. And he watched as the corporal raised his crossbow to reach for the restraints on his belt.

What he didn't see, until it was too late, was that Jasmyn had *turned*.

No one expected to see her rise like a banshee from her submissive pose against the wall. No one anticipated that she would take flight and swoop on the corporal, uttering an unearthly, screeching wail like nothing Barrak had ever heard.

She slammed into Stokes, and was all over him like a plague of demons.

Lachie Enright hadn't realised his plan had one fatal flaw: he had come undermanned. He hadn't expected much resistance from a physician and an aristocrat's daughter, and he hadn't counted on Jasmyn's anguish at seeing her father arrested, her disgust and rage over Meldrick's abuse and her fear and dismay at having her world turned upside down.

It was her father who had insisted she master the art of hand to hand combat, and her years of training were crystal clear in her mind as she took to the unprepared Stokes. When she rushed him, her primary focus was his weapon. All the momentum of her initial rush had gone to deflecting his bow, before administering a kick to the groin to fold him over, a kidney punch to open him up and a throat blow to stop him breathing, temporarily.

The crossbow had discharged.

In a frozen moment Barrak saw the grievous consequences of Jasmyn's assault. Ashen-faced and wide-eyed, Lachie Enright looked from Barrak to his own impaled shoulder, barely able to comprehend what he was seeing, then to Jasmyn, standing over the stricken corporal, breathing heavily in time with Stokes's own raucous gasping.

He pulled his shoulder forward on the shaft and grimaced as the barbs bit into his flesh. His eyes flared and he bellowed, more in frustration than pain.

Barrak's mind raced as he took it all in. The lieutenant's own crossbow had fallen to the floor when the errant arrow had slammed into him. Barrak's knowledge of both human anatomy *and* the construction of his kitchen told him the lieutenant would not be going anywhere. The door frame was solid hardwood, the type of timber from which nails were almost impossible to remove. The arrow was one of the new high-tech bolts, with barbs that deployed on impact. They were inhumane, disabling, ultimately lethal … Barrak thought they'd been banned.

Panic, fear and rage swept across Enright's face as he frantically assessed his position. His bow was out of reach. His sword arm was useless, hanging limply at an odd angle and inexplicably unresponsive. He tried his right hand but the angle and length of the scabbard wasn't going to let him draw his sword.

A chill of mortal fright ran through Lachie Enright as he felt blood trickling inside his shirt and down his leg.

'Stokes!' he croaked. 'Get up … Get up! Stokes!' His voice cracked with an edge of hysteria to it. Stokes gagged and coughed, still gasping for breath, but at least he was on his feet, starting to recover his composure.

Jasmyn was backing away from the crouching Stokes. Her nerve had deserted her now, and she looked shocked by her own bravado and the consequences of it.

Barrak took it all in, his racing mind compacting time.

In the end, it was the fear in Jasmyn's eyes as she backed away from the enraged Stokes that spurred him into action. He leapt forward with an agility he thought he'd left behind years ago. He grappled Stokes back onto the floor, his arm under his chin, trying to hold him down. But the smaller trooper was surprisingly strong and agile and rolled out from under Barrak and leapt to his feet. What followed was a blur of weirdly vivid images, Jasmyn in the corner near the bathroom, shock and confusion pressing her backwards, Stokes's sweating face contorted with exertion, so close to his own, the impaled Lieutenant whirling past, pale and soaked in bright blood, screaming incomprehensible orders.

Suddenly, Stokes had him pinned to the wall, a knee in his hip, a boot crunching down on his foot, but all Barrak's focus was on Stokes's hand and the ugly weapon in it, a short curved blade with rings for his fingers, which he struggled to raise to Barrak's throat. Barrak felt his eyes bulging with effort as he resisted with all his might, both his own hands clasped around Stokes's wrists.

Barrak looked past Stokes's ear and saw Jasmyn, clutching the corporal's crossbow.

'Leave him! Stop! LET HIM GO!' She was near hysterical.

The impaled lieutenant joined in the raucous pantomime. 'Drop that weapon! I'll kill you, you bitch ... DROP IT!'

Barrak felt the tip at his throat. An image of a pin and a balloon flashed through his mind and somehow he found more strength.

'Put the weapon down! Jasmyn! DROP IT! BITCH! ... CORPORAL!' The lieutenant tried to warn him, but all Stokes's attention was focused on the fight. He found another measure of strength and put it behind the blade.

Jasmyn was ranting, swearing, shaking the crossbow and banging it with her free hand. *How did it work?* None of her self-defence training had involved weapons.

'PUT – IT – DOWN!' Enright bellowed from the doorway.

A swish and a thud was all it took and Stokes's arms went limp. Barrak was blinded by a spray of blood. It felt warm and he tasted the salt in it. The dead weight of the corporal pulled him away from the wall. He went with it and felt the arrow lodged in the wall behind him brush past his ear. It must have gone straight through Stokes and missed Barrak by inches. Blinded still, he eased Stokes to the floor and only then wiped the blood from his eyes. He could hear Stokes trying to speak, trying to breathe, as though underwater. Gurgling and bubbling wails were all he could manage. Barrak saw him now, and the murderous brute was reduced to a scared boy in uniform, a boy with a slaughterhouse hole in his throat, staring up at Barrak with bewildered eyes.

Barrak tried to stem the bleeding but he knew it was useless. The bleeding told him the boy's jugular vein was severed. From the sudden limpness of his body and the lolling of his head, he guessed the bolt may have shattered his spine as well. He was cruelly conscious, unharmed from the neck up. *No … no! Orlan's mercy.*

He heard a thud as Jasmyn dropped the bow. She began to whimper, a ghostly keen that increased in volume then dissolved into tears and a murmuring repetitive plea, like praying. 'No, please, no… no,' she whispered, imploring the gods.

Barrak slipped a hand under the corporal's head and wiped some blood from his cheek. The lad looked up at Barrak and began to shake uncontrollably. Shock turned gradually to understanding and then a wave of fear flooded the poor boy's eyes. Barrak could hear Jasmyn's piteous whimpering still but not a sound from the lieutenant at the door.

'It's OK,' was all Barrak could think to say. The boy's trembling stopped abruptly and his eyes softened a bit as he looked into Barrak's. The corporal drew one more ragged breath through his shattered throat before the light left his eyes and the last of his breath seeped out of him.

Enright, dumb with shock until then, began to speak, quietly at first. 'Gods, what have you done!? Orlan's blood, you'll pay for this!' He pulled against the arrow and screamed for the pain it caused him. 'Is he dead? You'll hang for this, both of you! Get me off here!' the lieutenant bellowed.

He went on and on, ranting and screaming, struggling and bleeding, but Barrak had switched off. He picked up his bag as though he were alone in the house, going about his business, calm, unaffected. He picked up Jasmyn's bag and pressed it to her chest, eliciting a sob in response. Mechanically he gathered whatever else he could carry and ushered Jasmyn out through the laundry and onto the deck without a word, avoiding the impaled, ranting lieutenant and the blood-slicked floor.

He put Jasmyn's pack on her back, fastened it and ushered her along, out the back gate and onto the walking track above the beach reserve. She didn't speak or struggle or cry, but let him lead her by the arm, pliable as a sleepwalker. The further they got along the walking track that led to the pier, the more Barrak wondered when they would stop hearing the shouts and curses of the lieutenant following them on the breeze. Just when he thought they were out of earshot, his voice would come again, carried on the wind, bellowing threats or howling with frustration and pain, vowing retribution and justice.

As they paused in a copse of tea-tree above the wharf, Barrak was struck by the familiarity of his habitual walking track and he thought of the scant possessions he now carried on his back. He looked at Jasmyn's tear-stained face and then down at the young trooper's blood drying on his own arms and shirt. A wave of despair welled up inside him, threatening to overturn reason. In an instant, some internal alchemy transformed despair to anger, and then anger to rage.

He cast around wildly until he found a low-hanging dead branch, which he snapped off with a grunt and enough effort to unbalance him, infuriating him even more. He set to thrashing some nearby myrtles and tea-trees, hurling blasphemies and contempt with every swipe, until the branch snapped in half. This enraged him further and he pounded the earth at his feet with the snapped stick until it shattered completely. Still he wasn't satisfied until he'd kicked and stomped the broken pieces, damning them for all time.

Jasmyn looked on silently, her arms hanging limply by her sides, eyes wide and vacant, watching him as though he were a ghoul from a nightmare other than her own.

At the end of it, Barrak was red faced and breathing heavily, beads of sweat popping on his brow. He wiped his hands on each other then brushed himself off, soberly, reflectively, and stood for a time looking to the west where the sun was obscured behind late-afternoon thunderheads massing over the hills.

He tried a reassuring smile for Jasmyn, but couldn't be sure what kind of expression arranged itself on his face. He got only a blank stare and a double blink in response. A magpie chortled loudly overhead and the bushes around them stirred in a cool, humid breeze, which suggested a thunderstorm might not be far off.

They heard no more from the crucified lieutenant standing guard over the charnel house that had once been Barrak's kitchen.

Barrak took Jasmyn by the hand. 'We'll be losing the light soon,' he said softly and guided her gently onto the fork in the track that lead up to his old friend Thomas's house, overlooking the fishermen's wharf.

As they chugged past the last of the channel markers, Thomas spun the wheel and set course for the end of the breakwater. Nostalgia tugged at Barrak, making him long for simpler and happier times. The aromatic smell of his old friend's pipe smoke, the languid slapping of the waves against the bow and the scenes of aquatic serenity slipping quietly by, reminded him of the few special times in his student days when Thomas had convinced his father to let Barrak crew as a deck hand. Gulls squawked and argued and he watched Thomas at the wheel, relaxed, stoic, quietly alert, taking it all in through the salt-streaked windscreen of the old wheelhouse.

He knew how much Thomas loved putting out to sea. He knew this because Thomas had told him. *You know Barrak, there's something about the stillness before the sun's up, the mist still hanging on the water, smooth as a mirror. There's no hurry, you take it slow as you like ... out past the big orange channel buoy – the pelicans perch there and watch you go – out past the breakwater, and then you clear the point, throw a wave to the kids fishing off the rocks, maybe sound the foghorn ...* Barrak had heard him talk about it many times. *Then you're away, free as a bird. You're the gods-struck captain and it's just you, your crew, your boat and your wits and nothing but sea out there ... There's no feeling like it in the world ...*

But this was different, this was dusk, not dawn, an unscheduled sailing, and the two men stood solemnly side by side without a word.

Theirs was the kind of friendship that didn't necessarily require conversation. They'd been friends since school. At age eleven Thomas had come to the private college where Barrak had been schooled since kindergarten. Barrak, bespectacled then and bookish, had befriended the big gruff fisherman's son when others perhaps wouldn't have been so welcoming, and from that simple beginning a bond was forged that grew stronger through the years. This special bond between unlikely individuals would have been enough – Thomas was the most loyal and steadfast person Barrak had ever known – but what put it beyond question was what had passed between them decades later.

The city doctors had given up on Thomas's four-year-old daughter, Ruby. It was a particularly aggressive form of lymphoma, they said, and they had finally told him and his wife to take Ruby home and try to make the most of the time they had left. Barrak had been horrified when Thomas came to him, his painfully acute empathy for Thomas and his wife, and his great desire to help the little girl were, at first, overshadowed by his own fear and the daunting weight of such responsibility. He was only three years out of medical school then, and the words of his old professor still rang in his ears ... *Perhaps after forty years of practice, with diligence and constant study, some of you can expect to become competent prescribers ...* But Thomas had been insistent. Barrak was, he said, the only hope they had left.

There had never been any doubt really, Barrak just had to get over his own fear of failing his friend. In the end he had pawed through every Materia Medica and repertory in the university and hospital libraries for days and long nights, studied dozens of cases, anything remotely related, and observed young Ruby and questioned her mother and father over and over, until he was sure he had the most complete picture of her symptoms.

162

Eventually the remedy became apparent, that is, a remedy kept presenting itself and Barrak kept resisting it, because it was a remedy normally associated with diseases in the very old. But Ruby's symptoms were so unusual and so distinctive and such a perfect match for the remedy, that eventually Barrak realised it was the best and only choice. When he went to Thomas's house to administer it, he was shocked to see how Ruby's condition had deteriorated. She looked like a tiny, withered old lady. It was only then he was sure he had the right medicine. *Conium maculatum,* hemlock, a medicine derived from a strong poison and consequently one with particularly powerful curative qualities.

When Ruby rallied, he warned Thomas that spontaneous remissions from such serious diseases were not unusual and could last a short time or indefinitely, but Thomas wouldn't hear of it. Barrak had cured his little girl and that was all there was to it. Her recovery had indeed been remarkable and today Ruby was a healthy, vibrant and brash sixteen-year-old, making her parents' lives hell, just as she should.

This was why, when he and Jasmyn had burst in on Thomas that evening as he ate his dinner, he had put down his knife and fork with a chunk of sausage and mash still on it. One look at Barrak's face had told him his friend was in serious trouble. He ushered Barrak into another room, and before he was halfway through his story, Thomas had on his oilskins and boots and was telling his wife not to wait up, because he wouldn't be back until morning.

As they cleared the point and headed into open water, Thomas pushed the throttle forward a notch and adjusted course slightly. They both looked out the side of the wheelhouse towards the sun, which had emerged below a thick cloud bank to douse the mirror-calm sea in gold, before sinking, as it soon would, behind the western hills. Finally, Barrak broke their long easy silence. 'I best go below and check on Jasmyn.'

Thomas gave an affirmative puff from his pipe and nodded, a solemn look of concern on his weather-beaten face.

※

163

Meldrick carefully skirted the congealed pool of blood that took up half the kitchen floor, screwing up his nose with fastidious disdain. He looked down at the body on the floor for a long time, without a word. Several of his men were searching the house, clearing each of the rooms in turn, announcing their findings as they went. Finally Sergeant Mackie emerged from the main living area and stopped in his tracks at the sight of Meldrick standing over Stokes's crumpled body. 'There's no one here sir,' he reported evenly.

Meldrick lifted his gaze slowly and stared at Mackie for long enough to make the sergeant shift his stance uneasily and clear his throat. He then switched his gaze to the company medic attending to Enright, who was still slumped against the door frame, still pinned to it, but now only semiconscious.

Mackie followed his gaze furtively, hesitantly. The sight of Enright, slung like a coat on a hanger, deathly pale and barely conscious, filled him with dread and uncommon empathy. Gone was all the past animosity he'd felt for the annoying lieutenant. Enright had rolled the dice and lost. His career was over, and by the look of him, he'd be lucky to live.

Meldrick turned back to Mackie, his dark eyes simmering with anger and then suddenly widening as a surge of fury gripped him and he pounded both fists on the kitchen table, kicking up the paraphernalia arrayed on it like a miniature chorus line. 'Orlan's cursed blood!' he spat venomously and took the edge of the kitchen table and upended it, flipping it completely over to crash against the sink, its assortment of domestic minutia clattering across the floor.

He took two quick strides towards the medic and the wretched lieutenant. 'Wake him,' he demanded. The medic gave his commander a sidelong look of shocked disbelief as he juggled a syringe and a bag of intravenous fluid. Meldrick pushed past him and took Enright by the lapels and shook him. 'Where are they? What have you done? You, you ... imbecile!' Enright's head lolled and his eyes rolled. He groaned and mumbled incoherently.

'WHERE – DID – THEY – GO?' Meldrick demanded.

'How long ... how long have you been here ... like this?' Meldrick looked disdainfully at the lieutenant's wound, the protruding arrow and the bloodied floorboards, as if it were all an affront to military decorum.

The half-dead lieutenant's only response was more garbled gibberish.

Meldrick sighed and took his hands off Enright, straightened his lapel and patted his chest as if he were a schoolboy about to be dispatched to class. More with resignation than anger he looked around the room at the medic, Mackie and two other troopers, all frozen in cringing anticipation of their commander's ire.

He looked again at Stokes lying still in the corner. They all looked on, uncertain, appalled, as Meldrick strode back to the dead corporal and lifted him by the lapel, going down on one knee to heft his bloodied torso up onto his leg. A collective wince went through them as Meldrick shoved his fingers into the dead soldier's gaping wound. His hand came out bloodied and he held it up. 'Warm,' he stated emphatically. 'He's still warm.' He stared at Mackie and the gathered troopers. 'They can't be far!' His eyes took on a vivid, wild clarity. 'What the hell are you waiting for?' he roared. 'Find them! Go!'

The room erupted with activity as men shouldered weapons and jostled through the doorway. Mackie began barking orders, but Meldrick interrupted him: 'Sergeant Mackie, wait a minute. I have another job for you first.'

Barrak went below, down the steep stairs into the bowels of Thomas's trawler and then stopped to get his bearings. At the bottom of the steps was the widest part of the ship. On one side were the equipment lockers for the nets, weights, cables and floats, and on the other, coat hooks and lockers for the crew, where they would change into and out of their wet-weather gear. Aft were the storage compartments for the catch, which opened via hatches to the winching deck, and just to starboard was the old ice machine he remembered doing battle with during his brief career as a deckhand.

He turned and went forward, behind the stairs into the crew's mess, the cramped little common room where the crew would eat and spend any time they had between sleeping and working. With no crew crowded around the old table, it seemed more spacious than he remembered it, dimly lit by a single overhead bulb that looked like it hadn't been changed since he was last on board.

But there was no Jasmyn. She wasn't where he'd left her, but he thought he could hear her.

He went further forward, following the faint human sounds barely audible over the whining of the engine, through an even smaller hatch into the forward sleeping quarters, ostensibly the captain's quarters, so designated for the rare luxury of having its own washbasin.

This was where he found her, wedged between the end of the semi-recessed bunk that ran between bulkheads and the basin, sitting on the floor with her knees to her chin and a towel over her head like a shroud.

She looked up at Barrak with eyes full of bitter anguish.

He thought he smelled vomit and there was water on the floor. He guessed Jasmyn had made good use of the tiny washbasin to try to clean herself up. Her hair was wet under the towel and nothing remained of the morning's careful make-up, applied in another world, for another time. She was sunburnt, tear-stained and pale all at once, shivering, despite the afternoon warmth still trapped below deck. She bit her bottom lip to stop it quivering. Perhaps she had no more tears left to cry.

Barrak sank to his knees and crammed himself as best he could between the bunk and Jasmyn and put his arm around her. She made room and pulled herself close to him and pressed her face into his shoulder. After a moment Barrak felt damp warmth seep through his clothes, and it was clear there were tears yet to come. He held her tightly and the tears gave way to sobs, which gradually grew in intensity to great cathartic wrenching gasps. He could do nothing but hold her even tighter, as she heaved and clung to him like a shipwreck survivor.

He shut his eyes and an image came to him of his little boy Noah, bawling in his arms after skinning his knee in a tricycle accident. He whispered soothing inanities to Jasmyn just as he remembered doing with Noah, and held her tight and steady, stroking her hair and holding on for as long as it took, until the sobs began to subside. Eventually she relaxed in his arms a little and her sobs gave way to the occasional ragged, shuddering breath.

Still there were no words, and Barrak was silent too; the events of this day could not easily be reconciled for either of them. After a while it seemed as if Jasmyn might fall asleep, which would have been a blessing, but before that could happen, Thomas's head appeared around the door of his cabin. 'You better come up and have a look at this,' he said sternly. Barrak gave him a questioning look and dipped his eyes toward Jasmyn.

'I'm sorry. It's important. You're gonna need to see this, mate. I'm afraid it's not good, not good at all.'

Back on deck the two men stood on the port side of the boat, just outside the wheelhouse and looked back past the stern, towards the receding shoreline of Rylanswood. The sun had set but the western sky above the hills was still lit up warm and yellow, a bright stage under a descending curtain of dark cloud. The dying sun's reflection followed them across the darkening bay as light rain began to fall, misting the glow of a first quarter moon, trying to poke through gaps in the dark clouds overhead.

At first Barrak didn't know what he was looking at, but it only took a moment for the penny to drop. There was a second sunset flaring orange above the shoreline, but there was smoke, too, growing rapidly into a towering pillar above the shore. As they watched, the orange glow flared brighter, doubling and redoubling in intensity until a second trail of reflected luminosity fingered its way across the oily black waters to their vessel.

Soon, huge tongues of flame could be seen reaching impossibly high into the evening sky and swirling into a vortex of black and grey smoke as the blaze took hold and began to consume Barrak's house.

It was impossible to make out anything that clearly identified it as Barrak's property, and yet somehow, there was no doubt. The ferocity and speed with which it took hold surprised and appalled Barrak and he imagined he could feel the heat of it and hear the roar and crackle of the flames, even though they were miles away.

He felt Jasmyn slip her hands around his arm in the dark and hug it to her, putting her cheek against his shoulder without a word. He felt a kaleidoscopic array of emotions – anger, sorrow, rage, regret, relief, puzzlement, tenderness, self-pity … an endless parade. But nothing seemed to fit. He was numb, transfixed by the savage spectacle of it, but curiously detached. *Did this matter? Had the world not just recently gone completely stark raving mad? Was he even himself any longer? Whose house was burning across the inky bay anyway? Nothing made sense any more.*

Jasmyn held onto his arm as if it were a lifeline and stared at the shore. When she looked up at him and he saw the twin specks of orange fire reflected in her dark eyes, he felt something give way inside himself as he realised his home was being destroyed. The confusion of feelings began to coalesce into grief, a diffuse sadness he knew only too well. It was a path that could lead to a chaotic loss of self, with little or no possibility of redemption. It was a path he refused to go down, not again. Then somehow, strangely, he began to laugh. A dubious chuckle at first, but soon it became a robust belly laugh. Jasmyn squeezed his arm and rubbed his shoulder, trying to comfort him, and even Thomas clasped his shoulder for support. But the laughter had him in its thrall and the unholy glow of his burning home lit up the night as he guffawed and gasped like a madman, his secret love clinging to his arm as they motored on in his old friend's boat, into the darkness.

CHAPTER 12

GITAN KILLED A MAN when he was just seventeen, or so the story went.

It was in fact true. He killed him with a jemmy, the sort a builder or demolition worker might use to remove a difficult nail. He used it to remove Dennis Buckley from the face of the earth and he reckoned he'd done everyone a big favour in the process. He killed him with a single zealous blow to the side of the head that shattered his temporal bone and pulped his disturbed brain. Dennis was dead before his big witless body hit the ground.

Gitan was not his real name, but it did provide a certain anonymity, and perhaps even mystique. More importantly, it helped put some distance between his present-day self and some of the more unsavoury events of his past life. Few people in his orbit today even knew his real name, and those who did, never used it.

He was born Sebastian Gittiana, in the port town of Westhaven, to a father who worked six days a week on the docks and cut firewood on Sundays to make ends meet, and a mother who took in sewing and lovingly cared for her four children in the tiny portside tenement, which, in Seb's memory, was perpetually festooned with other people's garments. Most of Seb's early life was a blur, washed-out snippets of memory that just filled the space between his birth and the day he was reborn a killer.

It was a grey, wet, autumn day when that gormless animal Buckley stole everything from his baby sister, Petulia, leaving her broken and frail, until the day, six years later, when she ended her pain with a razor blade in a warm bath. Seb could still remember her on her knees in the front hallway, sheets of rain teeming down outside the open front door. Sometimes he thought this searing image was the only clear recollection he retained from his youth. He could still feel the clenching tightness in his chest and see the look of sheer desolation and terror in Petunia's eyes, a puddle of rainwater around her crumpled, dripping body and the fingers of both her small hands tangled in her long wet hair, as if she were trying to keep her head from cracking apart.

And he remembered the blood on her dress.

Seb was just sixteen years old, but that day he became a killer. Even though he would not actually kill for almost a year, that gloomy April day was nonetheless the day he became a steely-eyed, cold-blooded murderer. Killing Buckley became his religion, which he practised thereafter every day, in the privacy of his own mind.

They say things come in threes, and four months later, when his father was killed in a tree-felling accident, leaving Seb to care for the family, no one could have guessed that a third tragedy was already stalking his family. The day of his father's funeral, his youngest brother, Zac, fell ill with a fever, and three weeks later, he too was dead from pneumonia. Seb became the dedicated protector of, and provider for, what remained of his family. And there was no part of that role he took more seriously than ridding the world of the ever-present threat and general affront to humanity that was Dennis Buckley.

Buckley punched Seb once, breaking his nose and landing Seb on his backside, after Seb glared at him across the street in a chance encounter on the harbour promenade. There were witnesses. Seb did nothing in retaliation, but reported the incident to the local CSF station, insisting that an official complaint be lodged. Every chance he got after that, he let Buckley know he'd not forgotten him. And Buckley responded mindlessly, pushing and shoving, threatening and intimidating.

Two days after Seb's seventeenth birthday and ten days after the local physician had committed his sister Petulia to the mental hospital in Rylanswood 'for observation', Seb took the jemmy he'd bought months before and slipped it into his belt, curved side out for a good grip – *you don't want anyone taking that off you in a fight, son* – and took himself down to the local tavern where Buckley was known to be a frequent and enthusiastic customer.

Make sure he takes the first swing.

Seb made sure he did, by simply telling Buckley just what he was, in front of his assembled drinking mates.

Drunk and slow, Dennis's haymaker was easy to side step and exposed him completely to Seb's bar, which he swung with such inspired force that all who witnessed it knew Dennis was dead before he even hit the floor boards. So he was not worth defending really, and in any case, he was such a prick, no one considered him a particular friend. His drinking mates all looked at Dennis, bleeding and gurgling on the grimy beer-soaked floor, then at Seb, who looked a bit like he was just getting warmed up with the jemmy, and then at their half-empty beers on the bar. Each of them, to a man, finished his drink before stepping around or over the expiring Buckley and leaving the bar, as if each of them had suddenly remembered an important prior engagement.

'It's another dispatch marked urgent, Gitan.' The young squad leader gave his boots a cursory wipe and put the grubby yellow envelope down on the red-gum slab that served as Gitan's desk and conference table. Gitan took it and gestured towards a jumble of old wooden chairs, still arranged in a rough semi-circle around the fire from the previous night. 'Thanks, Symon. Take a seat. Relax. Throw another log on the fire if you like.'

Symon did just that and then spun one of the seats around and straddled it, facing his commander as Gitan opened the dispatch.

'Who's it from?' Gitan asked as he unfolded the sheet.

'Corey,' said Symon. 'Probably not good. The runner said he thinks their whole position may have been over-run, just after he left with this.'

'Orlan's blood.' Gitan sucked his teeth as he read the dispatch. He let it fall onto the desk and rubbed his beard, looking past his young lieutenant at the fire that had begun to smoke and pop.

'Are your people ready, Symon?' he asked solicitously.

'Born ready, boss, every one of them.'

Gitan liked the informality of the movement. There was no real hierarchy here, although there was a chain of command, no salutes or snapping to attention, just a common passion to put right what had been so deeply wrong with their society for so long.

Gitan looked into the eyes of his youngest squad leader. 'This is going to be the real thing. No more skirmishes and guerrilla stuff. Meldrick's got what he wants – martial law. No checks and balances. Parliament suspended. We're all he has to worry about now, and he's gonna come after us with everything he's got.'

'My troops are ready to fight, Gitan, and so are all the others. We'll fight to the last man, the last woman, no question.' Symon held his gaze with a look of such steely determination Gitan could barely detect a thread of fear in the young fighter's demeanour. The passion and integrity in his eyes almost broke Gitan's heart.

'I know you will,' he said with undisguised pride. *Let's hope you don't have to.*

As the young rebel squad leader left the small cabin that served as the camp's headquarters, Gitan ambled over to the fireplace and poked the fire absently, consigning the disturbing news to the flames.

He loved all of the men and women in his movement. They were, after all, his family and he was their fraudulent leader, masquerading as the great liberator.

He wondered, not for the first time, just how the hell he had ended up in command of a thousand-strong ragtag army of dissidents, hell-bent on fighting against impossible odds for rights and dignity and the sort of freedoms that had been denied their poor peasant families for generations. It seemed like his whole life had been an accident, and despite his dedication to his new, enlarged family and to the cause, he was rarely able to shake the lingering sense of being a grand imposter.

He served three years in a CSF hellhole for killing the man who raped his sister. *Unlawful killing mitigated by provocation.* But three years nonetheless.

It seemed like an eternity. Three years of dehumanisation, trapped in a dog-eat-dog world, peopled by men who were just like the man he'd killed and worse. At first he attempted to trade on the reputation of his crime and acted bad and mad, affecting a crazy-eyed hostility in order to be left alone. But that didn't last long. He was eighteen years old, too big a prize. It took a few weeks for the hierarchy of prisoners to figure out whose prize he was, but Seb had already made his own decision, he'd die before he'd submit to any further degradation.

'The Emperor', as the top dog liked to call himself, never did make it out of the prison hospital. It took him months to recover from his primary injury but in the end he developed some kind of infection that killed him. It had taken three guards to drag Seb off the Emperor, beating him with batons until he finally let go. And even then they kept beating him until Seb coughed up the Emperor's testicle. Then they stopped, shocked, before starting up again, even more enthusiastically, out of sympathy for the Emperor who, after all, was an inmate of distinction.

After the Emperor died, Seb was left alone for the most part. His mad-dog reputation was confirmed. Still, those three years seemed like three decades. At first he was indifferent, but as the months dragged into years in his cramped cell, the reality of what he had done gradually seeped into his soul, as the prison damp seeped into his bones. Eventually he couldn't close his eyes without seeing Buckley's crumpled head in his mind's eye. It was a terrible thing to take a life, even the life of a cur like Buckley. The wrongness of it, the finality, seemed a perversion of nature and he began to view himself as beyond redemption. His mind became fragile. Had there been another year to endure, he might never have surfaced.

Seb aligned himself with the misfits and crazies in the prison, which allowed him to keep mainly to himself. By the end he had become the default leader of the 'crazies', in their eyes anyway, and along the way acquired his nickname, due to the difficulty most of them had pronouncing his real name.

Through some kind of perversity he couldn't explain, Seb kept the nickname when he left jail. Once outside, he faced the consequences for his family of his actions. His mother seemed to have aged a decade for every year he'd been away, and by the time he was released, she was a ghost of the vibrant woman he'd known before Petulia was raped and his father and little brother had died. Within eighteen months she had fallen ill, and barely two years after his release she died from consumption. His one remaining brother had fallen in with criminals around the docks while Seb was in prison, smugglers of opium and other contraband. Eventually he got hooked on the stuff himself. Years later he simply disappeared, his wife and young child left with no idea of what had become of him, no pension, no explanation, not even a body to bury.

But Seb had left Westhaven long before any of that happened, driven away from the remnants of his family by his own unbearable guilt and shame for having let them down. He was at fault. As a young impetuous teenager, it had seemed so clear to him: he must protect his family, and exact righteous retribution. But the killing had left him unhinged. He could never have imagined the effect it would have, and now he believed it had sealed the fate of not only Buckley, but his own beloved family.

On the outside he drifted in and out of the border zones for a year or two, finding work in the mines and farms, drinking, gambling. Eventually he fell in with a troupe of travelling bare-knuckle fighters. This seemed to suit his defiled self-image. He was a deviant after all, and an outcast, and somehow, paradoxically, the violence of it helped to blot out the images of his original victim … or maybe it was the alcohol; after a while it was hard to tell.

But fighters have a short shelf life.

The drunker Seb became, the more of a liability he was to the troupe and, distressingly, the less the fighting blotted out his old memories. In the end, every opponent became a ghoulish zombie Buckley, and when he landed a rare blow, the face of his victim became that of the dying Buckley, dribbling and oozing bodily fluids on the bar-room floor all over again.

174

Eventually the troupe just up and left him one grey morning, while he was sleeping off the effects of a skinful of drink and a barrage of undefended blows in some two-bob fleapit. They bequeathed his mortal remains to a small, rough and ready mining camp on the outer eastern slopes of the Olympus Ranges. It was here that he found the rebel movement, or more correctly the rebel movement found him.

It was still in its embryonic form, but it picked him up, brushed him off and took him under its wing, because clearly he had nowhere else to go. Under its protection, Seb regained his humanity, and bit by bit came to realise who he was and what he was put on this earth to do. He rose like a phoenix from his own ashes, and before too many years had passed, he had become second in charge of what was then little more than a motley crew of radical dreamers and petty criminals.

Barrak ran his hand over the wide rock shelf and then sat down. It was a natural resting spot, affording both shade and a panoramic view of the open plain below. As he sat and unfolded his crumpled map, Jasmyn's head bobbed up through a jumble of boulders interspersed with goosefoot and cranberry heather. She hauled herself up and dumped her backpack unceremoniously on the flat ground with an air of exasperation and relief. Barrak shifted sideways to make room for her but she ignored him and reached into her pack instead, taking out her water skin. She took a long drink as she too took in the view of the plain below.

'I hope you know where the hell we're going,' she said without turning around. Barrak shook out the map and studied it in silence for a moment or two. Jasmyn sat down in the shade and leaned against the smooth, cool rock wall. 'Well, are we lost?' she asked, still looking straight ahead.

'Not quite. In fact I think we're right on track,' Barrak ventured.

They'd been walking half the morning, making for a line of mountains that were nothing but a hazy outline on the horizon when they set out, just after dawn. The plain was studded with porcupine grass, bush pea and the occasional umbrella acacia, twisted and struggling to live in this arid land, but as they'd plodded on, the distant mountains had risen up steadily before them. Unused to walking long distances, Barrak was surprised by how quickly they reached the closest range.

At first, the nearest of them seemed to be a relatively low range of foothills, but as they approached, it eventually obscured the larger mountains beyond, until it seemed barely scalable by mere mortals. Strangely, as they approached the foot of the range and crossed over a dry creek bed it seemed to have shrunk back to a manageable size again, and now, to Barrak's surprise, he guessed they were halfway up it, after only about ninety minutes of climbing. They would easily reach the top before noon.

Thomas's hastily drawn map and verbal instructions were designed to get them across the border far from any patrolled crossing points and as far as possible from the main road and the main eastern border checkpoint at Lomond's Gap. It meant crossing a rugged tract of country from Eyre's most remote farming districts to the massive Olympus Ranges far away in the south-east. It also meant climbing over the saddle of St Mary's Peak, which was the highest point at some 3400 feet.

This cross-country route would get them into Wojinski's Pound while keeping them a good thirty miles south of Lomond's Gap checkpoint and the nearby border town of Bowman's Rest.

Bowman's Rest had begun life as a mining camp but was now one of the biggest towns outside of the borders. It had a reputation as a classic outland town, rough and lawless and no place for the faint-hearted.

Wojinski's Pound on the other hand was a natural feature in the nearby mountains, surrounded almost completely by a ring of ridges. The only road access to the pound was through Bowman's Rest, where the river that drained the basin flowed out through the one and only gap in the mountains. The pound had been used for generations by outland farmers to contain and water cattle and sheep in the rugged desert terrain, but it also had a reputation as a hiding place for outlaws and more recently had been rumoured to be one of the main camps used by the rebel movement.

As Gitan flung open the cabin door, the morning sun hit him full in the face and a cool breeze stirred the leaves of the mighty river red gums towering over the camp. It was a perfect spring morning and he allowed the joy of it to wash away the misgivings left behind from the morning's dispatch.

He smelled porridge and set out to find it. The mess tent was hard up against the rock wall at the far side of the river flat. Already the camp was bustling and Gitan could feel an atmosphere of tension and excitement as his troops prepared themselves for another day.

Two squads were already geared up and ready for morning patrols. One would go upstream as far as the saddle and track along the ridge line and then back though the middle of the pound. The other would travel downstream to the main pass at the opening of the pound, almost to the outskirts of town, and then back up through the forest to camp.

He nodded and smiled as he passed one of the fighters from Symon's company. The youngster gave Gitan a broad grin and threw an elaborate mock salute and some other men yelled a greeting to him across the clearing. It was the dawn patrol just coming off duty and heading for the mess tent. Gitan picked up his pace, but they still beat him to the porridge line, grumbling, joking and shoving each other, but making room for Gitan. 'Morning Gitan. G'day, Boss.'

'You lot go ahead, I reckon you'll be hungrier than me,' he said.

He wondered if they really knew what was in store. Many of them had seen some action, skirmishes mainly, although in recent times there had been some major battles and he knew many of the troops in camp this day had been involved in taking the main border crossing at Lomond's Gap and in the pitched battle that followed a week later when a whole division of Meldrick's forces had come to take it back.

As Gitan stood in the queue making small talk with his people, he felt an old familiar worry creeping into his consciousness. Even after seven years as their leader, it never got any easier when a fight was in the offing or trouble was upon them. He felt an aching sense of responsibility and concern for the men and women who followed him. He feared for them and their families, for their safety, for their futures.

He had no fears for himself: the movement was his family now. There was absolutely no doubt he would lay down his life to protect any one of them. But never far below the surface was that unshakable feeling of being a fraud. He wondered what these young soldiers would think of him if they knew the truth about his past. He knew the exaggerated stories that had circulated over the years: *Gitan the defender of the weak; Gitan who killed a giant with his bare hands to protect his sister, when he was just a boy; Gitan, the bare-knuckle fighter who would take on all comers.* But what would they think of him if they knew the whole story, in all its tawdry detail? And what gave him the right to lead these people into battle, to kill or to be killed?

He knew what it meant to kill. And he knew that violence was like a cancer, an enveloping darkness that could destroy lives. Could it really be justified because the cause was noble and the enemy corrupt? And who defined what cause was noble and just … Did he not think his cause was just when he killed Buckley? *Was any end a justification for violent means?*

In recent months Gitan had been increasingly plagued by such questions. As he reached the front of the queue and took delivery of a steaming bowl of porridge, he wondered what the members of the movement would make of their leader's doubts. Would they still follow him?

So Gitan told himself for the thousandth time that he had no right to doubt. If he was fated to lead, then he must lead, without fear or prejudice. Each person must exercise free will according to their conscience, that was all anyone could do. Beyond that, it was up to the gods to decide their fates.

As they continued up the slope from their rest stop, they found themselves climbing rather than walking, clambering over great granite boulders and along narrow goat tracks of loose scree with nothing but the rocky slope and the odd stunted bush or scraggly tree between them and the desert plain far below.

Eventually Jasmyn began to relax and let the rhythm of the trek take her. An old skill returned to her, linked to a distant memory of some hideous school camp that had involved trekking in the western ranges of Tamouer. She remembered that, in the end, she'd taken pride in matching it with the boys in her troop. And it was like that now as she kept pace with Barrak, determined not to lag behind. Skills like that were never forgotten: *test each hand or foot hold, three points of contact, don't look down … easy, climb anything.*

Perhaps she was adjusting to the idea of being in the wilderness. It was surprising the difference just a few hours could make. When they first set out, at dawn, Jasmyn had been tormented by doubt – a palpable resistance like a wall of fear. But her pride had not allowed her to let Barrak see her hesitancy, so she had just bitten down on her dread and followed him into the frightful, alien wilderness without a word.

One of Thomas's men, a friend or employee, someone trusted anyway, had driven them through the previous night, up from the tiny fishing village south of Broken Bay, the smallest port Thomas could safely berth his vessel, up through the sparsely populated farmland and forests south-east of Silvendale and out into the hills beyond.

Twice they had needed to cover themselves on the floor in the back of the truck as they went through tiny, out-of-the-way checkpoints, attended by bored young troopers scarcely able to rouse themselves from their drinking or slumber long enough to wave the truck through, let alone wonder what a rusty old fisher's truck was doing driving through the bush in the dead of night.

They had stayed in an old hunting cabin, the same one Barrak had stayed in before with Thomas, years ago on a hunting trip. They arrived late and the plan was to snatch a few hours' sleep. But Jasmyn had not slept, not as far as she could tell. She'd tossed and turned on the hard, unfamiliar bed with strange-smelling covers, anxious and assailed by horrifying images of the death of the young soldier the previous evening.

They'd risen before sunrise and found themselves in a valley surrounded by low hills at the end of a narrow stony track that meandered along the valley floor above a dry creek bed and ended abruptly at the rustic old log cabin that had been their shelter for the night. To the east, the sun was still hidden below the crest of a low, sparsely vegetated ridge. Jasmyn had noticed a barely visible walking track through the scrub winding up the hill towards the brightening sky. After a breakfast of dry rations of dubious provenance, their guide led them up this track to the crest of the hill.

The little cabin was about as far out of her comfort zone as Jasmyn ever wanted to go and yet she was being impelled further. She longed for the familiar comfort of home, her own bed, the sounds and smells of her father's house, Alicia's breakfasts, a hot shower.

At the crest of the hill it got much worse. It seemed to her they were contemplating leaving the world as she knew it. At first, Jasmyn could not believe the contrast in the landscape. To the west, back down the hill past their cabin, the countryside was relatively green. There was even pasture here and there, together with bracken and eucalypts, and gullies thick with melaleucas and acacia. But to the east beyond the ridgeline it was like a Martian landscape, dry and rocky, orange and brown in the dawn light with stunted vegetation barely clinging to life. *How could it be so barren beyond the crest of one small hill?*

She'd sat with her head in her hands, on top of a big flat purple rock for what seemed like a long time, as Barrak and the guide took their bearings using the map Thomas had made for them and the guide pointed out landmarks in the distance. But all too soon the guide was gone and Barrak was standing beside her, patient and quiet.

As they struck out across the stony flats towards an impossibly distant mountain range, she kept pace with Barrak with a mixture of pride and quiet desperation. But she was straining against a deep instinctive imperative that urged her, at every step, to turn and run for home. Yet somehow, strangely, with panic leaping in her throat at every strange sound, she followed Barrak without a word of protest, out into the empty plain that was bright and dark with the long shadows of dawn, cool and incongruously warm in places, a hostile refuge of anonymity under a boundless desert sky.

It was barely noon when they reached the top of the first range – the mountains that had seemed so far away when they set out at dawn. From the first of the high ridges, they carefully picked their way down the slope into the valley beyond, following a faint trail that at times degenerated into little more than erosion gullies filled with loose rock and sand.

They entered a dell of wattle and eucalypts – a hidden forest occupying the valley floor, where the meagre moisture draining from the nearby peaks persisted in the rocky ground. They followed the valley for several miles, glad of the shade, before veering towards what appeared to be a gap in the rocky escarpment that would give them relatively easy access to a higher ridge beyond. The gap was bounded on either side by a jumble of giant angled slabs of granite, and these continued along the saddle to the main peak. Barrak was convinced the gap was the so-called trail over the saddle that Thomas had tried to depict on his sketchy map, which would take them into the pound.

More climbing, this time over great chunks of rock smoothed by rain and wind. It made for an untidy ascent and they used the spindly trunks of casuarinas and fringe-myrtles as hand holds, and their toes found footholds on weather-bared roots in the gravelly ground.

Higher up the slope a fresh breeze whistled through the stunted casuarinas, creating the only sound on the eerily quiet mountainside and giving some relief from the afternoon heat. Grasstrees occupied every available crevice, the more mature ones well above head height and leaning precariously out over the slope, coiffed with a wild explosion of grassy strands swishing about carelessly in the wind.

Jasmyn began to see the alien landscape as not entirely surreal and frightening, but strangely intoxicating in its isolation. Finding a secure nook amongst the rocks to rest, she looked out past the peak they had scaled that morning and the desert plain beyond it. For a moment, her anxiety felt a lot like exhilaration, and the wind in her hair put her in mind of an eagle soaring high over the rugged plain.

When she started climbing again, she realised they had almost reached the top. Just a few more feet, past one last wedge of rock, and she hauled herself up onto a wide flat saddle.

A little way along the ridge, Barrak stood sentinel still on the edge of a sloping slab of granite that lay across the saddle as if thrown down by an untidy god. He was perched a little too close to the edge for Jasmyn's liking, and gazing out over the wide expanse from whence they'd come.

Edging closer to him, but staying a little back from the precipice, she followed his gaze. The plain they'd traversed that morning was reduced to a band of ochre and red, speckled with grey-green vegetation. Further away she could just make out the low hills that had been their starting point at dawn. Beyond that, fingers of dark brown forest resolved into bands of brown and vivid green, a patchwork of farmland around the distant rural settlement of Silvendale, which was lost to the hazy horizon. To the south, she thought she could make out the blue of the ocean, but it too was almost indistinguishable from the white haze along the horizon.

She was struck by just how far they were from home and she wondered what Barrak was thinking as he stared into the distance. Was he wondering when he would ever see his home town again? Was he thinking about his house, built with his own hands, now a smouldering wreck at the behest of that swine, Meldrick? Was he plotting revenge? Or perhaps remembering a kinder epoch in his life, before fate snatched away his family, a time when life was idyllic and predictable, as we think it should always be? Did he feel fear gnawing at his heart, as she did, standing on top of the world with their home receding into the distant haze and an unknown future ahead of them?

Jasmyn thought again of her home, and it was her father who sprang to mind. To her surprise she had conjured him as a youthful new dad, holding her by the hand at the seaside. It had been such a long time since she had hugged her father; she tried to remember the last time. Staring at Barrak's straight back against the sky, she bit her lip and blinked back a tear, which might have just been the wind in her eyes, except the wind had dropped away to almost nothing.

The silence as they both stood and stared was unnerving. The quiet of the wilderness and the cool of the mountain air conspired to create its own alchemy, an electric tension. And it was therefore a wonder they both didn't jump right off the precipice in fright when a clear bright voice rang out like a bell, directly behind them.

'Don't move!' it said, with just a hint of panic.

'Let me see your hands,' the voice continued, sounding incongruously young and female. Barrak and Jasmyn both raised their hands theatrically, pantomime style, and turned around slowly even as the voice commanded them to do just that.

To their surprise the voice didn't immediately appear to have an owner, until, as if sensing their puzzlement, its owner showed herself, slowly rising from behind a copse of myrtle. The first thing Barrak noticed was her cheeks, rosy from exertion, against porcelain pale skin. A strand of blonde hair fell across her high forehead, defying the confines of a dirty grey peaked cap. She was just a girl dressed in what looked like grubby fatigues and a weatherproof military-issue trooper's jacket, complete with a quiver full of arrows, arrows just like the one loaded and cocked in her CSF crossbow and trained rock-steady at Barrak's heart.

'Who are you?' Barrak breathed incredulously.

'That is my question for you,' the girl snapped, thrusting the bow forward alarmingly as she adjusted her footing. Her eyes flicked from Barrak to Jasmyn and back.

He was about to speak again, but the girl cut him off before he had a word out. 'My name is Nadege. I fight for freedom, and you are my prisoners.'

CHAPTER 13

'WHY SHOULD I BELIEVE you?' Gitan demanded irritably.

Barrak looked across the table at the rebel leader through narrowed eyes and snorted out an exasperated puff of air. 'You have Thomas's letter, there in your hand. What more do you need?'

'Look,' Gitan hesitated, then drew in a short sharp breath and leaned across the table. He flicked the crinkled note at Barrak. 'Don't mess me around, Councillor. I trust Thomas, he's a good man. What I'm asking is why should I trust *you*?' He stared intently at Barrak as if trying to decipher a complicated map or puzzle.

Barrak kept quiet and watched as he withdrew to the fireplace and retrieved the remains of a thin cigar from the mantel. He set about lighting it with a stick from the fire and puffed it back to life. Rounding on his prisoner, he pointed the smouldering stub at him for emphasis and said, 'You come barging into my camp, dragging Princess Bloody Mooney with you and expect ... well, I dunno, what did you expect, exactly? Everyone to drop everything and pay homage to the great and noble councillor and his little girlfriend?'

Barrak shifted uncomfortably and worried at the leather strapping that bound his wrists, but remained silent.

'Because, you know, maybe we are a little busy right now, Councillor. And oh, I do understand that you have met with some misfortune yourself. What a strange experience it must have been for you to suddenly find yourself on the receiving end of the CSF's foul doings. How did *that* feel, Councillor? Something of a change of pace for you I would reckon, to be no longer dishing it out, but copping it in the neck yourself for once. You bloody aristocrats, you live in a fantasy world with no idea what the rest of us have to do just to live, *no idea* what it takes—'

'Listen!' Barrak's anger at the rebel leader's tirade suddenly got the better of him. Gitan froze, his cigar pinched between thumb and index finger like a conductor's baton, mid-symphony. He squinted fiercely at Barrak through a shroud of smoke.

'I'm a physician. I've already told you my position on the council is nominal. I play no part in formulating policy. I barely even go to the sittings. I *am* one of the masses, I try to help people ...'

Gitan leaned in close to Barrak, as though he might take a bite out of his ear. 'Oh yes, I'm sure that's just what you do, as long as your patients can afford your fee. What a struggle it must be for the great physician to make ends meet.'

'Actually it is, sometimes!' Barrak said, straightening his back with indignation. He thought about all the patients in the village he treated pro bono and the others with whom he bartered his services. 'But look, that's not the point. I know Enoch well enough and many of the other councillors and senators. None of them want this. They want peace. They *want* modernisation and a better life for all. The government's not the problem. It's Meldrick's misuse of CSF power. Meldrick is the problem.' Barrak trailed off.

Gitan glared at him and then spat an errant strand of tobacco sideways before grinding out the cigar in an overloaded ashtray, fashioned from a CSF ration-box lid. 'Oh, you think so, do you Councillor? You think Meldrick's the problem, do you? You and how many geniuses on the council did it take to work that out?' Gitan raised his eyebrows in mock surprise and tilted his head to one side. 'I mean, what tipped you off? Was it when he combined all of the security forces and took personal charge himself? Or was it when citizens started vanishing into thin air? No? Maybe it was when he filled the streets with his troops, declared martial law and suspended your bloody parliament!? Orlan's blessed bollocks! Wake up to yourself, Councillor. Do you want to know how long we've been trying to draw attention to Meldrick and his quest for power? Because *no one* has wanted to listen to us before. You people, with your privileges and your bloody complacency, happy to sit around with your heads up your arses while Meldrick had *us* declared an outlaw organisation and proceeded to hunt us down like dogs. Do you want to know how many good people we've lost trying to resist his thuggery? And now, now the shit's finally hit the fan, now you have the bloody audacity to come here with your blasted sob story ... Well, I'm sorry, Councillor, it's a little late. How could you not see this coming?' Gitan's tone mellowed and he surveyed Barrak coolly, taking his measure, before tilting his head at the sound of approaching footsteps.

Barrak pulled at his bonds and twisted to face the rebel leader more squarely. 'And what about you, Gitan? Targeting innocent civilians, blowing up hotels, using weapons that go against Orlan's most fundamental—'

Gitan's head snapped around and he cut Barrak off mid-sentence. 'That wasn't us!'

There was the briefest knock on the cabin door before a young man in fatigues burst in and strode towards Gitan. He looked so young, but carried himself like a leader, maybe one of Gitan's lieutenants. Gitan met him halfway across the room and inclined his head as the lad whispered urgently in his ear. Gitan responded with a question and the boy imparted more information, his wide, clear eyes staring over Gitan's shoulder at Barrak as he spoke.

Barrak could make out nothing of the whispered conversation.

'No, no, that was *not* us,' Gitan insisted, as he turned back to Barrak and his lieutenant hurried out the door. 'Just another of Meldrick's tricks to whip up fear and further justify his bloody oppression. Now, I have to go. You wait here,' he advised Barrak, not without a little irony, as he hurried out the door after his young lieutenant.

Suddenly alone, Barrak held his bound wrists up and examined them then dropped them in his lap. He let his forehead fall onto the table with a gentle bump. *Gods abide ... Where was Jasmyn? Should he try to find*

186

her? He raised his head and glanced around him, wondering if there was something with an edge to cut the leather straps.

He stood up and wandered over to the mantel. He noticed the cabin was made of rough-hewn logs, sealed on the inside with pitch or mud or something. The fireplace, chimney and mantel were constructed from mortared river stones. The room was stuffy with wood smoke and smelled like an animal barn. The fire was almost out, although the stick Gitan had used to light his cigar was still smoking.

Was Jasmyn all right? Damnation. Why was Gitan so antagonistic? Barrak had told him everything, the whole story, starting with Elias's disappearance. Wasn't it obvious that he and Jasmyn were as much victims of Meldrick's contemptible coup as anyone else?

He sank down into a chair by the fireplace just as Gitan burst in, looking harried. He advanced towards Barrak, drawing a hunting knife from a sheath at his thigh. Barrak flinched, but the rebel leader's body language betrayed no malice, so he held out his bound wrists hopefully. Gitan slipped the blade between his wrists and sliced through the straps.

As Barrak sat and rubbed his hands, Gitan paced back and forth and fired information at him.

'Things are starting to move very fast, Councillor. We expect a full-scale attack by Meldrick's forces sometime tomorrow. You shouldn't have come here. It's not safe. I don't know what Thomas was thinking.'

Gitan's manner had changed. It seemed he was no longer suspicious or antagonistic, merely distracted and no longer much interested in Barrak.

'You may have to fend for yourselves. I've got other priorities just now. Arrangements have been made for you and Ms Mooney, at least you'll have a bed for the night and an evening meal of sorts. The mess tent's down by the creek.' He turned and looked towards the door, his mind clearly racing. Barrak could hear shouted orders, clanking equipment and the crunch of boots on gravel outside.

'Stay close to camp tonight,' Gitan added.

'You may have to decide, you and Ms Mooney, whether to fight with us or try to escape the pound. It's not much of a choice, I know. I'm sorry.'

Gitan made for the door again then paused and turned again to face Barrak. 'One more thing, Councillor. What did you say the name of that boy was? The boy who disappeared from your town?'

'I didn't,' said Barrak, gathering up his jacket. 'But his name was Elias, Elias Arrowsmith.'

'Wait.' Gitan screwed one eye shut. 'Uh-uh, no, that's not right. Not Elias. Are you *shitting* me, Councillor?' His expression was hard to read.

'Of course not,' said Barrak. 'He and his mother are my patients and—'

'You better not be bullshitting me Councillor,' Gitan cut across him, 'because by Orlan's blood, if you are, if it turns out you're working for Meldrick, I promise you I will personally gut you and peg you out in the desert sun for the scrub dogs to feast on.' This last was said with a strangely airy lilt to his voice and a faint smile, as though it were a party invitation.

Barrak had no answer. He was taken aback by Gitan's strong reaction to the mention of Elias.

'Don't leave the camp. We need to talk more about this.' Gitan's final words seemed to hang in the air even after he'd gone to join the gathering tumult in the camp as it prepared itself for battle.

Barrak found Jasmyn by the creek, sitting on a log in a patch of late afternoon sunlight. Somewhere nearby there must be rapids – he could hear the soft babbling of water over rock beneath the noisy preparations in the camp. Jasmyn smiled wistfully as he approached. The sapphire blue of her eyes seemed darker and sadder than before.

'Have you escaped?' she enquired with something like a cheeky grin.

'Released on parole more likely.'

Barrak sat down on Jasmyn's log and rubbed his wrists, examining the marks left by the leather straps. For a few minutes they sat in silence. Jasmyn flung a stick into the creek and they both watched as it bobbed to the surface and floated downstream.

'We're in trouble again, aren't we Barrak?' she observed, watching her twig.

'It looks that way,' he said. 'I don't think anyone expected Meldrick to move so quickly against the rebels. They say CSF forces will be here by morning. He's obviously been planning this for a long time.'

'It looks like they intend to put up a pretty good fight,' she said, glancing over her shoulder towards the main part of the camp where frantic preparations were underway.

'I'm sure they will,' said Barrak.

'What are we going to do, Barrak?'

'I don't know.' Barrak massaged his brow and stared into the bushes on the opposite bank, as though an answer might be found there. A mudlark piped, inconclusively, somewhere amongst the undergrowth.

'Gitan says stay and fight, or run,' he offered.

'Stay and fight?'

'Yeah,' said Barrak dubiously, 'or run away.'

'And live to fight another day,' Jasmyn said, as if suggesting a game to a child.

By evening the air had thickened to match the tension in the camp. Overhead, the first quarter moon fought a losing battle with bands of cloud and the indigo sky above the mountain peaks to the northwest was lit up, intermittently, by faint bursts of ghostly fire. With each uncertain flash the ragged ridge line they had crossed that day showed itself in eerie silhouette, before dissolving back into blackness.

Occasionally the faintest rumble of thunder sounded in the distance.

Having been co-opted as kitchen workers to help feed the troops, he and Jasmyn had settled in around a campfire with the mess crew afterwards. As Barrak sat, hearing but not really listening to the murmur of conversation, half mesmerised by the glowing embers of the fire and half watching the light show above Jasmyn's head as she sat opposite him, he thought about the flames engulfing his house, then about Meldrick mentioning fire-burst weapons, his claim that he would do away with hundreds of years of prohibition, cast aside one of Orlan's most sacred principles in his sick pursuit of power. As the distant lightning flashed, he reimagined it as the detonations of such dire weapons and tried to imagine the devastation and the trauma that would be loosed on people by such dreadful devices. He recalled the flash and shattering burst of turmoil in the restaurant that day with Jasmyn, and the confusion and chaos that followed, the ringing in his ears that persisted for so long after the explosion. In the midst of battle, it would probably be a hundred times worse.

Having lost the thread of whatever conversation was going on around him, Barrak was suddenly restless; he needed to walk. He made his way towards Gitan's cabin, distracted by the scattered glow of other campfires. There was a murmur of conversation and bursts of laughter here and there and he thought he could hear music and singing somewhere amongst the trees.

Around one of the fires was a group of half a dozen men and women. There was Gitan, standing amongst them. One of the men clapped him on the back and another shook his hand and one of the women hugged him before he took his leave of their circle and slipped away into the shadows between the cyprus pines.

Was he doing his rounds? Yes, he was heading towards the next fire. This was the commander, visiting his troops on the eve of battle.

'*Gitan!*' Barrak said, keeping his voice low. He ducked around a copse of myrtle, trying to head him off before the next campfire, but Gitan had disappeared.

'Skulking around in the bushes is not a good idea on such a night, Councillor. People are nervous, you know.' Gitan spoke calmly as he emerged from the shadows at Barrak's elbow. Barrak flinched but Gitan smiled and wagged his head towards a small clearing. 'I've been wondering what to do with you. We need to talk.' They stopped between stands of cypress. 'Prophet's mercy, things are moving so fast, we don't have much time.' Gitan seemed agitated and looked around nervously, before settling his shoulder against the gnarled trunk of an old tree.

190

'Tell me about your connection to Elias.' He beckoned Barrak closer.

'I told you …'

Gitan raised a finger to his lips and frowned slightly, and Barrak lowered his voice. 'His mother asked me to look into his disappearance.'

'Is that all?' Gitan prompted.

'He worked for me once, as a labourer, when I was building a house.'

Gitan's manner made him nervous and he glanced around. Low murmurs came from the nearest circle of soldiers, their faces lit by the glow of their fire. They were oblivious to Barrak and Gitan in the shadows.

'When. When was that?'

'705,' Barrak said.

'Did he tell you about his travels? Anything about travelling east, or intending to travel east?'

'Only that he'd travelled and worked around the border zones … all over the place really, but no, nothing particularly about going east. What do you mean exactly, east? Into the forbidden zones?' Again, memories of his conversations with Elias drifted across Barrak's mind.

Gitan paused, watching Barrak, his expression guarded. Barrak heard distant music start up again, a perverse accompaniment to his conversation with the rebel leader.

'OK, you give me no choice, Councillor. I'm going to have to trust you. I mean, everything happens for a reason, doesn't it? There are no accidents.'

Barrak inclined his head quizzically but remained quiet.

'Perhaps there's a reason you arrived here when you did. I'm thinking it's time I put you on the payroll.'

Gitan was talking in riddles. 'What do you mean?' Barrak asked.

'I mean, you waltz into my camp the day before all hell breaks loose with some cock-and-bull story, but, well, I believe you, OK? And I trust you, and now you're part of this.' He gestured vaguely. 'But we're out of time, and there's no place in my world for fence-sitters. I'm afraid it's time to shit or get off the pot, Councillor.'

Gitan stepped forward and a sliver of moonlight fell across his face. Barrak took an involuntary step back. 'What would you have us do?'

'Listen carefully. Just a few weeks ago, Elias walked out of the wilderness.' Gitan pointed east.

'We captured him, which was easy, because he'd come looking for us. We interrogated him. That was easy too, because he had information he *wanted* to give us. And he wanted our help in return. He'd been to the end of the gods-smitten earth, and the people he met there sent him back with a warning, and to find out what the hell was going on *here*.

'People?' Barrak queried.

'Yes. People just like us. Not savages or wanderers. Civilised people.' Gitan snapped a twig off a bush and turned it over and over in his hand as he spoke. 'It seems they know a lot more about us than we do about them and they sent Elias back here for a reason. They wanted him to gather some information, information that was, apparently, very important to them. Something Elias said could have implications for us all.'

'What information?' Barrak asked, intrigued.

There was a rustle and the sound of footfalls around them. Some of his men, alerted by Gitan's injudicious twig snapping, had surrounded them quietly in the dark and appeared like ghosts in the clearing, before recognising their leader and withdrawing to their fire with a mumbled apology and a chuckle as they went. Gitan called after them, encouraging them to stay alert. 'That's why we pay you so much.' That got laughs all around and a few snorts of derision as they settled back around their fire.

'What else did Elias say?' Barrak urged.

Gitan looked at Barrak for what seemed like a long time, his eyes hard.

'Look, these easterners were facing some kind of threat. Elias didn't make it clear just what sort of threat, but for some reason the easterners were convinced the threat was connected to Eyre, connected to Meldrick and the CSF.'

Barrak shook his head as if trying to clear it. 'What?'

'I know, I know. We reacted the same way at first. But Elias convinced us. He'd spent months with these people. They trained him and they trusted him and they sent him back here, to find out just what was going on.

'I'm surprised you trusted him,' Barrak ventured.

Gitan didn't answer. When he spoke again his tone had shifted and he asked Barrak, 'Did *you* trust him, Councillor? I mean, you knew him. He worked for you for long enough. You must have formed an opinion. Did *you* trust him?'

'Yes of course. Absolutely.'

There was another lengthy silence.

'Look, I know things about people, Barrak. Why do you think you're still standing here? And I knew Elias was trustworthy. And besides, my enemy's enemy is my friend, right? I sent two of my men with him. Elias didn't say exactly what he was looking for, but he'd narrowed it down to the northern desert, out beyond the arrays. He knew something was going on out there, something the CSF was trying very hard to keep secret. So I agreed to give him two of my men. He never did say what he was looking for. He said he would only know what it was when he found it. But it was vital that he get that information back to these easterners. He intended to travel back there.' Gitan paused again.

'How far east?' Barrak asked.

'Far enough. Do you know how dangerous it is to travel all that way alone? Elias had done it once, maybe twice, and he was intending to go back there again. He was a brave kid, and yeah, I did trust him, implicitly.'

Gitan was looking past Barrak as if momentarily lost in thought. As he shifted into the moonlight, his expression was sombre.

'Trouble is, that was five weeks ago and we haven't seen Elias or my two men since. They should have been back weeks ago.' Gitan thought for a moment. 'At least we now know Elias made it as far as his home in Rylanswood, before ...'

Barrak nodded slowly but said nothing. There was no need to.

Besides which, his head was swimming with the implications of Gitan's incredible story.

Gitan gestured to Barrak to follow him. 'Come on, it's cold. We need some warmth.'

Barrak followed in thoughtful silence. He had so many questions but he was struggling to formulate even one.

They found Jasmyn settled in around the cooks' fire. It was radiating a welcoming glow against the chill night. She was deep in talk with one of the cooks, but they broke off their conversation as Gitan and Barrak approached.

'I was starting to think you'd got lost,' she said with her trademark grin.

'That was my fault,' said Gitan. 'I've been bending his ear.'

Jasmyn made room for Barrak on the great trunk that had been rolled next to the fire pit and Gitan pulled a camp stool close to the fire and put his boots perilously close to the glowing coals, opening his hands to the fire. Jasmyn's new friend excused herself and left the three alone.

'We've been putting together a plan for you and the councillor,' Gitan said. Jasmyn looked at Barrak and raised an eyebrow. He shook his head dubiously and looked pointedly at Gitan.

'What plan?' he demanded.

'Someone has to go east, Councillor. That's what we've been talking about, isn't it?'

Jasmyn reached across and clasped Barrak's forearm. 'Barrak?!' she protested; it was half question, half exclamation.

'What? When did this become part of the deal?' Barrak demanded.

Gitan was looking at his boots and wiggling his toes, testing the heat in them.

'Look, Brethrenhope, this is a war. And like it or not I'm the one who has to make certain decisions – military decisions. Now you've come here, the two of you, you've put yourselves under my command. This is what needs to be done, and I'm asking you to do it.'

Gitan looked from Barrak to Jasmyn.

'OK. I'm not going to have you beheaded for desertion or anything. We're not the CSF. That's not what we do. You can do what you like.' His expression threw down an unambiguous challenge to them both.

'What's he talking about, Barrak?' Jasmyn sounded alarmed. 'What's going on?

Gitan answered for him. 'It seems we have a common acquaintance in the councillor's young friend, Elias,' he began, 'our ambassador to the east.' Gitan attempted a quirky grin, but couldn't pull it off. 'He's quite the quester, Elias – that's what I'd call him – made in the mould of Orlan. Unusual for a modern-day Eyrean, such a thirst for knowledge, to travel all the way east like that.'

'What's all this talk about east?' Jasmyn interjected. 'Everyone knows there's nothing out there but desolation and strife.'

'I know. That's what we have been brought up to believe, isn't it Jasmyn?' Gitan snorted. 'Never was there such an inward-looking, insular people as us Eryeans. It's one of the things we're trying to change. We believe it's time to expand our boundaries and our consciousness. There is a wider world out there, whether we choose to believe it or not.'

Jasmyn eyed him suspiciously.

'Look Jasmyn, I've just been explaining to Barrak, Elias made contact with these people in the far eastern provinces. They're real. He lived with them for a time, and they sent him back to Eyre because they believed something going on right here in Eyre, right now, had some kind of serious implications for *them*.' Gitan looked intently at Jasmyn across the shimmering ether of the coals.

Her expression was unreadable – giving Gitan nothing.

Gitan switched his attention to Barrak. 'You know what this means, don't you, Councillor? It means these easterners could be our allies against Meldrick. They could be our only hope to even the odds.'

'My enemy's enemy is my friend.' Barrak's tone was thoughtful, restating Gitan's own axiom from moments before.

Jasmyn shot him an incendiary glance, which had anger and even betrayal embedded in it, and yet she remained silent.

'Exactly.' Gitan said, nodding emphatically.

Barrak shook his head and massaged his brow wearily. 'But you can't seriously suggest that Jasmyn and I travel all the way east with so little to go on.' Barrak let his incredulity carry him along. 'What would be the point? Even if we made it all the way east, we don't have the information Elias came looking for.' Barrak cast around him. 'And why us, for quest's sake? We're not equipped for an undertaking like this.'

'Maybe you were chosen,' Gitan cut in, cryptically. I mean, Elias's mother came to *you*, Barrak, she asked *you* to find Elias, and look what's happened since then – you've been accused of treason and murder, you're on the run. Thomas helped you get this far but why are you here? There really are no accidents, Councillor. Maybe it's fate.'

'But going east won't help us find Elias. We know Meldrick has him.'

There was a heavy silence between the three conspirators, brief but tense.

'I think we all know Elias is probably gone,' Gitan said quietly. 'It's about Elias's legacy now. He made contact with these people. I'm convinced from what Elias told me that these easterners *could* be potential allies. They could help us. But they need to know what's happening here. And they need to know what happened to Elias. Someone needs to tell them. Maybe the gods have chosen the two of you for that task.'

'NO!' Jasmyn's voice carried the weight of her long silence. 'What you're talking about is completely insane!'

Barrak could swear he saw Gitan flinch.

'Barrak!' Her tone snapped his attention back to her and he saw the steel in her eyes. 'I've listened to you two planning this ... this ... *madness,* and now I'm telling you something: you *are* stark raving mad, both of you!' She eyed them both hotly, daring an argument. 'Your plan is absolutely bloody *insane.*'

'Jasmyn listen—' Gitan attempted, but she cut him off.

'No. *You* listen. My mind is made up. I've come up with my own plan. I'm going back home to Tamouer! We should never have come here. We should never have run, Barrak. I have faith in the rule of law. Meldrick can't just throw his weight around as he likes.'

Gitan and Barrak exchanged a glance that suggested it was Jasmyn who was mad.

'Father will know what to do. He'll have a way to put Meldrick back in his box and he'll need your support, Barrak. We should go back, and the sooner the better. We panicked, but now we need to go back and find Father, join him and the others and resist Meldrick and his bloody coup, but do it properly, legally. There has to be a way. Father will know what's required.'

Jasmyn's passion seemed to be fading under Gitan's steady gaze. She might have expected him to be angry, even enraged, but instead he looked sad, and Jasmyn saw compassion in the rebel leader's eyes.

'I'm sorry Jasmyn.'

What did he mean he was sorry? Jasmyn tried to read Gitan's expression, and as she did so, a powerful intuition washed over her and clamped a band around her heart. She knew what Gitan was about to tell her before he even spoke.

'I should have told you this earlier but I didn't know how.'

'No,' she pleaded, her face stricken in the firelight.

'I'm so sorry, Jasmyn.' Gitan closed his eyes and drew a breath. 'Word reached me this afternoon—'

'No! Don't!' She held up a hand as if to stop his words, but he went on, gently.

'Enoch was arrested and charged with high treason. He was executed yesterday.' Gitan seemed deflated by his own words. He lowered his eyes and stared at his steaming boots.

A hush seemed to settle over the encampment after Gitan broke the tragic news. It was late, but still there was activity here and there. Barrak thought no one would be getting much sleep that night.

The mess crew were making ready, presumably in case the need came to decamp quickly, and the odd fragment of conversation or laughter still reached them from the nearby campfires. But a blanket of silence had enveloped the three figures who remained huddled around the mess fire.

Jasmyn had tried to protest, but some instinct told her Gitan had spoken the truth. Not only was her father dead but her mother's whereabouts were unknown, and an arrest order had been issued for Jasmyn herself.

Barrak tried to comfort her but she pulled away from him and for a time just sat and stared into the fire quietly, her eyes dry.

After a time, Gitan outlined his plan for getting Barrak and Jasmyn safely out of the pound. He spoke quietly, and at one point Jasmyn slid over towards Barrak and put her arm through his, hugging it and resting her head against his shoulder, still staring into the fire, comforted by the quiet conversation but not really hearing the content or adding anything to it.

Gitan had arranged for them to travel with a group of cattle drovers, who would take them out of the pound and set them on a course to the east. It seemed foolproof. At this time of year the drovers were a common sight, coming and going from the grasslands to the east, through Bowman's Rest and into the pound, moving cattle down from the winter grazing lands into the pound for its summer pasture and permanent water supply. A group had just delivered a mob of cattle and would leave the pound tomorrow to go back for more. Travelling along the stock route from the pound and out through the outskirts of Bowman's Rest, they would raise no suspicions.

For a modest bribe they had agreed to take Jasmyn and Barrak and supply them with drovers garb to help them blend in, and Gitan had arranged for some scanty supplies and essentials including maps of the region to the east, towards the outer markers.

The drovers would take them as far as what Gitan called the junction, where the drovers would head north, to the grazing lands. At the junction was a trading post and hotel of sorts, the last settlement before the Barrier Range, the outer marker on the main trade route to the east.

Barrak had no knowledge of the region Gitan described and he felt a deep unease. But their fate seemed to be sealed and he found himself unable to raise further objections.

Gitan assured him a small amount of gold would be enough to pay a guide to take them east into the wilderness beyond the Barrier Range.

As Gitan talked, Jasmyn gradually subsided until her head was resting in Barrak's lap. She was quite still but Barrak could tell from her breathing she was not asleep. It was obvious Gitan had other more pressing concerns and Barrak realised he had spent much longer with them than he should have.

Gitan began to excuse himself. 'I'm sorry, I've got to go, I still have an evening briefing with my group leaders. There's not much more I can tell you. The drovers are sympathetic, they'll look after you as far as the junction. Beyond that you'll be following in Elias's footsteps. There's a large arid region and then grasslands extending for many miles. Elias talked about a mountain range, higher than any of our mountains, many days' travel to the east. The eastern ocean and the easterners' city is just beyond that. You'll know when you see the mountains.'

Gitan looked from Barrak to Jasmyn and gave her an uncertain smile.

'You're going to survive this, Jasmyn. We will put this thing right, eventually, and your father will be avenged.'

Jasmyn sat up and nodded with a glazed expression. 'I'm sorry, I'm just so tired. I need to sleep.' With that she got up and stumbled towards her billet for the night.

'Will she be all right, Barrak?' Gitan asked, watching her go.

'Don't worry, I'll look after her,' Barrak said quietly. But as he watched her forlorn figure recede into the shadows, Barrak feared he had little to back his promise.

The camp was already alive with clamorous activity by first light, and this roused Barrak from a fitful sleep. He found Jasmyn already up and sharing coffee with a woman and boy who were part of the droving team they'd be accompanying. She seemed subdued when Barrak joined them for a breakfast of porridge, day-old camp bread and black coffee. But it looked as if the few hours' sleep had done her good.

After breakfast they gathered together their meagre possessions, including the package of supplies he'd found inside his tent with a note from Gitan. There were maps, a compass, a flint and a large hunting knife, plus a smaller utility knife with a combination of functions. There were also several packs of CSF combat rations, which Barrak knew from talk around the camp were much prized by the rebel fighters whenever they could get their hands on them.

The droving team was ready to move not long after sunrise and so were Jasmyn and Barrak. Jasmyn was a competent rider, but Barrak was still uneasy, even after the team boss assured him his mount was the most placid they had. He was also perturbed that they would ride out of camp before he had a chance to consult Gitan again. Everything had happened so quickly the previous day. In the morning light, this plan to go east seemed half-baked.

There was some commotion and shouting amongst the drovers and a couple of loud whistles. Barrak's horse seemed to know the time had come to move, and their group of a dozen or so drovers edged forward as he and Jasmyn took up the rear, with a sweeper riding a few lengths behind them.

The camp was on full alert and preparing for battle. Individual squads were grouped together in their ranks with weapons at hand and armour on. Some of the group leaders were briefing their fighters. Other teams were milling around excitedly, talking, chiacking, encouraging each other. As the column of drovers moved slowing along the narrow path, with the creek on one side and the ranks of massing rebels on the other, Barrak noticed some were not so animated, and looked nervous and pale. He noticed one young lad vomiting under a red gum and two young women nearby, crouched down together, burning incense at a makeshift shrine.

As they neared the bend that would take them out of the camp, he spotted Gitan standing on a rocky rise under the spreading canopy of a huge river red gum. As they approached, the gathering grew quiet, to hear their leader.

'You wish we had more fighters, Corey?' Gitan was addressing someone near the front of the crowd.

'Gods abide! No! And have to *share* the glory of trouncing Meldrick's miserable army?'

'Look, if we are fated to die today, it would be a tragic loss, enough to scar the lands of Eyre for generations. But if we *live* and drive Meldrick back into the dungeons of his own cursed Citadel, then, the fewer we are, the greater the honour!'

A poignant hush had settled over the clearing, and every eye was on the rebel leader.

'Rather, brother Corey, spread the word. Anyone who has no stomach for the fight is free to go.' Gitan paused and surveyed his troops. 'Today is the Feast of Lillian. It's barely even acknowledged, coming on the heels of Orlan's Festival. Hardly even remembered anymore. But when the future history of Eyre is written, this day *will* be celebrated. Hearts will stir whenever this day is named! And those of us who fought this day and came home safe, will stand tall on Lillian's Day.'

The drovers had slowed to a halt, their eyes on Gitan. Even the horses seemed to be taking an interest.

'We *will* live to see old age, and each year we'll rejoice at the mention of this day and raise merry hell with our friends. Out will come the stories, you'll show your scars, yet again, to your grandchildren and say, "I got these fighting the great oppressor on Lillian's Day". Old people forget. Eventually everything is forgotten. But we *will* remember the feats of this day. And then our names will be recalled, as familiar as household words: Corey of Westhaven, Ottens of Tamouer, Chapman and Taylor, Kelly of Silvendale.' Gitan indicated some of his company commanders and got a whoop and a cheer from each of their teams.

'And *this* story the good parent will tell his child, for Lillian's Feast will never go by, from this day until the end of time, without we in it being freshly remembered, we happy few, this band of brothers and sisters.'

Gitan spread his arms wide and then he went on solemnly. 'For those who shed blood with me this day will be my family. And the well-to-do of Tamouer, lying in their beds right now, will feel themselves *cursed* they were not here with us today … and they will hang their heads in shame, when anyone speaks, who fought with us – upon Saint Lillian's Day!"

Gitan's raised his arms and a deafening shout went up from the throng of fighters, shattering the calm of the woodland with raucous cheers and clanging weapons and sending a chill up Barrak's spine. His mount, forgetting its placid nature for a moment, bridled and reared, almost unseating him, and only settled again as the drovers urged their beasts forward. This took Barrak right past Gitan, standing on his rocky dais under the old red gum. The rebel leader stole a sideways glance as they drew level and Barrak would swear to it later, that Gitan winked at him.

In an instant, they were around the bend in the creek and starting up the steep grade leading out of the camp, leaving behind the cacophony of Gitan's assembled troops.

Would this be the last he would see of Gitan and his rebel gang?

The chill he felt at Gitan's speech was with him still, in his bones, and he shivered in the damp morning air under the canopy of the gums.

Jasmyn brought her mount alongside and stared forlornly at him. 'They're all going to die, aren't they Barrak?' she said tremulously.

Barrak searched for an answer but all he could find to say was 'No,' and then repeat it, shaking his head. 'No.'

But the rhythmic gait of his horse made it seem that both he and the beast were nodding in unison instead.

CHAPTER 14

IT RAINED THROUGHOUT THE third and last day they rode with the drovers, not solid rain, more like a heavy mist: enough to wet oilskins and hats but not enough to churn the track too badly, even with the passage of eleven horses.

Not that their route could rightly be described as a track. A few hours out of Bowman's Rest, three days earlier, it had diminished to a set of barely visible wheel ruts, and by lunch, a vaguely perceptible trail that looked like it had never even seen a wheeled vehicle, and was marked out more in the minds of the drovers and plodding instinct of the horses, than on the ground itself.

And riding was not an apt description either. The days were timeless and the pace languid, with the crew content for their horses to mooch along, lazily nosing their way under the sun's ecliptic from dawn to dusk.

Blessed with fine weather the first two days, Barrak and Jasmyn settled into an easy rhythm, the afternoon sun warm on their backs, enriching the landscape as it unfolded before them with its sandy ochres and vibrant reds. The low desert vegetation, mainly saltbush and spinifex, was thick in parts, due to unusually heavy rains, which the cattle herders said had been the best in ten years, turning what would normally be a dust bowl into a veritable desert garden.

Each day's passage was marked by their steady progress through a peculiar landscape of grey-brown monoliths, scattered across the otherwise featureless flat lands, often with half a day, or a whole day's journey between them. These marked the tempo of their trek, with each hazy peak gradually growing in stature through the long day, until it dominated the landscape, mocking the vast flatness of the desert plain all around it, and the insignificance of the band of humans passing unnoticed to the north or south.

The nights were cold and clear and the deep desert sky was sprayed with rime, a shock of stars, brighter and more prolific than Barrak had ever seen in the hazy skies above Eyre. The drovers knew their camps well, and found scarce bands of stunted grey box or wattle to provide shelter and wood for the fires. In the bone-gnawing cold of the early hours, in the tiny tent that he shared with one of the rouseabouts, Barrak was hugely grateful for the drovers' wool-lined swag. But he worried about Jasmyn. Even though she had struck up a friendship with Isabel, whose son was Barrak's tent-mate, she seemed distant, quiet through the day and retiring early after the evening meal, not even a shadow of her usual gregarious self, leaving Barrak searching in vain for a way to reach her.

The droving crew abandoned them late on the third day, as a defiant burst of gilded light broke through the clouds to the west, painting the sky's grey underbelly crimson and mauve. As Barrak watched their companions climb a gentle rise away to the north, on another invisible track, he knew only two things for certain – the rain was setting in and he already missed his horse, whose tilting haunches were still visible, but only just, through the rain-mist.

Due east and down a long gentle incline was the so-called junction – Isabel had pointed it out, barely a half hour's walk – and now there it was, spotlit on the wide valley floor by a sunburst from the west, the curious light having grown in intensity in the last few moments, as had the shimmering rain.

In that moment, Jasmyn was a stranger to him, her expression unreadable under her wide-brimmed drover's hat, which had begun to overflow onto her already slick oilskins. Hunched in resignation and clutching her swag – rolled skin-out against the weather to protect it and all her worldly possessions – she looked at Barrak in the gathering gloom with a hooded expression he could only take for reproach.

As they neared the ramshackle trading post, it seemed larger, more imposing but also more run down than it had appeared from a distance. It was surrounded by a swathe of rocky ground, whether natural or artificial was hard to tell in the dimming twilight.

A wide verandah ran the length of the front. Ancient wicker furniture, decayed almost to extinction, was scattered to the left and right of wide timber steps, which were themselves worn smooth from boots and time. On either side, two lengths of guttering hung down from the edge of the roof, giving the place an air of disappointment. Rainwater cascaded off the rusted roof and over the verandah railing, splashing noisily on the rocky ground. Barrak noticed one front window was broken and another had been boarded up. The paintwork had long ago been given up for lost and the surviving window panes were thick with dust and cobwebs. Yellow light glowed warmly from inside and there was a curious musical sound like wind chimes.

When they reached the shelter of the porch, rain was already beating down and a squally wind had sprung up, stirring a rusty hinged sign into tortured lament above the entrance. Struggling to decipher it as they shrugged off their swags and shook the rain from their oilskins and hats, Barrak made out, *Dodsiadly's Merchandise And Bar, Romes To Let*. He wondered who or what a Dodsiadly was, as he pushed open the door and stepped into the subdued yellow light of a wide foyer.

The two of them stood for a while, tasting the ambience of the place. The foyer was lined with all manner of exotic and time-worn artefacts. Right at his elbow was a huge and mottled lion, frozen mid spring, as if pouncing on unwary guests. Around the walls on hooks were strange tools, farm implements, obsolete weapons, pots and gourds. Faded pictures in dusty frames paid tribute to grim men in old-fashioned suits and sour women with hardship in their eyes.

To the right the space opened into what was some kind of store, with sparse merchandise scattered on open selves. To the left was a bar lounge, gaudy with what looked like party lights strung out above a long timber bar.

Directly in front was a reception counter, surrounded by wire mesh. As Barrak's eyes adjusted to the dim light he could see a shadowy figure inside the cage, staring out at him with yellow eyes shot with red. The innkeeper bobbed his head up and down as Barrak approached his cage and glanced at the counter where a crossbow lay, ancient, rusted, and apparently loaded.

'Git yers lost in the dark, ranger?' wheezed the innkeeper. A tangled mane of hair clung to the sides of his head, but was altogether missing on top. Barrak could see now that his skin was mottled and there was sickness in his eyes. A faint stench emanated from the cage, like something had died in there.

'It's barely dusk,' said Barrak. 'We just want lodgings for the night and a meal if there's any available.'

The wizened hotelier angled his head and stared at Barrak, then glanced at Jasmyn. 'We don't commonly git many ladies in these parts, ranger.' A reptilian tongue flicked around his scaly lips, then he turned and looked towards the bar.

Barrak followed his gaze. The wide dingy space was sparsely furnished with wooden tables and chairs and some bar stools and benches along the wall. Two figures sat at a table in front of the bar under a dim electric chandelier. The only discernible feature was the whites of the eyes of the man facing them, which seemed to draw what little light there was. Sitting stone still, he stared at Barrak.

'What means d'yer offer to make good f'yer room? That's if I got one?'

Barrak discreetly showed him the smallest of his gold coins. 'Two rooms, old man.'

Jasmyn grabbed Barrak's arm and squeezed hard. 'Uh-uh.' Barrak took her point; he didn't much want a room to himself either, not in this place. 'Give us just one room, with two beds, preferably with its own bathroom,' he added as an afterthought.

The innkeeper snorted and reached for a ledger. 'Bathroom, eh?' he gave a wheezy chuckle, shaking his head slowly. 'Y'can wait over there by the bar if you want, I'll git yer key. See 'bout some eats then too ... an' somethin' to drink, eh ranger?'

Jasmyn stayed close as they moved towards the bar and edged along it to the far end, keeping their distance from the men at the table. Neither he nor Jasmyn acknowledged the men, but both felt their eyes on them as they passed.

No sooner had they taken up their stools at the far corner, than one of the men rose, scraping his chair raucously on the timber floor. He was tall, almost touching the dilapidated light fitting, which chose that very moment to flicker and fail, leaving the room in near darkness, but for the party lights. Long ropes of dark hair fell to his shoulders and a ragged beard partly obscured his pale face. A coat of some kind of animal hide barely contained his huge frame. He swaggered towards the bar, the coat flaring out as he swung himself around before settling on a bar stool. As he landed, he roared 'Haaarh', a manic laugh with no sense to it, then stared towards the corner where Barrak and Jasmyn sat, trying to ignore him.

'Lost yer sheep, drover?' His voice was deep, gravelly and too loud in the quiet bar.

Barrak sighed. The big man was staring straight down the bar as if it were a bow-sight, smiling a demented smile, eyes unnaturally wide. Those parts of his face not covered in hair were scarred or tattooed, and one earlobe was grossly stretched around an animal bone. Metal studs and gemstones decorated his eyebrow and nose. A livid scar ran down the side of his face from the corner of his eye, through his beard to his chin.

'Well drover, shouldn't you be out tryin' t' round up them chickens?' he slapped the counter and yelled *Haarh* again, this time even louder, and glanced at his mate, then back at Barrak.

In the pause, they heard rain drumming on the tin roof.

'You hearin' me chicken man?

Barrak looked away. Jasmyn squeezed his arm.

'Y'best know it, drover, I don't much like bein' ignored,' he continued in a low, gravelly rumble. 'Now it's customary for new guests here t' buy a round o' drinks for the whole bar. It's called a *shout*. Yep, you shout everyone in the bar – me and all ten o' me mates.' He gestured towards his sole companion then slapped the bar again. This time his *Haaarh* extended itself into a loud, wheezy giggle that only stopped when he abruptly pushed himself to his feet.

From the corner of his eye, Barrak saw the other man stand and move towards the bar too. But Barrak's attention was on the tall brute. He was massive. Barrak stood up and began to back away, further around the corner of the bar, keeping Jasmyn behind him.

The brute advanced. 'Now, drover boy is just bein' plain rude,' he growled.

'Yeah, maybe he don't wanna share,' a voice hissed from the shadows. The brute's mate had appeared right by Jasmyn's side. She barely stifled a scream and recoiled, trying to squeeze herself between Barrak and the bar.

'Don't wanna share his little *princess.*' The smaller man was half the brute's size, ugly as a gargoyle and similarly festooned with bones and skin, an ugly ornament in his face with his nose grown around it. The oversize brute had stopped right in front of Barrak, staring. The whites of his mad, bulbous eyes were shot through with vivid red seams.

'Look, we don't want any trouble. We're just passing through here.' Barrak's protest fell hopelessly flat.

'Well it looks like you've already got trouble.' The giant thug smiled an ugly smile and raised his eyebrows as he carefully drew a knife the length of his great tattooed forearm from behind him. 'Trouble for plain bad manners,' he added, admiring the blade.

'And fer not sharin',' said the gargoyle, reaching around Barrak and making a grab at Jasmyn's hair. A burst of instinct swung Barrak around on his toes, his right arm coming in a flat arc, his fist slamming into the bridge of the gargoyle's nose. He went down like a sack of potatoes but seemed to bounce right back up, as if made of rubber.

The tall brute grabbed Barrak and almost pulled his arm from its socket, wrenching him away from Jasmyn and getting the huge hunting knife right up at his throat to immobilise him, just as the gargoyle, now dripping blood from his smashed nose, took Jasmyn by the arm and spun her towards him.

She gave a yelp and bought up her knee, but missed the mark, then tried to slam the heel of her hand into his face, aiming for the nose. But he dodged the blow and took hold of her again, this time by both arms, so she could do no more damage. She screamed and writhed, hurling barely comprehensible expletives out into the room.

Barrak felt the cold of the blade on his skin and wondered if his throat was already cut, and then a burst of orange-red light erupted in the corner of the bar.

Everything stopped.

The brute eased the knife away from Barrak's throat and peered at the fiery glow of a struck match, bathing the corner booth in orange and lighting the face and shoulders of a figure no one had seen sitting there in the dark, watching the whole show. The four of them were frozen in a tableau for an instant, then the gargoyle loosened his grip on Jasmyn, and she pulled away. The flame was sucked into the glowing end of a cigar, leaving just the little pulsing cauldron of red and a hint of smoke.

'Now what have I told you two vermin 'bout comin' in here monsterin' civilised folk?' The voice from the shadows was not loud, but richly resonant, honeyed, with a hint of gravel and plenty of authority.

No one spoke. Rain drummed.

The cigar end brightened to hot red, and a cloud of pungent fumes fogged in the party lights. A chair creaked and the cigar end rose. The brute beside Barrak tensed and his knife disappeared under his coat. The gargoyle seemed to shrink.

The man was still not yet visible beyond the reach of the bar lights but his voice came across to them smooth and loud – apparently addressing Barrak. 'I will not ask you to excuse these misguided cretins, sir. They deserve no consideration, neither yours nor mine.' He stepped into the light, and glided smoothly between Jasmyn and the gargoyle. He was taller than Barrak but still a head shorter than the brute, even in his hat, which he had kept on indoors. He looked like a farmer, in his long straight coat and wide-brimmed hat. Most of his face was in shadow, but Barrak could make out a square jaw with a large and odd-looking chin, and a long beak of a nose. He gave the faintest nod in the direction of the tall assailant and said, 'This one, I'd like to see gutted with that offensive blade of his and left out in the desert, but I doubt even the wild dogs would touch his poisonous flesh and rid us of his wrongful incarnation.'

Then he turned on the gargoyle. 'And this misbegotten wretch was the product of some unholy congress between goat and snake I'll wager, with Diabolus himself blessing the union. He deserves nothing better than to be flushed in pieces down the nearest sewer.'

He turned to Jasmyn and touched the brim of his hat in deference. Apparently the man was confident enough to turn his back on the two filthy brutes. 'I apologise, ma'am, on behalf of all good people, east and west, for the wrong he has done just by breathing the same air as you, let alone putting his foul hands on your person. For that, I have a good mind to cut out his black heart, right here and now, but for the further upset it would cause your good selves.'

The farmer turned his attention back to the tall man, who had stepped away from Barrak a yard or two. He puffed his cigar into a fury of bright embers before drawing down a lungful of smoke, all the while giving the dirty brute a penetrating stare. 'These two mindless degenerates will be leaving us now and taking themselves back into the godless wasteland from whence they sprang.' As he spoke, smoke poured from his nose and mouth as if his innards were on fire.

To Barrak's surprise there was no argument. He was steeling himself for the outbreak of more violence, but the brute said nothing and met the farmer's eyes with a blank stare, barely tinged with resentment. The gargoyle had already withdrawn, gathering something from the table they had occupied and making for the door.

The giant thug backed away, keeping his eyes fixed on the farmer and as soon as he had put some distance between them he sneered, 'You got a gods-bane nerve, Bishop. You'll do this once too often, I reckon, and it'll be yer undoin'.'

The farmer seemed to raise himself slightly on his toes. He leaned

210

towards the retreating brute and flicked his coat open as though to reach for a weapon. Barrak caught the glint of metal that might have been a sword under the long jacket, and as the man turned he saw the same on the other side. Two swords on the one man.

The tall thug scrambled to grab his things from the table and hurried to the door, twice glancing over his shoulder at Bishop, before he reached the exit and was swallowed by the teeming night.

It was midnight when Barrak checked his watch, and he couldn't account for the time gone missing. To his surprise, Jasmyn had gradually returned to something like her old self in the company of the strange and charismatic Bishop, as he regaled them with tales of the outlands and educated them on the geography and culture of the wild lands. The unpleasantness of their arrival at Dods Junction was quickly dispelled by a glass or two of surprisingly good wine, which Bishop had insisted upon, and a plain but tasty meal he had also insisted on buying them, as recompense for the appalling welcome they had endured. Besides which, he confided, he alone possessed the vital knowledge of just what could and could not be eaten from Dodsiadly's menu without serious risk to life and limb.

He had started by making light of the two louts who had accosted them in the bar and then acknowledged that they, and others of their ilk, were dangerous and should be avoided at all costs. He had insisted that Dods give Barrak and Jasmyn his best room, one that did actually have a bathroom, and told him to put the kitchen on notice that if they poisoned anyone that night, they would have Bishop to answer to.

He was urbane and knowledgeable, quite unlike Barrak's expectation of outlanders. Clearly Jasmyn was charmed and intrigued by Bishop's unusual accent and idiom. He was quite tall, slim but strongly built. His age was impossible to gauge – he could have been forty or sixty. His skin seemed strangely pale and somewhat incongruous with his jet-black hair, greying over one temple only, and a silver moustache. His strong angular features were set in a head that seemed slightly too big for his body. But strangest of all were his eyes, dark and penetrating even in the dim light, even mesmerising. They held his audience whenever he spoke and when he listened they were full of empathy and interest. His eyelids drooped as if he were always on the point of falling asleep, even when his gaze was at its most penetrating. The eyes, together with his long face and aquiline nose, gave him the look of a wise and watchful raptor.

His laugh was infectious and the conversation between the three of them became more relaxed and engaging as the evening wore on. Barrak felt more and more at ease, and it was plain Bishop had Jasmyn in the palm of his hand with his easy charm. For now at least, she had recovered a little of her natural buoyancy. He seemed impressed by their resolve to travel east in search of a missing family member, as this was the way they had decided to explain their quest. He told them of some of the most notable perils they might encounter and gave advice on how to avoid the worst places. He offered maps to compare with their own and advice on how to structure their journey.

On the subject of guides he was informative, if a little sardonic. When Jasmyn told him their intention had been to stop at the junction for as long as it would take to hire a guide, Bishop had chuckled good-naturedly. 'It would be a lucky traveller indeed who found a guide at Dodsiadly's who wasn't bent on taking all their money and leaving them stranded,' he mused.

And so it was, by the time Barrak looked at his watch and realised it was midnight, they had already agreed that Bishop would act as their guide. He would take them east as far as 'his own little piece of paradise' some three hundred miles away. In any case, his plan had been to leave first thing in the morning and be on his way, and as the three of them were the only guests at the junction that night, who knew when a suitable or trustworthy guide might otherwise be found.

The next morning dawned grey and bleak. The barrier ranges to the east were shrouded in low misty cloud. An insipid orange glow, leaking through the grey where the ranges fell away to the north-east, was the only sign of cheer in the morning chill.

Regal and pale as marble in the low morning light, Bishop stood tall in his coat and hat – a drum major in search of his marching band – as Barrak and Jasmyn descended the front steps with their meagre possessions bundled in their swags.

He had already brought up his vehicle, which was making a throaty, throbbing sound and had smoke or steam issuing from the back as if there were some fault. Bishop's vehicle was not unlike the sort of utility truck used by farmers, and even his friend Thomas around the wharf, except it had a rigid canopy over the truck tray, presumably rigged for Bishop to sleep in during his long trips. And the vehicle's chassis was much higher off the ground, with oversize wheels and wide soft tyres, apparently designed for rough terrain. Attached to the front was a large bull bar, and underneath it, some kind of winching mechanism, presumably to help get the vehicle out if it were bogged. But there was not a crystal array anywhere on the thing. Strangest of all was the loud chugging motor.

'Combustion motor, Barrak,' Bishop declared as they set off, following a road that was little more than a set of wheel ruts, leading out of the junction and veering to the north. 'Devil's own technology where you come from, I'll warrant, but out here, it's the only thing practicable. No array techs out here, or charge ports, and batteries are rarer than hen's teeth.' He looked at Barrak to gauge his reaction.

Jasmyn looked uncertainly at Bishop from her position between the two men on the wide bench seat and asked, 'What does it run on?'

'Anything!' Bishop declared. 'When I can get it, refined impellent from a trading post or town along the way. But Dods didn't have any, not a drop, so right now we're running on used oil from his kitchen.' He smiled at Jasmyn. 'I do apologise for the smell. Gods help us, we'll be bringing the fumes from his wretched kitchen with us.'

They veered further north, heading for a pass, which Bishop attested was the best way across the Barrier Ranges that ran deep and high further to the south. As they chugged and bumped along, there were long silences, which verged on awkwardness at times, and they watched the landscape change as the range gradually loomed up beside them.

At times Barrak felt an uneasy sense that Bishop's charm could easily shift to mockery when some comparison or another was made between the easy life inside the boundaries of Eyre, and the austerity of the outlands. Perhaps it was the harsh light of day, or the grim reality of their approaching the Barrier Range, the outer marker of the Eyrean border zones, or maybe it was the strange and enigmatic energy that seemed to emanate from their new-found guide, but Barrak never again felt as comfortable as he had the night before. Perhaps it had just been the wine after all. In any case, he was increasingly aware of his own tendency to hold back parts of their story, not wanting to let Bishop know too much about their place in Eyrean society, or how badly out of favour they were with Eyrean authorities since Meldrick's coup. And he thought it unwise to align himself too closely with the rebels. In the end it seemed enough to cast themselves as residents of Rylanswood, who had set out to find word of Barrak's nephew, who had ventured east and not been heard from. He had left Bishop to assume what he would about Barrak's relationship with Jasmyn.

It took the best part of the day to reach the pass and then labour up and over it. Bishop assured them the going would be easier and much faster on the other side. It was almost dusk before they made it down into the low foothills on the eastern side of the mountains.

They struck camp in a clearing by a creek, a small oasis in the barren foothills, treed with some of the same cypress pines that had been prolific back in the pound, as well as oak-bush and a few gnarled mallees. Dusk came early as the sun dipped below the mountain pass, and so Barrak and Jasmyn busied themselves getting a fire going and preparing a meal before the light was lost altogether. As they toiled over the fire, they kept their conversation to the task at hand, but Barrak could see in Jasmyn's eyes that she shared his concern: *Had they been too hasty in allowing this strange outlander to be their guide?*

And there behind them, in the deepening dusk, was the Barrier Range, one of the outer markers of Eyrean civilisation. They had done the unthinkable, something neither of them could have imagined a week ago, they had left Eyre and entered the forbidden zones. And they had done it with barely a second thought, and in the company of the strangest of strangers, a mysterious outlander, with whom they were now all too heavily invested.

Bishop himself seemed preoccupied. While Barrak poked at the fire and Jasmyn looked to the rice and vegetables, Bishop wandered the boundary of the camp, paying close attention to the ground, looking at tracks and signs left in the dirt. Bit by bit he zigzagged along the creek and then up a low rise to a ridge running along the edge of the glade. There he stood for quite some time in the gloaming, scanning the country to the north, where the foothills shrank away and flattened out into desert. He came back down to camp and offered no explanation for his ramblings, and no one asked. The evening passed with a simple camp meal and some stilted conversation around the fire, which was in stark contrast to the conviviality of the night before.

All retired early, Bishop to his truck and Barrak and Jasmyn to their small tent.

By mid-morning the following day the trio were crossing an endless plain of red sand and saltbush, with the distant range on the northern horizon. Bishop attempted a travelogue from time to time on some point of dubious interest. Mostly they travelled in silence, watching the unchanging landscape or dozing in the cab of Bishop's droning desert vessel.

These were the badlands, Bishop explained, also known as the Lesser Western Desert, degraded land where nothing useful grew for lack of nutrients, and in any case – except for the current year, which had been unusually wet – a virtual desert with little or no rainfall. No one lived here apart from the odd tribe of hardy nomads who rarely crossed the low mountains they could see in the distance to the north. Occasionally traders plying the east–west route between the Eyrean border zones and the central provinces crossed this arid country. Ahead another half-day's driving was the 'thriving metropolis of Europa', as Bishop called it, a remote desert town that marked the intersection of the east–west and southern trade routes.

He had ceased to quiz Barrak and Jasmyn about their story, which was patently thin and, Bishop probably knew, largely untrue. Barrak felt a growing unease about their guide's readiness to accept his passengers' dubious story, with the alacrity of someone whose own history and motives were not necessarily transparent. A conspiracy of mistrust seemed to have settled over the travellers and Jasmyn was slipping back into morose introspection and sorrow.

By mid-afternoon they were again heading more or less due east. All trace of cloud had vanished and the barren plain baked under a white-hot sky; an arid wind coming out of the north sucked the moisture out of them. As they crested a small undulation, the road, such as it was, fell away before them, stretching for miles ahead, through a barren stony valley, where a line of figures wobbled mirage-like in the heat haze rising from the plain. Barrak made out tall loping creatures, camels weighed down with a cargo of humans and goods, traipsing in single file towards the east. They lost them in the low ground between one rise and the next, and as they topped the next hill, Barrak fully expected to see the camel train just ahead of them, but there was no sign of it. The road ahead stretched straight and flat for miles, with no sign of camels or traders. He scanned the country either side and even stuck his head out the window and looked back behind them. The traders and their animals seemed to have vanished. Bishop said they must've taken a side track, but Barrak had seen nothing resembling another track.

The mystery of the vanishing camel traders stayed with him for some time and added to his unease.

Europa was home to a dismal collection of humanity, marooned like flotsam at the crossroads of two desolate byways. The first sign of habitation was the track widening to a dusty roadway with a ditch choked with waste of various kinds running beside it. Humpies made of rough mud bricks and boughs started to appear here and there and grubby urchins, skinny as grasshoppers, gawked at them with wide eyes in bony heads, before darting away as the vehicle approached, fear apparently trumping curiosity.

Bishop pulled the vehicle to a halt in what passed for the main street, near the crossroads. The intersection was strewn with a bit of gravel to keep down the dust and around it were a handful of more substantial structures, some built of poorly masoned stone or rough-hewn timber, although overall mud brick was the building material of choice. Opposite them was a building with a second story and windows that Barrak took for a town hall or possibly a tavern of some sort. Alongside them was a store. Bishop was quickly out of the truck, crossing the roadside ditch via a couple of wide planks. More planks served as shelves on either side of the entrance. On the left, the shelves were sparsely stocked with pumpkins and tired-looking root vegetables. To the right the shelves were bare, but for three large flagons of yellow fluid.

A boy clothed in rags and mud, pushing a cart with smoke issuing from it, held out something on a stick to Bishop, a burnt offering. Bishop waved him away and the boy cowered as though he expected a blow. The few people wandering the streets looked gaunt and grim, their clothes not much better than the urchins' they'd seen on the outskirts. Unlike the bold boy with his grilled delicacies, they seemed intent on staying clear of Bishop's vehicle.

A buckled woman and small girl passed by on the other side of the road and Barrak caught them staring at him and Jasmyn. Their faces showed something more akin to wide-eyed horror than curiosity. As Bishop came bursting back out of the store the woman picked up her little girl and hurried away down the road.

Bishop stopped and grabbed two of the three flagons from the shelf. Barrak got out and helped him load the third. He assumed the yellow fluid was fuel for Bishop's combustion engine.

It was already late afternoon, so Barrak asked Bishop if he planned to stay the night.

Bishop slammed the back door of the truck and wiped his hands on his pants. He eyed Barrak dubiously and made a noise in his throat like an edgy horse. 'Not recommended, Barrak.'

'That looks like a hotel across the road,' Barrak persisted, hopefully.

Bishop lifted his head slightly, so Barrak could see his piercing eyes. 'Trust me Barrak, you do *not* want to be in Europa when the sun goes down.'

After leaving Europa they travelled on until the light was almost completely gone. They ate only dry rations that night after pitching camp a few miles off the track and Bishop forbade a fire, citing the warmth of the evening. But Bishop was clearly on edge, and after their frugal meal he declared they would need to keep a watch that night.

They took it in three-hour stints, Bishop first. He gave Barrak an old crossbow from the back of the truck to keep with him on his watch.

In the chill before dawn, after his watch, Barrak couldn't sleep and watched Bishop through the open tent flap as he wandered the camp in the low light of the setting moon, his twin swords at his sides, smelling the wind and tilting at shadows. The constellations plunged through the black desert night as he dozed, with his head half out of the tiny tent, and he listened to the night creatures and to Bishop's furtive footfalls. Keeping time with it all was Jasmyn's slow steady breathing at the other end of the tent. He wondered how she slept so soundly and envied her the knack.

The next day was hotter by far than the previous two. By midday, the desert heat had turned the truck's cabin into a baker's oven. Gradually the flat terrain gave way to low dunes and erosion gullies, sometimes hidden from view and ready to trap the unwary driver. A barely visible track threaded its way between these obstacles.

Ancient hills, their bones exposed by time, seemed to close in on them from the north and south-east. Eventually the track began to climb up into a mountain pass. This soon narrowed into a kind of ravine with craggy sandstone cliffs on both sides as the pass became ever narrower and steeper.

It was even hotter in the ravine than on the plain.

Bishop's old engine banged and laboured in the heat, struggling up the steep climb. Then the tyre blew.

218

They all got out and stared at it. As Barrak concentrated on the tyre, Bishop scanned the surrounding landscape. Then he moved along the length of the vehicle inspecting the ground. At the rear he got down on his hands and knees, sifting through the sand. Barrak turned to watch, and saw him stop, then wrench something clear of the sand.

It was a leather strap, still half buried in the sand, with short metal spikes sticking up out of it.

'What the hell is that?' Barrak asked.

Bishop didn't answer. He was back on his feet, wrenching open the back door of the truck.

'It's some sort of trap, isn't it?' Barrak said.

'Get in the cabin, both of you,' Bishop said quietly.

He pulled something from under a tarpaulin in the back of the truck and unwrapped the covering. It had a timber handle, exactly like the butt of a crossbow. But it was not a bow. Extending from the handle were two long cylindrical metal barrels, fused together.

'Get Jasmyn in the cabin of the truck now, please,' Bishop's voice was still calm. 'Go,' he urged and pushed past Barrak.

Barrak took Jasmyn by the arm and they climbed into the truck. Bishop had come around in front of the vehicle and was pointing the weapon towards the side of the ravine. He had the butt against his shoulder, just as you would a crossbow.

Looking up through the windscreen of the truck, Barrak saw movement, figures running and ducking and bobbing along the ridge line amongst the crags and boulders – there were people up there.

At that moment the air cracked and a loud explosion boomed over the cabin. Barrak ducked instinctively as an explosion of dust and sand and fragments of rock came off a crag at the top of the ravine. There was no sign of the bobbing figures on the ridge anymore.

'Gods!' Jasmyn whispered.

Bishop had swung around and was pointing the thing up at the other side of the ravine now, shifting back and forth on his feet.

Boom. Another cloud of dust and sand sprang up amongst the cliffs and a loud crack echoed off the side of the ravine.

219

Bishop paced around the front of the truck and back again, scanning the ridges. He broke open his weapon as if it were jointed and removed two small red canisters from the back of the barrels. There was a wisp of smoke. Bishop paced some more, watching the high ground. Jasmyn and Barrak looked on in silence. After a few minutes he seemed satisfied and climbed back into the truck, laying his weapon down across the back of the cabin behind the seats.

Sensing more than seeing Barrak's questioning expression, he said, 'Yes, I know, old Orlan wouldn't be amused, would he? What do you people call them? "Fire-burst weapons" isn't it?' Bishop's tone was clearly sardonic and mocking. 'I call it persuasion and insurance; scares the living daylights out of those desert people, the little buggers.'

'Where do you get such a thing?' Barrak asked him.

'My little blaster? Something like that can easily be acquired, at a price, from traders. I've got contacts.'

'Are they dangerous, these desert people?' Jasmyn interjected.

'The nomads? Not so much. Some can be. Not like the vermin you encountered back at the junction. They're opportunists. These ones were probably hoping we'd leave the truck, so they could help themselves. They wouldn't have been expecting a fight. But still, they might return once they get their nerve back. Best we get this tyre changed and be on our way.' Bishop wrestled the truck jack from under the seat and climbed back down, apparently unconcerned.

They reached the top of the ravine and the land levelled out into a rocky plateau the colour of rusted iron. Occasionally they saw a sparse stand of low twisted mallees clinging to life in the red sand.

Barrak could barely make out the track, but Bishop seemed to know his way and paused only occasionally to take his bearings. By the time they had topped the ravine, high cloud had rippled in from the north-west, giving some relief from the afternoon sun, and as the plateau opened out, the sky away to the north began to darken.

As they settled into the rhythm of the plain, Barrak plied Bishop for advice about how best to continue their journey east from Bishop's place. He was evasive at first and questioned whether Barrak and Jasmyn really wanted to make such a dangerous trip, once again citing the many perils and the great length of the journey.

'I mean, those desert people back there, they're one thing, but further east there's whole bands of maraudin' vermin like the ones you met at Dodsiadly's, only worse. Those two were just a couple of outcasts. And further east there's savages too, and in the grasslands and mountains, wild animals, dangerous ones ...'

In the end he suggested their best option might be to make contact with a suitable group of traders heading east, who might be persuaded to take them along, for a price.

Bishop nodded at the gathering clouds to their north. 'Desert storm brewing.'

A column of cumulonimbus was boiling up into the vacant blue, unfurling cream and gold in the late afternoon sun. At its base was a mass of dark cloud, rolling over the red plain like a celestial reaper. Barrak had never seen anything like it.

Just as it seemed their path would take them past the storm to the south, the track veered to the north. Bishop adjusted course, following the ghost of old wheel ruts, tinted by the late afternoon sun, before heading straight for the centre of the storm.

'Better hold on,' said Bishop lightly, 'this could get interesting.' The desert storm was like a giant mushroom, its bourgeoning column piling up into the vaulted sky. The setting sun lit the plain all around in barely natural shades of red and orange and mutated the darkening cloud mass to mauve and indigo. Forked lightning discharged from its dark underbelly, straight into the ground.

Bishop stole a glance at them both.

'Can't we go around?' Barrak asked.

'No, we have to stick to the road,' murmured Bishop. 'Gods abide, it looks a bad one.'

It came on them more quickly than they expected and swallowed them. In the space of just a few moments, they were in near darkness. Ahead the gloom flickered white and rosy with lightning every few seconds. Bishop slowed to a crawl. Rain started to fall in great dollops, smacking against the windscreen, and the crack and rumble of thunder drowned the grumbling engine. The unnatural night brought Barrak up in goose bumps. In the side mirror he could still see a golden halo of light, back where they had come from.

A squally wind buffeted the truck and rain lashed the windows. They found themselves in a forest of gnarled and stunted trees, tortured by the whipping wind, lit up every few seconds in a pink burst. Bishop's knuckles were white on the steering wheel, his head thrust forward as he tried to pick his way through the trees, the faint track now lost. Jasmyn's face was gaunt and stoic as flashes lit the cabin, dazzlingly bright and impossibly close together.

Thunder cracked all around them.

Once, Barrak imagined he saw Bishop's skeleton, glowing like a carnival ghoul as an ominous bolt sizzled the cabin to white-hot radiance and deafened them with a hellish crack, all in the same instant. A second near miss a moment later, and his eyes darted to the side mirror. In it he saw a shattered tree just behind them spout a great tongue of fire up to the heavens, before receding from view, swallowed by the rain.

When they came out of the trees, Bishop increased his speed. Perhaps he realised they were past the point of no return and an act of faith was needed. No one spoke, they just rode it out, held together in the common space of heightened awareness and truncated time.

When the storm finally spat them out onto the empty plain, Barrak wondered what had happened to the afternoon. The sun was already gone and the first sky gods flew unblinking in the purple dusk. The trio spoke little in the calm after the storm. It was as if they had just woken. The cool night air was crisp, cleansed of its oppressive humidity.

And so it was at once unexpected and still no surprise at all when, just a few miles on, Bishop announced, 'This is it,' and turned the vehicle to the south and drove along a line of trees that could never have grown naturally in such a straight line. Before long, he swung the vehicle around in a sweeping arc and the lights showed them a collection of buildings, strange and incongruous in the desert. They were set out like a country estate, barns and stables, some in good shape, others dilapidated, behind new wire fences.

Finally Bishop pulled the vehicle up in front of what could have been a manor house in Tamouer's most salubrious suburbs. It had an air of antiquity about it. Built mainly of stone, parts of it appeared, even in the moonlight, to be ancient and crumbling. The front seemed new, refurbished and neat. Curving around one side of the homestead was a long line of towering trees that Barrak couldn't identify in the dark, their thick foliage whistling and swishing in the stiff breeze .

'Welcome to Bishop's Paradise,' he said as they got down out of the truck. To Barrak's surprise and amusement he discovered that those very words were engraved on a brass plaque next to the front door.

CHAPTER 15

THEY'D SHARED AN ORDINARY evening meal, Bishop apologising for the paucity of his provisions, due to his long absence. But there was something else – Bishop had seemed distracted. There was no sign of the gregarious and charming raconteur they'd encountered that first night at Dods Junction. In fact the atmosphere around Bishop's large antique dining table had been tense and the ambiance of his big old house was frankly a little spooky.

They were such a long, long way from anything and anyone familiar. Barrak and Jasmyn betrayed their unease with every furtive glance, every hesitant word, and in the end it was a relief when Jasmyn pleaded exhaustion and Bishop showed them to their room to make themselves comfortable for the night.

'Don't you feel it? This place, it's creepy.' Jasmyn plonked herself down on the bed.

'Why?'

'I can't say why, exactly, it just is. Quest, Barrak, don't you ever trust your instincts?'

Barrak shook his head and shrugged as he unzipped his backpack and peered inside.

'And as for Bishop ... well, I for one won't be sorry when we say our goodbyes. He's so ... well, you know what I mean, don't you?'

'Yeah, I do know what you mean, he's a strange one.' Barrak was still rummaging.

'Creepy,' suggested Jasmyn, 'just like his big old house.' Jasmyn looked searchingly across the room at Barrak. 'Have we done the right thing, Barrak? Are you sure this is what we should be doing?'

'I don't know Jasmyn. But we didn't have too many options.' Barrak pulled his coat out of the pack and put it to one side.

There was a longish pause before Jasmyn spoke again. 'What if we just went home?' She said it earnestly, her voice small, her eyes wide. Barrak stopped his rummaging and looked at her. She had dropped her guard, deliberately; she was letting Barrak see her vulnerability: Jasmyn, who was normally so confident, sometimes feisty and irreverent, always full of good humour. He wanted to make everything all right for her and it stung him that he probably couldn't.

'It wouldn't be safe,' he tried, somewhat lamely, 'and we've come this far already ...'

Jasmyn smiled sadly at him and nodded. She was willing him to convince her.

'And we promised Gitan, and Elias ...' Barrak faltered. 'For Elias's sake, someone needs to go and ... I don't know, it feels like it should be me. I feel it's something I have to do.' He gave Jasmyn a tortured, puzzled look. He was struggling to understand his own justification.

Jasmyn straightened her shoulders and bit her lip. 'I know. You're right. We do have to go. We have to do it, together. It's just that, Barrak, I'm scared.' Her voice was small again, and again Barrak was disarmed by her honesty. He pushed himself up from his pack and went to her and sat on the bed and put an arm around her. She leaned into him and sighed.

'I'm scared too,' he said softly, 'but things will look brighter in the morning. And we'll get Bishop to take us to the nearest settlement or town or whatever and find some traders, just like he said. We've still got some gold. We can pay them, and they'll take us the rest of the way east. It can't be that far – we've come such a long way already – it can't be much further.' He squeezed her shoulder. 'Anyway, I think we're past the point of no return,' he added with a snort.

Jasmyn laughed quietly, unconvincingly, for a moment.

He went on detailing a rough kind of plan to her and the more he talked the better Jasmyn said she felt about things. It had the same effect on Barrak. After a while he fell silent, and they sat together, relaxed, until Jasmyn said, 'Barrak?'

'Hm?'

'Do you think my father's really dead?'

Barrak sighed softly.

'I don't know, Jasmyn. I hope not. But we both know how ruthless Meldrick is.'

Jasmyn nodded against his chest.

'We should get some sleep,' Jasmyn said, stirring. 'Are you as tired as I am?'

'Yeah, but I need some fresh air first, and I want to have a little look around.'

'Now?' Jasmyn was incredulous. 'At night?'

'I won't be long, I just need some cool air in my lungs … It's been so hot.'

'Well, be quick – I won't sleep a wink until you get back.' She looked at him, annoyed. 'Better take your coat, too. You know how quickly the temperature drops at night, and by the way,' Jasmyn moved over to the door and tapped on it twice and then again, three times. 'Two long and three short, that's your code, because I'm locking the damn door.'

The moon was a bright, white lantern in the void above Bishop's circular driveway, suspended in a gap in the dark canopy of the alien trees. The wind had dropped and the night was chilly as it approached the icy small hours. Barrak shivered. He'd forgotten his coat after all. He still hadn't got used to the way the temperature dropped in the desert at night, away from the moderating effect of the Eyrean Sea.

He wandered aimlessly, thinking of Jasmyn as he crunched over gravel. And about Enoch. He still found it hard to believe him dead. Responsibility lay heavy on him as the words of his old friend came back to him: *Make sure you look after her, Barrak.* It was almost as though he'd had some prescient knowledge of what was to come.

As he walked along the driveway, silver wire glinted in the moonlight and beyond it he could see a long shed, half hidden in the shadows of the trees – a shearing shed, Barrak guessed, although there were no signs of sheep. He hesitated and looked back towards the house. He'd already passed another large outbuilding, close to the drive but still obscured by the line of trees. Something about it caught his eye, there was light coming from it, and he could hear something running, which sounded like one of Bishop's infernal motors. He doubled back towards it. Maybe Bishop was working late.

He found himself before a set of old-fashioned barn doors. He pushed one and it creaked open, a small, loud noise in the still night. Inside, taking up one corner, was an old farm truck, out of service, up on blocks, looking like repairs had long since been abandoned. The shed was large and empty but for the truck. He took a few tentative steps into the cavernous space. It was dark and still warm from the day's heat, and yet, strangely, Barrak felt a chill as he entered. The floor was dirt and spongy underfoot and there was a musty smell hanging in the air, not the smell of a garage, not of mechanical things, more earthy – a farmyard smell.

As his eyes adjusted, Barrak moved past the truck and saw that light was spilling into the shed from an opening in the back corner. That was the source of the steady mechanical purr, louder now.

On the back wall of the shed were wide workbenches and big double troughs with water taps and spraying nozzles. Stacked along the benches and to the sides were timber crates and large metal storage bins.

To the right of the benches the light was leaking in and he could see there was something hanging from the ceiling, swinging slightly, even though he felt no breeze. It was some kind of apparatus for hoisting heavy loads and it was hanging by a metal chain from a rail attached to the ceiling. As he moved through the opening into the smaller shed at the rear, he saw there were more hoists.

He touched the nearest one and it turned, rotating easily and revealing to Barrak's surprise two large curved metal prongs, both honed to a sharp point.

On the back wall was a prominent white door with a window. A bright light in a protective metal grille hung from the bulkhead above the door.

More hooks hung from the rail between Barrak and the white door. The floor in this smaller back room was concrete, with drains covered by small metal grilles, spaced in a line down the centre of it.

Surprised by his own temerity, he crept toward the white door, which seemed to be the source of the rhythmic humming. He had to remind himself to breathe. Large knives, saws, axes and other implements of uncertain purpose were hanging along the walls. He'd seen similar ones outside over the workbenches.

Unease settled on him and again he felt strangely cold despite the humid warmth of the old farm shed. Clearly this was some kind of workshop for dealing with farm produce – meat processing, a slaughterhouse. Suddenly he had a powerful urge to get out, to return quickly to Jasmyn, but a perverse curiosity drove him on towards the white door with the window.

He brushed past the last of the hoists and pressed his face to the small window in the door. It was obscured by filmy dirt and the room beyond was dark. But there was enough light for him to make out dim shapes, carcasses hanging inside. It was as he thought, a coolroom for meat storage. He wondered what Bishop farmed; he never had asked him. Morbid curiosity overtook him and he reached for the door handle and pulled.

The door opened with a smack of separating seals.

His hand went out, searching for a light switch. Instead, there was something cold and clammy – a carcass. He recoiled and a shiver went through him, even as he noticed the sudden drop in temperature. His eyes were adjusting rapidly to the dimness of the coolroom, with the meagre light spilling in from outside.

Again he had the urge to get out.

The carcasses resolved themselves in the gloom, six hanging in pairs toward the back, and the odd one out, hanging just behind him, near the door.

Pigs, thought Barrak: pale and smooth, but without the bulk, the skin still on. Hanging upside-down, their long bodies reached almost to the floor, with cropped necks and strange thick forelegs and ...

An isolated part of Barrak's brain knew what he was looking at well before the rest of his mind allowed the truth to penetrate his consciousness; the part of his mind that retained his knowledge of surface anatomy from physicians' college was mapping the anatomical markers on the hanging carcasses: *the iliac crest ... the twin columns of the erector spinae ... inferior angle of the scapula ...*

Human carcasses!

His conscious brain was numb and unbelieving, even while the instinctual processes of his physical body began to kick in.

He let out a strangled groan, expelling the breath from his lungs as if it were poison. A chill entered the top of his head and ran straight into the marrow of his spine. Simultaneously a hot flush rose up from his groin and turned into a wave of bilious nausea which quivered all the way to his numb face.

His knees went out from under him and he sat on the cold floor. Then he leaned over and vomited. Something cold nudged him. He shoved it away and let out a grunt of angst and scrambled frantically, still on his backside, out through the coolroom door. The carcass that had been near the door, still swinging from his touch, dragged its fingertips across the floor as if bidding him goodbye. This one had yet to be fully processed and its inverted bloodless face, moving like a pendulum in the doorway, seemed to share his horror and dismay.

Barrak steadied himself enough to deliberately take a deep breath and hold it for a moment of calm. But panic took him again and he scrambled to his feet and slammed the coolroom door and leaned on it for a second or two before making his way along the line of hoists, batting them aside with his forearms like a man lost in a thicket.

He reached the opening to the dark garage and paused, resting his hands on his thighs, gasping for breath like a sprinter at the end of a race. He glanced back as though expecting pursuit by ghoulish carcasses, then saliva swelled in his mouth and he was bent double again, retching over and over with waves of nausea sweeping through him.

Get a grip. More deep breaths. He straightened and turned to make for the barn doors. Suddenly, from the darkness, hands were on his chest, grabbing his arm – a face came out of the darkness. He gasped and jumped back, jerking himself free.

'Barrak!' Jasmyn's face followed him as he recoiled.

'Oh shit!' He breathed. 'Gods!' He wiped the vomit away from his mouth.

'Barrak?' she hissed urgently. 'Barrak, what's wrong?' Her eyes were as wide as saucers.

'Oh, quest . . .' Barrak breathed, reaching out and taking Jasmyn by the arm. Her face crumbled. Seeing Barrak in such a state terrified her and she grabbed hold of him and shook him.

'Barrak!'

Her cry focused Barrak and he put his hand over her mouth. 'Quiet, OK? We have to get out of here,' he whispered, trying to sound calm. 'Just keep your voice down.'

Jasmyn squirmed away from him when he relaxed his grip. There was anger in her rigid stance and her clipped whisper chastised him for his rough treatment. 'Then tell me what's going on, what are you doing in here?'

'I can't explain now. We have to go. We have to leave now and we're taking Bishop's truck.' Barrak's tone was unequivocal as he grabbed her by the arm again and started to move.

Jasmyn wrenched free once more. This switch from fright to calm was almost as disturbing as finding him so distraught in the first place. *What did he mean, taking his truck?* 'No! You tell me what's going on. Barrak!'

'Listen to me.' Barrak took her by both arms and shook her. 'There–is–no–time!' There was a violence in him Jasmyn had never witnessed before and it scared her.

Barrak softened his tone, pleading with her now. 'This one time just do as I say.'

'Just tell me what's going on ...' Jasmyn's voice cracked.

'Orlan's blood! Look, it's Bishop, he's a ... he ...' Barrak couldn't find a suitable word.

'What?'

'Look, you were right about him. He's ...'

'He's what Barrak?' Jasmyn's voice was barely a whisper, beseeching him for an answer she knew she didn't really want.

He's going to kill us,' he announced simply.

Jasmyn sank in his arms and he went down with her, until both were on their knees. She clung to him, breathing heavily.

'Now, no more questions, Jasmyn. We need to move. Looking past Jasmyn he noticed for the first time that the barn had windows along one side. Moonlight was spilling in and he could see the homestead across the way.

'OK? Go to the truck. I'll go back to the room and get our things. Then we get in the truck and go, simple. OK?' Even as he spoke, Barrak tried to remember what Bishop had done with the keys to the truck. Was he in the habit of leaving them in the ignition?

'OK.' Jasmyn sniffed back a tear and resolved to stay calm.

Barrak could smell soap in her hair, and over the top of her head, he eyed the homestead through the barn windows. And that was when his heart stopped. A light had come on, a light in what he was sure was Bishop's bedroom.

Jasmyn felt him tense, but he covered it by turning her around and pulling her towards the double doors. They peered out. Jasmyn caught her breath when she noticed what Barrak had already seen, and to make matters worse, another light went on – in the living area. She fell away from him, crouching down as if getting ready to sit on the ground. Barrak held her up.

'Oh no, no ... no.' She pulled away from him again, repeating the words softly, like a mantra. Barrak worried that she would run, overcome by her fear of Bishop.

'Listen,' he said, shaking her briskly. 'Listen ... OK. Change of plan.'

'What are we going to do?' She seemed more composed now, but her eyes were full of fear, beseeching Barrak.

'Stay here.' Jasmyn shook her head.

'*Hide* here, just for a minute. I'll get the truck.'

'Barrak!' she hissed, but he was already moving, his hand signalling her to stay. He ran across the gravel driveway to the truck and crouched low on the driver's side, out of view of the house. He couldn't see if the keys were in it, so he carefully opened the door and felt around for them.

Nothing.

He scuttled to the back of the truck, leaving the driver's door open. He remembered seeing Bishop's so-called blaster and the crossbow in the back. The handle turned and the door squeaked loudly in the still night.

'You and y' girlfriend planning a little trip?' The polished gravel of Bishop's voice chilled him to his core. Barrak turned around slowly. Bishop was twenty feet clear of the back of the truck, moving in an arc but keeping his distance, the blaster pointed at Barrak's chest.

'Where is she?' Bishop snarled, his eyes hidden in shadow, his mouth like a scar. He had on his long coat and Barrak could see at least one of his swords at his waist.

'Where's who?' he responded, watching Bishop intently as he moved around.

'A comedian!' Bishop said sardonically. 'Don't worry. I'll find her, even if she wants to play games ... *especially* if she wants to play games. I'll find her and you won't be around to protect her.' Bishop adjusted something on his weapon with a click, not taking his eyes off Barrak. 'She's a prize, our Jasmyn is,' he reflected. 'She's one I might keep around for days, even weeks, if she's lucky.' He gave a barren chuckle and steadied his weapon. He had stopped moving now and it occurred to Barrak that he'd been moving around just to open up the angle, so when he fired he wouldn't risk hitting the truck.

Barrak opened his mouth to speak but the barrel flashed red.

Blackness followed.

He had a vague sense that he'd been airborne. His chest was buzzing, numb. He couldn't remember how to breathe and the strangest sensation was creeping along his backside and back.

It took him time to realise he was moving, being dragged along the ground. Then he drew breath and a searing pain shot through him, squeezing a raw wince from him. He tried to dig his heels into the ground and twist but the pain of it made him seize up. Bishop had him by the collar and was hauling him along. In his confusion he could only think how strong Bishop must be to drag 180 pounds of dead weight.

Barrak's hands went to his chest, expecting to find it mangled, but it felt intact. Sticky with blood it burned with a sharp searing pain. He wondered how he wasn't dead and whether he would live, and then he struggled anew, ignoring the pain, digging in his heels, twisting and crying out with the hurt of it.

Bishop dropped him. He saw the flash of a boot and the butt of Bishop's weapon smacked into the side of his head once, twice.

Through the ringing in his head Barrak still heard Bishop's gruff, mocking monologue.

'Stop wriggling around you dog's arse. And stop your damn moaning. That was just a bit of seasoning, peppering you up with a bit of salt.' Bishop laughed humourlessly. 'What's all the fuss about? You'll be feeling no pain soon enough.' He had Barrak again by the collar and almost lifted him off the ground with a disturbing amount of force.

Barrak saw now that he was being dragged through the doors of the garage, and panic rose up in him. He tried to calm his mind and think.

Outside the door, Bishop paused, as if wary of the darkened shed. 'Where's that little playmate of yours? She's gonna miss all the fun,' He twisted around to see where the nearest hook hoist was and then yanked at Barrak's collar again, dragging him towards it.

Barrak saw Jasmyn first. She'd followed them in through the barn door, holding Bishop's old crossbow out in front of her. Bishop had turned away, looking to the back of the shed, but Barrak could see the steely resolve in her stance. As Bishop turned and caught sight of her, he let go of Barrak's collar and let out a low menacing growl. 'Now then, little missy, that's not a toy. Better put that down before—'

Jasmyn never spoke a word. There was a swish and a dull thud; Bishop finished his sentence with a grunted exhalation of breath. Barrak scrambled away to one side, struggling to stand, but only getting as far as his knees. A tight searing pain spread across his chest.

In the moonlight spilling through the window, Barrak could see Bishop with both hands around the shaft in his chest. He was pulling at it fitfully, trying to rid himself of what had no business sticking out of him. His teeth were clenched in an ugly snarl as he stared at Jasmyn with his hooded dark eyes. Hate and shock twisted his face as he glanced at Barrak, still struggling like a new-born colt to stand.

Bishop let go of the shaft in exasperation; it wasn't coming out. 'Ah y' damned whore!' he bellowed, then winced and coughed painfully.

His head lolled, but he was just inspecting the shaft. When he looked up again there was malice in his eyes. 'Ha! Looks like you missed everything important, like my black heart for instance, which means now you are *mine*!' His voice ramped up to a guttural roar, his teeth bared like an animal.

The blaster was at his feet and he saw it there, but ignored it.

He threw back his coat and drew the sleek three-quarter sword from its sheath with a spine-chilling zing. Once more he looked down with annoyance at the offending shaft protruding from his chest, then he flashed a ghastly smile at Jasmyn.

'We were gonna have so much fun, you and I,' Bishop pointed the tip of the long blade at her as if taking aim. He drew a ragged painful breath. 'But now I'm afraid I'm gonna have to take off that pretty little head.'

As Bishop stepped toward her, Barrak lunged, grabbing hold of his back foot. It was enough to unbalance Bishop and he fell to his knees. Barrak scrambled backwards as Bishop reared up and rounded on Barrak, bellowing like a wounded beast. Barrak felt the air disturbed above his head as he ducked the blade swishing inches above.

It took Bishop a moment to recover from the over-swing and Barrak scrambled backwards, crabbing over the ground until his hand fell on Bishop's abandoned blaster in the dirt. He hauled it around and held it up, just in time to catch the blow from Bishop's sword, a vicious vertical strike, that could have split Barrak asunder. Instead it cleaved the timber butt of Bishop's blaster and stuck there, the blade deep in the timber stock.

Bishop wrenched the blade so hard it pulled Barrak up to his feet. They were face to face with the tangle of weaponry between them. Bishop's eyes were black, his face as pale as bleached bone, his yellow teeth bared in a predator's snarl. A bizarre tug-of-war ensued until Bishop turned it into a merry-go-round, swinging Barrak around in a circle. As the barn turned past him he saw no sign of Jasmyn by the barn door. Bishop used the extra purchase to wrench at the sword again and it finally came free, sending Barrak sprawling onto his back. But he had the blaster in his hands still and it was pointing straight at Bishop. Bishop froze, realising the tables had turned.

Barrak's finger found the trigger and squeezed.

All he got was a dull click, which brought a smile to Bishop's face. He rested his sword tip on the ground and laughed. Then he returned his sword to its scabbard and chuckled some more, coughing as he slid it home. He looked down again with irritation at the shaft in his chest. 'Well, well, Barrak …' was all he said as he approached him slowly, his breath laboured and noisy.

Bishop took the weapon off him easily when Barrak swung it at him. He threw it in the dirt. Barrak reached out and took hold of the shaft in Bishop's chest and twisted it and Bishop bellowed as he brought his big fist down on Barrak's head and laid him face first in the dirt, stars and chimes ringing in his head. He pulled him up by his hair and hit him again, a disdainful, casual blow to the side of the head but with such force it spun him around and he slammed into the old farm truck. He slid down its side onto the spongy ground.

Bishop picked him up by his lapels and dragged him along the ground again, straddling Barrak's feet as they dangled in the dirt. Barrak felt his head lolling. He saw Bishop's ghastly face as though he were watching through thick glass. Part of him knew Bishop was dragging him towards one of his hook hoists; part of him didn't even care. He couldn't feel his body anymore and wondered whether he would feel the hook as it pierced him.

The only sense he had left was his vision and that seemed to be dimming. It was filled with Bishop's hellish visage.

When blood spurted from Bishop's mouth for no apparent reason, his eyes lost their zeal. His head tipped sideways as if he were pondering a puzzling issue. Barrak felt himself falling, and as he fell, he was surprised to see Jasmyn's face appear, her teeth clenched and her eyes ablaze with purpose. She held something in both hands, arms straight, as if she were striking a massive gong.

The sound of the gong must have put Barrak to sleep.

It took Barrak some time to focus. He was on his side staring at dark sandy ground. Further away was Jasmyn, sitting, staring straight ahead, but not at Barrak. Her arms were relaxed by her sides as though in meditation. It took Barrak several attempts to get himself up to a sitting position and an even more concerted effort to get unsteadily to his feet.

The constant hum of the coolroom accentuated the quiet, as did the cool white moonlight, which laid a neat, window-shaped geometry over the ground where Jasmyn sat. Beside her lay a bulky mound, clothed in black.

As Barrak limped slowly towards her, Jasmyn's eyes tracked him, but her stare remained vacant. Closer to her, Barrak could see her face was covered with a dark sheen, her hair matted and stuck in thick untidy braids to her face. He reached down, painfully, and took hold of the implement that rested on the ground beside her. He couldn't tell what it was or its purpose. At the end of a long handle was a short, thick, heavy metal spike. The grip was sticky with blood as he gently pried Jasmyn's fingers from around it. Her hand and arm were also thick with blood.

She looked up at him, the whites of her eyes in bright contrast to the dark sheen on her face. She was covered with congealed blood and small fragments of matter. Barrak lifted her by the arm and she came up easily. He cradled her under his arm, ignoring the shooting pains in his chest, and turning her away from Bishop's body.

Bishop lay face up. Barrak tried not to look. The air hung thick with the sweet foetid smell of death and a glance revealed that Bishop's face was a dark pulp and his chest a bloody, ragged mess.

He took Jasmyn out through the barn doors, retrieving the crossbow from the dirt as they went. He made her stand for a moment in the chill moonlight while he closed and bolted the barn doors.

Back inside Bishop's house, Barrak washed Jasmyn's blood-soaked clothes and laid out fresh ones, her only spares, while she showered. When she emerged she seemed to have come out of her trance somewhat, but disconcertingly she still didn't seem to know where she was.

She insisted on tending to Barrak's wounds and set about it almost light-heartedly, as though Barrak had been injured playing sport. It appeared that Bishop *had* shot him with salt, or sand or some other non-lethal substance. His chest was badly bruised and abraded, and one or two of his ribs might be cracked, but there was not much more damage. Barrak was worried about his head: he had a huge lump on one side and on the other his face and jaw were swollen. Something felt displaced and the side of his head clicked whenever he worked his jaw.

As Jasmyn tended to him he felt a hot rush of guilt as he wondered how long she had been there alone with Bishop, while he lay unconscious. He wondered if her locked mind would ever allow her to recall what she had done.

Barrak was impatient to get far away from the place as quickly as possible, but he also sensed the need to take it slowly and not cause Jasmyn to panic.

Once the first aid was complete, he packed the truck with whatever he could find that might be useful, including some dried provisions, two large water cans and four more of the flagons of yellow fluid that powered Bishop's combustion motor. He found bolts for the crossbow and checked that they were compatible.

The worst moment came when he realised he would have to retrieve the keys, which must have been in Bishop's coat.

After that they drove for hours, heading due east away from the descending moon, across a flat rocky plain lit up in radiant, silver monotone. Barrak took it slowly, even once he had the knack of driving Bishop's truck. The moonlight was enough to drive by, but he was still uncertain of the terrain. He drove on for hours without stopping, slowly and deliberately in the uncertain light, wanting to put as much distance as he could between themselves and the horrors of the night.

He only stopped when the first light of dawn began to brighten the eastern sky.

And then, once they found some high ground, affording a view out to the east, he stopped the truck to wait for the dawn to bring sufficient light to plot the route ahead.

Jasmyn seemed quiet and fragile as they stood on the stony rise and greeted the pale dawn with rare relief. Back to the west the sky was still pitch dark in contrast to the east, and Mars descending, glimmered like a chink in the night, not a degree or two off the setting moon which itself had turned a bloody red as it hung in the sky, marking the coordinates of Bishop's baleful hacienda.

Jasmyn turned and saw the ruddy disc in all its unnatural glory. It was a full lunar eclipse, which she surely must have recognised, but the eerie sight broke her open and she whispered *gods* and sank to her knees. Barrak settled down on one knee beside her and she clung to him and wept and clenched his coat in fists of anguish. She went on sobbing and railing and gripping Barrak like a cursed soul, adrift in her grief and shock, until the lurid bloody eclipse had passed and the first shard of solar fire broke over the eastern horizon.

CHAPTER 16

JASMYN WOULDN'T SLEEP IN the back of the truck and Barrak never questioned it. She would travel all day in the damn thing, but when night fell, the tent became her refuge, flimsy and inadequate as it was. Barrak understood, right from the first night, that it was her safe space.

After the morning of the blood moon they drove all through the day, carefully picking their way across the shifting landscape as it changed from desert scrub to grassy savannah, which was even flatter than the desert country they'd just traversed and sparsely populated with patches of low hopbush and scraggy acacia, with rare clusters of bush cypress and eucalypt scattered here and there. Gone were the massive craggy ranges of the Western Desert, replaced by eroded hillocks. Barrak navigated around these, keeping their overall heading due east and deviating only for the odd erosion gully.

That first night, when Jasmyn hauled the tent out of the truck and set about erecting it, Barrak helped her put it up without a word and positioned the truck right next to it for shelter. Then he gathered wood and built a nice big fire on the other side of the tent and they both slept in the flimsy thing with the crossbow loaded and laid across the opening.

Barrak got up twice and stoked the fire and they had the comfort of its orange glow through the side of the tent all through the night, until the early hours when they finally both fell into a deep sleep, waking with the first chill light of dawn, snuggled up together against the cold, like pups in their woolly swags.

'How much further I wonder,' Jasmyn ventured as they packed up their meagre camp the next morning.

'It can't be much further,' Barrak said. 'Need to keep our eyes peeled for mountains to the east. Gitan said we'd know when we saw the mountains.'

'I can't wait to get there. It's quite exciting really, isn't it Barrak?'

Barrak smiled warmly and nodded, but a cold tightness tweaked his brow and he felt troubled by Jasmyn's state of mind. She still wasn't herself. It was as if she'd not quite emerged from the catatonic state he'd found her in, that night, in Bishop's barn. She seemed to be functioning normally in every way, but part of her had gone missing.

He supposed Jasmyn had withdrawn into a protective bubble, where the dire realities of their circumstances were less obvious. He assumed the same protective shell was in place to hold back the memories of that night and he certainly had no desire to coax her out of it.

Nevertheless, Jasmyn's optimism about their prospects was a little disconcerting. On the one hand, her buoyancy did help to brighten his mood at times, but when he applied the rule of his own assessment to their plight, it did mess with his head just a little that Jasmyn was so blithe. In the end it made the responsibility for their predicament weigh more heavily on his own shoulders.

He concluded there was nothing for it but to go along with Jasmyn's enthusiasm and be grateful for it.

'Yeah, although I'd be happier if we could find that east–west trade route, so we know we're on the right track,' he said reasonably.

'Oh, I'm sure we'll come across it soon enough. It's got to be out there somewhere.'

In the end they drove for two more days, with no sign of mountains to their east. And they never came across anything that looked like a road, not even a track or set of wheel marks, nothing remotely like the so-called trade route Bishop had mentioned when he'd suggested they travel with traders.

Perhaps it had all been a lie. Or perhaps, in their panicked flight from Bishop's, they'd missed the trail altogether, if there was one – gone too far north or south. It occurred to Barrak they should perhaps travel north or south for a time now, in the hope of picking up the trail. But which one and for how long? He feared it would only waste their fuel and provisions and possibly get them even more lost.

In the end they'd agreed, with an optimism almost wholly contrived on Barrak's part, to keep heading due east, and before long they would see the great dividing range Elias had told Gitan about, the mountains that separated the desert and the plains from the eastern ocean and the city of the easterners.

The country returned to semi-arid saltbush for a while and for most of one whole morning they saw what looked like endless rolling sand dunes to their north. By midday of the next day they were crossing land again dotted with the ubiquitous bush cypress, which gave way to a scrubland populated with scraggly low gums and occasional stands of she-oaks. At one point the trees thickened up to low tangled bush and they had to backtrack to find more open ground. After that, the terrain opened up again, into a wide flat grassland, thick with high native grasses and trees scattered more sparsely on the plain but taller and more robust, no longer stunted by lack of water.

They'd taken to sharing the driving, because steering the unwieldy truck over rough terrain played havoc with Barrak's ribs. He even tried to catch up on sleep, lost during cold nights crammed in the pup tent. He'd had a lot of trouble sleeping on the hard ground. His bruised ribs made it almost impossible to find a comfortable position and his damaged jaw tended to throb and ache whenever he lay flat. So Barrak had developed a habit of sleeping only lightly and sometimes kept deliberate watch, unsure as he was of their safety in the wilderness at night.

Through the days of flat monotonous terrain, if neither was dozing, they talked a lot – and more and more their talk went to the past and they shared things they didn't already know about their hitherto mundane lives in Eyre. They talked politics and gossip and personal dramas. Barrak opened up to Jasmyn about how his wife and child's

241

death had affected him and Jasmyn told him about her dalliances with unsuitable boys and men. They talked and laughed about the awkward time long ago at the university and Jasmyn even admitted she had had a schoolgirl crush on Barrak then.

They avoided the subject of their current plight, and Bishop's name was never spoken. Barrak knew it never would be, even though his undead spectre still hovered as a malignant presence in Barrak's subconscious, feeding his increasing sense of dread and anxiety.

It was only as the afternoon shadows lengthened that the talk would turn to practical things like finding a camp site and firewood and whether there was any sign of mountains visible in the distance. Well before dusk they would find an accessible piece of high ground and pull over and hike to the crest of it to look to the east to see what they could see, and sometimes from such vantage points they would spy a likely spot to make camp.

One night they sat for some time around a fire they had built up to glow warm and smokeless, using a ready supply of old mallee roots found in a copse of trees near their camp. It was a still night and milder than any they'd had so far. The boundless black sky swarmed with a celestial conflagration like none Barrak had ever seen.

Jasmyn had made herself a seat scooped out of the dry sandy ground and was luxuriating in the warm glow of the fire as she gazed up at the stars. Barrak guessed she was still hungry, just as he was, although she would never say. Surely she knew as well as he did that their provisions were almost gone, their water even lower, and they were down to the last half flagon of the weird yellow fuel that powered the truck's banging motor. And yet she seemed relaxed and almost cheerful in the firelight. Barrak on the other hand had felt a creeping sense of despair throughout the day. The wilderness seemingly went on forever, there was so far no sign of any mountains.

'Do you see Scorpio?' Jasmyn pointed almost straight up, sighting along her outstretched arm as if taking aim. 'One degree of Scorpio,' she said, closing one eye to take better aim. 'That's our star, right there,' she said. 'Bet you didn't know that, did you Barrak?'

'You know me, I wouldn't know a constellation if it fell on me,' Barrak said gracelessly, trying, but largely failing, to match Jasmyn's uncanny buoyancy.

'I know, but that's our point of synastry, yours and mine, in Scorpio.'

Barrak grunted, watching Jasmyn's soft features in the firelight. There was no doubt about the state of protective denial she had carried with her from the dreadful night at Bishop's. He saw more clearly than ever how it helped her manage her reality and he concluded it was a blessing. He also realised with a tiny mental jolt that he was envious.

Jasmyn went on. 'It's the degree at which *your* destiny point coincides with Neptune and Jupiter, and *my* Moon sits right over the top of it, same degree, precisely. It's remarkable.' Jasmyn sat up a bit straighter and looked at Barrak with a mischievous expression. 'That's what I saw when I snuck a look at your chart, back when I was first studying. When I was a kid, you know, with that crush … and of course seeing that only made it worse,' she giggled and slid back down into her hollow with a sheepish grin. 'But I think I get it now. Neptune demands we have faith; Jupiter, the guardian angel, expands the boundaries of our consciousness, and they both sit on your north node, which is your destiny point … don't you see?'

Barrak tried to see but his mood of gloomy pragmatism didn't really lend itself to celestial flights of fancy and his head was throbbing, as it tended to at night, although, as usual, it brightened him up quite a bit to listen to Jasmyn's animated discourse.

'And my moon, my security, my trust, is connected to you at that point, so I don't really have any choice but to have faith, do I?' There was a disarming sweetness in Jasmyn's tone and her eyes were soft and dark, yet bright in the firelight.

'I don't want you feeling all responsible or anything, y'know – no one planned this,' she went on, addressing herself to the heavens, her hands clasped behind her head. 'Maybe we really do just need to have some faith. Maybe there is some higher purpose to all this. Maybe, just maybe Barrak, we're exactly where we're supposed to be.' Jasmyn turned around in her sandy hollow and looked at Barrak across the coals.

'You mean lost in the middle of nowhere? Out of supplies? Gone too far to turn back and no idea where we're going?' Even as he spoke, Barrak felt a pang of remorse for his gloomy summation, in light of Jasmyn's optimism. But nothing seemed to faze her.

'So,' she said in response, 'we don't have much choice do we? If this is what destiny has planned for us, if this is the end, there's nothing much we can do about it now. Besides it's always darkest before the dawn,' she pronounced as she rolled back and turned her face to the star-smudged sky.

Later that night as they settled into their swags, with the fire freshly stoked and crackling outside, Jasmyn rolled over and kissed Barrak on the cheek, the sweetest, warmest, most comforting kiss Barrak could imagine, and then in no time she was snoring gently while Barrak lay wake, as was his wont, alert to the night noises outside and to his own demons inside. It sometimes seemed he drew solace and repose from watching over her as she slept, hearing her steady breathing. Sometimes her father Enoch's worried eyes would drift before him and his words too, beseeching Barrak, *Whatever happens, you'll always look after her won't you?* It was Barrak's penance and his responsibility. If watching through the night was all he could do to keep her safe, then that was what he'd damn well do. He stoked the fire twice more, and gauged the progress of the night by the plunging stars, before sleep finally took him in the chill small hours.

In the morning, before the sun was up, Barrak set out for a nearby ridge to take a bearing for the coming day's travel, leaving Jasmyn to make a fire and see what could be done about breakfast. The top of the rise opened up a vista that was all too familiar, an arid rocky plain stretched out red in the first orange blush of dawn, peppered with saltbush and acacia scrub but not much else. Every time they thought they had left the desert behind, they seemed to come upon it again. The middle distance looked more hopeful with a swathe of grassland, and further south were darker patches of what looked like forested hills. In the far distance was a line of black ranges, which held some promise.

To the east, a stone blue moon with a bright balsamic rim hung above the distant hills, in a sky still indigo and barely washed with colour, and there was Jupiter too, brash and bright, vying with the brilliant moon to see away the last of the night.

Before he turned back to camp, something caught his eye on the flats, just below his lookout. As he stared, it intrigued him all the more, because he couldn't identify it. It was a square thing standing up on the ground – not a tree stump or rock, its shape was too regular for that. The first creeping rays of dawn caught it and flung a dark ribbon of shadow from it, out across the pebbled flats.

He started down the far side of the hill and quickly came upon the thing standing like a monument in the middle of a wide flat area of rocky ground. It was pure white, but pink in the new light. It stood the full height of a man and more, coming straight up out of the dirt, about four feet square and standing on a wider plinth with sculpted columns in each corner and overhanging capping like a solid stone roof. Atop that was a smaller square block of white stone.

He walked around it slowly and examined the alien thing in the dawn light. It looked brand new, but when he finally reached out and touched it he could feel that it was pitted and worn with age.

Marble. Carved from solid marble and curiously ornate.

His toe hit something in the ground and he stumbled. Lying half submerged in the glowing red dirt was a man, a marble man, lying on his back.

Barrak got down on both knees and examined the stone figure. The first thing he noticed was that the man had been carved with eyes downcast. He brushed away some sand to get a better look at him. The sculptor's art had captured sadness in his down-turned eyes, and he looked forlorn. He wore some kind of uniform, with a curious hat with one side turned up, suggesting a jaunty sense of irreverence, in contrast to his melancholy expression. The stone man held a weapon in his hands, one that looked for all the world like Bishop's blaster. But it wasn't held, rather the barrel was pointed at his feet and his hands were clasped on top of the upturned butt of

245

the thing, as though the stone warrior had vowed to use it no more.

Barrak looked from the figure in the dirt up to the pedestal and saw now that he had fallen from his place atop the monument.

This thing was built to last. But why here?

He looked around him and as he did he saw that the rocky landscape had a pattern to it. Lines of rocks protruding only inches from the ground seemed to line up in geometric patterns of parallel lines radiating to four corners from where he stood. If he hadn't been standing in the middle of a barren desert Barrak could easily have imagined the lines of rocks marked out roads that intersected just where the marble man had stood, looking at his boots, guarding a vanished crossroad in the vast emptiness.

As Barrak returned to camp he found Jasmyn had contrived a pot of tea from the fragrant leaves of a tree the drovers had shown them and a porridge of millet and oats, which was pretty much all they had left in the way of food. She asked what had taken him so long but Barrak found he had no answer that would adequately explain the strange stone monument.

As he'd trudged back up the hill to the camp, he turned the image of the lone sentry in the middle of nowhere over and over in his mind and the inexplicable nature of it left him feeling uneasy and, if anything, even more lost and confused than he had felt before, and frightened by the vastness of the wilderness. He thought he would show the statue to Jasmyn, but in the end there seemed little point and all he told her about was the promise of some hilly-looking country away to the east.

Tidak pulled the arrow back slowly, steadily, breathing into the tension building in his back. He felt the stiff feathers against his cheek as he sighted his prey along the shaft of one of his own handmade arrows, just the way he'd done a hundred times before. The muscles of his forearm and shoulder sang with pain and strain as he bent his Kahzit bow just a little more, breathing gently but deeply into his core and projecting his *hunters mind* onto his prey, willing it calm and simultaneously asking the Great Spirit for permission to take its life.

He felt the gaze of his father, Kajha, upon him like the warm sun in spring, quiet and all but invisible in the thicket behind him. He could *feel* Kajha's expectations and hopes, his own *parent mind* combining with his son's, helping him to succeed.

Tidak added another prayer to the Great Spirit: *Please don't let me miss.* He exhaled gently, slowly, and felt a great calm come over him, steadying his bow arm, and then, all at once, as if by some wizardry, his arrow was in flight, the shaft having loosed itself from his soft grip, as if it had its own *hunter's mind*. It flew flat and straight and Tidak held his breath and watched for a small eternity as it pieced the air, rotating slightly and speeding unerringly, sickeningly, towards its target. He winced as the arrow sliced into the flesh of the young doarht. At the very last instant his quarry had reared, causing the arrow to strike it low in the front flank. If it hadn't moved, Tidak was sure it would have been a perfect, clean throat shot.

The quiet of the bush was shattered.

A shock of birds exploded from the surrounding trees and the young buck bellowed, wild-eyed, kicking at the air. It hit the ground and collapsed onto its knees with a grunt, all thrashing legs and dust as it struggled back to its feet. It seemed to feint one way as if testing its footing, almost falling again, before finding its strength and bounding away into the scrubby forest.

Kajha was already at his son's side, having broken cover, and together the two hunters lunged into the clearing.

'Great skill, Tidak,' Kajha said as he scanned the ground, wordlessly marking the spot where the buck had fallen, the disturbed sand, a smear of blood on a leaf, erratic tracks and a snapped twig where the animal had burst out of the small clearing and away. But he stood back and let his son gather the signs, watching him proudly, pleased that he had missed nothing.

'This way, Father,' Tidak said. 'He has my arrow in him and is sorely wounded but I fear he may run for a day or more before his spirit leaves him.'

Kajha saw his son's brow was furrowed with concern for the

wounded animal. But he was pleased to see that Tidak held his back straight and his hunter's eye was still sharp and clear. He guessed Tidak was worried that his shot had not been clean and felt the weight of the doarht's suffering upon him.

'Your arrow was true, Tidak,' Kajha said evenly. 'The doarht's suffering was written in the sky long before we came upon him. The way it jumped up, at the last instant, that was deemha.'

Tidak nodded solemnly to his father, inwardly feeling a warm glow at his approving words. 'We must hurry,' he urged. Young Tidak, tall and slender in his fourteenth year, his dark skin glistening with a sheen of sweat, led the way out of the clearing and into the low scrub beyond.

Tidak used every bit of his bushcraft as he led the chase, taking care to tread softly on the ground and leave no trace of his passing. This was instinctive, an integral part of his upbringing. He read all the signs left by their quarry. Some were obvious, a drop of blood, a broken twig or a tuft of fur snagged on bark … these he barely acknowledged at all. It was the lesser signs, a slightly bent blade of grass or a small pebble dislodged in the sand, these signs Tidak pointed to, murmuring quietly as he passed, to make sure Kajha knew he had seen them all.

While focusing his attention on the hunt, Tidak also kept his danger eye open around him and constantly sniffed the wind and occasionally stopped to listen intently to the sounds of the bush before proceeding. He knew Kajha was doing the same, perhaps even more so. Every Dzahn hunter knew how easy it was for the hunter to become the prey.

They went on like this for some time, through the midday heat and into the afternoon, until the sun hung low in the west. They had tracked the wounded beast through the low scrubby bushland into a forest of stunted bush cypress, struggling to grow in the arid half-desert, and then on across a wide grassy plain where the cypress became fewer and fewer until there were none at all. After a time the grassland dipped into a shallow ravine, and when they reached the bottom they found pools of water there from the last rain and the welcome shade of a few great spreading river gums along its edge.

They tracked along the river bed until the trail took off up the opposite side of the ravine. The doarht's signs indicated the animal was very weak and would not get much further.

The light was failing.

When Kajha gave his son a querying look, raising one eyebrow slightly, Tidak declared: 'We should make safe here for the night. I think the creature will drop soon and go no further. With luck we will end its misery before the sun is up.'

That night, as Tidak lay trying to sleep, his mind was busy with the excitement of the hunt. There was some fear, too; the sounds of the night creatures seemed so much louder and closer in the wilderness, far from the comfort and security of the village. Suspended between the low boughs of one of the river gums he could feel Kajha nestled against him in his night harness, and for once, his snoring was more a comfort than an annoyance as he lay awake with images of their great adventure racing through his mind. For this was Tidak's om-sahdu – no ordinary hunting trip but a week-long odyssey in which father and son travel far into the wild areas beyond the customary hunting grounds in search of the man-boy's spirit sign, or Wasu, which would mark his crossing into manhood as a fully-fledged hunter. It was a time of great challenge and excitement, as the boy must lead the expedition and choose the way as well as display his hunting and tracking skills to provide food for the pair. The father must only give counsel if asked and act only if there is great or unexpected danger.

As Tidak lay awake, listening to the howling night creatures and to Kajha snoring beside him, he wondered what form his Wasu would take. He had heard many stories, of dramatic confrontations with lepoyds or pachyds, or in one case, the story of a great river fish jumping from the water practically into the hands of a young om-sahdu. He knew that usually the Wasu was much more subtle, and father and son must keep their spirit eye clear in order to see the sign when it came. Tidak couldn't help hoping for something that would make a big story, a story that would be told around the fires for many moons to come.

It was barely midday when Barrak and Jasmyn came to the river. They had travelled for several hours over a wide grassy plain, hemmed in by hills to the north and south and skirting sometimes quite dense groves of eucalyptus. Through the morning, the distant hills had inched up on them and shifted to the north-east. A few times they had seen wild animals grazing in the distance, but they were unlike anything they'd ever seen in Eyre and they'd fled at the sound of the truck before they got a close look at them.

For the first time they had started to experience real trouble getting the truck over soft ground, and twice they had been bogged. Both times, by sheer luck, they had been within reach of a large enough tree to use the winch to pull themselves out.

But this was different, this was more than just another small creek or erosion gully, this was a flowing river and possibly quite deep. In some ways it was to be expected, because now there were mountains not only away to the north-east, but also smaller forest-clad hills not far away to their south.

It seemed they had finally left the desert behind them.

They turned north and followed the river until the terrain started to steepen and they approached some wooded foothills where the ground was rocky and uneven and they had to navigate through and around copses of trees and shrubs. Eventually they came to a wide flat stretch of stony rapids where the water was shallow and Barrak calculated they could get the truck across.

They made it across the river easily and up onto the opposite bank, only to career straight into a sand bank where the truck immediately sank to its axles, settling there with a groan and a shudder, as though it knew it had found its final resting place.

This time there was no anchor close enough for the winch and although Barrak made a half-hearted attempt to dig the thing out of the sand, his spirit was never really in it and it painfully aggravated his bruised ribs. In any case, they had no more fuel. The last flagon had been emptied into the beast a few hours before; the truck had been living on borrowed time anyway.

They unloaded their possessions and set up the tent on some flat ground alongside a red gum, not far from the rapids. Jasmyn tasted the water and it was good and sweet. Just downstream from the rapids there was a deeper pool, almost waist deep, which would be perfect for washing.

By late in the afternoon they had established a good fire of coals and a large dry bough, which could be gradually fed onto it, was blazing away and drying Jasmyn's clothes hung all around it on sticks. The camp already felt established and Jasmyn was warming herself by the fire, wearing Barrak's big lamb's-wool coat when Barrak came back from a patrol around the area.

He had walked up through the long grass to the ridge line half a mile away and beyond that he'd seen the land slope gently away into a wide flat valley of grass and mixed forest. Looping back to the north, he followed the river up to where wedges of trees hugged the gullies and the foothills became steep in their ascent toward the nearby ranges. Crouched low in the long grass he'd spied some rylabies grazing in amongst the trees and he'd stayed low and still like a hunter and watched them for a time.

'I think I could shoot one with the crossbow, if I can get close enough,' he confided to Jasmyn back at the camp, as she dried her hair by the fire.

'You should try,' she encouraged, looking sideways at him from under a curtain of hair.

Barrak spent the rest of the evening fussing over the crossbow and familiarising himself with all its workings, and by dusk he had inscribed a target on a nearby eucalypt and set himself at an appropriate distance to practise his shooting. By the time he returned to camp it was getting dark and he was annoyed that he had lost one of his three bolts in the long grass.

That night, the absence of a meal was a topic neither mentioned and Jasmyn seemed to be compensating with various attempts to domesticate their camp: logs for seats and a sheet hung from the truck for shade, slung up between branches of the red gum, and a clothesline for drying. Barrak had taken the shovel from the truck

251

and dug a toilet in amongst some bushes downstream from the camp and well away from the river, and collected an oversupply of firewood. It was as if they were setting up a permanent camp. They shared the unspoken fear of leaving the security of a water supply and the truck, albeit now useless for transport.

There dilemma was clear, stay with some semblance of security, or strike out on foot into the unknown.

Their conversation was subdued and intermittent that night around the fire and each lapsed into periods of reflection, staring at the fire and keeping their thoughts to themselves. The last thing Jasmyn said before they slept that night was to ask Barrak if he really thought he could shoot some game with the crossbow.

'I think so,' was all he could say. 'I'll find that other bolt in the morning.' As usual Barrak didn't sleep much, in fact even less than usual, due to pangs of hunger and the disturbingly loud noises of the night creatures. He envied Jasmyn her ability to sleep through it all, but in the early hours even she was awake to the terrifying roaring of some creature of the night, whose frightful yowling was unfamiliar and seemed alarmingly close to their camp.

By first light, Barrak would have sworn he hadn't slept at all, consumed through his long night watch by images of flighty rylabies and his obsessive stalking of them, crossbow in hand, with his imagined quarry always just out of range or darting away before he could shoot. Sometimes the half-formed dream creatures would morph into Bishop, malignant and menacing, in the sights of his hunting bow.

The hunters found their wounded prey just before sunrise. It was nestled in a hollow near the top of the slope on the opposite side of the ravine. It was shivering and barely breathing when Tidak found it and he felt a great wave of compassion and sorrow for the creature, realising it was just a youngster like himself. Tears ran down his face as he thanked the Great Spirit and apologised to the doarht for his own poor marksmanship, causing it so much unnecessary suffering.

He cut the doarht's throat quickly with his hunting knife.

Tidak crouched with his prey while its spirit slipped away and it was only then he noticed Kajha was not beside him, but had continued up the slope to the top of the ravine. Something about Kajha's stance alerted Tidak right away – something was not right. He watched Kajha crouch down slowly as if stalking prey and reach for his spear and bow while staring intently at something beyond the top of the ridge.

Tidak eased himself quietly up to join his father and peered over the top of the escarpment. Nothing could have prepared him for what he saw there and he let out a gasp before ducking back below the ridge line and sitting down heavily in the rocky sand where he remained frozen for a few moments before looking up questioningly at Kajha. Kajha remained completely still but for a reassuring hand, which beckoned him back up to his side. Tidak held his breath for his second glimpse over the ridge, but still couldn't make sense of it. It hurt his head to look, because what he saw just didn't seem to fit.

The top of the ridge opened up a view along a rocky saddle to a slightly higher peak, almost within arrow range of where they stood.

On top of the nearby peak was something that looked like a tree, but it was nothing like any tree Tidak had ever seen. Its trunk was smooth and straight, straighter even than a spear, and it was huge. The tree-thing had what looked like branches, branches which came out a short way and then curved and went straight up. The branches turned into broad flat things that looked like shields, but bigger than any shield, and so straight and flat.

Strangest of all, the branches were exactly the same, and it was something about this sameness that disturbed Tidak's mind: nothing grew like that, so straight and true.

Further up the trunk were things that might have been flowers, but clearly weren't. They were shaped like giant shells, except they were perfectly round and also huge. There were four shells and they seemed to be opened in all different directions, pointing towards the four winds.

Tidak closed his eyes and opened them again, but the tree was still there. The more he looked at it the more his head hurt. As he tried to figure it out, he realised that if the thing hadn't grown there, it must have been made, like a spear or a ceremony pole.

Suddenly another thought occurred to Tidak and he ducked back down, landing on his backside in the sand again. *What or who would make such a huge ceremony pole. and put it in such a place?* The thought filled him with a sickening fear and he began to tremble. Seeing his distress, Kajha slowly lowered himself down below the ridge line and gave Tidak a reassuring squeeze on the shoulder, but the worried look on Kajha's face gave him little comfort.

'What is it?' Tidak asked quietly, tremulously.

Kajha's weather-beaten old face shifted into a solemn, sad look of concern, which only made Tidak more frightened. Suddenly another thought popped into Tidak's mind.

'Is *this* my Wasu?' he asked quietly.

Kajha's eyes widened and the sadness suddenly seemed to mix with anger and even a flash of fear, or something. It made Tidak even more uneasy.

'No. Certainly not!' Kajha said, shaking his head solemnly. 'No. No. This is something else.'

'But what, Kajha?' Tidak implored. 'What is it then?'

Kajha stared right past Tidak as if looking at something in the distance. Tidak didn't like the look on his father's face; it was not like him.

'Yar-wu-bahn,' Kajha barely breathed the word, as if it were an incantation.

Tidak didn't really know what the word meant, although he had certainly heard it spoken a few times before, usually in the same sort of breathless whisper. Sometimes, late at night when all the younger ones were in bed and the old men told their fire stories, some of them would use this word, and always the word was spoken with eyes wide in mock awe and fear. He had heard it whispered amongst the children sometimes, too, as they tried to scare each other with their own versions of the fire stories.

But he had never really taken the idea seriously, and besides, he didn't really understand exactly what the word meant. As close as Tidak could work out, it meant, *from the time before this.*

As usual, Barrak couldn't say when he woke; the vague wash of light across the inside of the tent at some point became bright enough to turn his intention from trying to sleep to meeting the day. Some mornings at this point he would adjust his position enough to ease the aching in his chest and relax enough to fall into a blissful scrap of sound sleep, until the sun itself illuminated the tent, bright and hot, but not this morning. This day was full of intent, and an early start was warranted.

A pool of mist hung over the river bend below their camp where the water ran deep and the grassy plain beyond was heavy with dew. Barrak left Jasmyn to doze in the tent and put on his jacket against the cold and gathered up his crossbow and the two remaining bolts. The morning was still and quiet, but for the high-pitched chirping of bushlarks and silvereyes foraging amongst the yam daisies and spurge along the river bank. A lone kingfisher studied him from its post on a low branch slung over the creek.

Before the sun broke over the low eastern hills he was on his way, pausing by his improvised target from the previous evening to search the long grass for the lost bolt, which was easy enough to locate in the brightening dawn light. He set off north-east through the long grass, which quickly soaked his pants and boots with dew, moving quietly and keeping low, straightening up occasionally to peer over the top of the nodding seed heads to get his bearings. After a time, he came upon what looked to be a game trail, where the grass was disturbed and partially flattened. He followed it away from the river for some time until it seemed to peter out into a kind of clearing surrounded by a ring of eucalypt and acacia on one side and rising ground and thicker trees beyond that.

Barrak sank slowly to his haunches and held his breath.

Rylabies. Dozens of them, grazing the short new grass along the edge of the trees. One of the group nearest Barrak raised its head and sniffed the air, its erect ears twitching as it chewed, before returning

255

its attention to the grass. Barrak edged forward and reached slowly for the old crossbow. It was only then that he realised he should have had the thing loaded and cocked already and he cursed himself for not thinking through his preparations.

He froze as the nearest animal straightened its long back almost like a person would. It seemed to look straight at Barrak. Its small pointy head pivoted left and right and then it leaned forward, balancing itself on spindly forelegs and loping slowly forward, drawing its long flat hind legs up under it before settling again on a new patch of grass. Barrak edged forward. Rylabies were good game and excellent meat, Barrak knew, but notoriously skittish and hard to catch.

Without warning or reason, a hue and cry of squawking cockatoos rose like a dotty white cloud from a towering eucalypt on the edge of the clearing. The delicate heads of the grazing animals rose up as one, swivelling in unison towards the tree. In a moment the whole troop was bounding away across the clearing in the opposite direction, and in a heartbeat or two the whole lot of them were lost to the long grass and scrubby bush of the flats, leaving Barrak crestfallen and eyeing the scrub at the base of the big tree suspiciously, wondering what the hell had spooked his prey.

Barrak returned to camp empty-handed, but for the rusty old crossbow, and by the time he got there he had brooded himself into a mood of livid disappointment. He flung the crossbow into the sandy dirt near the fire in disgust and it bounced up and banged against one of the large branches Jasmyn had across the fire, supporting the billy of tea she had heating. The steaming canister nearly toppled and some water lapped out, making the fire hiss and smoke.

Jasmyn shot a scowl at him.

'Blast!' He spat out the expletive and speared one of the crossbow bolts into the ground beside the fire. 'There's no damn way I'll ever get close enough to shoot one of those things. Too bloody skittish. Gods be damned!' He flung the remaining bolts at the red gum near the tent and they clattered to the ground.

'We've got no chance of actually killing something we can eat. I dunno what the hell I'm doing! We're buggered. Damn it, by Orlan's bloody spirit!' Barrak shouted at the skies and kicked a cloud of dusty sand up, some of which blew back over the fire and Jasmyn's tea. This too earned a yelp of annoyance.

Barrak dropped down into the sand by the fire and put his head between his knees. His hands went over the top of his head.

'We'll be all right, Barrak,' Jasmyn ventured tentatively. She was shocked by Barrak's tirade and also worried about him. She didn't think she'd ever heard him curse so much.

'We can try again, we'll get something. I found some berries down by the creek. They might be edible and we've got water. We'll be OK.'

'No! We won't!' Barrak swiped his hands down and slapped the ground on either side of him. 'We won't be OK. We'll be dead. We're going to starve, because we have no damn food, and no means of catching any food!' He felt close to tears, which surprised him a bit. He was even more surprised because he felt neither embarrassment nor shame at his outburst or his suddenly fraught emotional state. Nothing seemed to matter anymore. It occurred to him just how exhausted he was from lack of food and sleep, and his head was pounding.

He felt Jasmyn's leg brush against his back and then her hands were on his shoulders, massaging the tight muscles. Her touch calmed him right away and he let her knead the knotty cramps away. He was heartened and soothed by the simple, pragmatic and oddly reassuring words she came up with next. 'Well, you could be right. But I think no one learned to hunt in a day.' Her tone was matter-of-fact and comforting. 'We'll keep trying. I think maybe I'll come with you next time ... isn't that what you do? Hunt as a pair ... I make some noise and scare them towards you ... that's what hunters do, isn't it?'

Kajha helped Tidak to skin the doarht and then watched while his son sliced along its belly and removed the innards. They paused for a while and sat around the carcass gorging themselves on the still-warm liver – this would help them to gain the strength they'd need to carry the meat back to the village. They both knew what it meant to make a kill like this, so far from the village. Meat could not be wasted. The kill meant it was now time to start the journey home. It would be an arduous one, they were further than Tidak had ever been, and although the beast he had shot was young, it was still almost fully grown, and they must hurry to get the meat back before it spoiled.

They had dragged the beast down the slope to the edge of the creek to do the butchering. As they crouched in the sand, Tidak was filled with an unfamiliar swirl of feelings, which seemed to be doing battle in his chest. On the one hand he was still unsettled and feeling afraid of the tree-thing they'd seen just over the nearby ridge; he was anxious that they be on their way. It was the first thing that had really scared him on their trip, and now he had a surge of longing for the comforts and safety of home. He thought about his mother, as he slurped down the dripping meat.

But on the other hand he was starting to feel a bit annoyed and disappointed, knowing that his om-sahdu would soon be over. It appeared that the best he could do for his spirit sign was this doarht. In truth, he knew most young hunters would be more than satisfied with a doarht. But Tidak was known to be a skilled hunter amongst the youths of the village. Already he had three kills to his name, the first one almost two years ago. He had had such great expectations for his spirit sign, his imaginings had run wild with all the famous fire stories of great and unexpected Wasus.

He would keep his eyes sharp on the return journey. It was not over yet; it would take them at least two more days and nights to return to the village.

Man and boy looked up at each other and laughed to see the doarht's blood slathered all over their faces and arms. Feeling quite sick from the richness of all that meat, Tidak washed himself off in the creek, scrubbing his hands in the coarse sand, and then set himself to the task of cutting up the carcass. He managed most of it and only needed Kajha to help him twist and cut free the hindquarters. They laid the meat out on a bed of bracken to keep it free of dirt and then wrapped it up using the animal's hide, Each helped the other to secure the load using their sleeping sling straps and ties, so the heavy burdens could be carried squarely on their backs. Tidak had the forequarters and the loins and Kajha had sliced through the ankle of one of the hind legs to make a hole and threaded the hoof of the other leg through, so the hindquarters could be carried slung across his back.

They started up the steep embankment of the creek and by the time they reached the top, Tidak's load seemed to have doubled in weight and he was starting to doubt his ability to carry it all the way back. But as they struck out across the plain, Kajha set an easy pace, which was barely even a trot, and the going became easier.

CHAPTER 17

BY LATE MORNING THE day was already hot and a dry north-westerly wind had sprung up and burned away the last of the dampness from the earth. Barrak crouched low and listened to the wind whispering in the long grass all around him as he checked his crossbow and fingered the two spare bolts in his belt. They had walked a good hour from their camp.

He peered over the top of the grass and saw that the rylabies were still oblivious to his presence downwind of them, grazing languidly on the grass amongst a grove of eucalypts. Some lay prone, relaxing like lords in the shade.

He looked away to his left but there was no sign of Jasmyn. The plan had been for her to circle around to the other side of the trees through the long grass, and once she was opposite Barrak, to make some kind of commotion and drive the rylabies towards him. But the grass had swallowed her and all he could see now was a lone hawk quivering and bobbing on the rising thermals, high above where he'd sighted her last.

How would he know when she was in position? Would the animals smell her as soon as she was upwind of them? Barrak didn't want to miss another chance.

Crouched low, he began to inch forward, threading himself like a needle between the stalks of grass. Nearer the trees where the animals were grazing, maybe fifty yards further on, the tall grass abruptly thinned out. He held the crossbow to his chest and parted the stalks with his left hand, moving slowly and deliberately, scarcely breathing.

So focused was he on his own stealth, it took him some time to realise he was not alone; something else was moving through the grass next to him, in parallel.

He caught a glimpse of it where the grass thinned out into a game trail, the dusty brown haunches plainly visible for a moment. As it moved into a thinner patch and its form became clearer, the long straight back was almost as high as Barrak in a crouch.

The muscles at its shoulder rippled as its legs pumped silently, its immense feet padding through the grass with barely a sound, almost as though the great beast were weightless. Just before it dissolved back into the grass he caught a glimpse of its massive head and jowls, blunt nose pointed ahead intently, ears pinned back … then it was gone, its ragged haunches disappearing in the grass without a crease and the long tasselled tail sweeping low behind.

It had paid him no heed at all; the great, prowling predator knew its craft better than Barrak and was entirely focused on the hunt.

At first he was frozen in shock and fright, a lump pounding in his throat. An eddy of warm air wafted the smell of the thing into his nostrils, a rank musky odour like a mix of carrion and game, which sparked a primordial reflex in him. He was hard pressed to curb the panic that rose up in him like hot bile. Somehow he contained himself and turned slowly and set a course through the grass square to the lion's track, carefully at first then faster, until he was bashing through the grass without restraint, tight fear rising in his throat.

He stopped to get his bearings, but to no avail, he was adrift in a sea of grass with no means of navigation. He struck out blindly again through the grass, oblivious now to the commotion he was making, going in what he thought was the direction taken by Jasmyn.

He must find her, warn her. He went to call out but then thought better of it.

A cold sweat chilled him and his breathing was ragged. Suddenly he was on open ground, a stand of black box to his left, tall coolibahs opposite. He ran into the clearing and stopped, bent over with hands on knees to catch his breath.

The still morning was shattered by a sound that prickled Barrak's skin and quivered his bowels. It rent the air and filled the clearing like a solid, brutal presence. Barrak glimpsed the great maned beast rising to its feet in the shadow of a coolibah on the far side of the clearing, a male, lounging in the shade, waiting for the female to make the kill. It glared at Barrak with regal offence and roared again, louder this time, incredulous at the sight of Barrak, and baring its great yellow canines in a yawning gape.

Barrak didn't know he'd dropped the crossbow or even that he had turned away, somehow he was just running, but it didn't feeling like running, it felt like flying; his legs were like springs, barely touching the ground and yet propelling him with impossible force. He was making for the trees. A calm, still part of his mind told him he would never make it and if he did, would not have time to climb up anyway – but he ran all the harder, his head held high and mouth agape like a sprinter's. He wondered what it would feel like to be eaten, and if he would be conscious while it happened.

As he closed the gap to the trees he began to hallucinate. He saw a tall, dark-skinned boy standing at the foot of one of them. Every detail of the crazed vision was crystal clear to him as he ran headlong towards the apparition: the sheen of sweat on the boy's smooth skin, the braids in his long hair, the fine detail of his animal-skin skirt and decorated vest, even the long spear complete with feathers and tassels, which the boy held with steely resolve in both hands. To Barrak, it seemed like a good idea to run straight towards the apparition; perhaps it was a portal to some other dimension where he would not be eaten.

The boy paid Barrak no attention at all as he flashed past, which, in a way, confirmed to Barrak that he was a phantom of sorts. Instead he lunged past Barrak and raised his spear, his eyes alight with zeal and avid determination.

Barrak slammed into a tree and leapt for a branch. He heard the beast bellow again but in a different way, it sounded wrong, curtailed in mid-roar, then there was a human scream, high-pitched, but forceful and strong, like a battle cry. There was a thud and a scuffle. He stopped scrabbling for the low branches and turned around slowly, strangely calm now in the face of his imminent death.

The scene before him was hard to fathom. The prone beast lay with its front legs splayed out, its massive paws held out towards Barrak as if inviting an embrace. Its colossal jaws were working up and down as if chewing the air, and a rhythmic grunting, like a low, strangled growl, was issuing from the beast's cavernous innards with every breath. It was flat on its belly and yet turned slightly to the side. Its haunches were raised up, with one of its hind legs moving rhythmically, kicking up dust, as though it were still trying to run, but with only a single working limb.

Stranger still, as Barrak took a tentative step towards the felled giant, were the two human legs writhing frantically, as though birthing themselves from the soft furry underbelly. Only then did he notice the shaft and tip of a spear protruding from the animal's side, bloodied and glistening in the bright noon sun.

Suddenly Barrak was pitched forward onto his knees. He'd been pushed. The sad and angry eye of the lion glared at him with glassy contempt as it chewed out another throaty protest. Then there was a new figure, dark and semi-naked, like the apparition he had seen before, standing up tall and straight on tip toes beside the lion, back arched and with a long spear raised up … before plunging it down into the wounded beast once, twice and then a third time.

'Tidak!' The man screamed and cast aside his spear. He seemed smaller to Barrak without the spear, and older, sinewy, even a bit frail as he bent and took hold of the ankles of the trapped youth. He pulled to no effect and as he did he turned to Barrak, his eyes desperate with panic and urgency. Finally regaining his composure, Barrak rushed in beside the old man and threw his weight against the belly of the beast and tried to roll him as the man hauled at the boy's legs, but the animal was too heavy. Then they both threw their weight against the brute and it groaned and gurgled out a final protest. It was enough, and finally the boy wriggled free, coming up like a lost diver gasping for breath and brushing dirt and sand from his sweaty, blood-smudged face.

The three eyed each other, standing in a rough circle, each studying the other and unsure of what they were seeing, almost oblivious to the great fallen beast at their feet. The man was torn between relief at seeing the boy safe and fear and suspicion of the tall light-haired stranger. The boy's eyes darted from Barrak to his father and back to Barrak. He was clearly wary of Barrak, too, but his eyes were bright and sparkling, as though he were about to burst into laughter or scream in terror. Barrak summed them both up, guessing they were father and son – real, not phantoms – wilderness dwellers like the ones he'd heard about.

This was the scene that greeted Jasmyn as she stepped hesitantly out of the long grass into the clearing. She approached the group quietly and it took a few moments before anyone noticed her. When she caught Barrak's eye the look on her face was an exquisite mixture of shock and baffled amusement. Tidak met Jasmyn's stare with one of equal astonishment and wonder. She floated past Barrak and made directly for the older man but then paused and stared aghast at the fallen beast.

The boy's father took a couple of steps away from her and Jasmyn looked at him and smiled uncertainly. Then she came forward and stretched her hand out towards him. He looked blankly at Jasmyn's hand. She smiled and inched forward, then reached out and took his hand. He gave a start and tried to take it back from her, but then relented, looking down at their joined hands in puzzlement as Jasmyn shook his hand gently up and down.

Once he got the idea he joined in and pumped Jasmyn's hand enthusiastically, then he returned her smile and broke into a laugh. Pumping her hand even harder, he looked around at the boy and Barrak and gave them a broad, gap-toothed grin.

The boy was smiling at his father too, but when Jasmyn caught his eye, his grin fell away and he dropped his eyes to the ground and examined the footprints in the sand and his own hands went behind his back and he inched around a bit to put Barrak between himself and Jasmyn.

This was his Wasu!

It was almost too much for the boy. He had killed a lion! This was the greatest hunting feat that even the most skilled warrior could hope for, the kind of spirit sign a young om-sahda could only dream of. Maybe he had wished too hard for a special Wasu.

It had happened so quickly.

He was just walking through the bush and suddenly a crazy man and a lion were charging towards him. He hadn't had time to think at all, if he had, he would have climbed a tree and waited for the lion to eat the man.

So fast.

The lion was already pouncing and he had jammed the end of his spear into the ground and let the lion come onto it, just the way he had been taught to, if attacked. Then he had been trapped under the lion! Somehow in the process he had saved the life of a Hakeah. Surely this was the most remarkable Wasu ever. And now here was a Hakeah woman too, like a crazy, beautiful goddess, possibly come from the White Sea itself, and when she looked at Tidak it made him wobbly at the knees and put dragonflies in his stomach and his face felt like it was burning.

Tidak was overwhelmed. He hoped he had not offended the Great Spirit by wishing for too much.

That night Barrak built the fire up to prodigious proportions to ward off wild animals, now that he knew the source of the frightening night noises and the reality of the threat. He kept adding branches to it until Jasmyn bade him stop, because it was already a veritable bonfire, lighting the whole camp with a fierce glow and intermittently launching swarms of red embers that were sucked away into the night by a stiff breeze, swirling and racing over the dark plain and, thankfully, extinguishing themselves in flight before descending into the long grass.

The curious foursome had positioned themselves on the windward side of the fire, Barrak and Kajha together, with Jasmyn and Tidak like wallflowers on either side. Each time Barrak tried to engage

Kajha in some kind of conversation, Tidak's eyes would wander or he would pick at his feet or poke at the fire or look up at the stars, anything to avoid Jasmyn's gaze. That she made the young man so nervous charmed Jasmyn, but she wanted to find some way to put him at his ease.

That afternoon, it had taken some time to establish any means of communication with the two hunters, and even then it took quite some convincing to persuade Kajha to backtrack to their camp rather than continuing on his way.

Kajha had helped his son skin the lion quickly, furtively scanning the edges of the clearing all the while for signs of its relatives. The skin would become Tidak's most prized possession and a source of great prestige amongst his people. Once the animal was skinned, Barrak had watched with keen interest as the old man expertly dissected a tenderloin from its back, leaving the other side in his haste, before shepherding them all away from the kill, downwind and out into the long grass, staying clear of the trails of trodden grass, which Barrak had finally understood to be stalking tunnels, used by the predators.

There had been a thorny moment as they approached the camp, when the hunters first caught sight of the abandoned truck. This had stopped them in their tracks and Kajha had protested vigorously and made it clear they wanted no part of the thing. Barrak had managed to reassure Kajha, taking him to the truck, which the old man inspected gingerly, finally seeming to accept that it was no threat after all, then Barrak and Jasmyn welcomed the two hunters to their meagre camp.

Eventually, with gestures, and words full of inflection and emphasis, if little actual understanding, and with the aid of scratchings and maps in the sand, Barrak and Jasmyn had established an understanding of sorts with the old man. Kajha seemed to appreciate their situation and he had explained graphically that he and the boy were travelling east, to a place that Barrak assumed was their home or village.

The two hunters had already carefully slung their loads of doarht meat high up in the branches of a red gum and then Tidak helped Barrak establish a fire, before Barrak took over from him and got carried away with it. Once it had burned down to a good bed of coals, Kajha roasted the tenderloin and divided the meat up carefully into four portions. It was at once the strangest tasting meat and the best thing Barrak had ever tasted, such was the extent of his hunger. As they sat around the fire after eating it, Barrak was sure he could feel the nourishment of it coursing into the very core of his body, like an elixir, soothing his jangled nerves and relaxing his fraught muscles. He had never experienced anything like the hunger and deprivation that he and Jasmyn had endured in the last few days, even though it *had* only been days since they'd eaten. After the meal, he and Jasmyn attempted more conversation with Kajha, using words and gestures and pictures in the sand, and Jasmyn tried hard to include Tidak, but he just wouldn't be coaxed – he seemed painfully shy.

Later, when they all fell silent, Kajha kicked a toe-full of sand toward the young lad and said something in their strange, lilting tongue in an imperative tone. He nodded at the boy and gestured with one hand as if urging the boy to some sort of task. Tidak dipped his head and looked coyly at Jasmyn and Barrak and back to Kajha and then replied in the manner of adolescents everywhere: he mumbled something in a surly tone and cast his eyes down, finding a twig and tossing it into the fire.

Kajha gave a universally understood *harrumph* and sat back slightly, folded his arms and glanced towards Jasmyn, making a short and mysterious statement to her and including Barrak with a sideways glance and what looked like a wink. Even though they understood none of the words, Jasmyn and Barrak knew from the tone that the old man was goading the boy in some way.

Tidak responded with a terse and belligerent pronouncement of his own and spat into the fire. Barrak was sure now that the two hunters were father and son – the dynamic between parent and adolescent was unmistakeable in any language.

This got a gruff, dismissive response from the old man. *Please yourself then,* was Barrak's guessed translation. But then the old man seemed to get his dander up and went on, raising his voice and clearly urging the boy to do his bidding, repeating the same phrase twice and the hand gestures too.

Finally Tidak relented and shot his father a petulant frown, then slapped the sand on either side of him with both hands and pushed himself to his feet. He approached the lion skin where it had been stretched over the fork of a branch, positioned near the fire to dry it. He examined it closely for a moment or two, as best he could in the firelight.

The wind had died away and the stars were bright in the clear night sky as Tidak stepped back from the lion skin. He raised both arms up, hands clasped together, fingers pointed aloft and then drew his arms down on either side of him, slowly, gracefully, as if parting the heavens. As he did this, a stream of words issued from him, but they were not like the language they had heard the two hunters speaking. It was more like chanting or even singing, with a delicate but discernible rhythm and cadence that distinguished it from conversation. The boy repeated the same gesture to the night sky and then he began to tap one foot on the ground and move his body to an unheard rhythm, sweeping his hands through the air. He went on chanting in perfect time with the delicate and graceful movements of his dance, spinning and jumping on the edge of the darkness.

Jasmyn sat up and stared at the boy across the fire. She was instantly mesmerised. Gone was the adolescent awkwardness of a painfully shy boy. In its place was an accomplished performer, barely confined by gravity as he jumped and glided in the soft sand, his lithe body lit by the firelight against the curtain of the night.

Bit by bit Tidak's dance took on form and narrative; it was his story of killing the lion and his exaggerated gestures in the beautifully flowing dance depicted him first walking nonchalantly through the bush, then stopping to rest, then all at once the surprise and fear of the attack … As he danced his voice rose and fell, chanting the story of his great escapade, and even with no knowledge of a single word, Jasmyn felt all the emotion and excitement and wonder in the boy's telling of it.

The boy got a good laugh from the audience when he did Barrak, running like a frightened child and trying to climb an imaginary tree. And as he went on and the story reached a climax, the excitement rose in Tidak's voice and he kicked the air, virtually cartwheeling towards where the skin was hanging. The old man joined in the chant for a bar or two, by way of encouragement or embellishment, and at the same time, shook the end of a branch he'd been feeding into the fire, sending up a storm of embers to add theatrical effect.

Tidak emerged from the swirl of sparks, wearing the lion's skin.

He stalked around the edge of the fire, his voice taking on a different pitch and intonation. Now it was the lion's story. He stalked and snarled and pounced. Tidak had become the lion as he prowled the perimeter between firelight and darkness, and to add to the drama, the old man sent more embers billowing up into the night and chanted his punctuating contributions to Tidak's telling of events.

As Jasmyn watched in awe, she felt there was great respect and compassion for the lion in Tidak's telling of his tale, and to her surprise she found tears suddenly welling in her eyes and running down her cheeks as Tidak subsided slowly into the sand and lay still under the lion's skin, depicting the creature's last moments. She shot a furtive glance at Barrak, a little embarrassed, and wiped away her tears. But Barrak didn't notice because he was on his feet giving Tidak a rousing round of applause.

The boy poked his head out from under the skin and looked around with a slight sense of panic for the source of the strange noise. The old man looked at Barrak with a hint of annoyance and then gave a perplexed grimace. Jasmyn decided she better join in and started clapping her own hands modestly and smiled at Tidak and then at Kajha. The old man nodded and his old face cracked into a grin and he looked at his own open palms as if they were new to him, then back at Jasmyn. Tentatively he started clapping his hands too. Tidak crawled out from under the skin and stood up and smiled broadly at his audience and gleefully joined in the hand clapping himself.

Jasmyn watched as Tidak carefully hung the skin back on the drying branch and was overcome by a swarm of emotions; partly

269

she was missing her home in Tamouer, but partly she felt a strange and unaccustomed rush of maternal longing, an urge to wrap this gorgeous, shy boy in her arms and take him with her, back to Eyre.

All at once she realised that wasn't it – what she really wanted was to go with the old man and the boy back to wherever they had come from and see what kind of world had created *them*.

CHAPTER 18

AT THE END OF a long and arduous day's trekking, Barrak began to realise that the language spoken by the two hunters, a strange melodic tongue that had seemed so alien at first, was actually closer to his own language than he'd realised. In some ways it was almost like a dialect of Eyrean.

There were still plenty of unfamiliar words and these had to be explored with sign and simile, but that first night out, around a small, smoky camp fire, trying yet again to communicate with Kajha, it had struck him like a minor epiphany that many of the words were actually the same or derived from the same root as Eyrean words. The grammatical structure was similar, if a bit loose, and the rest was all just a matter of inflection and pronunciation. The main difficulty arose because the Dzahn, as the hunters referred to their people, had a great many other unique words, which were mysterious to Barrak.

By the second day spent walking with the bush men, Jasmyn had made the same discovery, and to her delight, this was how she'd broken down Tidak's shyness. Once he had become her self-appointed language coach, his defences had melted away and an easy friendship quickly developed. She was charmed by the boy's openness and ready acceptance of the two foreigners, and it fascinated her to be immersed in his world. As they threaded their way through the landscape, Tidak brought it to life with his commentary, pointing out what plants could be eaten and sometimes foraging for a sample for her to try, naming birds and animals and, once he realised how interested she was, taking time to point out some of the more subtle signs of Dzahn bushcraft.

Tidak seemed so unaffected and so totally present in what he was doing, that it brought a smile to Jasmyn's face just to be with him, and once or twice when he wanted her attention he would simply take her hand in his, as naturally and easily as if they were children in pre-school, exploring the world.

At other times Tidak would abruptly attune himself to his father and he and Kajha would become serious and cautious, calling for quiet or directing them to conceal themselves in the scrub, while together they would examine signs on the ground or gaze towards the horizon, or sometimes, just listen intently to the wind, before satisfying themselves it was safe to move on. Once, Kajha took them on a wide detour, circling far to the north and adding hours to their journey just to avoid something, which neither Kajha nor Tidak seemed inclined to explain.

After two days travelling on foot with the hunters, Jasmyn and Barrak were exhausted. Tidak and Kajha were weighed down with the doarht meat and their two charges had nothing but their own meagre possessions, but Kajha had refused all offers to share some of the load, no doubt fearing this would slow them down even further. Stopping early to make camp in the late afternoon on the second day, Barrak had sensed Kajha's frustration. He supposed the two hunters, left to their own devices, might have pushed on and reached their destination before dark that same day.

The next morning dawned clear and crisp, but with a hint of approaching summer, which took the edge off the morning chill. Tidak couldn't contain his anticipation any longer, and his enthusiasm was contagious; even Barrak felt rejuvenated after a rare, sound sleep, and he had a spring in his step, as if the two days of hard walking had improved his fitness, despite his injuries. Jasmyn caught the bug too and chatted excitedly with Tidak as they set off into the rising sun.

Later that morning, as they came down out of some low, wooded hills, a wide grassy plain stretched out before them with a lake to the south, and to the north, a dark rift in the landscape ran along the horizon and lost itself in the morning mist.

As the morning warmed away the mist, the rift resolved itself into a long escarpment that bounded the plain and ran north and south as far as the eye could see. Finally they came to a river that ran along the base of the escarpment and tracked along its edge until they found a crossing, adjacent to a cleft in the high ground on the opposite bank.

They crossed the river and followed an indistinct trail up through the gap, a steep wooded gully strewn with boulders the size of houses, creating sheer rock faces and narrow goat trails in between. As they zig-zagged up through the trees, it was like climbing a giant's stairs. It took them past a double waterfall, spectacular and pristine, and beyond that the trail was lost to an open, gently sloping woodland and the plateau above. They followed the water that fed the falls, moving upstream along its meandering course through a high, hidden valley.

The foursome entered the Dzahn village around midday, treading a well-worn trail along the south bank of the creek, babbling over pebbles, with small sandy beaches either side and steep banks marked with flood debris. The definition of the trail, the smell of wood smoke and Tidak's mounting excitement told them they were getting close, and before long, Barrak spied a couple of children cavorting in the grass up ahead.

Soon they were surrounded by bronzed urchins of all sizes, half naked, darting in and out of the banksias and eucalypts and back and forth across the trail in front of the strange foursome. Tidak had his lion's skin about him like a cape and swirled and roared and pounced on the children as they squealed with delight. Others began a game of chicken with Jasmyn, seeing who dared run closest to her and, if they were really game, reach out and touch her lightly as they passed. Jasmyn laughed and waved at the children and whooped with delight herself whenever she was tapped.

By the time the village itself came into view, the track was lined with spectators young and old, come out to welcome the hunters and their outlandish entourage. Wide eyes tracked Barrak and Jasmyn and a babble of greetings and excited exchanges flew back and forth between the villagers and the hunters. But something drew Jasmyn's attention away from the romping children and curious villagers and her eyes locked onto a lone figure standing high on the river bank, up ahead beyond the crowded track.

The bronzed and muscular figure was like a statue in his stillness, naked to the waist, a spear in one hand, the other by his side. Lean and taut, the tall young man had a warrior's stance and his head was tilted back slightly, giving him a vaguely aloof bearing. His penetrating stare met Jasmyn's like a challenge, intense and candid. Jasmyn felt the blood rising to her face and a flutter in her chest, before she averted her eyes and gave her attention back to the milling children. But she could feel his gaze on her yet, and almost against her will, she found herself sneaking another glance at the stunning figure.

His hand came up in a salute and his voice boomed out deep and clear above the general hubbub: 'I see you, Tidak!' There was gravitas in his pronouncement as he paused, and yet there was the barest hint of mischief too, in his otherwise solemn expression.

'I see you, my young brother,' he went on. The tall warrior's gaze was now fixed on Tidak and his face was lit with a fierce intensity.

'My brother, Tidak, I see you are now a slayer of lions and a hunter amongst hunters.' All at once the warrior's serious face broke into a huge smile which lit up his whole powerful body and he raised his spear up and boomed out a loud and forceful chant, 'Wa-Suuu!' There was a heart-beat of perfect silence along the river bank, before the chant was amplified a hundred times by the crowd: 'WA-SUUU!' The sound of it resonated in Jasmyn's bones and made her neck tingle. Tidak raised the lion skin high above his head and shook it and let out an ear-piercing scream like a battle cry, 'Ahh-yeeeeyaahh!'

His brother responded in kind, shaking his spear at the sky, and the villagers joined in, creating pandemonium that only subsided when a woman burst onto the trail in front of the foursome and grabbed Tidak, hugging him with affection so fierce and sustained, that Tidak had to struggle free to catch his breath and avoid mortal embarrassment. Then she turned her attention to Kajha and kissed him on the cheek and hugged him too. Her smile was as bright and clear as a summer's day and spoke of pure happiness and relief.

'Why have you come here?' the old man asked a second time, his brow crinkled with a hundred lines etched deep in the rugged terrain of his face. Even in the gloom of the cramped hut, the elder's eyes were bright and intent on Barrak and seemed to convey not only curiosity but some measure of compassion and patience too.

Barrak sensed, more than saw, other eyes on him too, watching from the shadows. But the others seemed content for the old man to do the talking … *the village elders*, Kajha had said. He strained to understand the head man's thickly accented question and tried to focus on the ancient clansman's face, but his head seemed to be swimming, wood smoke stung his eyes and his mouth felt claggy and rancid from the strange, milky, spiced tea they had given him to drink.

Why? Barrak finally understood the question, but his mind was blank. *Why indeed?* Barrak could not clear the fuzziness from his head, which was throbbing worse than ever now, and he began to feel nauseous. *Was it the strange tea?* He felt as if his brain was inflamed and he searched in vain for a sensible explanation to give the old man.

Kajha launched into a monologue, addressing the old man in a quiet and measured tone which was both respectful and gentle. The ancient clansman nodded solemnly several times as Kajha spoke, and in between, looked thoughtfully at Barrak and smiled at him kindly. Kajha seemed to be telling the old man the story of how he and Tidak had found the two strangers lost in the wilderness; in the end, after what seemed an extraordinarily long explanation, the venerable old bushman seemed to be satisfied, though presumably no one present was any the wiser on the question of 'why'.

The old man then seemed to deliver a kind of benediction, waving a hand gracefully in front of Barrak and speaking with some authority and intensity to Kajha and eventually smiling and patting Barrak on the hand and then waving him off.

Straightening up out in the open air Barrak took a deep breath, which eased the nausea somewhat, but reminded him of the ever-persistent ache of his bruised ribs. His head still pounded and his eyes were unequal to the brightness of the late afternoon sun.

'What was the verdict?' he asked his companion. Kajha gave him a sideways look, as if Barrak was a naughty schoolboy, then smiled and nodded as though Barrak had made a joke he understood.

'It is time to rest now, my friend,' he said gently. 'Dimali says you are welcome, but he is unquiet,' Kajha confided. 'He believes you are … not whole.' Kajha looked concerned; Barrak believed he was right to be. 'Tomorrow I will take you to Shabbah.'

Barrak already knew what this Dzahn word meant, because it had come up early on in his conversations with Kajha, when he had sought to explain his own occupation. And so tomorrow, it seemed, he would be taken to consult the Dzahn purveyor of medicines.

Barrak woke in alarm. It was light. *Dawn? No. Where was Jasmyn?* He fretted for a moment over her disappearance and the loss of the tent. It took him a few more moments to remember where he was. Light filtered through the thatch of the little shelter he'd been assigned. *No, not dawn. He hadn't slept that long, it was still the same day.*

Late afternoon.

He remembered seeing Jasmyn rounded up by a group of the village women, just after their arrival, just before his visit to the elders. He had no idea where she was now. He felt a strange mixture of relief and concern. *She is safe, at least.*

Barrak's head felt a little better but the nausea was worse. *God, that's what had woken him, the nausea.* He crawled out of the low opening of his hut and got his bearings as best he could. His hut was on the edge of a circle of dwellings – was it some kind of guest house? – with a river frontage.

Barrak made for the water, but he only got part of the way before vomiting under a bush, just above the bank. There was a clammy sweat on him and he sensed a fever was not far off. He slid to the sandy verge and went down on his hands and knees to drink, scooping water onto his face and head. The effort left him exhausted, and he lay on the sand on his side, knees drawn up in a foetal curl. He let his breath come slow and deep to ease the nausea, and it seemed to work, he began to feel better.

Lying quite still with his face on the cool sand, he looked across the deep-flowing channel on the near side of the river, which was just a few feet wide. He stared vacantly at the opposite bank where wider shallows trickled and murmured over grey and brown river stones. At that moment a powerfully odd sensation broke over him: he felt he had lain in this very spot and done this very thing before. It was the strangest feeling, and as it came over him, he noticed something on the opposite bank, half submerged in the shallows. It was a small animal, brown with shiny slick fur, flipping over pebbles with its wide duck-like bill. It seemed to notice Barrak just as Barrak noticed it, and held his gaze for a moment or two before scampering across the stones on its stubby webbed feet and slipping deftly into the deeper water with barely a sound and just the slightest splash from its wide flat tail.

Once the nausea passed Barrak had been enveloped by overpowering fatigue and it was all he could do to get himself back to his little hut and crawl into his swag. That night he slept the sleep of a child, the most restful he'd had for weeks, and didn't wake until dawn was well past and the sun was climbing through the branches of the eucalypts outside his shelter.

Groggy from sleep and yet with a new-found clarity of purpose, he crawled out of his hut and stretched and looked around him.

His first order of business was to find Jasmyn.

Other shelters were dotted around amongst the trees and he heard voices coming from one nearby. He felt suddenly awkward and embarrassed, as if he were an intruder. He struck out in a direction he knew, down towards the river, skulking behind the nearest dwelling. It had a low stone wall at the back, about chest height, and what seemed to be a chimney. On top was a thatched roof which sloped up to above head height at the front. The side wall was a patchwork of some kind of animal hide, stretched tight over upright sapling trunks.

Past the back of this, he caught sight of a much larger structure, with no walls on three sides and thatch on top. In front of the ramshackle pavilion was a fire, smouldering in a pit surrounded by stones. And sitting on a log beside the fire was a single old man, wiry and brown from the sun with tufts of grey, wispy hair crowning his head. He looked like the elder Kajha had taken him to see the day before, but he couldn't be sure. The old man removed a kind of smoking pipe from his mouth and flashed Barrak a toothless grin, but Barrak was already moving away towards the river.

He followed the river upstream to a natural ford, where the water ran fast and shallow. Large rocks had been positioned, deliberately by the look of them, to make a dry crossing possible, and Barrak put them to use, hopping across and up onto the opposite bank.

He was on a promontory of land bordered on both sides by a sweeping bend in the river. There were no more dwellings apparent, but there was smoke in the air and he thought he could smell something cooking. Female voices caught his attention, and as he peered around a copse of trees, he saw a group of women in the shallows on a small sandy beach, washing clothes in the river. One turned and saw him and yelped an alert. The others turned to look too and giggled, covering their faces and chatting excitedly.

Jasmyn was not amongst them, so he doubled back and continued downstream.

He came to an area of ground that had obviously been cultivated, with terracing and crude irrigation channels running through it from one side to the other. It took up the bulk of the isthmus of land inside the tight river bend. There was a variety of plants in rows and it reminded him of the comfarm plots and produce gardens back in Rylanswood, although the plants were unfamiliar and looked a bit stunted and sparse, despite the irrigation.

He continued on a path that bisected the garden plot until it joined another trail. Here Barrak almost ran smack into a villager, who emerged suddenly from a line of scrub where the new track curved away into the bush. He looked surprised and sheepish, and hurried on without a word. Barrak walked on, following a hunch and a distinct odour.

In amongst some scrub he found a group of latrines, each strategically separated from the other by low bushes and backed by a copse of flowering wattles.

Now it was starting to make sense. A washing area and then latrines … all downstream.

He helped himself to one of the units, which comprised a nice box to sit on with a thatched roof. It was a luxury after being obliged to just scratch in the dirt these last two weeks. By their depth and position in relation to the river bend he assumed the toilets were constructed to allow natural sand filtration, with the effluent seeping into the river, cleansed by soil microbes and river sand and entering downstream from the village.

He back-tracked the way he had come, now with a clear sense that the main part of the village must be upstream.

Moving back past the scrubby precinct that included his own hut, he came again to the long roofed structure, which he now assumed to be a meeting house of some sort. The old man there had been joined by another. The two cronies laughed openly at him and yelled incomprehensible instructions to him and pointed him up-river. Barrak began to see that the village was built around two large sweeping river bends. He found a trail that took him upstream past more bush dwellings.

Wrens and honeyeaters flitted amongst the trees and a thin haze of wood smoke made silver rays of the sun filtering through the canopy. He could hear faint voices and children's laughter carried on the breeze from somewhere nearby, barely distinguishable from the faint murmuring of the river.

But he saw no one. Mid-morning … he supposed people were about their work, whatever that might be.

At the next river bend was a massive fallen red gum with fang-like bare roots half exposed to the sky and reaching up as high as two men.

As he moved around it Barrak realised it had been used as a bridge. Where the base of the giant lay flat against the river bank, large steps had been carved into the trunk. The fallen tree ran at a gentle angle towards the opposite bank, where one great bough projected outwards like an architectural feature and the rest had broken off in the ancient fall, or long ago rotted away in the mud.

Barrak crossed the tree bridge, which had long since lost its bark to the friction of feet, leaving a smooth, undulating timber course.

Children scattered as he came down off the tree bridge and then stalked him in the bushes, peeping from their hideouts in the foliage along the river bank. He came past another large thatch-roofed structure in the centre of a cleared area bordered on three sides by the second sweeping bend in the river. More children were gathered in the shade of this structure and they stared at him as he passed, whispering and giggling. Through the trees up ahead he could see smoke rising from amongst more dwellings.

There were voices, clearer now, and he heard Jasmyn's distinctive laughter ring out amongst them.

Past a giant red gum arching over the river and more little lean-tos on either side, he entered a large clearing. Jasmyn was sitting on a log, one of three arranged around the edge of a large smouldering fire pit.

A great boulder, flat and smooth on top, was positioned nearby and three older women were gathered around it, pounding something on the giant rock. Two more women, much younger, barely out of their teens he supposed, were gathered around Jasmyn, one next to her on the log nursing an infant, another standing behind her doing something to Jasmyn's hair. A little girl, maybe only four or five years old, with double braided pig-tails, sat right at Jasmyn's feet with her arm crooked around Jasmyn's calf.

But for hearing her voice, Barrak might not have recognised her. Gone were the travel-soiled borrowed clothes which had been her only wardrobe through their days lost in the bush. She was outfitted like the other women in earthy soft animal hide, tanned to an ochre hue, a single garment tied on one shoulder and cinched at the waist with a plaited cord. Leather sandals were on her feet and as she caught sight of Barrak, he noticed that she already sported the delicate red and black painted stripes across her cheeks that Barrak recognised as a fashion necessity amongst the Dzahn women.

'Barrak! Gods! I didn't know where you were. They said you were sick. Said you were resting. Are you all right?'

The girl with the baby moved to another log as if to make room for Barrak and the others by the boulder watched with interest, shifting their attention back and forth between the two outlanders as Barrak approached. The woman braiding Jasmyn's hair seemed to pay him little attention, but for a shy smile as she went on with her work.

'I'm fine, I think I needed some sleep, that's all. Quest's end, I'm hungry … Where is everyone?'

'I don't know … hunting? Don't know. This place is amazing isn't it Barrak … can you believe it?'

'Merciful gods, what have they done to you?' Barrak studied Jasmyn with mock shock and amusement as he sat down next to her.

I know, I know. Marvellous isn't it? They insisted, you know … it's like I've turned up at a bush spa or something.'

Barrak looked around at what seemed to be a cooking fire and food preparation area. *What were those women pounding on that rock?* He sniffed around for some sign of food.

'Is there anything to eat?' he enquired delicately, hopefully.

Jasmyn snorted and looked at the angle of the sun in the trees. 'You've missed breakfast by a few hours.' Jasmyn said something to the women by the rock, which he couldn't quite catch. She seemed to be streets ahead of him already in learning the Dzahn dialect.

They chatted and compared notes some more, with Barrak telling her of his discoveries downstream and Jasmyn told him the village had goats, domesticated animals, and there was milk and cheese. This explained the strange milky drink he remembered having the night before. She told him they grew some produce – local bush food – using the river to irrigate their crops, and Barrak told her he had seen the produce garden already, and the natural sewage treatment set up downstream. Jasmyn had been given fish from the river for breakfast and Tidak had promised to take her foraging for eggs and show her how to find bush honey.

One of the women appeared beside him and handed him a curved wooden platter, smooth and polished. On it was a blob of mash or thick gruel and lying across the blob were some nasty-looking strips of something that might have once been meat. Scattered about the gruel were some shrivelled up things that looked like raisins.

He didn't need any encouragement, he was so hungry he'd have eaten anything.

To his surprise it was incredibly good, belying its rough presentation. The mash had a neutral taste, a bit like potato or rice but with an agreeable nutty flavour, and the strips were intensely flavoured smoked fish or perhaps eel. The shrivelled things tasted like a tomato crossed with a berry and were sweet and salty and spicy at the same time. It might just have been the best thing Barrak had ever eaten, second only to Kajha's loin of lion, and the woman, seeing how he'd finished the first plate so quickly, took away his plate and brought him back another big serve of the mash.

Barrak was still licking his fingers when Kajha came wandering into the clearing and knelt down beside the two newcomers.

'I see you are rested, Mahnu.' Kajha used the Dzahn word, which Barrak had come to understand meant something like *friendly stranger,* or in another context, *respected opponent.* He smiled benignly at Barrak and Jasmyn in turn.

'And you have eaten well? It is good.' Kajha took the empty plate and handed it to the little girl at Jasmyn's knee.

'But now we must go. The Shabbah is waiting for you.'

CHAPTER 19

THEY WALKED IN SILENCE as Kajha led him back over the bridge and along the trail, travelling away from that part of the village Barrak had already seen. A short distance along, the track forked and Kajha took him to the right and up a gentle incline. To the left Kajha pointed out an enclosed area, fenced in by crude post and rail with a large structure standing along one side of it. It was much like the other meeting houses, but more solid. This was a training ground, for here, at last, were some of the village's young men. About a dozen were sitting on the ground, observing two figures standing and going through the motions of a stylised fight, one clearly the instructor, the other his hapless victim. Kajha said something Barrak didn't quite catch.

Further up the trail Kajha again gestured to their right and made comment, something about a meeting place. Below them was a flat area bounded by a small curved rocky escarpment which extended up to meet the ridge line ahead of them. In front of the escarpment was a wide area of flat ground and beyond that, extending back towards the training field, was a small rounded grassy hill. It looked to Barrak almost like a natural amphitheatre.

The track steepened and they reached a hairpin bend that was high enough to catch a cool breeze; it opened up a view over an opposing ridge line. Below was a natural basin, ringed by the two ridges and sloping gently down to the outskirts of the village. Goats grazed on the pasture in the basin, and away to the north, where the land flattened out towards the river, there were more small dwellings.

A fence had been built across the opening of the gully, which amused Barrak, because clearly the steep ground was no match for the goats' climbing skills and one of the animals was standing just on the verge of the hairpin, munching wild goosefoot and enjoying the view along with him and Kajha.

'This Shabbah – he's a healer?' Barrak enquired delicately of his guide.

'Shabbah is a fool,' Kajha stated simply, staring straight ahead, his assessment seemingly for the edification of the goat as much as Barrak. 'He talks in circles and sometimes he talks shit …' Kajha paused and looked thoughtfully at Barrak. 'But he is a wise fool. Some believe the old ones speak through him. Some say he walks with the spirits.' Kajha looked at Barrak gravely and then started up the track again. 'You can hear for yourself what Shabbah has to say to you.'

They reached another hairpin bend, where a smaller trail, not much more than a goat's track, ran away and down to the left onto a narrow, lop-sided saddle. Around another bend it dropped and opened up into a wide flat area below the main ridge. On one side of the flat ground was a steep escarpment and on the other a drop-off to the valley, a hundred feet below.

A ramshackle structure of sticks and thatch and skins hugged the cliff below a jutting overhang and Barrak noticed smoke leaking from the space between the structure's roof and the cliff.

'Shabbah waits for you,' Kajha said, giving Barrak a gentle push towards the shack before turning and retreating.

Barrak stood for a time in the warm, late-morning sun. A cool breeze whispered through the thick, thorny undergrowth at the base of the cliff. A raven stopped its hopping and foraging around the remains of a cooking fire in front of the shack and stared at Barrak with its dead, white incurious eyes, before squawking rudely and throwing itself off the precipice.

Beyond the shack he could see the ledge of flat ground was wide enough to accommodate patches of grass and what looked like a vegetable garden. The structure itself was more elaborate than the other dwellings he'd seen, if somewhat misshapen. It hugged the escarpment and seemed to be incorporated into a cave, below a jutting overhang. At the front, a doorway was constructed of substantial cut limbs, gnarled and grey with age; the walls were composed of bundles of sticks held together with the same binding Barrak had seen before, made from woven strips of some kind of soft pliable bark or hide.

A strange decoration hung by the door, made to an intricate design from feathers and bones and polished river stones. As he approached the door he examined the thing closely and found it had a mirror at its centre. It was the first manufactured item he'd seen in the village.

He took a deep breath and pushed aside the goat-skin flap that served as a door. His exposure to the morning sun rendered him blind in the darkness of the hut for a few moments, but gradually he discerned a figure squatting on the ground at the back of the room, lit by a narrow shaft of light from the incomplete roof. He had his back to Barrak and he seemed to be tending something on a small fire on the bare ground where the shack met the hollowed out cliff face. Barrak waited for some kind of acknowledgement from the Shabbah.

Should he say something? He cleared his throat.

No response.

The room was lined with skins and lit only by a chink of sunlight from the opening in the roof, which was nicely sucking the smoke up and out. Bunches of drying herbs hung from rafters and there was a timber and thatch bed along one wall covered with more skins. Leaning against it was a stout stick of polished wood with a curved end like a walking stick. It too was elaborately decorated with feathers and stones, much like the talisman at the front door, and next to that was a crude timber chest, its top inlaid with river stones and shells.

Barrak was startled when the Shabbah stood up abruptly and, still with his back turned, held something up above his head. Fumes from the steaming bowl combined with the wood smoke and swirled up and out through the gap above.

A long animal-hide cape hung from the medicine man's shoulders and long ropy strands of braided hair reached down to his lower back.

Pieces of bone and shell, woven into the braids, clattered together as he wagged his head from side to side and chanted quietly in a low resonant bass, which wavered alarmingly in tone. His chant stopped abruptly and was followed by a rapid-fire staccato 'Tcha, tcha, tcha,' as the bowl came down and the spindly figure turned to face Barrak.

His round, ageless face was painted with black and red in the same style as the village women, but with the startling addition of a vivid blue band of colour in the centre of his forehead. He had a triple string of shells at his chest and plain circular earrings, which appeared to be gold or at least some kind of metal. He wore the traditional ochre tanned robe in the fashion of the village women and old men and he gathered his cape around his shoulders as he sat down before the small fire and beckoned Barrak to do the same.

He put the bowl carefully on the ground and pointed a bony finger at Barrak. 'Your journey is written in the sky, Hakeah. It was a word Barrak had come to understand meant, stranger from the west, or sundowner. 'I have seen your troubles, you and the woman,' he claimed quietly, lowering his finger. 'You should have died ... But the sky god has spared you. The people say she is spirit mother to the boy, Tidak.'

Barrak said nothing, but nodded respectfully as if the Shabbah's words actually made sense to him. He could see the Shabbah more clearly now, as his eyes adjusted fully to the gloom. The frail bushman's eyes shone like gemstones and seemed to peer right into Barrak, such was the clarity and intensity of his gaze.

Barrak felt a wave of unease that came and went, only to be replaced by a much stranger feeling of familiarity, almost as if he had been acquainted with the Shabbah before.

'Drink this,' the Shabbah said simply and handed the steaming bowl to Barrak.

Barrak took it from him and caught a whiff of strong fumes and gave the old herbalist a dubious look.

'Go ... go ... drink. It will help you to see clearly.' He waved an impatient hand at Barrak.

Barrak took a sip. It was bitter and strong. Aromatic fumes, pungent and searing, went up his nose and made his eyes water. The medicine man eyed him critically and leaned across the fire.

'Who are you?' he asked deliberately, eyes narrowed.

'Barrak … Brethrenhope,' he said uncertainly, putting the bowl down and hoping that a conversation might distract them from the pungent tea. 'Councillor to the …'

'No. No … NO!' He wagged a bony digit at him. 'Drink it. Drink … It will help.' He watched intently as Barrak took another sip and tried not to gag.

'Who *are* you?' he asked again, tilting his head, beads jangling, and peered keenly at Barrak.

Barrak thought he was misunderstanding something in the question, but there was no translation, those three words were essentially the same in Dzahn and Eyrean.

'I'm a physician,' he began doubtfully, 'I'm a Shabbah, like you.'

The strange ascetic hissed at him and then grunted in disgust. 'Hear me, Hakeah.' He paused thoughtfully, long enough to confuse Barrak, when no more words followed.

'Drink now,' he urged and sat patiently while Barrak forced down several more sips, before getting up and repositioning himself on Barrak's side of the fire, right beside him. With his face uncomfortably close to Barrak he demanded for a third time: 'Who *are* you?'

This time Barrak felt his confusion was tinged with annoyance or even panic. He could smell the Shabbah's breath on him. 'Look, I'm just a man, an Eyrean … we're trying to go east …' Barrak pulled back from the leering healer; he felt confused, he was losing his train of thought.

'Parghhh!' The Shabbah was clearly frustrated. The old sage groaned as he pushed himself to his feet and shuffled to the bed and snatched up his ornate stick with one hand and beckoned to Barrak with the other. 'Come,' he said simply and flung open the goat-hide door.

The tea bowl emptied itself onto the fire, seemingly without Barrak's help, and a cloud of bright vapour hissed into the air above him. Barrak watched it bend and twist in its accent, before shooting out through the opening above, like a frightened ghost.

Barrak was sitting cross-legged in the sand and facing the door … although he could not recall having turned around, so he guessed he must have levitated, because his body was starting to feel quite weightless.

The Shabbah had lost patience and gone out, dropping the flap shut, but his words seemed to echo around the shelter. *Who are you?* For a moment Barrak thought he had the answer but it slipped away, and besides, he was distracted by the flapping goat's skin, which seemed to be mouthing words at him, and the shack itself was pulsating and expanding. Now Barrak was standing at the door, without any recollection of making the journey there. He took one last look at the interior of the shack, which had expanded so impressively that it now resembled the Temple of Orlan's Blood back in Tamouer and, come to that, he thought he heard Cardinal Jasper Selwood's urbane voice inviting him into his 'conjurer's lair', so he threw back the goat's skin and stepped out into darkness.

Above him is a void of blackness so deep and immense it seems to be sucking at his weightless body. Barrak tries to curl his toes to hang on to the sand and stares agog at the stars above him.

It occurs to him, but only vaguely, that it is supposed to be midday. The stars captivate him. They are impossibly close and bright, yet delicate and distant. He observes the cosmos as if he can gauge the depth and breadth of it and recognises constellations he never knew by name as if they are old friends.

A shower of sparks adds colour to his heavenly realm and only then does he see the Shabbah is tending a brightly burning fire, which looks like it's been burning for years.

They are standing together on solid ground, floating in space. Barrak knows the village and the river are below them, but when he looks down he sees only more stars, to complement those above. It makes perfect sense, they are at the centre of it. He hears the Shabbah's voice inside his own head once more, asking him for his identity. He thinks he has the answer this time, but it no longer seems to matter.

'Look ...' The Shabbah tells him as he draws a line in the translucent sand with his riotously decorated stick. 'Here is your path.' The Shabbah's line in the sand is bright and shimmering and seems to stretch the length of the medicine man's rocky promontory.

'*You* follow your path through time, without courage *or* wisdom.' He retraces the line with his stick a second time, marking out Barrak's craven journey through life.

'The hunter runs with only bow and spear and he is unafraid of the hunt. But you ...' the Shabbah jabs his shaman's stick at Barrak for emphasis, 'you carry too much with you through time. You carry your past with you like a rotting corpse ... and you fear the future.' The coals of the Shabbah's timeless camp fire burn bright in his eyes, which pierce Barrak's timorous soul as he stands opposite the healer in the centre of the sucking night.

'But time is not like this.' The Shaman scribbles away the straight line he has drawn in the sand and points his gnarled wand up into the lurid heavens instead. 'Time is like this,' he declares and sweeps his stick across the night sky in a great curving arc, casting a trail of fire into the yawning blackness of the heavens. The phantom embers sizzle and burn bright and white, just like starlight, and he sweeps his magic stick all the way around and completes the circle. It dominates the sky above them and blots out the stars. Barrak is on his knees in the sand, then he falls back on his haunches, appalled by the intensity of the perverse circle of fire the shaman has cast into the void as though it were just a party trick.

'Now, Hakeah ...' The Shabbah's voice has become disembodied, it seems to be inside Barrak's mind, which no longer enjoys the refuge of his skull.

'*Who are you?*' The question reverberates into the heavens.

Barrak lowers his head and looks at the ground, where his hands are supporting him, but instead of hands he sees the great padded paws of Tidak's lion, planted firmly in the sand. He looks up at the circle of light – the Shabbah's demonstration of the circularity of time – and it vanishes in a blink, without trace, revealing again the star-spattered night. The medicine man is eyeing him with curiosity. Barrak lifts one paw and holds it up to the starry sky. It is once more a human hand, except now it is composed of a thousand stars in the shape of a hand. Starting with the fingers, the stars dance out into the heavens, and bit by bit, his hand disintegrates and is sucked away into the night sky, forming new and unknown constellations.

Barrak falls to earth and rests his forehead in the sand – he can't look anymore.

'Don't be afraid, Hakeah,' the shaman counsels him gently.

Barrak can feel the sky pressing on him and his head becomes thick and slow as if sleep is close. Dreamy images flit across his mind and he attaches himself to one he recognises, one that feels familiar and safe. It is a swimming creature, the aquatic marsupial he saw down by the river. It is swimming through sparkling clear water.

Descending.

Barrak follows it. Deeper, into water that becomes dark, murky. Barrak feels fear … wants to hold back but can't.

He is sucked down. Deeper. He can't breathe.

'Don't be afraid Hakeah …'

Barrak relaxes a little and instantly he *is* the river possum, tugging at the water with his supple swimmer's body, feeling the currents, sensing the contours of the bank. He swims down and down into the murky depths as though he knows his destination.

'What do they mean, Tidak, when they call me spirit mother?' Jasmyn asked casually, as the two of them sauntered along the sandy track, curving away from the river bridge and up a slight rise. The sun was high and the air was still and warm. Overhead, a canopy of tall eucalypts painted the pair with dappled shade.

'They think the old ones sent you to protect me …' Tidak called light-heartedly over his shoulder as he ran ahead to a fork in the track. 'This way,' he said, beckoning her to follow. He ran ahead again and when Jasmyn caught up, Tidak was leaning against a fence composed of branches and saplings and pointing into the clearing beyond, where a group of young men were gathered. 'Look,' he said excitedly. '*This* is where they practise.'

Jasmyn caught up to him and leaned against the fence next to him. 'I don't understand Tidak ... they think I am a spirit?'

Tidak laughed. 'No! But they say it was deemha, the way you appeared with the lion ... I wished so hard for a great Wasu ... and then you came along. They think you were sent to protect me, by the spirit of my mother ...' Tidak tailed off and there was a gleam of sadness in his eye.

'Your mother, Tidak?' Jasmyn said quietly.

Tidak turned to her and staunchly blinked away a tear.

'Binta is my mother now. She and the other women and Kajha and my uncles have cared for me well, but she did not give me life. I was born to Kara, her cousin. She was taken when I was very young.' Tidak smiled his amiable, frank smile and Jasmyn felt a rush of empathy once again for the young lad and wanted to reach out to him, but instead she asked him, 'What happened to your mother, Tidak?'

The young hunter paused and swallowed, but his gaze was steady and clear as he looked up at her with the sadness of an old soul in his eyes. 'She was *taken*,' he said emphatically, and for a moment there was fierceness in his eyes and even a brief flicker of anger before he abruptly turned his attention to the young men on the training ground, letting Jasmyn know the matter was closed.

'Look! My brother Nimbarra is teaching the Har-barch. He is the best. No one can defeat him.'

Jasmyn shrugged off a chill from Tidak's stoic words and tracked his gaze to the young men on the training ground. Tidak's older brother was the handsome young warrior who had stared at her so disconcertingly when they entered the village the day before. Nimbarra was standing in front of a line of some eight young men or boys, some not much older than Tidak. Each was holding a club. In turn, each one stepped forward and took a hefty swing at Nimbarra. And each time Nimbarra shifted and ducked and unbalanced his attacker, using the attacker's momentum against him and disarming him. As he did this he counted out the steps and exaggerated each move for the group.

As Jasmyn and Tidak looked on, a group of young women joined them along the fence to watch the action. Jasmyn guessed, from the giggling and jostling for position, that this was perhaps a favourite pastime of the village girls.

Nimbarra heard the commotion and glanced their way, just for an instant, without breaking stride in his demonstration, taking care not to be distracted, as the next trainee came charging at him. In fact he seemed to deal with him even more easily, almost disdainfully, smoothly side-stepping the lad, lifting the club from his adversary's grip and laying him almost tenderly on the ground. Then he looked up again at the spectators along the fence.

This time a hint of surprise crossed his face when his eyes met Jasmyn's. He held her gaze for only a moment, just long enough for his eyes to brighten and a faint smile to touch his lips, and also long enough for his next student to sense an opportunity. In a flash he had his legs around Nimbarra's neck, flipped and rolled him and brought him down to earth with a thud.

Tidak let out an audible wince as the young girls gasped. Nimbarra got up looking flushed and embarrassed. He brushed himself down and Jasmyn was sure he stole a sheepish glance in her direction as he fought to regain his composure. The trainee who had got the better of him was grinning broadly. Others amongst his students were laughing uproariously and all appreciated the irony of the situation and the exquisite embarrassment of their instructor.

Nimbarra shrugged off his wounded pride and broke into a huge grin himself and congratulated his self-satisfied assailant, commending the winning move to the other students and even re-capping the technique.

When he glanced again at Jasmyn and Tidak, he could not have missed Jasmyn's approving smile, and Jasmyn was sure she noticed his eyes brighten, before he returned his attention to his class and barked an order to regain their attention.

Barrak is weightless, sinking, falling like a leaf, into darkness.

Without warning, a mindless terror comes at him from the dark waters in the form of flashing teeth. His heart and mind explode with horror, as his river possum's body is shredded limb from limb.

But the pain and fear quickly recede, as he is freed from his physical body.

He is dying … and yet the fear recedes even further, leaving only a feeling of wonder and anticipation. As his trembling consciousness enters another realm, the last fading image of his former world is Shabbah and his cup of magic poison, which had brought him undone and seemingly, ultimately, set him free.

He floats down, or perhaps up … it doesn't seem to matter. There is only his mind and another gentler, quieter mind, outside his own, calming him. He struggles with this because now a kaleidoscopic chronicle of his past life starts to play out in front of his mind's eye.

It goes on forever, and is over in a moment.

He comes to rest on a slab of cold, hard rock, or so it seems in this ethereal dream world. Fear returns to him suddenly, a dark, cloying, human fear … fear of death. He is entombed … All around him are shadowy figures, bending over him, peering at him with concern … or perhaps curiosity. He wants to recoil but he is no longer in his body. His mind quails.

They speak silently to him, and their one collective, singing word dispels his fear completely.

In that instant the gathered figures begin to glow, with beads and streams and pulsing jets of luminosity, which course through their strange, long-limbed bodies like fluorescent blood or sap, in colours beyond comprehension, the lilac and rose and gold of a celestial conflagration … just like trapped starlight, alternating with the shimmering, vibrant greens and blues of vital, living energy.

It runs through them like shining streams of liquid crystal.

One figure reaches down to him, with an arm impossibly long and slim and glowing, the slender fingers reminding him of something amphibian. She has Persephone's smile and Jasmyn's eyes.

With one touch he is taken into their group, he is part of them and their starlight flows through him too. Now he recognises them, they are all there, Persephone, Noah, his parents, his ancestors … they pour their light into him and he understands, then, what it is: knowledge and love and timelessness. A gentle sigh of quiet recognition passes through him, because it feels like he's remembered something he'd forgotten long ago. And what's left of Barrak, which is hardly anything at all, smiles a small smile and he reaches up and let's himself rise into their arms.

The figures all around him morph into a web, a network of branches or vines, all inter-connected and growing, pulsing with the same vibrant glowing energy. He is part of it, a vast web of light and knowledge. He is moving upwards, faster. Everything is expanding and quickening and he is taken up with it. The branches of the pulsing vine expand to an awesome intricacy, a galaxy of light and life, and finally Barrak can see that it has become the universe, expanding forever all around him. And yet he is connected still, to every point of light, every consciousness, every person who has ever lived. It is perfect and he understands …

… he understands …

… everything …

A shudder goes through his universe of light and there is a mighty contraction.

Gravity rushes in.

His orb of light crumbles and density gathers all around him. His boundless mind grasps for what he has understood. It was so clear, like the crystal points of light, but it is slipping away. He can't hold on. He is falling.

It was so perfect, so clear, so right … But it is fading …

It is gone …

It can't be …

The world has closed in.

A howl burst from Barrak like the bellowing of a wounded beast. With his lungs heaving, he woke, flailing in the sand. He jerked bolt upright, his eyes raw in his skull and a cold sweat all over him. His ragged, heavy breathing hurt his chest and his mouth was so dry, his tongue felt swollen, like a slab of pumice in his mouth.

Shabbah held out a cup to him and he recoiled from it at first, startled by the healer. But then he took the cup and, once he'd identified it as water, drank it all down, too quickly, spilling it down his chin and coughing from the shock of it in his dry throat. He looked wide-eyed at Shabbah, who returned his gaze with understanding.

'Be calm Hakeah,' he said quietly. 'The Taikkim root can be harsh but it shows us many things.'

Barrak's addled mind tried to formulate a response that might convey to Shabbah something of what he had experienced, but instead his mouth filled with saliva and he lurched away to the side and vomited. He kept on vomiting for several minutes, until he was as void as he was wretched.

Shabbah returned with more water.

Barrak noticed the sun was gone over the western hills and the colours of burnished dusk lit sparse fingers of high cloud to the east. The whole afternoon had passed. The mocking laughter of an unseen kuckkalah rang out across the vivid, still valley.

'Taikkim takes us to the centre of things,' he continued. 'It is the way of the Shabbah, but the journey is different for each person. Sometimes we must journey into the underworld, to confront the dark spirits.'

'Must we ... ?' Barrak sputtered and coughed and drank more water from the shallow wooden cup. Part of him was angry that the Shabbah had poisoned him with his dangerously potent concoction, without his consent or even so much as a warning. But before his anger could ripen, it was overtaken by a sense of wonder that was like an echo, a fading image, of the amazing epiphany he'd had whilst he was under its influence. He blinked and shook his head and then rubbed it vigorously.

The shaman smiled at him.

Barrak couldn't grasp it at all. It was like a dream, half remembered in the semi-conscious state of waking, but then lost in the clear light of morning. But it wasn't a dream. It was real ... It was ... *everything.*

He had understood everything.

Parts of it were still with him, pieces of bright, brilliant knowing.

But as his mind reached for the fragments, they fell away, like a slippery fish escaping overboard. He was overcome by a sudden sense of loss and exquisite frustration as he realised he couldn't hold onto the experience … or what he had learned.

He looked up wordlessly at the old herbalist, with what must have been an agonised expression, and Shabbah smiled warmly, with knowing in his eyes.

'Yes, of course Hakeah. In the end we must accept the dark spirits, they are part of the hunter, part of the warrior, part of the whole person … Is that how it was for you, my friend? Was it demons or the wise ones? Sometimes it is both.'

Barrak was wordless still. He frowned and wiped a sleeve across his mouth, before nestling the water bowl in the sand, all the while eyeing the old sage with keen interest.

'Both … I think,' he finally managed to croak. 'They were … *amazing* …' Barrak was appalled by the inadequacy of words.

'They are part of us all, Hakeah, the demons and the wise ones, the light and the dark. We must make peace between them … it is the only way to be whole.' The Shabbah eyed him dubiously, as though he were a slow student.

'Surely you have Taikkim, or something like it back there …' He gestured to the still bright western sky. 'Journeying to the spirit world is the only way to find answers, it is the source of the healing powers … you must know this Hakeah …' Shabbah trailed off as though he had lost interest and looked past Barrak towards the edge of his little plateau, in the direction of the village.

It was only then that Barrak noticed the sound of rhythmic music, drum beats drifting up on the still air from the village. He saw the Shabbah had changed his clothes and was sporting a lion's skin cloak, complete with an elaborate headdress fashioned from the skull of the lion. While they'd been speaking the Shabbah had been painting his face in bright, detailed patterns, using his mirrored talisman to assist in the task.

Barrak stood up gingerly and moved a few steps closer to the precipice, which was edged with small boulders. He peered over into the valley. A large fire was burning and people, small like figurines, were gathering in the meeting place below, in the area Barrak had thought looked like an amphitheatre. High-spirited voices and laughter rose up to him and he saw an animal on a spit being positioned for the fire.

He looked questioningly at Shabbah, who was putting the finishing touches to his make-up.

'You will need some time, Hakeah, to think about your visions,' he advised Barrak earnestly. 'You will not forget what you saw today. It will stay with you, in your hunter's spirit. We will talk again about this. But for now, we must go.'

Barrak frowned at the old spirit guide.

'Tonight is the celebration of Tidak's om-sahdu.'

Shabbah stood up and strode over to his hut and returned the mirrored talisman to its place by the door. He came back with his feathered wizard's staff in hand, raised it above his head and declared, 'The whole village celebrates tonight, and you must celebrate too, my friend. We will wrestle your demons another day.' And with that, the resplendent shaman led the way along the precarious narrow trail that would take them down to the village and the gathering place of the river people.

Jasmyn felt the rhythmic pounding of the drums vibrating through her core and danced with abandon, flinging back her head and watching the embers rush past her and swirl high into the night sky as she gyrated in the warm glow of the fire.

No one had warned her about the strange, fruity, milky drink and by the time she realised it was alcoholic, it was too late. She was feeling loose and wild and there seemed little point to inhibitions, as everyone around her seemed to have abandoned themselves to the beat of the drums and the effects of the Dzahn festive drink.

But she was dizzy and she beckoned to Tidak over the sound of the drums; she needed to take a break.

Back on the grassy hill away from the fire it was cooler and she wondered how late it was. It seemed the whole village had been at the celebration but now it was mainly just the young people still partying, maybe some forty people milling around the huge bonfire, dancing to the drums or sitting in groups on the grassy hillock.

Jasmyn thought it was sweet that Tidak had sought her out especially to dance with her, but she suspected he wanted to get back to carousing with the other teenagers. She'd spied him earlier hanging around with some of the young village girls, with an uncharacteristically self-conscious awkwardness to his manner, which could mean only one thing.

She suggested, half-jokingly, that it was time he went to bed, but he just laughed at her.

'Just remember whose om-sahdu this is,' he yelled over the noise.

Now that she'd sat down, she realised she was feeling quite woozy. She wondered where Barrak was and suddenly felt a pang of longing to share with him what was, after all, the first carefree and enjoyable day they'd experienced for some time.

She'd seen him earlier, looking haggard, when he came down from his meeting with the Shabbah, and when she'd questioned him, he'd been reticent and a bit weird about it. She'd talked to him again briefly when the roasted meat was served, but after that he'd just disappeared and presumably missed the whole ceremony, with Kajha telling Tidak's story, the acknowledgment of the elders and the Shabbah's ritual blessing.

Tidak and Jasmyn sat together for a few moments catching their breath in companionable silence. Staring absently at the milling pack of dancers around the fire, Jasmyn realised her eye had settled on Tidak's brother, Nimbarra, gyrating and shimmying amongst a group of young people. In her tipsiness, she stared unabashed for a moment or two, enjoying his athletic and muscular dancing. His smooth dark skin shone with sweat in the firelight.

'Look, there's your brother Nimbarra, isn't it?' She gestured towards the dancers and Tidak looked up and nodded.

'He dances like a marsh hen, doesn't he,' the young boy observed drily.

She asked Tidak how old his brother was and he told her Nimbarra was in his twentieth summer. *Only nineteen, just a boy,* thought Jasmyn, and as if on cue, Nimbarra looked up, straight at her, with that same frank, arrow-like stare he'd aimed at her before and she was hard pressed to feign nonchalance and continue her conversation with Tidak.

The effects of the celebratory drink were still with her and she had begun to suspect there was something more than alcoholic fermentation involved in its making. Jasmyn decided her best option would be to make for her hut and get some sleep, so she suggested Tidak re-join his friends, as she was sure he was eager to do, anyway.

She had begun to feel strangely removed from herself, but nonetheless keenly aware of the surreal and bizarre situation she was in; at the same time, she felt oddly excited by it. It made her crave Barrak's company even more, to talk with him, to try to make sense of things, to find out how he was feeling about this strange and fascinating new reality into which they'd been plunged so suddenly.

As she picked her way along the trail that led to the tree bridge, her central landmark within the village, she was glad of the crescent moon lighting her way home, but only then did she realise she still had no idea where Barrak's sleeping quarters was.

She paused at the bridge and looked down at the river. The quietly gurgling water was lost in the night shadows and the only clue to the water's course was a patch of sandy beach, lit pale and creamy by the waxing moon. It was quiet now, except for the distant whooping and drumming.

How had this happened to them? How the hell had she ended up in a place like this? Awe, trepidation and excitement all seemed to be coursing through her, in a confusion of inebriated emotions.

She stepped gingerly towards the tree bridge, trying to make out the steps in the shadows.

A twig snapped, loud in the still night.

She turned quickly, and there he was, Nimbarra, his dark form gleaming in the moonlight. His smile was warm and friendly, a smile that slipped away in a moment and left him looking a little coy as he lowered his eyes to the broken twig he held in his hands. He tossed the snapped stick to the side of the trail.

'You are leaving so early, Lateah.' He said it simply, with just the slightest questioning inflection. And Lateah was a term of endearment ... Jasmyn thought so anyway. She thought it meant esteemed one, a term of affection and respect for a female elder, but she had also heard it used to address a child, and for all Jasmyn knew, it might have other connotations too.

'Yes, I'm very tired, Nim ... Nimba ...' Jasmyn knew his name, she couldn't think why on earth she was stumbling over it.

'Nimbarra.' The young warrior said plainly and put his hand up in the Dzahn gesture of greeting. He proffered a broad grin, his teeth capturing the pearly radiance of the moon. 'I am brother to Tidak. The night is dark. You should not walk alone, I will walk with you,' he suggested.

'Thank you, Nimbarra, but I think I'll be OK ... I'm a big girl,' Jasmyn replied demurely. Thank gods it was dark, because she felt herself begin to blush.

Nimbarra shifted his stance uncertainly and licked his lips. He seemed puzzled. 'No, Lateah, you are slim ...' he hesitated and swallowed, 'but womanly and round,' he added hastily, and then he seemed a little panicked and unsure how to proceed, before blurting out, 'but still with sturdy hips and firm of breast ...'

The stunned look on Jasmyn's face stopped him in his tracks. She was definitely blushing now. He shifted his weight and examined his feet, clearly mortified, having realised he was out of his depth with this strange woman.

The effect of his perfectly proportioned man-boy's body, his bare shoulders and arms shining in the moonlight, combined with the look of embarrassment and doubt creeping over him, was enough to melt Jasmyn's heart and rouse her instincts, both maternal and otherwise.

She let out a sudden yelp of laughter, which sounded so loud in the quite forest she put a hand quickly to her mouth.

Nimbarra relaxed and let out an audible sigh. His broad smile returned and Jasmyn said: 'All right then, yes, Nimbarra. That would be lovely, walk with me, if you don't mind.'

His smile seemed to brighten his whole person and he laughed in relief and bounded ahead of her like an excited pup. Jasmyn allowed herself a grin and even a subdued giggle as he led the way across the bridge, and when they reached the clearing beyond, he set off in the direction of Jasmyn's hut, the location of which he seemed to know already. As they went he struck up a conversation with his characteristic candour and naiveté, which Jasmyn was already starting to find quite beguiling.

CHAPTER 20

The passage of time amongst the Dzahn was marked only by the changing seasons and the phases of the moon, and the days since their arrival at the village quickly turned into months. Barrak's bruised ribs had finally healed, with the help of the Shabbah's herbs and poultices, and no longer caused him any real restriction of movement or very much pain.

At times he still felt like an intruder amongst the river people and spending time with the Shabbah in his rocky eyrie, got him away from the routine of the village. At least with the Shabbah there was a common vocation, and Barrak was fascinated to learn the medicinal uses of unfamiliar indigenous herbs. Shabbah was generous with his knowledge and patient in his instruction, and it comforted Barrak, perhaps because it was a link to his lost life.

Shabbah shared his own experiences of exploring the spirit realm using what he called the spirit medicine, made from the Taikkim root. Sometimes Shabbah also referred to it as the plant of the dead. He talked about the dark spirit of the hunter – the shadow spirit – and they discussed the symbolism of the river possum, which he said was Barrak's spirit guide from the animal realm. Barrak began to understand the old spirit guide's ways, through exploring with him his own Taikkim-mediated experience.

But they only talked about such things sparingly.

Barrak knew why.

What the Shabbah referred to as the spirit realm, this alternative reality to which the Taikkim root had transported him, was beyond physical reality and could not be easily grasped or explained literally. Understanding grew only gradually.

One of the most enduring images from his 'journey' was encountering the spirit of his dead wife, Persephone, and finding that she and Jasmyn seemed to merge into one spirit.

'Perhaps the lesson is to let go, Hakeah,' Shabbah had counselled him when he asked him what he thought.

'We must all learn to let go of those we love the most.'

Shabbah knew without being told how Barrak felt about Jasmyn, and his counsel regarding Barrak's vision had a strange synchronicity, because as the weeks passed, it became obvious to Barrak and to most of the village people that the young warrior Nimbarra was smitten with Jasmyn and seemed to be pursuing her. Jasmyn made light of it to Barrak, as though she dismissed the whole idea out of hand, due to Nimbarra's youth. But it wasn't that simple.

It seemed no taboos had been breached, no one in the village appeared to disapprove. In fact, right from the start Jasmyn had been accepted as one of their own. Bizarrely, they seemed to think she was reincarnated from some Dzahn ancestor. Spirit mother. Barrak had struggled a little with this. What did that make him … the goat's breakfast?

He knew that Jasmyn had been badly shaken by their experiences in the wilderness. It had almost brought her undone, and forced her into a kind of protective denial. But now, in the comfortingly secure setting of the Dzahn village, she was recovering herself and coming back to reality. But Barrak couldn't help wondering whether Jasmyn had embraced the Dzahn way of life so readily because part of her was still seeking psychological refuge from the horrors of the recent past. And though she made light of it, Barrak suspected that the sense of security and comfort Jasmyn found in village life was inextricably linked to Nimbarra's infatuation with her. And perhaps she was a little gratified and flattered by the young man's attentions after all, despite his age, or perhaps even because of it.

One day, after Barrak told Shabbah about their encounter with the monster, Bishop, he counselled him again and offered a possible explanation.

'She is running from death, Hakeah, a vision of death so awful she cannot face it, and so the only thing to do is turn her back and run, run from what can't be accepted. What better than to run straight into the arms of Nimbarra? He is youthful and strong and alive. He is the opposite of death. So, it is natural, she chooses life, she flees from death … We all do, Hakeah.'

Gradually Barrak became more and more interested in the routines and practices of everyday life in the village, and as he grew stronger, he spent less time with Shabbah and aligned himself more with Kajha and his hunting group, the oldest of the hunters still active. He had to work for acceptance because it seemed the last thing Kajha's group wanted was a clumsy novice with little or no bushcraft ruining their hunt. Eventually it was agreed that Barrak would join their group, and after that, they were gracious and patient with him, if a little condescending. He was treated like a young novice hunter. Perhaps, in the end, there was an element of sympathy, too, because it must have seemed to them that the young warrior, Nimbarra, was trying to steal his woman.

Jasmyn herself made every effort to preserve Barrak's pride and she went out of her way to spend time with him; in some ways she was even more demonstrative in her affections towards him. But there had been a subtle shift in the fabric of their relationship – a relationship that had never been formulated in words – its unspoken substance only ever half-known and intimated in the private world of their unconsummated intimacy, like a secret glue that bound them together.

The more she sort to define the new boundaries in subtle ways, boundaries that had been mysteriously and deliciously blurred in the past, the more it stung Barrak. Every small change in her was evidence that Nimbarra's infatuation with her might not be entirely one-sided. But pride demanded his complete complicity in re-drawing the boundaries and that he join Jasmyn in the pretence that those boundaries had been in place all along.

Perhaps it was pride, too, that impelled him to persevere with Kajha's hunting cadre; after all, that was what the Dzahn river people did, they hunted. And it was a constant preoccupation, finding enough food to feed the people of the village.

Barrak estimated that the village numbered about 150 souls in all, and he marvelled at the way the little society operated as an organic, integrated unit. There was a natural rhythm and what seemed like a collective will that permeated the village, giving every individual a sense of their place in the natural world of the Dzahn and an instinctive understanding of what needed to be done and when. Barrak found he was envious of this sense of belonging and, bit by bit, as he settled into the new reality of village life and overcame his initial resistance to it, he found he very much wanted to make himself part of it.

There were at least a dozen hunting groups, each comprising four or five individuals. And day to day, with little discussion or argument, the objectives for the day's hunting were allocated with ease and understanding, with any debate settled quickly by Kajha's group of hunting elders.

Not every group went out every day, and on rare days, no hunting party went out at all. But depending on the weather, the availability of game, the season, the phases of the moon and many other factors, of which Barrak was conspicuously ignorant, the day's activities would be easily and often wordlessly decided upon. But the Dzahn were not entirely dependent on hunting and gathering food. They had developed some considerable industry in cultivating several of the native plant species that were suitable for cropping and much care and attention went into maintaining the Dzahn goat herd, which provided milk and a ready supply of meat for special occasions.

Game was plentiful in the surrounding countryside, and what, to Barrak, seemed a bewildering array of other natural food sources, some surprisingly appetising and others, like the big, plump, creamy-coloured grubs which Tidak once dug out of a rotting log and offered him, were less so. Tidak had laughed at him and joyously bitten off and discarded the heads of the ugly grubs, swallowing the rest with relish, rolling his eyes and rubbing his stomach as he did.

The country the Dzahn occupied was so different from the arid wastelands they had crossed to the west. In some ways it seemed to be even more fertile and abundant than the farmland and hinterlands of the Eyrean Sea. There were forested ranges to the north and east of the plateau, and below the falls, the river quickly became deep and wide as it meandered towards the nearby lake. To the south were marshlands and then flat grasslands extending as far as the eye could see.

There seemed to be little the people could not make use of in their environment, and village fare was rich and varied. Already Barrak had sampled several types of fish and delicious crustaceans from the lake and the river. Hunting parties that ventured out onto the plains often returned with doarht, the Dzahn's favourite meat, and closer to hand were plentiful rylaby, which the expert Dzahn hunters found embarrassingly easy to shoot with their powerful and accurate hunting bows. There had also been waterfowl from the lake, a spiny ant-eating animal with sweet, strong-tasting flesh, and once, a giant reptile as long as a man was caught and cooked to tender perfection in an oven of hot rocks covered by coals and earth.

All the hunters, young and old and even the children, prided themselves on their expertise in crafting their hunting weapons, and it was part of every child's upbringing to learn to make their own full-size kahzit bow. Some of the older men, who'd retired from hunting, were regarded as expert in various crafts, and the young hunters would seek them out for their advice in the making of a new bow, spear or arrow.

Barrak learned that metal spear and arrow heads, when they could be procured, were much preferred over sharpened stone and a prized possession amongst the hunters. But it was unclear where the metal for them was obtained.

Some of the older men and women had specialised in other work, like crafting domestic utensils or curing and shaping animal hides for use in clothing and bedding, or construction of the village's rudimentary buildings. Village life was a matter of co-operation and communal effort. Gender roles were not strictly defined. Barrak noticed that many of the hunting groups included young women and the older women often organised their own expeditions to the lakes and rivers to fish and hunt.

The men too, were not averse to foraging for wild fruits and roots or wild honey or tending the gardens when, for whatever reason, the conditions were not conducive to the hunt. Generally the women took a leading role in food preparation and caring for the young, although these roles too were interchangeable and the village as a whole took on the task of rearing the young, regardless of whose particular offspring they were.

And when it came to the preparation of a meal, which involved the roasting of a good joint of meat, such as doarht or goat, you could be sure the men would be quick to come forward, claiming particular expertise and technique which, as Jasmyn noted with wry humour, was just like men anywhere, when the job of searing animal flesh on a fire was at hand.

But there was one anomaly, one aspect of Dzahn life that both he and Jasmyn found hard to fathom. It was their warrior training, which they pursued obsessively and which seemed to take up so much of the young men's spare time. They took great pride in their prowess as warriors, perhaps even more than their ability with hunting bow and spear, and this was a quality that the young women of the Dzahn valued most highly in a prospective mate.

The fighting club seemed to be exclusively used in combat training and was purpose built for the task. Essentially it was a stone axe, made from an especially stout sapling of one or two particular species. Much attention went into the weighting and binding of the club and also the hardness and the finish of the stone head, which usually had one blunt side and one sharpened edge.

Often the clubs were highly decorated, much like the Shabbah's medicine stick.

While the warrior's battle club had no place in hunting, there was some cross-over in the other direction. Barrak had witnessed at least one session of warrior training in which a target of dried grass and sticks, fashioned to look like a human figure, was set up in the training field and riddled with arrows shot in quick succession from hunting bows by trainees on the run.

Training was serious. Competitions were held and the winners celebrated as heroes. But try as he might, Barrak could not get to the bottom of just what the men were training for.

A strange seriousness and intensity came over the young men whenever they entered the dedicated training ground. It was like a bushland military academy, and within its precinct there was a strict discipline and code of conduct that was strangely at odds with the relaxed attitude pervading the rest of Dzahn life. There was no doubt that a threat existed from somewhere outside the village which was at once imminent and deadly serious. And yet most of the time life went on as though there was no threat at all. He started to wonder if the village suffered from some kind of collective paranoia.

When he asked about the reason for the training he always received vague and evasive answers.

He once pressed Yenta, one of Kajha's hunting group, for an explanation. She would say only that the world outside the valley and the nearby hunting grounds was full of danger.

'What kind of danger?' Barrak had pressed her.

Yenta's deep blue eyes had fixed on Barrak with unexpected intensity. 'The deadly kind,' she had said simply.

'What do you mean … What … who is this deadly enemy?'

'Don't ask me that, Mahnu,' she had snapped at Barrak, sharp and impatient. 'We never speak their name. Not ever. It is bad deemha, and you must not ask. Not even think of asking.'

Jasmyn had tried to get some clarification from Nimbarra, but to no avail. She told Barrak she'd been quite annoyed, because Nimbarra had spoken sharply to her, too.

He had conceded that the Dzahn did have a dangerous enemy, but then he'd forbidden her to speak of it again. Barrak thought that normally anyone, especially a young and brash suitor, forbidding Jasmyn anything, would have riled her. And yet it seemed she had accepted it and let it pass because of the intensity the question had evoked in Nimbarra, just as Barrak had observed in Yenta.

It had left them both perplexed and more than a little bothered.

'I'd never seen him look that way,' she confided to Barrak later. 'And he's never taken a tone with me before . . .' she trailed off a little awkwardly, 'but you know, there was something else, something he said that was strange. He said it was forbidden to even speak the name of their enemy, for fear of drawing them closer to the village.'

Far from the village for the first time since their rescue, Barrak was infused with a strange cocktail of exhilaration and anxiety. This was the same wilderness that had almost claimed his life. Its vastness and harshness were unchanged and it evoked a lingering trace of the fear and desperation he had felt when lost in it.

But now he felt less vulnerable, as if the sparse skills he had learned restored some confidence and even pride, and the beginnings of an understanding of the serenity with which the Dzahn moved through their landscape.

This was the first time he had been included in a hunting sortie of more than one day and he had taken it as vote of confidence, an indication that he was no longer considered a complete liability.

It was their second day out. After skirting the lake and travelling north across the wide grassland that separated the Dzahn valley from the blue ranges on the northern horizon. The four of them had made camp in the foothills, before climbing a low pass through the mountains all through the early part of the next morning. On the other side was hilly country with mature open woodlands on the eastern slopes extending out onto a fertile grassland, which was known to be a good hunting ground for doarht.

But now they were stopped, crouched along a rocky rise, marking the last of the foothills and overlooking the first of the wide northern plains. Kajha's barely perceptible hand signal had instructed Barrak and the youngest hunter to stop and stay low, below the rocky ridge line. Meanwhile, he and Yenta had crept up onto the crest of the ridge.

Not for the first time Barrak marvelled at the stillness and patience of the Dzahn hunters. The two of them had been watching something down on the plain for half an hour, in total silence and with barely a movement, except for one or two whispered comments.

But something was wrong. Even in his own limited experience he knew this was not consistent with the usual rhythm of the hunt, and there was tension in the quietness of the two hunters and a note of concern in their barely audible whispers.

Finally Kajha signalled to Barrak and the youngster to come up. With all the stealth he could muster, Barrak edged up to Kajha's right side. The leery old hunter seemed to have relaxed a bit and he shifted his position and leaned out across one of the boulders, no longer taking quite so much care to conceal himself. He raised his arm and stretched it out along the top of the boulder, pointing. 'Do you see, Mahnu?' he asked quietly.

Barrak squinted in the direction Kajha seemed to be pointing but could see nothing remarkable. He raised a hand to his forehead to shield his eyes from the bright morning sun.

The horizon was marked by a misty line of grey ranges. To the north, mature eucalypt forests of the mountains gave way abruptly to sparse and scrubby woodlands along the verge of the rocky foothills and, as the ground levelled out, the scrub was confined mainly to the banks of a small creek meandering along the northern fringe of the plain.

But directly below them was only a vast grassland, rippled like the ocean by a fresh breeze, and like an ocean, concealing any minor feature in its vastness.

'There!' Kajha gave his extended finger a shake. 'Do you see now?'

Barrak followed his finger and finally he saw what Kajha saw, in the middle distance, directly in front of their position. Barely more than a spec at first, bobbing on top of the grass, and then clearer, as the taller grass fell way, a small figure was surging through the long grass.

'Yes. Yes, I do see, now,' Barrak enthused. 'What is it?'

'It is a human person,' Kajha said with quiet conviction.

It was just like hunting. Once they were in the grass, before it got too long and they lost sight of each other, Kajha used hand signals to spread them out, not too wide, and then they set a course to intercept their quarry.

A few minutes later it was hard to say who got the greater shock when Barrak came face to face with their prey in a sparse patch of low grass. All heard the ear-splitting, high-pitched squeal, which went on and on, shattering the morning stillness until every winged creature in the valley had taken to the skies in panic. By the time the three others arrived in the clearing, Barrak was wrestling with a creature not even half his size but twice as feisty. He had instinctively grabbed the little girl after she started screaming but before she could gather her wits enough to run off into the grass.

The little girl's terror was most likely heightened by Barrak's outlandish looks, because once Kajha took hold of her and turned her away from Barrak and said some soothing words to her, she stopped screaming, but she didn't stop struggling to get free, not until Kajha talked her down with his quiet, calm and reassuring manner.

But even then she sat tense and brittle on a flattened patch of grass, with Kajha's arm around her, her wide eyes accentuated by the hollowness of her emaciated face, which was covered with dirt and what might have been dried blood.

Barrak and the other two looked on as the gentle old hunter took the girl's small hand in his, a tiny hand clenched up like a rock, white-knuckled, grazed and gritty, holding onto her only possession with grim determination. Slowly, with gentle movements and whispered assurances, he coaxed her fingers open one by one, until finally the contents of her grubby hand fell to the ground and rolled a few inches over the flattened grass.

No one spoke a word.

Barrak stared at the small red object as if it were an aberration of nature, which, in some ways, he supposed it was. Recognition collided with puzzlement in his mind and he looked to his companions. Kajha wore a dark frown and when he caught Barrak's eye there was intensity and alarm in his gaze. Yenta glared at Kajha and exhaled a long weary breath that wheezed out of her like a groan, a groan resonating with fear. The youngest hunter just stared wide eyed at the thing on the ground and bit his lip.

The waxy red cylinder lying at the girl's feet was open at one end and capped at the other by a distinctive metal disc. Barrak knew what the thing was right away, but he still could not grasp the significance of the girl having it in her possession. It was a spent cartridge, identical to the ammunition Bishop had used in the weapon he called his 'blaster'.

A chill seemed to settle over the quiet group standing around the ragged girl, and as if on cue, a gust of wind blew across them and set up a whisper through the nearby stand of tall grass. The youngest hunter drew a short breath and spoke a word that Barrak didn't recognise, but he only got it half out before Kajha cut him off mid-phrase with a sharp look of caution, a hard stare that came at him like an arrow.

The little girl looked up at the hunters and began to wail. Her eyes filled like tiny green wells and then overflowed, the tears pouring out of her like a spring and making spidery trails down her muddy face before soaking into her tunic. Barrak wondered that the body of the poor wasted child held moisture enough to produce so many tears. But she wailed all the harder, tears falling like rain, and her disquiet spilled out over the grassy plain.

CHAPTER 21

JASMYN STARED AT BARRAK with soft eyes and smiled in a familiar way, creating an almost tangible harmonic of warmth and compassion in the space between them. Barrak half turned away from her and cast his gaze out over the foothills and nearby lake, cobalt against the near shore, fading gradually to a misty white haze where it met the sky.

'It sounds like your mind is made up,' he said evenly.

'He loves me, Barrak ... without any strings attached. I can't explain it. It's like it's pure, somehow ... natural. No one has ever been this way with me before ...'

Barrak wanted to say something, anything. Something to reassure her that he understood. Just some words or even just a sound to relieve the strange sensation of hollowness in his chest. But the buzzing swarm of thoughts and emotions welling up inside him stubbornly refused to resolve itself into speech of any kind, and instead, he took a single, vapid breath, and stared into the distance.

He remembered Jasmyn telling him about all the misfits and miscreants she'd attracted in the past, up to and including Meldrick he supposed, and he wondered what it was about her that always seemed to attract the wrong sort of man. Maybe Nimbarra was the first good one ... With that thought came an avalanche of self-reproach. Why had he not declared his love for her sooner? The answer was right before him. Because it wasn't until right now, this very moment, that he'd even allowed himself to acknowledge it, finally ... fully.

'Barrak.' Jasmyn touched his arm gently. He let the warmth and affection in her touch flow right through him and it lingered in his heart and lightened it somewhat. He knew that she loved him in her own way. Nothing would change that. And he knew that his love for Jasmyn was a rare and peculiar thing, conceived through nurture and care, enriched by time and the twists and turns of fate, and ultimately fired in the crucible of hardship. It was a love, timeless and resilient, but, as the Shabbah had pointed out to him, it was a love that must not grasp.

He didn't need the Shabbah or even his own Taikkim-enhanced dreaming to tell him this. He had known it for a while, maybe always. It was a love pure enough that it could let go, and not be diminished.

'I want to have a family. Maybe this is my time. Nimbarra can give me that, and you know the whole village is one big family ...' Jasmyn had taken on a slightly pleading tone as if she felt she needed to convince him. Barrak felt a tear well up in one eye. It might have been the mention of family, or maybe it was the chill morning breeze. All at once he had a fleeting image of the children he and Jasmyn might have had together and it seemed strange that this had never occurred to him before.

But now it broke his heart. He blinked away a tear, kept his gaze averted and exhaled slowly.

But do you love him, Jasmyn ... do you? His inner voice railed with hurt and anger, petulant inside his head. Could you possibly ... like I love you? He was surer than ever that Jasmyn was more in love with the village as a whole and all it offered her, than with Nimbarra himself. Or was that his pride talking?

Somehow he was struck dumb, and instead of speaking, he found himself nodding in agreement.

Jasmyn's life in Eyre had been cruelly snatched away from her, as had her family. And she'd experienced such horrors in their flight from Eyre ... She was twenty-seven, the time of the progressed lunar return. He didn't know much about the planets, but he knew this was the time in a woman's life when she experiences a tremendous urge for family, security ... children. No wonder her every instinct was to grasp this one haven of security in what had become, for her, a dangerous and frightening world.

Jasmyn seemed to be reading his mind.

'Barrak this could be my chance for a normal life …' She paused and gave a short, sharp snort of self-derision. 'Did I just say that? Normal life … hah! You know what I mean … It could be a good life … simple, honest … in some way.' She paused to let Barrak speak but he just kept nodding and staring into the distance.

Jasmyn grew more insistent. 'My life in Eyre is over. We can't go back there. We'd be arrested, or worse. And besides, how would we even get back there? And to go on … to go east, like Gitan said, well that's just crazy. What do we know about the east, for quest's sake?!' She paused as if she'd become uncertain of her argument.

Barrak thought about Enoch and Elias and Elias's mother, and he remembered his discussion with Gitan in the forest that night and tried to imagine what did lie to the east of the little village that had become their home.

She said his name again and gave his arm a small, urgent squeeze, perhaps a little exasperated by his silence.

He turned to her now with a crooked, half-baked smile. 'I know. I know. You're right. This does look like the best option. Maybe it is the best option, for you … But I'm not so sure.' He flicked a quick glance over his shoulder out across the lake. 'Maybe my place is to go east.'

As he turned back to her, Jasmyn's eyes were full of hurt, not her own, but Barrak's, reflected back at him with the sweet and genuine empathy which, when her guard was down, was what made him love her the most. It was as if she'd only just now realised the full implications of her declaration for Barrak, the heart-breaking quandary in which it left him.

Barrak saw doubt flicker in her eyes and he was glad to see it, even as he chastised himself for feeling so.

Past Jasmyn's shoulder he could see the canopy of the big river gums above the heart of the village and a patch of river and a hint of smoke below the tree tops. Something had caught his attention, a sound, discordant and unusual, a sound that seemed to carry almost too clearly through the trees from the distant village all the way to the high ridge where they stood.

He was distracted by the strangeness of the sudden noise for a moment but Jasmyn was talking again.

'Barrak, I don't know what to say to you. We've been through so much together. Sometimes I wonder if you really know how much you mean to me ...

'I don't want to lose you ...'

A second noise took all of their attention this time and Jasmyn spun around to look towards the village. There was no mistaking it, it was a high-pitched scream, distant and thin but chilling in its intensity, rising quickly, only to end in mid cry, cut off with dreadful finality.

There was a frozen moment, but only a moment, as they stared wide-eyed at each other, then with a single mind they were on the move, scurrying down the rocky path from the ridge. What had been a leisurely twenty-minute stroll up to the lookout in the early morning sun, seemed to take no time in reverse, and almost before they knew it, they were on the flats by the meeting place. The only thing that registered with Barrak as they scrambled down, was a fleeting glimpse of the Shabbah as they passed, a look of dread and sad knowing in his eyes as he silently watched them go by ... that and more impressions of upset reaching them from below, another scream, voices raised in alarm, a flash of flame through the canopy as they descended.

At the junction of the paths there was an eerie and unnatural silence. The silence quickly broke into mayhem. Loud screams erupted simultaneously from either side of them, desperate screams, tinged with horror and fright. A figure burst from the bushes, one of the village women, clutching an infant in her arms, terror and determination blazing in her eyes. She glared blankly at them for an instant before adjusting her line and dashing into the bushes beyond the clearing. She had appeared and vanished in an instant, like an apparition, the only sign of her passing was the sound of her crashing through the undergrowth, and a single shouted word which seemed to hang in the air, marking the spot where the bush had swallowed her.

'Run!'

There followed a thunderous boom which shook the leaves of the trees and filled the serene village glade with its brutal percussion. With the sound still ringing in his ears, Barrak found himself rushing across the tree bridge, making for the village centre.

The scene there pulled him up to a dead stop.

The clearing was devoid of people, but for a lone figure near the main cooking fire. Two figures really. Tidak was on his knees in the sand, cupping the head of a prone form in his hands. Barrak knew right away the crumpled figure was Kajha. He wasn't sure how he knew, whether it was the stillness of Kajha's body, or the wracked expression on Tidak's face. By the way Kajha seemed to have subsided partially into the ground, with one leg twisted under him, he knew Kajha was dead.

Barrak felt an odd pang of relief for Kajha, that he wouldn't have to witness what was to come. But the feeling was as fleeting as it was perverse and was quickly overwhelmed by a deep and visceral sense of foreboding and a dire sense that the world was about to be turned on its head, in a way that was unimaginably cruel.

His foreboding took on organic form as a figure rose up right behind Tidak, looming out of a thickening swirl of smoke and yellow flames, which cracked and flared in the roofing thatch of a nearby dwelling. Barrak's feet seemed to be rooted to the spot and he stared at the great hulking figure, transfixed by its grim and imposing appearance, horrified by its proximity as it strode towards Tidak.

A trick of perspective made the brute appear two or three times Tidak's size as it cleared the smoke and paused, seeing Barrak by the bridge. Barrak met its blank one-eyed stare and a gut-churning memory of the two brutes in the bar at Dods Junction came back to him.

This one was bald with a garish network of black tattoos extending over his skull and down the left side of his face. A patch of livid flesh had grown over the socket of his missing right eye. A full beard, turned mainly to grey, together with the paunchy gut hanging over the front of his black leather trousers, showed this one was past his prime.

As he caught Barrak's eye, his gnarled face broke into a leering grin, exposing a row of blackened stumps and a single gold tooth. His one and only eye glinted with apparent delight, and he seemed to be saying, 'Yes, you just watch this!'

Only then did Barrak notice the huge metal axe as the paunchy brute hefted it high and wide, moving forward and then planting his back foot for balance.

He wound up with a huge backswing. The curved metallic blade was the size of a dinner plate, dull and black in the morning sun, as though light itself could not abide the rusty, blood-stained cleaver.

Tidak sensed the danger, or perhaps he'd seen the look on Barrak's face. He tensed to spring up but it was too late. The bearded troll grunted with the final exertion of his strike.

But, there was another cause for his grunted exhalation. He let the axe fall to the ground and his left hand went to his neck, examining the arrow shaft that had appeared there, beyond all expectation. Barrak could see it had gone right through, the arrow head protruding from the other side. The look of exaltation in the brute's eye turned to surprise and then swiftly to anger. He grasped the shaft and bellowed, his eye darting from Tidak to Barrak and back again before finally swivelling to take in his assailant.

Nimbarra was running straight at him, loading another arrow and stretching his bow to full force, without even breaking stride. Barrak remembered seeing Nimbarra and the young men doing a similar exercise in the training ground, using a thatched target.

The ogre bared his stumpy teeth at Nimbarra and bellowed like a wounded animal, jutting his thick ugly head towards him. He hefted up the axe, double handed. Nimbarra loosed the second arrow. It struck the brute slightly below and at an angle to the first, giving the bizarre impression of a collar of arrows. It had pieced his larynx and cut the brute's bellowing off to a choked gurgle.

Tidak rolled out of danger and his brother took three shortened steps before dropping to one knee, not ten yards from the enraged enemy. The wounded cyclops rounded on him, raising the axe across his body with a mute grunt of frustration and rage. Jets of blood spurted from the second wound, which looked like it had severed a major blood vessel, but there was no sign of it fazing the big bastard.

Nimbarra crouched calmly, his bow already reloaded in one seamless movement as he'd dropped to the sand. He let the beast take a step towards him, just to square him up, then he let the third arrow go, almost delicately, not quite from full bow tension, with precision. It sliced into the rampant giant's one good eye and jarred to a stop inside his skull. That arrow would be ruined.

The axeman grunted. One great boot seemed to waver in mid-air for a moment, as if looking for solid ground, and one hand came away from the axe handle and shot up towards the shaft in his eye but then stopped half way, as if uncertain of its purpose. And that was all. Tidak's would-be executioner crumpled to his knees and fell forward with a dull thud and a loud snap as the arrow in his eye broke off, twisting his ugly head grotesquely to one side.

Nimbarra shouldered his bow and lurched forward, whisking his fighting club from his belt as he ran toward the fallen brute. In one fluid movement he planted a foot next to his head and swung the club in a long scything uppercut, skimming the sandy ground and smashing with full force into his skull. There was a loud pop as the back of his skull opened like a lid, revealing its pulpy organ. Nimbarra landed lightly in the dirt between the dead brute and Tidak and stowed his club, squatting there, tense and alert, scanning the clearing in one direction, then the other. Satisfied, he put a foot on his dead opponents shoulder and extracted the two good arrows and replaced them in the scabbard.

'Why are you still here, brother? You know you should be away, to the hiding place.'. He took Tidak by both shoulders and shook him gently and held him at arm's length, looking him up and down, checking him for wounds.

'You know your place, Tidak, the ones who have escaped, they will need you ...'

'But Kajha ...' he interrupted his brother weakly, nodding towards their father's body.

'Our father is dead. He fought well, Tidak. You know he would want you safe.'

Barrak approached, walking towards the crouching brothers as if in a trance. Nimbarra caught his eye, but only briefly, before looking past him and scanning the edge of the clearing and the bridge behind him.

His expression said it all. Where is she? Where is Jasmyn?

With a sinking sensation, Barrak realised he had run on ahead and crossed the bridge, momentarily forgetting about Jasmyn in his shock and distraction. He followed Nimbarra's gaze and they both saw her, but they'd heard her first.

It was not so much a scream as a strident wail of protest. Jasmyn's arms and legs were flailing in the air, because one of the giant brutes had her around the waist, heaving her off the ground and swinging her from side to side as if that might subdue her.

This one was taller and younger than the beast Nimbarra had felled. He had a strangely elongated face which gave him a sour and ugly expression. Long straight black hair hung to his shoulders and a lurid red and blue snake was tattooed down one side of his face and neck, seemingly continuing down his lean muscled left arm, where it emerged from his armour.

His mad, malevolent eyes were shot with red and there was frustration and malice in the grim set of his crooked jaw as he struggled to contain Jasmyn. He exuded an evil presence, which seemed it might not abide a lack of killing for long.

Nimbarra didn't hesitate. He flashed past Barrak, closing the gap to the brute in a moment. But even as he launched himself like a spear at Jasmyn's captor, another figure had descended the bridge behind the first and was lined up beside him. This one was shorter, with a great welt of frizzy, matted hair all about his fat head, thickset like a massive bull.

Slung at his side was a blaster, which he snatched up, but too late. Somehow Nimbarra was above him, soaring impossibly high, his legs still running in the air. He flew at the head of the stocky brute and deflected his weapon with one hand; in the other, his fighting club was arched above him. The blaster boomed and the tall one flinched and bellowed and raised a foot off the ground, as if he'd been shot.

The blaster-wielding brute hit the ground in a mess of arms and legs. Nimbarra's club flailed in a fury of blows with more bone-popping crunches.

The tall one threw Jasmyn like a rag doll onto the river bank. And then he had Nimbarra, stopping his club with one huge hand while the other took hold of his hair. The young warrior was slick with his last victim's blood and rotated nimbly, kicking free. But before he could fully regain his balance, the tall brute caught him with a savage blow to the back of the head and Nimbarra fell forward onto his hands and knees. Barrak and Tidak rushed in and the thug turned to meet their charge with bared teeth and a savage snarl, as he reached for a bladed weapon at his belt.

But Jasmyn beat them to it. She came out of nowhere, flying through the air. She hit the brute between the shoulders, clinging on like a monkey and throwing him off balance. She gouged at his eyes but was quickly thrown aside, only to be replaced by Tidak and Barrak, who slammed into him and brought him to his knees. Nimbarra was back on his feet and for a moment it appeared they had the upper hand.

What happened next was unclear.

Barrak remembered seeing Tidak whisked away, somehow spirited out of the fight and Jasmyn screaming ... and that was all.

He woke with grit and blood and his own swollen flesh between his teeth. His head was on the ground and his arms were immobile, bound behind his back.

Groggy and confused, he couldn't really see, but he could hear a gods-awful noise; it must have been what brought him back to consciousness. The noise was terrible. An unearthly keening wail, strident and appalling, and then there was a stream of venomous abuse. It took Barrak a moment to realise that it was Jasmyn's voice because he'd never heard her, or any human, sound quite like this.

He tried to blink the sand from his eyes. As his vision began to clear, he saw dark figures were gathered around, there must have been ten or more. He could see Jasmyn was on her knees, her hands bound in front of her, her neck arched with tendons taut as she faced the clearing. Screaming.

He became aware of a series of dull smacking thuds. With each thud Jasmyn yelped. He raised one knee to wipe more of the sand and muck from his eyes.

He could see the tall brute, kneeling in the dirt. He had Nimbarra by the hair and his bloodied fist slammed into him with sickening force. He hit Nimbarra again and again as though toiling at a repetitive task, his face grim-set with zealous determination and bile. His victim was almost unrecognisable and blood covered them both. With each blow Jasmyn moaned and roared and hissed like a wild cat, screaming out what she would do to Nimbarra's attacker in terms lurid and graphic and studded with expletives.

The lanky brute would not desist; he was overcome by some kind of demented blood lust. And it was clear Nimbarra was already dead.

The brute paused as though exhausted by his efforts, suddenly aware of the crowd gathered around. A dozen of his feral band stood in a rough circle, many of them with captive villagers bound and cowering at their feet. There was a moment of quiet, as if the scene was distasteful even to such a horrid assembly.

This seemed to anger the tall one and he bellowed in frustration. He took Nimbarra by the hair and dragged his limp form with great effort to the milling boulder in the centre of the clearing. He flung him against the side of it, looking around at the feral congregation again as though seeking acknowledgment of some kind, but all he got was an uncertain murmur. He bellowed his rage and suddenly a long blade was in his hand, shaped like a short sword. He had his victim by the hair and hoisted him up with a mighty effort, holding his limp form almost off the ground and laying his head and shoulders across the edge of the stone's flat top.

The air above the clearing was filled with Jasmyn's shrieking and the horror of the gruesome scene became even more surreal as the brute set his bloodied arm to sawing away at Nimbarra's neck with his blade.

Barrak screwed his eyes shut. Then he glanced sideways at Jasmyn, but he couldn't bear to see her distress. She was moaning in a low throaty wail and her forehead rested on the sand as her outstretched hands kneaded the dirt in front of her. Barrak looked away.

It seemed to take forever.

Gradually a chant began, keeping grotesque time with the murderous brute's sawing. Apparently this was a ritual the assembled maniacs could identify with. Rhythmic clapping was added to the chant and it rose to a crescendo until finally a cheer went up.

It was over.

Barrak opened one eye to see the tall bastard holding Nimbarra's head up by his long hair, thrusting it high in a gesture of victory, showing off his trophy to the cheers and hoots of the assembled mob.

Abruptly, Jasmyn was on her feet, having somehow wrenched herself from the grasp of her captor and freed her hands. She ran at Nimbarra's killer, shrieking wildly. Barrak struggled to his feet and lurched forward, but was felled and ended with his face in the sand again. He rolled to one side to see Jasmyn, terrified for her, willing her to stop and stay quiet.

The brute saw her coming and gave her all his attention, dropping Nimbarra's head carelessly to the ground. She slammed into him but he turned at the last moment, letting her momentum carry her past, then caught her by her arm and dragged her in to him, putting a hand around her waist and hugging her to his besmirched body.

'Yeaah, that's it, my lovely, come to Battle,' he growled with a mad grin, his eyes darting around, playing to the crowd. Jasmyn shrieked and swore, stomping and kicking and letting loose another vile stream of abuse.

'Arrghh. I like one with fight,' he emphasised the last word as he threw Jasmyn to the ground, clearly annoyed by her flailing boots, despite his claims. Jasmyn crabbed away from him on her back and he rounded on her and tucked her up under his arm as easily as he would a child.

'Come on, my little wildcat – let's get married!'

He gazed around the crowd again, leering and looking for their approval.

Jasmyn kicked and squirmed and freed herself, dropping to the ground and scything a roundhouse kick into the brute's knee, dropping him to the other knee, but only for a moment. He came up with an angry scowl and lurched forward, bellowing out his rage as he took her by her hair and slapped her hard, knocking her to the ground before gripping her by her upper arm and dragging her towards the edge of the clearing.

Barrak lurched to his hands and knees, but a weight fell on him like a ton of bricks and pushed him to the ground so hard it forced all the breath out of him. Then a boot pushed his cheek into the dirt and held him there.

The theatrics were finished and the brute's manner was again malicious and wanton, as he hauled Jasmyn towards a copse of wattle. Jasmyn barely resisted, she was groggy and her head lolled. The thug dropped her to the ground and knelt down in the sand, pushing himself between her legs. He leaned forward and put his face close to hers and whispered something into her ear. Coming to her senses Jasmyn tried to wrench a hand free, but he had both her arms pinned. She struggled in vain and, finding herself trapped, she spat forcefully in his face. He grunted and shrugged a shoulder up to wipe away the spittle and raised his hand to slap her again.

But ... Battle had been so intent on Jasmyn, he hadn't seen what the others in the clearing had been observing for some moments, the approach of another member of the bandit clan.

He walked purposefully across the clearing towards Battle and the girl. Perhaps, had he not been so preoccupied, Battle might at least have noticed the hush that had come over the group, as they watched the imposing figure march across the clearing, a hint of authority in his calculated stride.

Barrak watched too, his ear pressed to the dirt, a knee in his back and his bound arms twisted painfully behind him.

He observed the newcomer was shorter than Nimbarra's killer, thickset and big-boned. A mane of red hair caught the morning sun. He resembled the others, with heavy leather boots and black leather trousers adorned with the usual patches and chains. A copper-coloured breastplate was partially obscured by a deer-hide jacket, fastened with a large bone clasp at the front, and trimmed with fur at the collar.

As he drew level, Barrak noticed the flame-haired bandit lacked the tattoos that were commonplace on the others he'd seen. He wore just a single gold earring dangling from his lobe in the shape of a zodiac cross. At close quarters Barrak could see the clasp across his chest was actually a human mandible.

He turned and assessed Barrak with an indifferent stare as he strode past, his eyes obscured behind eyeglasses tinted a curious blue. Barrak felt he was being sized up by a massive, orange-crested, alien insect. And he noticed the blaster – just like Bishop's – held nonchalantly at thigh level, as the gnarly brute passed by, and a thick leather strap running diagonally across his breast plate, with rows of little red canisters.

But the one who called himself Battle had noticed none of this as he hovered fervently over Jasmyn, licking his lips, his hand raised to strike her again.

The first he knew of it, the barrel of the blaster was at his ear.

The orange-haired brute had not even raised the weapon from the casual hold he had on it, slung low, at arm's length. He'd just sauntered up to the tall one, prone over Jasmyn with his bum in the air, and poked the end of the barrel into his ear.

Battle froze and tried to turn towards his attacker, but the muzzle, hard in his ear, wouldn't allow it.

'That's enough Battle.' Flame-hair's voice was gravelled but clear and emphatic. 'You'll damage her.'

Battle ducked his head from the barrel and turned to face him, still down on one knee but wild-eyed and tense, like he was ready to leap up at his adversary.

'Dust you, Ling. I claim her, she's mine,' he growled irritably. 'Find your own win.' He glared defiantly at the blaster-wielding creature called Ling, as if daring him to back up his demand.

Ling stayed calm, almost placid, and the barrel hovered level with the kneeling Battle's face. Ling's only move was to stretch a thumb up to the weapon's trigger mechanism and pull down on it. A sturdy metallic click sounded across the clearing.

Battle jumped to his feet and took a step back. The end of the barrel followed him as if it had its own agenda. Ling raised his head, the slightest of nods. 'You're rank, Battle. You have no place. One like this must be taken to Mebbor. You know this, you fool.'

Battle tensed and his eyes clouded with rage. 'I said, I claim her, Ling! Now leave me.' The lanky brute took a step towards his antagonist and that was the end of the conversation. In a blur, Ling's blaster described a 180 degree arc and he threw all his weight behind it, off a single step. The timber butt smacked into the side of Battle's head with such force, it damn near lifted him off his feet. He hit the ground with a thud and an exhalation of air that drew a communal wince from the assembled audience, and Battle's crumpled heap of lanky limbs lay still, unconscious or dead for all anyone knew.

CHAPTER 22

Jasmyn tried to stop shaking but she couldn't. She felt cold to the bone, even though the warm afternoon sun was full on her. She willed her leg to stop quaking and she shifted her weight on the hard rocky ground, but to no effect, her muscles were no longer hers to control. She spat a curse under her breath – Control yourself! But she could feel it rising up in her, like a long dark cloud, rolling towards her, a cloud of pure terror, which came with an almost irresistible urge to run. That was irrational, because there was nowhere to go, not with her ankles shackled with short stout cords, designed to limit her steps to little more than a shuffle or small hops, and her hands bound so tight that her wrists were already chafed red raw.

Next to her on the rocky trail were two villagers she had known well enough after months living amongst the Dzahn. One was a young mother, a cousin to Nimbarra, and the other a young teenage boy, one of Tidak's compatriots. The mother sat with her head in her hands, crying again. Jasmyn wondered fearfully what had become of her baby, just a toddler in its second year. The boy stared vacantly into the distance, his expressionless face devoid of the light and animation the Dzahn usually had about them in any setting. The two seemed like strangers now, oddly disconnected and separate from Jasmyn, even though they were physically joined to her on either side by a length of rope running between their bound hands. She wondered fleetingly how they felt. But Jasmyn was preoccupied with her own battle to contain her fear. This had become a precarious balancing act, because her fear could be displaced, but only by one thing. Anger.

Whenever she caught sight of Nimbarra's killer, a white-hot rage welled up in her like magma, filling every corner of her consciousness and dispelling her fear completely, instantly, like some kind of alchemist's magic. It had become her elixir and it had sustained her through the hours of their forced march through the heat of the day. Increasingly she found she craved the anger, like an addiction. It was preferable to the fear, but frustratingly, she couldn't control which one would hold sway from one moment to the next. And through the wild fluctuations between terror and rage, she had begun to perceive the fragility of her own mind, like cracks opening up in a massive dam wall, a wall holding back an ocean of madness.

And so it came again: just as the one they called Battle, Nimbarra's murderer, emerged from the edge of the track and began working his way along the lines of prisoners, so emerged her hatred, like a rampant genie. She embraced it, she drank it in, greedily, allowing it access to every cell in her body, and it rewarded her by dispelling her fear.

Her trembling eased.

Battle caught her eye and became more violent in his rousing of the prisoners. Instead of prodding them with the length of sapling he carried for the purpose, he began to strike the cowering prisoners viciously with it. He watched Jasmyn as he went about his savagery, as though he sought to punish her by inflicting pain on the others. Jasmyn glared at him, projecting hatred.

As he approached, watching her watch him, he leered at her and caned the boy next to her for good measure. She turned away. She would not give him the satisfaction of holding her attention. Neither did she scream nor hiss nor rant at him any longer because her anger had turned and become calmer in some way. She would bide her time. She would wait and remain vigilant and eventually the right opportunity would come. And then, she would kill him.

She would kill him with cool precision, just as Nimbarra would have done, without blinking, and she would avenge Nimbarra. She must nurture her anger and her hatred and wring the last drop of passion from it, so that when the time came, she would strike without hesitation.

Battle would die at her hand, it was her promise to herself and Nimbarra.

It sustained her.

By the time Battle planted a great worn and muddied boot by her side, Jasmyn had allowed herself to become a cauldron of hatred and spite and it had done its job, she felt no more fear and her limbs were steady. She studiously ignored him and dared the lanky brute to strike her where she sat, because if he did, she would not move and he would have to strike her again and again, and still she would not move until, eventually perhaps, the bear-like Ling, the bandits' leader, would come and stick his blaster in the miserable bastard's ear once more. He moved on and she took it as a small victory, but flashes of fear crept past the battlements of her anger as he passed. Besides, she had little choice but to get up, as the other five in her group were already on their feet, pulling her upright by their combined momentum as they began to move off along the track.

The sad and motley caravan was soon on the move again. Ahead were two other groups, with Barrak and Tidak bound together in the front group of four, then another group of six, then Jasmyn's group and a smaller group of five taking up the rear. The dozen or so bandits emerged from their resting places and began to move along the track, most of them showing little interest in their captives. The orange-haired Ling surveyed the line of prisoners briefly and muttered a few peremptory commands, but it was the sadistic Battle who seemed to have appointed himself the drive master and he continued to berate and bludgeon the captive villagers unnecessarily as they shambled along, moving as well as they could with bound ankles and hands.

The shackles restricted her stride, and the pulling and jostling from the others made the going exhausting. Jasmyn's hip ached terribly and her feet were blistered.

It had been the first time they were allowed to rest after several hours of a forced march, but although the bandits ate, no food or drink was offered to the captive villagers. After the attack, their captors had driven them up into the densely forested high country to the west of the village. Presumably this was how they had stolen into the village undetected. They'd been forced across a precarious high saddle and zigzagged down the steep slopes beyond, into a valley with a river running through, not unlike their own. Halfway down someone in the second group had lost their footing and the whole group had slid off the narrow goat track and tumbled and skidded down the steep slope, most of the way down to the river flats below. It was a terrifying moment. The six were severely shaken, abraded and bruised but it didn't stop Battle, the sadist, from beating them for their trouble until Ling had to intervene again, to reign in his over-zealous lieutenant.

After crossing the shallow river they had followed the course of a lesser, dry creek bed through another valley running east before turning north and scaling a steep slope to a sparsely vegetated ridge line which sloped gently up and away to the north-east. Their brief rest stop had marked the uppermost elevation of that ridge, and as they set off again now, they were on a downward slope.

As they descended, the sun was sinking towards the west and starting to lose its heat. There were perhaps only three hours of light left in the day. It was obvious now that their route would take them down and out of the low foothills onto the flat lands beyond.

Jasmyn felt a deep sadness that this day would end and the sun would rise again on a world devoid of her brave and tender lover, a world corrupted by the violence of these vile savages, in which hope would be a rare commodity. But she clung to hope nonetheless and consoled herself that with the coming of night, the darkness might provide her with an opportunity to wreak her revenge. It hadn't occurred to Jasmyn that her imaginings were wildly unrealistic, that she and the other captives were securely bound and that the bandits were heavily armed, seasoned killers with numbers and size in their favour. Or that, for the most part, the captive villagers were cowed and defeated, terrified and despairing. Despite it all, her rage burned bright enough to give her hope. She would find a way. She would kill Battle. She didn't realise that, having no further plan than that, might be a recipe for disaster.

They made camp far out on the sparsely grassed flatlands, still within sight of the mountains they'd crossed earlier and in the lee of a low rocky escarpment. In fact, there was already a camp established in this place. A small contingent of the bandit clan had been left behind to tend the camp while the rest, the ones who had come to the village, a hunting party no less, had been dispatched on their dreadful mission. There was a large tent and several smaller ones and fires already burning, hugging the escarpment for shelter along the sandy bank of what appeared to be a dry creek bed.

On their approach, with the low sun at their backs, they'd seen the smoke from the fires and a few figures moving about. Jasmyn had been perplexed by strange objects positioned around the camp, which she couldn't identify. From a distance they appeared almost the size of tents but darker and more irregular in shape and glinting oddly in the late afternoon sun, golden flashes of reflected sunlight dazzling them as they shambled on towards their dubious destination. Getting closer, the things resolved into strange irregular shapes with mechanical workings and a saddle suspended between two large black tyres at the back and one at the front. They were vehicles of some kind, with the configuration of a child's tricycle, but much bigger.

Reaching the outskirts of the camp, there came ironic cheers and whoops from the resident bandits and these were answered by the hoots of their captors. It put Jasmyn in mind of the atmosphere back in their village, when a hunting party returned from a successful hunt, and that sent a chill through her and made the skin at the nape of her neck prickle and crawl.

The prisoners were quickly bundled into cages on wheels, strange contraptions made from old dark timbers worn smooth by time, with vertical metal bars. The cages were lined up along the western edge of the escarpment, and from hers, which she shared with three other prisoners, she could see a number of other similar cages. They were

331

rigged up like trailers, one already attached to a three-wheeled vehicle as though ready to be towed.

If she pushed her face right up into the front corner of her cage and looked past the cage beside her to the next one along, she could see Barrak and Tidak in it. Barrak was doing the same and he called to her in an urgent raspy whisper, which told her his throat was as parched as hers from lack of water. 'Jasmyn, are you all right?'

It was the first time they'd been close enough to speak since being bound up in their groups for the forced march. Earlier, in the aftermath of the attack, Barrak had tried to come to her, tried to call out to her, but he'd been tightly trussed up and any attempt he made had been met with violent oppression. Jasmyn didn't answer him right away. It was a strange question under the circumstances.

'What do you think?' she said dryly, trying to make it sound like humour, but it came out sounding snippy and despondent. There was another long pause; she supposed Barrak wouldn't know what to say to her. What could he say after all?

Seeing Barrak straining with his face pressed to the bars of his cage, brought on a deep sense of sorrow in Jasmyn; it welled up in her and there were flashes of anger and bitter resentment too.

After a moment Barrak said, 'Don't worry, it's going to be all right.'

Another strange assertion.

At that moment he jumped back from the front of his cage and out of sight, as one of the gangsters lurched forward and smashed an iron bar against the bars. 'No talking!' he barked.

Jasmyn set herself against the timber slats at the back of her cage. She tried to smile for the childless mother sharing her cage, but it seemed she was already lost to grief and despair and she looked at Jasmyn glassy-eyed and blank before casting her eyes down at her feet. Outside there were strange, loud rumblings which rose and fell in pitch as some of the bandits drove their machines around on the flats in front of the escarpment. She caught glimpses of them throwing up great clouds of dirt and leaping over small humps in the landscape, the great hairy oafs, hunched over the steering bars of their three-wheeled vehicles as you would to ride a tricycle. Anger welled up in her again. These brutes were like mindless, thuggish children, separated from their toys for too long and now obsessively playing with them in the dirt. Had they no shame, no remorse for their vile deeds?

Through the bars of her cell she watched the sun descend toward the distant hills. Her hands and feet were still tied, but she'd been uncoupled from the other prisoners in her group. Her feet throbbed and her left hip ached deep in the joint. Her face was swollen and tender, where the brute, Battle, had slapped her.

In the distance the sun was expanded to twice its natural size by its proximity to the earth. It hovered over a gap between two peaks and glowered, a torrid orange-red, fit to match Jasmyn's simmering rage.

The insistent throaty throbbing of the brutes' giant bikes was loud and unsettling and wouldn't let up, lending an edge of annoyance to her anger. Quite suddenly it dawned on her how distinctive the noise was and how it would carry across an undisturbed wilderness. She remembered how Kajha and Tidak and the other hunters would sometimes grow quiet and watchful out in the bush, seemingly listening to the wind. She realised now they had been listening for the far-off, discordant sound of their enemy's conveyances. It all made sense to her now. And the bandits had stalked the village stealthily, leaving their noisy contraptions far away. But she would never really understand why they had not warned her and Barrak that the Dzahn people had such a fearful enemy.

The plunging sun expanded further and its hue deepened. It made a fiery cauldron of the gap between the two distant hills and wisps of cloud reached up around it, glowing angry red and bright gold. It had an hypnotic effect on her. She knew it was a sunset made vivid and colourful by smoke haze hanging in the western sky, the smoke of their burning village, and so the warm amber glow painted across her cell appalled her and the scene took on a ghastly fascination.

Normally, such a spectacle would have been one of beauty, to be remarked upon and appreciated, and Jasmyn was swept back through time to her father's house in Tamouer, overlooking the bay and the western ranges: a radiant sunset and she herself bathed in its warm glow, a cool drink at her hand.

But her reverie was short-lived and flashes of the morning's carnage abruptly returned to her, the village burning in the bright morning sun, Nimbarra fighting for his life, a bandit holding a child by its ankles. She gasped, as if slapped, and an involuntary whimper escaped her. She drew her knees up to her chest, but still she couldn't avert her eyes from the sun's death throes. The giant roiling orb had touched the earth and was sinking into the gap between the peaks. Jasmyn imagined instead it was rising up through the broken mountain from the bowels of the earth, a fiery subterranean god, enraged by the deeds of men, rising up from his underworld realm to finally deal with the iniquity of humans. The sun seemed to quiver like a molten mass and great arching spirals radiated bright red and amber and grasped at the sky, like minions of an angry deity. Jasmyn could almost believe the gates of hell itself had burst open, beyond the mountains, away to the west, where the broken Dzahn village lay.

As the sun sank into the earth, Jasmyn remembered another setting, the baleful blood moon over the desert in the pre-dawn chill, months ago, before they were lost and then found. It seemed an age since then. And riding on its heels came flashes of memory and disturbing images that were new to her and yet strangely familiar, horrid and yet perversely comforting. Imagery vivid and raw, of how she had killed Bishop with the spiked smith's hammer, back in his dreadful work shed on that full-moon night.

She remembered clearly now the thrilling surge of savagery as she drove that spike into his head, the giddy orgasm of transcendent mastery as it breached his skull and she knew she'd taken his life. And she recalled how the violence had overtaken and compelled her as she made sure of her kill, half driven by fear that Bishop would rise like a ghoul and half spurred on by the irresistible power of it.

A deep chill trembled through her and it occurred to Jasmyn, as she watched the dying sun, how curious it was she'd not remembered anything of this incident before. It had been as if Bishop had just vanished, albeit fortuitously.

She concluded the memory had returned to her now for good reason: it was inspiration, a prescriptive recollection to help her plot Battle's demise, and give her the nerve to carry out her mission. Her anger began to solidify and stabilise in her, and she realised for the first time that anger really could conquer fear. And so she fed that anger with images of doing to Battle just what she had done to Bishop and she thought she felt the numbness of shock finally recede for good and her mind becoming clearer.

CHAPTER 23

Barrak watched the setting sun too, but he was distracted and saw only the portent of coming darkness. It was a backdrop as he kept watch and strained to hear the voices of some nearby bandits, hanging around a campfire, judging from the occasional waft of smoke. Meanwhile, Tidak, lying on the floor behind him, worked away at Barrak's ropes with his improvised blade.

Barrak's heart pounded; anxiety was like a band around his chest.

The infernal throbbing of the bandits' desert bikes would make it almost impossible to hear anyone approaching.

This new tension had driven out the numbness, despair and creeping fear he'd felt during their forced march through the hills. Everything had changed when they reached the camp. For one thing, when he saw the cages and vehicles, Barrak realised this was not their final destination. It meant they had more time. When they were put into cages and their captors started to make camp, it felt like a reprieve of sorts, some breathing space at least, and it gave Barrak a shred of hope.

Later, when Tidak revealed he had found a broken arrowhead in the dirt after the massacre and concealed it in his mouth all day, everything changed; there was not only hope, they could now begin to shape a plan of sorts.

Tidak worked feverishly with the arrowhead, lying back to back with Barrak. It was awkward work, trying to saw away blindly at Barrak's ropes, going purely by feel. The arrow head was not really fit for the purpose and the ropes were hard and tough. When there was movement at the front of the cage Barrak raised his hands to alert Tidak and he would stop and lie still, pretending to sleep. Once, when this happened, the arrowhead slipped from his grasp and it took some time to find it again, searching blindly at his back on the cage floor.

As he worked away at Barrak's bonds, Tidak watched the girls who shared their cage, Mahalia and Mimu. They were huddled in the corner, holding each other for comfort, watching Tidak with breathless trepidation in the failing light. He watched them watching him as he worked and remembered them all playing together as children. In some ways he still saw them as the carefree companions of his youth, but it wasn't really the case. In recent years the bond between himself and Mahalia had grown stronger and, as they'd left childhood behind, she had begun to look at Tidak in a way that made his heart skip. It was at once exciting and strange, and sometimes, made him feel awkward and even embarrassed amongst his other friends.

By the time Tidak's om-sahdu had come, there was an unspoken understanding between the two of them and Tidak had come to relish the warm glow he felt whenever Mahalia was near and the familiar comfort of her touch. It reminded him of their childhood when they would wrestle and play together, but now, when Mahalia touched him, the familiarity had an exciting edge of anticipation and mystery about it. When Tidak had returned victorious from his om-sahdu, it had been Mahalia's face he had sought out amongst the crowd, and the glowing smile she gave him that day, bursting with pride and affection, had sealed the deal. From that day on, he and Mahalia and all the village seemed to know that the two of them would one day make a life together.

But everything had changed in the course of a single horror-filled day, and the world was now a different place.

Tidak looked into Mahalia's soft dark eyes in the dimming light as he concentrated fiercely on cutting Barrak loose, but he no longer felt like himself. The carefree Tidak was gone and he felt the troubled spirits of Nimbarra and Kajha heavy upon him. There was a stone in his heart, and he felt a sense of great foreboding and fear, not for himself but for Mahalia. He glimpsed vague images of a dire future he could barely imagine.

It was up to him to protect her. The urge to defend her was so intense it made him want to cry tears of desperation and scream in frustration. But he channelled it all into willing that arrowhead to slice through the ropes, and he sweated in the dimness of their prison, looking into Mahalia's eyes for reassurance and strength. She tried to oblige him, but he saw such a veil of despair and fear in her eyes, it spurred him on all the more and made his heart sink at the same time.

The last strand of the rope snapped and suddenly Barrak's hands were free. To avoid drawing any attention they stayed where they were and just swapped tasks, with Barrak using his free hands to cut Tidak's bonds. It was then Tidak noticed Mahalia had something in her hand, which she had been fiddling with all along, nervously turning it over in her fingers.

'What is that?' he whispered. She held it up, but it was too dim to see.

'It's a hair pin,' she said simply. Tidak realised it was a split bone pin, which the women used for pinning their hair and sometimes for fastening items of clothing. All at once a frenzy of ideas started swarming through his head. The pin could be useful, maybe as a weapon. He had Mahalia hand it to Barrak to examine.

'Yes, yes,' Barrak whispered as he turned it over in his hands, trying to examine it in the dim light.

Barrak hadn't given much thought to getting out of the cage once their hands were free. He'd had vague images of fighting their way out when the cage was opened, although realistically there would have been little chance of success. But this could do it. He had seen something like it done by a locksmith back home; perhaps this pin could be used to open the big old padlock on the cage door.

'Dust Ling. I'll worry about him.' Barrak and the other three captives strained to hear what was being said around the campfire near their cage. Barrak was pretty sure it was the voice of the one they called

Battle, Nimbarra's killer. Barrak was almost exhausted, there was a jabbing pain in his shoulder, and his fingers were painfully stiff. His mind was consumed with desperate frustration. It seemed like hours he'd been working on the lock with the bone pin and was starting to doubt its worth. Perhaps picking a lock was not as easy as an expert made it look.

The night was dark – devoid of any moon and the silence in the camp meant Barrak was at pains to work quietly. Most of the brutes must have been sleeping, but a conversation had started up around the nearby fire and Barrak and his cell-mates tried to make out what was being said.

'You're on yer own Battle, I'll have no piece of it. Ling has made it plain enough – fresh meat walks itself.' This from an unknown brute, his voice a low murmur.

'Have a heart, you mouse,' Battle's tone was scoffing and yet cajoling. 'Just think of the sweet meat. A young female, slow roasted. Look at these coals.' There was the sound of coals being stirred with a poker.

A chill breeze entered the cage and one of the girls barely managed to stifle a whimper. Tidak sucked in a sharp breath, grabbed Barrak's arm and squeezed it hard. The voices were faint and partly snatched away on the night breeze, but they had all heard clear enough what Battle was suggesting. Tidak tried to calm the girls. They had begun to sob and moan. He set about untying their hands, hoping to distract them.

Barrak's neck hairs stood up and his heart seemed to be bouncing around and knocking up against his windpipe. He recalled the brutes they'd encountered back at Dods Junction and Bishop's apparent rescue of them, and then the bodies in Bishop's coolroom. It was all starting to make some kind of ghastly sense. The fright of it seemed to clear his head and focus his thoughts and he set to work urgently with the bone pin, strangely with a new and clearer image of the internal workings of the lock and how he might use the pin to trip the mechanism: *If he leveraged the bone against the outside edge of the keyhole, put enough pressure on the internal pin he thought he could feel,*

just enough pressure but not enough to break the bone tool, and at the
same time applied some downward pressure ...

'You're cooked Battle, it'll be Ling sucking your bones in the end, if you're not careful, brother.' The cautioning tone of the other bandit seemed to leave some room for negotiation.

'Maybe we'll have the princess,' said Battle in a quiet, conspiratorial tone with a mocking edge to it.

His companion's answer was lost on the breeze and there followed an eerie pause. Barrak thought he felt something move inside the lock. He gently maintained pressure but feared the bone pin was close to snapping. He felt an odd mixture of feverish anxiety and icy calm.

'Yeah, bit tough I'll bet.' Battle wheezed out a low laugh and coughed.

'Besides, I think Ling wants to keep her for himself, or gift her to Mebbor,' the other bandit observed dully.

'Luck to them!' growled Battle. 'She'll have their balls off, I reckon, both of them.'

The two joined in a wheezy chuckle at this.

Barrak felt something turn in the lock and there was a loud click. He held his breath, hoping to the gods the bandits' laughter had covered the noise. Ever so carefully he slid the lock open and removed it gently from the door latch. He paused for a moment to listen and prayed the hinges wouldn't squeak when he pushed the door open.

'One of the young females, then,' Battle said. 'I'll gut her down by the creek and we'll put her on this for a spit, slow roast her whole, over the coals. Oh yeah. Mmmm.'

His companion swore noncommittally and spat into the fire.

'The small one in there. Shouldn't take more than a few hours. We'll have it for breakfast.' Battle's tone was cajoling, almost pleading.

'Jesus, Battle ...'

'We'll just say she ran away,' he breathed in a husky whisper.

Barrak looked around at his cell-mates; he could just make out the girls' haunted, wide eyes and Tidak's arms around them both, trying to calm them, trying to keep them from crying out. He pushed the door and it swung open, creaking loudly, and he winced as he slid out onto the cool sand and crouched there, nerves jangling, his hands splayed on the ground, as though he were about to start a sprint. He looked back into the cage and took in a breath to whisper something to Tidak, but his words caught in his throat.

Something was on his hand.

Something heavy, crushing it painfully into the ground. There was a crunch of boot on gravel and Barrak twisted around to look up at the dark figure that, in the dimness, he could only assume was the murderous Battle. He was a black shadow, strangely crowned with a faint orange halo. It took Barrak a moment to realise it was the moon's disseminating orb, just risen above the escarpment and half shrouded in cloud; it hung bizarrely over the bandit's head. Battle exuded a low menacing snigger but said not a single word. Barrak could see nothing of his expression in silhouette but he heard clearly enough the short metallic zing of a knife coming out of its scabbard and caught a glimpse of the blade rising up yellow in the moonlight.

'No, no, no,' the shadowy brute said in a weary, disappointed tone as he pressed his boot down harder on Barrak's hand for emphasis. The moon blew itself out of the cloud bank and illuminated the scene as Battle looked down on Barrak with a glum set to his mouth and the long curved blade of his hunting knife pointed accusingly at him.

But Barrak's eyes were fixed on the bandit's chest.

He blinked deliberately to clear his vision because something was amiss with his eyes. He thought he could see bright red dots, like pin lights or fireflies, dancing on the brute's chest. He gave his head a little shake and blinked again, but the hallucination didn't clear. *Perhaps he was about to pass out.* The brute noticed Barrak staring and followed his gaze, tucking in his chin to look down at his own chest. At that moment, a puff of wood smoke wafted across them and the points of red light on his chest were suddenly transformed to ghostly shafts of red light, pencil thin and hovering weirdly in the space in front of Barrak's eyes. Superstitious awe filled Barrak because he had no idea what he was looking at.

But Battle knew.

His knife arm shot up and the other hand went across his chest as if to brush away the fireflies; his upper body twisted and arched as though it had no time to wait for his legs in its haste to avoid the dancing points of light. Simultaneously he let out a terrified yowl of indignation and fear.

Suddenly the air was filled with loud percussive shocks as if giant wings were beating up into the night sky. The killer's scream changed to a series of short sharp grunts and the darkness to Barrak's left cracked with vivid flashes and streaks of coloured light that lit up the surroundings like a chaotic dance party. Above him, under the moon, Battle seemed to be keeping time with the flashes, in a wild uncoordinated dance of his own, his arms flailing about like a convulsing drunk as he staggered backwards past the side of the cage.

The noise and light ceased as suddenly as it had started and Barrak noticed a warm mist settling over his face and arms. Darkness returned. The pause that followed was probably only a second or two, but to Barrak it seemed much longer, and what he observed in that strangely elongated moment had a dream-like quality to it and at the same time a clarity, as if time had stood still altogether.

He heard Battle's big body hit the ground with a thud and an exhalation of air and then, for some time, a sound like someone half submerged trying to sing a tune. Jasmyn called his name, her voice loud and strident, and unseen, someone quietly *shushed* her. In the dim moonlight out past the cage in the low scrub he saw shadowy figures moving, keeping low, crouching and then moving again. He could hear Tidak and the girls breathing heavily inside the cage and the distant, alarmed voices of the sleeping bandits rousing themselves through the camp.

Strangely, he was not at all surprised to see a face appear before him, peering around the far side of his cage. The newcomer looked at Barrak, his eyes clear and calm in the moonlight, a long metallic object in his hands held up level with his shoulder, the end of it pointing out into the night, scanning. The way he held the thing, Barrak thought for a moment it might be something like the bandits' blasters, but in the moonlight, its shiny black surface looked alien and complex. Clothed in black, his young face was disguised by thick black streaks smeared across his cheeks, and a large round helmet was strapped at his chin. The crouching fellow half smiled, then turned serious. He extended an index finger and put it to his lips, then put out one hand, holding it level, palm down, before gently lowering it, *stay down* the gesture told Barrak.

All at once the pause was over. Fire burst from the young man's weapon and streaks of it raced over Barrak's head. He recoiled against the cage door and swung around to see another figure – Battle's reluctant dining companion perhaps – doing his own death jig to the dancing light.

Abruptly the darkness was gone altogether and Barrak twisted around on his knees and looked up into the sky at what could only be described as a small sun, hovering in the night sky. He cowered in disbelief, taking the advice of the young warrior, then for good measure he slid under the trailer. From this vantage point he could see where the bandits' tents were spaced out along the sandy creek bed in the lee of the escarpment.

The whole area was lit up, half as bright as day, by the garish red glow of the ungodly thing hanging there in the sky. Flashes of light at ground level and bursts of staccato sound came at him from the northern edge of the escarpment, as clutches of crouching shadows moved ghostlike through the camp, firing their bizarre weapons in short repetitive bursts, as if a storm were ripping through the camp.

Not far from his hide, he could see two bandits, rousing themselves around the campfire. One was on his hands and knees, searching frantically for something on the ground, the other sitting up, a blaster in his hands, waving it wildly from side to side as if searching for a target. A line of little dirt explosions came tearing across the sand, bisecting the campfire, making an explosion of embers and ash and continuing straight through the torso of the one on all fours, virtually cutting him in half. An instant later, a second line of destruction tore up the sand and

343

rent the sitting brute from thigh to opposite shoulder, shattering his weapon and tearing off an arm, pieces of which flew out into the night in ragged chunks.

Two helmeted figures emerged near Barrak's trailer, using the back of the cages for cover in the unnatural light. One of them planted his boots a few yards from Barrak's face and stood there, examining the dying bikers around the campfire, his weapon trained on them and his head tilted slightly to one side. His companion crouched with his back to the scene, carefully scanning the ground beyond the campfire and nearby tents. The sitting bandit who, by some quirk of biophysics, was still upright, gurgled and coughed and frantically propped himself up on his one good elbow while the spurting stump of his other arm waved about for balance, as though he still proposed to stand up. The near soldier's weapon burst into life again, pitching the struggling brute sideways into the sand.

Barrak was appalled by the destructive capacity of the weapons, which seemed to fire an impossible number of projectiles in short bursts. There was a chill in his gut and he pressed himself into the soft sand as the night erupted further into a maelstrom of noise and confusion. He saw two bandits burst from the cover of a nearby tent. The soldiers cut down both as they ran barking towards them, but not before one got off a misdirected shot from his blaster, slamming into the trailer above Barrak.

'Reload!' yelled the young gunner and dropped to a knee. The other fired into the night all the more passionately, raking the area beyond the line of cages with ruthless enthusiasm. Barrak could no longer see what he was firing at, as acrid sweet smoke filled the air and small metal canisters rained down, some of them pinging off the metal struts of the trailer and littering the sand in front of his face. They were burning hot.

The young soldier yelled again as he slammed something home into his weapon with a loud metallic click and then both were firing again, shoulder to shoulder, moving away from Barrak. Flashes of fire from their weapons lit up the swirling smoke in a night turned mute with the deafening percussion of battle. Barrak was stunned and the strange smoke stung his throat. Yet even over the hectic din he could hear the soldiers yelling unfamiliar abuse as they fired: 'Come and get it, you fuckers! Fucking vermin!'

Abruptly the firing stopped and silence rang in Barrak's ears.

Finding his eyes closed he opened them to see the soldiers carefully skirting around a number of bandits' bodies, one of them prodding at a tangle of limbs and torsos with the end of his weapon. Another short burst of fire made Barrak flinch and it was echoed by a distant crackle on the other side of the camp, and then another over by the escarpment. A lurid pink fog hung over the camp. The smoke, which smelled like firecrackers, was illuminated like supernatural swamp gas by the dimming light in the sky as it floated down, almost to ground level. And just before the artificial light died away altogether, through the clearing smoke, he caught sight of other soldiers standing openly in the camp now, milling in a rough circle and fanning out, weapons at the ready still.

The young fighter helped him up and Barrak felt like an old man. He dusted himself off and followed the young man into the ruined camp. They made their way toward the circle of men and approached the one who seemed to be in command, standing at the centre of his troops, calmly issuing orders in a clear, loud voice.

'Let's get some lights on over their Dex, quick as you can. Then we'll secure a perimeter, if you please.

'Darko – better start thinking about a watch roster and assign a squad to burn these bodies. Somewhere downwind, preferably.

'And stay frosty for Christ's sakes, there may be more of these fuckers lurking around, not quite dead enough to sooth *my* weary soul.'

With that, the commander shoved a cigar into his mouth and reached for something at his belt, something that looked a lot like a smaller version of the weapons his men had been using. He drew it and pointed it at arm's length at a prone figure, bearded and bloody, lying outside a nearby tent, trying to sit up despite a split gut spilling

345

viscera and one leg half shot off. There were three sharp cracks and the broken brute went back down for good. The commander didn't skip a beat as he went on with his instructions to his men before replacing the weapon and then taking the cigar from his mouth and pointing it at the approaching soldier, who had Barrak in tow.

'What have you got there, Jasper? Taken some prisoners, have you?' He raised one brow at the young soldier, keeping the other one in frown formation, a hint of a smile about his otherwise serious face, because both knew no prisoners were taken in this kind of operation. A short burst of gunfire rang out not far away as if to confirm the point.

Commander Axel Striker's shaved head and regular features made his age hard to gauge, although his face showed signs of wear and hardship, and he had the leathery skin of an outdoorsman. At average height, he had a working man's build and a boxer's stance and was dressed in something like a military uniform, although, in Barrak's experience, it looked more like hunting attire. A utility belt at his waist was bulky with unfamiliar objects and a holster for his weapon. At his waist was a three-quarter length sword, the likes of which was all too familiar to Barrak. The sword grip and the way he wore the weapon reminded him uncannily of Bishop and his twin swords.

His dark ribbed pullover had nondescript patches at the shoulder that might have been epaulettes of rank, and his trousers had pockets at the thigh and swirls of differing tones, all grey and black in the moonlight. At his feet was a small backpack and helmet.

His expression was hard to fathom in the moonlight, as he watched the kid approach with Barrak at his side – perhaps a mixture of parental concern and world-weary angst, infused with a little humour or irony, as if he were about to tell a joke.

'No Strike, I think they might be *Eyreans*,' the young soldier ventured with a hint of wonder in his otherwise professional tone.

Only then did Barrak notice Jasmyn had been released from her cage and was coming up behind him, striding ahead of her rescuer and making a beeline for Barrak. She grabbed his arm and pulled him towards her.

'Merciful gods!' She looked up at him with wide eyes, tear tracks all down her dust-smudged face. She held Barrak's arms and looked into his eyes. A swirling jumble of emotion – shock, horror, wonder and relief – seemed to be vying for supremacy in her eyes. Then she gulped in a huge breath and shoved an arm through his and hugged it to her. Standing up a little straighter, she turned and stared wide-eyed at their rescuers.

'Fuck me, Jasper, I think you're right,' the commander said, shaking his head slightly as if perplexed himself and blowing a puff of smoke away on the night breeze. 'Eyreans. Fuck!'

'Looks like they've been living with the Zanies, sir, until the Narbool got 'em.'

'Hmm, well, they're bloody lucky Eyreans then, aren't they?' the commander observed dryly.

Jasmyn was puzzled and a little disturbed by the strange names, which sounded like unfamiliar expletives, but, despite his distinctly odd accent and idiom, it appeared the commander was talking about them, as if they weren't even there, and apparently without much respect or sensitivity to their plight. Almost like her old self, she was beginning to take exception to this, and was considering making a comment to that effect, when the recently returned calm of the night was split by the throaty roar of an engine firing up.

It was one of the bandits' bush machines, the distinctive *blat-blat* of the engine filling the air, as it revved urgently up through its gears. It was soon joined by a second, doubling the ruckus.

The commander yelled, but his men were already taking action: 'Flare!' he bawled. 'Light 'em up, Dex!'

'Hugo! Hugo! 30 cal. Quick as you like. Nail that fucker.' The commander threw down his cigar and spat. 'Jesus,' he said quietly to nobody in particular.

Another of the artificial red lights burst to life above them and the field of carnage, which had once been the bikers' camp, was bright again in the surreal pink glow, a dome of light against the black night. Already halfway to the edge of the dome and lit up like actors on a stage were two bikers, hunched over their machines, the urgent throaty wail of their engines piecing the night with such a strident noise, it almost seemed the machines themselves were fleeing the scene in panic.

A soldier nearby had dropped what looked like a tripod onto the ground. It was attached to the long thin barrel of a weapon, longer and sleeker than those carried by the men. The gunner was down on one knee, his face pressed to the stock of the weapon, adjusting something on top as he looked down the sight.

'Steady, Hugo. Make sure of it, son,' the commander murmured.

The rose light made the two bandits seem closer than they were and, as they accelerated towards the curtain of darkness, Barrak caught a glimpse of Ling's flame-red hair, made gaudy in the pink light. He was just ahead of his companion.

There was a short sharp *thwack* and the weapon bucked in the sand. A moment later, the trailing biker flinched and fell, half his lower back blown away. His bike skewed sideways and the engine note increased to a scream, then choked. The machine pitched forward and sideways, throwing its rider up and over, the large rear wheels rising up before crashing and tumbling, gouging up a large plume of dirt.

The single note of Ling's bike continued unabated but he himself was obscured from sight by the plume of dust, and to make matters worse, he was already entering the dim umbra of the descending flare's light dome.

Hugo's weapon bucked a second time.

As the report of his second shot died into the night, a palpable tension came over the company, a moment of dead quiet. Every ear was honed to the sound of Ling's motor, waiting and hoping to hear it falter. The silent moment lasted longer than it could possibly take for a result until Hugo himself broke the spell by swearing in frustration as he stood up and slapped his thigh and swore again, casting his helmet to the ground for good measure.

'Good shooting, Hugo. No one could've made that second shot, you know.'

Hugo nodded his acknowledgement to his commander but he was

clearly not consoled as he snapped up the stand of his weapon and solemnly gathered up his gear. 'Sorry, Strike,' was all he said as he mooched away to the irritating sound of the biker's engine receding into the night.

The commander hunted down his cigar, apparently having decided it had some life to it yet, and brushed sand from it, then patted his pockets. 'Fuck it,' he muttered noncommittally, perhaps referring to the escaped biker or perhaps the sandy cigar, or even the lack of a flame to light it with.

More figures had gathered around the commander. One of them, flanked by two soldiers, came forward and reached out with a lighter. He thumbed the lid and flicked a flame to life, holding it in front of the commander's face. The commander leaned forward and turned his head sideways to light the stub from the flame, and as he did, he looked past the flame at Barrak and Jasmyn, squinting intently at them, as if seeing them for the first time.

'Thanks Doc,' he said as he straightened up, still staring at Barrak and Jasmyn.

The man with the lighter wasn't like the others. He didn't really look like a soldier at all and had no weapon. He was older and dressed in civilian clothes. In fact he was quite well dressed, if somewhat crumpled. He looked more like a university professor than a soldier, except for the large heavy-looking dark-blue vest he wore over his clothes, which Barrak guessed, from its colour, was some kind of military-issue body armour. He snapped the lighter shut and stepped back, casually following the commander's gaze to Barrak and Jasmyn.

Jasmyn still hadn't said a word and Barrak surmised that she was having as much trouble as he was processing recent events. His sense of relief was like a mad euphoria welling up inside him, but at the same time there was excitement that made his innards tremble; somehow it was all mixed up with a feeling of indignant anger and fear, like a delayed reaction to what had nearly happened to them at the hands of the bandits. Overlaying all of that was sense of disbelief, as though he was in a bubble or dreaming. Jasmyn gave his arm a good hard squeeze; as though she might have guessed he needed someone to pinch him. It seemed he was expected to say something but it was taking him some time to assemble the words.

'Who *are* you people?' he finally managed.

The commander spat out an errant thread of tobacco and stole a conspiratorial glance at the man he'd called Doc.

When he looked back at Barrak he had a grim set to his jaw and an intensity in his eyes, almost like alarm or rage, but infused with a hint of humour – as if he alone knew something, and it amused him.

'We're Historians,' he said, clear and simple, making it sound a bit like a challenge.

CHAPTER 24

As THE BUS PULLED away, young Axel tried to wrench his hand free, but his mother had such a firm grip on him, he couldn't get loose, no matter how much he tugged and squirmed. It wasn't fair, he was only seven and no match for his mother's determined grasp. He leaned towards the departing bus, straining to peer up at the high windows. *Why had he started to cry?* He had promised himself he wouldn't, but it had come on him so suddenly, a flurry of sobs and tears, like a baby. He was angry with himself, and with her.

When he'd started up, she bundled him away quickly. Was she embarrassed? Had his tears made her feel awkward in front of the other people seeing off the passengers? And it meant he hadn't been able to give his father a final hug, or say to him all that he'd planned to say.

It was always the same, the giant trundling wheels rolling away and the misty rain shimmering in the yellow light spilling from the bus's windows. And his father's profile in silhouette, looking straight ahead and not back at Axel at all, as the bus pulled away into the night. *I love you, Daddy.*

'Shit! All right, yeah, just give me a minute Darko.' Axel Striker sat up in his swag under the low-slung hutch that was his only shelter from the desert dew and the weather. The tepid blue of dawn's first light filtered through the flimsy canopy, which was all beaded up with condensation.

Jesus! That same dream.

He'd had it many times over the years, but this was the second time he'd dreamed of his father since setting out on this particular operation. It was always the same dream and always the same feeling, a loop of memory enshrining a real event: the night at the bus station, the last time he ever saw his father. And the feeling was stronger than ever, tremulous dread, the fear of a young boy who had understood for the first time that his father's trips away really *were* dangerous. But there was pride too. He remembered how proud his father had been to be admitted to the Guild of Historians as a delver, or at least he thought he remembered. Perhaps all he really remembered was his mother talking about it, as she did so often in the years after he was gone, and the gold-framed Certificate of Marine Archaeology from the Guild's Academy of Antiquity which, even to this day, had pride of place on his mother's lounge-room wall.

Striker had as much respect as anyone for historians and their work, but quite understandably there was some ambiguity in his attitude to those seekers of history's truths, and it was perhaps no accident that his work as a soldier had become the protection of historians.

Darko Mars, Striker's second in command, poked his head around the flap of Axel's hutch and winked at his commander. 'Sorry, Strike, fuck'n early, I know.' Darko jerked a thumb back beside his ear. 'It's this Eyrean bloke, he insists on talking to you. Must've wet the bed, I reckon,' he added gruffly.

Striker came out of the hutch in a crouch and pushed off the sandy ground with one hand as he straightened up to look at Darko and the surly Eyrean. Darko lifted a brow and flashed his commander a look that seemed to say *he's all yours*, and then melted away into the pre-dawn shadows. Striker arched his back and tipped his head first one way then the other, stretching out the night tension in his neck, all the while watching the tall Eyrean with his mad bouffant of sandy hair and a look of thunder brewing in his eyes.

'Sleep well?' Striker ventured dubiously.

The thunder in the Eyrean's eyes seemed to coalesce and he glared at Striker. It was plain from his appearance that he had not slept well, if at all. His stern mouth opened and then, finding no words, closed again.

Striker blew out a long breath and slowly passed a hand over his stubbled skull.

Barrak took a half step towards Striker and said suddenly, 'What did you mean last night, when you said you were *historians*?' Barrak fixed the commander with a dark stare.

Good question thought Striker. He had the uncomfortable feeling that this strange Eyrean had somehow got inside his head, fronting up outside his tent at the crack of dawn and waking him from his dream – that dream. As he held the Eyrean's stare, a random thought occurred to Striker, that the pride he felt for his historian father had formed a protective shell, protecting him from the grief and sadness of his father's loss. The thought rattled him momentarily and he blinked it away and tilted his head slightly, looking inquisitively at the Eyrean.

'Well,' Striker began as he turned and reached inside his hutch for his boots, 'well, I don't know about you, but in my book, we're all a bit like historians, aren't we?' Striker sat down and began pulling on a boot. He'd always considered the Protectorate to be closely allied to the Guild of Historians. Soon after joining the Protectorate he'd gravitated to special operations and quickly gained experience on remote digs and archaeological sites, providing security for guild personnel as they went about their work, often in dangerous regions well outside the reach of the Protectorate's secure zone. He'd certainly never had much of a taste for domestic security around Harbour City, and today his unit was one of the most experienced of the Outland Stealth Units, teams that could penetrate deep into the uncontrolled zones and operate undetected.

'After all, what could be more important than searching for answers, finding out what happened to the ancients?' Striker watched Barrak closely, assessing him as he started on the second boot with a small grunt.

There had been a hugely significant archaeological find way out west and his unit was the obvious choice for the mission, which involved venturing further than ever before into the dangerous western regions. The job was to take a fresh team of historians out to the dig site and bring back the team they were relieving, which included the project's director and revered historian, Truman Clay. They had been on their way back when they'd crossed the fresh trail of a group of Narbool, mustering live captives.

Looking up at the Eyrean as he laced his boot, Striker thought Barrak still seemed a bit perplexed. 'We're a special protection unit, assigned to the Guild of Historians. We're escorting a team of diggers back to civilisation.'

'Civilisation?' Barrak demanded derisively, looking around as dawn was about to break over the barren plain. 'Where's that?'

Striker ceased to tussle with his boot long enough to give Barrak an even, sombre look.

'East,' he said matter-of-factly. 'Harbour City. Due east, about four days.'

Barrak huffed and snorted then repeated, 'Four days?'

Striker really couldn't read the Eyrean at all. He'd never actually met one before, just heard stories about them. He assumed from his twitchy demeanour that this one must've been pretty badly traumatised after his near miss with the Narbool and he would need time to adjust. Be that as it may, Striker had a mission to run. The Eyrean man and woman had decided after some considerable deliberation in the earlier hours of that same morning not to go back into the wilderness with their Dzahn companions and it had been more or less agreed that they would travel east with Striker's unit, but he'd be buggered if he was going to let them distract him from his primary objective, which was getting his diggers safely home.

'Walk with me,' he said, standing up and going past Barrak, down into the dry creek bed and on towards the sandy escarpment. He was thinking about how his men had concealed themselves through the night, expertly melting into the landscape all around the camp and marking out the night in careful shifts, alert and watchful for the unlikely return of the Narbool. Their camp, if it could be called that, was a few hundred yards along the dry creek bed, upwind from the scene of the previous night's attack. Striker's men were already up and about, emerging from their night lairs and making ready to depart. Not for the first time, Striker felt great satisfaction and pride in his men; he marvelled that he had such confidence in their ability to secure an area, that he was able to sleep in his hutch, and with his boots *off* no less, even out here in a wilderness controlled by the Narbool.

Further up the creek they saw two soldiers putting the finishing touches to a mound, six or eight feet high and twice as wide. The massive pyre was composed of the bodies of the slain bandits and their infernal machines, piled up untidily into an appalling amorphous sculpture. As they paused to watch, one of Striker's men skirted the gruesome charnel pile, sloshing liquid from a container onto the corpses and machines.

'Will more of them come?' Barrak asked as they watched the grisly scene.

'No. This lot were a long way from home,' said Striker. 'Besides, we scare the living shit out of 'em.' Striker popped a quick glance at Barrak and gave an off-beat chuckle.

'Anyway, they won't be able to find us once we're on the move; we're pretty good at not being seen,' Striker continued. 'These bastards prey on the weak and the vulnerable. Sometimes they go after the Dzahn, but that's actually pretty unusual, because the Dzahn fight back.'

Barrak just nodded, drinking in the information.

'They must've been surprised to find you two out there. What were you doing with the Dzahn, anyway?'

Barrak ignored the question. 'What did you call them?'

'Narbool.' Striker said it slow and clear as though teaching a child.

'These Narbool, they use ...' Barrak searched for the right words, 'they eat ... do they ... do they *eat* human flesh?'

Striker looked at Barrak and arched both his eyebrows in mock awe and nodded his head in an exaggerated fashion. 'Yes, they do, the filthy fuckers.'

He'd heard stories about Eyreans, that they were naïve in the ways of the real world, isolated as they were in their eccentric society, which eschewed contact with the outside world. But it was still hard for Striker to believe a person could be completely ignorant of one of the harshest realities of life.

He returned to his question. 'You didn't answer me, Barrak, what were you doing out there, with the Dzahn?'

Barrak didn't know why, but he gave Striker only the abridged version of the story, how they had set out looking for a missing relative who had travelled east and how they had become lost and were found by the Dzahn and stayed with them, until the attack of the Narbool. He told him he was a member of the High Council in the Eyrean Parliament, but he wasn't confident enough in Striker to divulge the full story of political upheaval back in Tamouer and their having to leave for fear of arrest, or of their encounter with the rebel leader, Gitan. Nor did he mention that they had a much more explicit reason for reaching the east coast: to try to make contact with the people Elias had encountered there.

So his story must have sounded pretty thin as he related it to the commander, shadowing him around the camp as Striker spoke to his men. And even though it seemed plain enough that these probably *were* the easterners that Elias had told Gitan about, Barrak just wasn't ready to trust Striker yet.

Too much was still unknown.

Who were these so-called Historians? And what was the nature of this militaristic Protectorate, which clearly had the use of fearsome weapons? He found it hard to imagine this civilisation Striker referred to, this Harbour City. Would it be as grand as Tamouer and the thriving provinces of the Eyrean Sea, or would Striker's idea of civilisation turn out to be something more akin to the seedy townships they'd seen clinging to life on the outskirts of Eyre and out in the western deserts? Above all, Striker's weapon, the sword he wore, gave Barrak a bad feeling. It looked just like the one Bishop had used.

The company was gearing up for departure with quiet efficiency. No orders were barked, no real hierarchy was apparent; Striker's manner with his men was consultative rather than prescriptive and each man's task seemed to fit seamlessly into the operation of the whole.

The last to emerge from her hutch was Jasmyn and a humorous murmur went around some of the nearby men as she sat in the sand blinking at the rapidly brightening dawn and grabbing for her boots as the flimsy canopy she'd slept under was whisked away and bagged up by a hovering trooper. Barrak went down on one knee and handed her a small slab of oat biscuit which he'd preserved from a ration pack one of the soldiers had shared with him earlier. She looked dubiously from the biscuit to Barrak and rubbed her eyes.

'Breakfast,' Barrak advised evenly and gave her a crooked smile.

At that moment the sun broke over the cloudless eastern horizon and there was a muted *wharumph* as the bikers' funeral pyre ignited and a ball of flame ascended and then morphed into a column of black smoke, which rose straight up into the glacial dawn sky. An ironic cheer went up from some of the men.

'A message to our Narbool mates,' said the trooper packing Jasmyn's hutch as he watched the dark plume rise over the escarpment. A ripple of murmurs went through the camp, erupting into an appreciative hoot or shout here and there.

'OK ... let's get ready to move,' Darko Mars' gruff voice sounded harsh over the subsiding ruckus in the crisp morning air.

Jasmyn's boot flew past Barrak and skidded into the trunk of a scraggily tree. She hurled several expletives after it and threw down her small backpack, following it onto the ground and wrestling the other boot off with considerably more exasperation and effort than would have been necessary if she had just loosened the laces a bit.

'Damn-gods-blasted-stupid-boots!' She punctuated each word by pounding the ground with her second boot before sending it flying after the first, seeing it off with a final expletive that surprised both of them, having been co-opted from the ribald banter of the Easterners. 'Fucker!' she yelled fiercely after the flying boot.

Striker appeared, making his way back through the group to see what the commotion was about. The company had pretty much halted, realising something was amiss. Striker assessed the situation with a glance at Jasmyn and nodded at Barrak with an expression he found hard to read, somewhere between sympathy and annoyance.

'All right, this looks like a good enough place to stop.' He raised his voice without really shouting. 'Break. Lunch!' The word went along the column and Barrak heard the distinctive whistles he'd noticed before, like bird noises, which were the soldiers' way of communicating with those securing a wider perimeter out in the bush.

Jasmyn had her back against the trunk of a large tree, her arms folded across her chest and her face a stern mask of annoyance

'Those blisters, they're still bothering you, aren't they.' Barrak eased himself down beside her with a grunt.

Jasmyn tossed her head and snorted as if blisters were the last thing on her mind. She looked away from him, back along the track. She didn't want him to see the tears starting to well in her eyes.

He knew the borrowed boots had been bothering her. Her soft hide shoes from the village had been ruined during their forced march and someone amongst the company had found a spare pair of boots for her. But they didn't fit. She'd been tense all morning, her mood alternating between manic and morose ever since they set off. Normally she would have coped with such a problem stoically, but Jasmyn was a ragged, jittery patchwork assemblage of her normal self, and perhaps not surprisingly, blisters had been the last straw.

'Are you all right Jasmyn? I mean, you know, I'm worried about you.'

Jasmyn blew out a small puff of air and blinked several times in rapid succession. That made the tears come, little pearls dropping onto the sand. She grimaced and willed them to stop, swiping with annoyance at her cheek.

'Yeah, yep. I'm OK. It's just, I can't …' She took a couple of short sharp breaths to contain a sob.

Her voice cracked and almost faltered. 'I can't close my eyes … you know?' She turned to Barrak now and her look of haunted desolation made his own breath catch in his throat.

'I can't close my eyes without seeing him.' She scrunched her brow and her mouth dropped. Barrak saw her small hand clench in the sand too, as she tried to compose herself.

'And seeing what that … that … *animal* did to him.'

Barrak touched her shoulder sympathetically. He wanted to take her in his arms and hold her, but Striker was back and hovering over them, a concerned frown on his face.

'Is everything all right? Anything I can do?'

'Can I borrow one of your medipacks?' Barrak asked quietly.

Striker nodded and backed away towards the track and the clearing up ahead, where the others were gathering.

Jasmyn had begun to compose herself and her hands were on her cheeks. She looked at Barrak wide-eyed and shook her head slightly.

'I just can't stop it.'

'I know,' Barrak said gently and put a hand on hers.

'And when it starts, I get this tightness and my heart feels like its pounding, right up here.' Jasmyn put a hand to the base of her throat. 'And I can't stop thinking and it just gets worse and worse … and there's more and more images and thoughts and I think I'm gonna go crazy because it just won't stop and then I just want to run, run away, but I can't because it's all in my head and it's closing in on me, like some massive awful weight.' The words tumbled out of her.

She looked up at him with an expression of such wretched sadness, his heart ached, and he was frustrated that there seemed so little he could do for her. At home, with his dispensary at hand, he would have quickly made her a good strong blend of bitter, anxiolytic tinctures and a mixture of essences to treat the shock. But here, in the wilderness, he felt powerless.

'You know it's just your mind that creates these images, these pictures. They're not real. You can step out of your thinking mind and just be the observer.' Even as he spoke, Barrak retrieved a memory of his meditation training and the words of the monks who had mentored him through his breakdown in the mountain monastery long ago. But it was more than that; the Shabbah's medicine had given him a much more immediate and direct experience of this other, objective mind. It was as if the medicine had taken him right into that other mind, which could observe without judgment. He suddenly realised he understood it much better now than he ever had with the monks.

'If you use your observer mind, the images will lose their power. Just watch them and recognise them for what they are, just pictures that don't really mean anything. You don't have to attach yourself to them. You can just let them go.'

She appeared to be about to speak but then said nothing.

'And when you get overwhelmed with anxiety, like you just described, use it then too. Use your observer mind to look at the fear and anxiety, go into it, *examine* it.'

Barrak took her hand in his and smiled.

'Try it now. *Watch* the sensation as though it was something to be investigated. Try to get inside it. What's its texture? Does it have a feel, a colour, is it hot or cold ... do you see?'

Jasmyn concentrated, wearing a mild frown, and her eyes seemed distant for a time, then her face softened and she smiled. 'Yeah, yeah. I think I see. That seems to work, at least it helps.'

Barrak gave her an encouraging smile, which he tried to imbue with his most confident and reassuring bedside manner, but in reality he felt just as uncertain as Jasmyn looked, judging by the dubious smile she gave him in return. And as he gently eased the sock off her left foot, the medipack arrived as if on cue, along with Hesta, one of the historians, the same young woman who had lent Jasmyn her spare boots in the first place. Together they tended Jasmyn's blisters.

Never had such care and attention been given to such an ailment and in the end her wounds were cleaned and salved and bandaged. In the process Jasmyn's spirits noticeably lifted and Hesta proved to be a sympathetic carer and a good listener. The three of them chatted almost like old friends, despite the difficulty they still had with each other's unfamiliar accents.

When they'd finished, Hesta left quickly to try to procure some food for the three of them before it was all packed away. Barrak found himself sitting, still holding Jasmyn's foot in his lap, and now that Jasmyn was much more relaxed, they were both struck by the peace and solitude of the place and the simple intimacy of the moment.

When Hesta returned she had retrieved one of Jasmyn's far-flung boots. She also had half a ration box for them to share.

As she handed Jasmyn her boot, Barrak was sure he detected something pass between them, something in the nature of the secret and mysterious communications that pass between women, a nod or a wink, too subtle for male perception.

Before Barrak could decipher any of it, Striker came past and beckoned to him, while the soldiers in the clearing were making ready to depart. With a tilt of his head he motioned Barrak toward a piece of higher ground on the other side of the track.

'Is she gonna be all right d'you think?' he asked Barrak as they got out of earshot.

'She's shaken up pretty badly,' Barrak offered. 'We both are.'

'Some people never recover from an encounter with the Narbool,' Striker observed dryly.

'That's nice to know,' Barrak replied even more dryly, thinking Striker had all the subtlety and compassion of an ox.

Standing at the top of the low hillock Striker had his back to Barrak looking out to the north. A breeze whistled through a scraggy stand of she-oaks near the crest of the hill and Striker raised a hand and pointed past them at the distant horizon.

'See that, over there?'

Barrak tried to follow his pointing finger but could see nothing but a wide expanse of grassland, parched brown and silver and dotted with the green crowns of widely spaced eucalypts. To the north-east the relentless monotony of the plain yielded to a line of low ranges, shrouded in purple haze and angled like the haunches of giant beasts, reclining on the edge of the world.

It occurred to Barrak that the land was changing again, becoming more fertile, more like the lands around the Dzahn village. And they seemed to be gradually descending, coming down from an arid plateau, which must have been in some kind of rain shadow, with its own peculiar desert climate.

'Not down there,' Striker wagged his finger at the horizon, 'beyond the ranges. That long brown smudge, looks like a dirty cloud.

'Yeah, I see it.'

'That's the Narbool. Their city, they call it Babylon. Thousands of them live there.' Striker looked at Barrak inquisitively, but Barrak said nothing, just returned the look with alarm in his eyes.

'They mine black ore and extract oil from it. Use it to make impellent for their bloody precious machines. The smoke from the processing fouls the air all around the place. You can smell it for miles.'

'Is it safe for us to be this close?' Barrak interrupted him.

'Yeah it's OK. The Narbool are dim-witted brutes, and we choose our battles.' Striker surveyed Barrak coolly.

Barrak returned his stare, trying to gauge his disposition. 'Then why did you come after the Narbool back there? If your mission was to escort the historians, why did you go out of your way to attack them? Why would you take such a risk?'

Striker narrowed his eyes, and again Barrak felt awkward and uncomfortable under his frank gaze. 'That's what we *do*,' he said simply, as if explaining something terribly obvious. 'If we find Narbool, and it's safe to do so, we exterminate them, especially if they have prisoners.' Striker cast his gaze back towards the distant shroud of smoke. 'Trust me. You wouldn't have wanted to end up in Babylon.'

Barrak frowned. This seemed to annoy Striker, almost as if Barrak were feigning ignorance of something obvious. 'Killing Narbool is one of the *prime* imperatives of the Protectorate, always has been. Clay and his diggers know this. They wouldn't have it any other way either. Nobody would.'

Striker was glaring at him now, as though confronted by a strange and hitherto unknown species. 'How can you not know this?' he asked, exasperated. 'The hostility between ordinary people and these animals goes back to the Fall. Is it not the case in Eyre?'

Suddenly on the defensive, Barrak thought about telling Striker

362

of their encounter with the Narbool-like characters back at Dods Junction or about the ensuing drama with Bishop. He found Striker's manner annoying. *What was he implying? That his and Jasmyn's knowledge and understanding of the world was in some way deficient because Eyre lacked a population of murderous buggy-riding cannibals?*

Striker had already more or less implied that he thought Eyreans were backward in some way, sheltered from and ignorant of his so-called real world. But to Barrak's way of thinking, nothing he had seen so far, outside the borders of Eyre, would dissuade him from his very Eyrean point of view, that the world beyond the outer markers of his homeland was a primitive badland of lawless savagery. Perhaps the Dzahn had found a way to isolate themselves from the worst of it by returning to a simpler way of living in the wilderness areas, but they were terribly vulnerable. And as for these easterners, despite their surprisingly sophisticated weapons and peculiar fascination with ancient history, they clearly lacked the sophistication of Eyrean culture and seemed to be undisciplined and violent, nothing more than a product of their environment.

Striker seemed to sense that he'd struck a nerve with the prickly Eyrean and when he got no answer he just shook his head and turned away from Barrak, starting back down the hill.

Before long they were moving again and for the most part they passed quietly through a landscape that alternated between open grassland and swathes of eucalyptus scrub, which was gradually becoming more like a true forest with taller, straighter trees.

By mid-afternoon they had left the dry, scrubby grasslands behind altogether and were walking permanently in the shade of towering eucalypts with occasional patches of satinwood and myrtle in the lower storey. Their progress through the forest was easier than Barrak expected and he remembered Kajha telling him about how the Dzahn sometimes used fire to burn away the undergrowth in forested areas to improve the hunting. The fire would encourage new shoots to grow, bringing in grazing animals, and the clearing of otherwise thick undergrowth would allow for free passage and easier hunting. He felt a stab of sadness as he remembered his old hunting mentor. He guessed this area had been burned many times before, which was to their advantage because the terrain seemed half wilderness, half parkland, with clear ground and good visibility between the sometimes densely packed trunks and occasional patches of low scrub.

For the most part the group observed an unstated rule of silence as they walked. Often the only sounds were the occasional whistles and signals of the soldiers patrolling the periphery of the group, and these were sometimes almost indistinguishable from the birdcalls of the surrounding bush. Certainly Striker seemed preoccupied with moving the group safely through the landscape and was disinclined to involve himself in superfluous chat.

The repairs he and Hesta had done on Jasmyn's blisters seemed to have worked and perhaps his spot of bush counselling had helped too. As the day wore on, in the cool of the forest, her spirits lifted, and as her mood improved, she engaged Barrak in muted conversation as they walked, mainly sharing observations and impressions of the easterners or speculating about their destination and what manner of civilisation they would find.

Nothing more was said about the attack of the Narbool, nor her decision, which he knew had been difficult, to go east rather than accompany Tidak and the others back to find the remaining Dzahn villagers. Secretly of course Barrak was glad that, in the end, civilisation – or at least the rather dubious promise of it in some form or another – had won her over. In any case, the momentum of travelling with the Easterners was having a positive effect on them both and he was pleased to see Jasmyn regaining her equilibrium.

The company came to a halt as the forest abruptly ended, giving way to uneven ground and a rocky, sparsely vegetated ridge line. Below them, a wide vista was illuminated by a vast sky, grey and white and uncommonly bright to eyes long adjusted to the shade of the forest.

It was as Barrak had thought all along, they had been travelling on a high plateau. This was the edge of it.

He moved up to join Striker and some of his men strung out along the ridge looking out over the flatland below. They made no attempt to conceal themselves. Striker had one foot up on a boulder, affecting an explorer's pose. Above the grasslands, hung a grey expanse of cloud, heavy with impending rain and lined with white and bright silver along its western edge.

The air had an electric feel.

Above them and away to their left, the sun suddenly burst through a ragged gash in the shark-skin sky and bathed the plain below with radiation so rich and lurid it turned the grassland to an other-worldly tableau of gaudy greens and burnished gold.

Away in the distance, something drew Barrak's eye with its unusual shape and its contrast of dark bronze against the fluorescent green grassland. It looked like a discarded dish leaning against a box. Perspective and the curious light wreaked havoc with Barrak's perception and he blinked and refocused on the thing, trying to identify it. They were not at all high up, maybe only two or three hundred feet, but the dish was a long way out on the plain. At that distance he guessed the thing would have to be enormous, a giant's dish, and the box it was leaning against, perhaps a substantial building. He looked around himself, somewhat bewildered, and noticed that Striker and his men were looking at the thing too.

He caught Striker's eye and Striker smiled uncertainly at him.

'What is that thing, down there?'

Striker stared into the distance for a few moments and then back at Barrak, narrowing his eyes slightly. 'It's a relic,' he said simply and moved sideways, a bit closer to Barrak, scrutinising him like he might a new recruit. 'An ancient relic, from the old world, from before the Fall.'

Barrak's look of consternation and uncertainty seemed to irritate Striker anew and Striker shook his head and began to turn away from him.

'But what *is* it, exactly?' Barrak demanded.

'Who knows?' Striker returned dismissively, over his shoulder. 'Not really my department. You should ask the professor.'

CHAPTER 25

THE SUN WAS ALREADY gone – sunk below the ridge where they had all stood some thirty minutes prior. The last of its burnished light caught the upper rim of the strange dish-shaped structure as Barrak craned his neck to look up at it. It was huge, perhaps 200 feet across, and slumped against the great stone building below, one edge crumpled and partially buried in the ground while the opposite edge swooped parabolically up into the sky to a height of some 100 feet or more.

As they'd approached, it had resolved into an open mesh structure, composed of metal struts crisscrossed to form a massive dish and supported by a now mangled superstructure that might once have attached the colossal thing to the top of the great solid cell-block of a building. Up close it was obvious the thing was a ruin. The superstructure was a tangle of twisted metal struts from a time when it had fallen from its anchor on top of the building. Barrak reached for one of the bent metal struts where it protruded from the ground and, to his surprise, it virtually crumbled at his touch, such was the extent of the corrosion.

He backed away, suddenly concerned for the safety of the rusted giant, and craned his neck once more to look along its curved edge.

The sound of camp being struck reached him on the charged evening air, which carried the heavy scent of impending rain. Distracted as he was, he virtually backed right into Truman Clay, the head historian, whom Striker called the professor, and it startled him as Clay put a hand on his shoulder to steady them both. 'Wooah there, Councillor.'

As Barrak wheeled around to face him, he offered Barrak a smile that was at least half awkward grimace.

'Impressive sight, isn't she?' He tipped his head towards the dish and then surveyed Barrak with sleepy eyes behind black-rimmed spectacles. His gingery hair, greying at the temples, was barely visible under the hood of a military-issue anorak.

'Do you know what it is?' Barrak asked him, aware that this was the first time he had spoken one-on-one with the so-called professor. Clay assumed the demeanour of a studious and patient tutor.

'Well, we don't know exactly. Communication of some sort, obviously.' Clay looked past Barrak and up at the towering structure and put his hands on his hips. 'We do know it dates back to the very beginning of the Digital Age. So, really quite rudimentary technology.' Clay's gaze came back down to earth and he peered at Barrak over the top of his black rims.

'A bit like what we have today, actually.' Truman Clay's thin smile and a little chuckle told Barrak he was quite pleased with what he clearly considered a very apt and ironical aside, even if it was pretty much lost on Barrak.

'Communication?' Barrak repeated.

'Yes. But you see, originally, it pointed up at the heavens. Makes you wonder doesn't it, who they were trying to communicate *with*?' Clay was looking up at the sky now. 'Looking for answers to their troubles in the great beyond, perhaps?

'It's one of the great mysteries; we really don't know what it was used for.' Clay scrutinised Barrak. 'We may never know, I suppose.'

'Well it's just about ready to fall down, I think,' Barrak offered, showing his hand and rubbing together his thumb and fingers, still stained with corrosion from the strut he'd touched.

Clay tucked in his chin and looked even more intently at Barrak over the rim of his spectacles. 'It's over 800 years old, you know Barrak.' He said it succinctly, as if it was part of a lecture.

Barrak felt his scalp tighten.

'No one knows how it's survived so long. Virtually no other metal structures have, not from *then*. Most metal structures from back then are reduced to little more than iron oxide in the soil.'

Barrak was eyeing him with suspicion, but he went on: 'We think it must have been some kind of alloy, built for strength and flexibility but inadvertently giving it tremendous longevity. The base building is a different story, of course. Bluestone blocks and double reinforced concrete. Built to take the weight of the bloody thing. We should build everything like that, things'd last a thousand years.'

Clay was clearly on a roll, but he stopped when he saw the look on the Eyrean's face. He reminded himself that he was talking to an Eyrean. In his student days he himself had presented a thesis on Eyrean culture and considered himself something of an expert on the subject. Eyrean culture was insular and sheltered, bordering on xenophobic. He should tread carefully.

Barrak shook his head disparagingly. The eccentric researcher's ideas about the dish seemed far-fetched. How could the thing possibly be that old? However, he was nagged by a vague uncomfortable feeling, as if he was a schoolboy caught with his homework not done. He shook it off and changed the subject. 'What do you know about these Narbool? Why do they do what they do? Do they really prey on humans?'

'Ah the Narbool. Yes, well it's pretty rare for them to actually eat human flesh these days. Slavery's more their thing now, forced labour in the mines around that filthy city of theirs. Probably what they had in mind for you and Jasmyn. Well, you anyway.' He shut his eyes and affected a shudder. 'God only knows what would have become of her. Doesn't bear thinking about, does it?' Clay squinted at Barrak. 'On the other hand I'm not so sure what they had in mind for you. Too old to work, too tough to eat.'

Clay grinned, but when Barrak's stony expression told him his joke had fallen flat, he cleared his throat and frowned instead. 'No. No. Some still do it, but relatively few. Appalling damn creatures. It's like a bad habit, left over from the bad old days, I'm afraid.'

'Bad old days?'

'Well, you know, the dark age, after the Fall. No infrastructure, no law, no food production. No nothing. Dog eat dog, so to speak.'

It seemed that every answer Clay gave him just raised more

questions, and the more outlandish and unbelievable his assertions the more sceptical Barrak became. Before he could formulate his next question a fat dollop of rain smacked him on the head, followed by a cavernous boom, which reverberated and rolled across the plain. By the time Barrak and Clay dashed the short distance back to the half-made camp, the heavens had opened, emptying thick sheets of rain, flattening the lush grass and turning bare ground into an instant bog. They found their way to one of the smaller bluestone outbuildings, where the majority of the company had already retreated for shelter and followed the faint glimmer of an oil lamp through the curtain of white, down into the hush of the dank old building.

There they found their companions gathered like brethren along the dark side of the musty old cavern, away from the glassless windows where the driving drops sprayed and frothed on the old stone sills.

As his eyes adjusted to the dimness Barrak recognised Striker and heard Darko Mars nearby muttering something about tracks being washed away.

'If they're searching for us, wouldn't this be an obvious place to look?' Barrak demanded.

'They won't be looking for us,' Striker intoned evenly. 'They don't come looking for this kind of trouble, and besides, they never come *here*.'

'Why not?'

'Evil spirits,' Striker said, po-faced.

A low humorous murmur rippled through the assembled group.

'Superstitious buggers,' muttered Darko Mars.

Darkness came and the rain barely let up at all. Some of the crew had laid a fire in another of the ruins, which had enough of a roof to ward off the rain. Damp kindling made it difficult to start but eventually they got it blazing and most of the company gathered around, drawn to the fire as humans always are, to warm themselves and enjoy the glow of it. When the flames died down and a good bed of coals had been achieved, they cooked a *doarht* and a young rylaby (which the soldiers called *roo*), both of which had been shot at dusk, before the rain. Portions were shared around to supplement the dwindling rations and provide some much-needed protein.

Barrak's piece was charred on the outside and still bloody in parts and tough with sinew throughout. It even had some singed fur still attached. But he devoured it with relish, doggedly chewing every gristled morsel and finally sucking every last drop of marrow from the remaining piece of bone. He was amazed how his body craved the protein and juices. He could've eaten anything.

As he licked his fingers he saw Jasmyn across from him doing the same, holding her small charred joint in both hands, hunched over it with an air of canine devotion, tearing and nibbling at it, pausing only to lick the juices from her hands and wrists. *Look at us,* he thought, *high-bred citizens of Eyre.* He allowed himself a chuckle, and a memory of prime rib, served in some long-forgotten restaurant, passed across his mind's eye. He marvelled that they had survived at all and he understood something that he never had before, about the resilience of humans to withstand all kinds of deprivation.

Eventually the rain eased to a steady drizzle. They gathered along the dry side of the old building, nestling in groups on the sandy floor. The solid bluestone had been laid bare by time, no floors, no ceilings, no window frames. It felt old; it smelled old, like a sunken tomb.

Striker sat with his pack wedged between himself and the wall for comfort. Beside him was one of the small transportable lamps sitting on the flat top of a ration box for a table. Beside the lamp was an open jar, its lid set neatly beside it. Striker dipped a piece of cloth into the jar and gently ran it along the length of his sword, which he had laid flat along his thigh, the sword tip held off the sand by the instep of his boot. On either side were groups of soldiers and diggers similarly gathered around their small orange flames, as though around campfires.

They talked and smoked quietly and somewhere a card game struggled to make sense in the dim light. There was snoring too and not long ago there'd been a change of watch. But it was quiet now for the most part, almost peaceful. The receding storm rumbled in the distance and the doorways and windows were lit at unexpected intervals by faint, far-away flashes. As Barrak and Jasmyn sat together in the dim umbra of Striker's lamp watching him oil his sword, Darko Mars sat nearby, rolling a cigarette. And there were three or four others, soldiers whose names Barrak did not yet have straight.

Barrak felt a companionable bonhomie in their company and began to relax, just a little, for the first time in days. But Striker's sword made him nervous; it still reminded him of Bishop. He wasn't sure Striker could even see him in the shadows and so it surprised him when Striker addressed a question to him, out of the blue.

'You're wondering about the sword, aren't you Barrak?'

Barrak sat up a bit but said nothing.

'Maybe you're thinking a sword like this is a bit ... redundant, is that it?'

'No. Actually I was thinking I've seen a sword like that before, up close.' Barrak leaned into the light. 'But now that you mention it, it does seem a bit primitive compared to your other weapons.'

'I'm a believer in preserving traditions, Barrak, honouring the old ways. There's value in preserving those things. Our forefathers had a code of honour, which guided them in combat and in everyday life too. The Way of the Blade, they called it.' Striker held the sword edge up to the lamp and examined it in the feeble light.

'That's why you don't use a weapon like this against the Narbool. They have no honour. Narbool blood would defile a weapon like this.' Striker looked up from the blade and focused on Barrak as best he could in the semi-darkness.

'The professor tells me modern weapons like ours are prohibited in your land, is that right?'

Barrak nodded. It made him think about Meldrick's proclamation in the parliament and he imagined Meldrick and his security forces getting hold of weapons like the ones he'd seen Striker's unit use on the Narbool. It chilled him.

'You see, gaining weapons like those hasn't just helped with the fight against the Narbool. It's changed the course of our history.' Striker paused. Darko Mars struck a match and lit his rollie.

'Shall I tell you a little bit about our history, Councillor?'

Barrak nodded and settled in closer to the commander. Jasmyn shimmied up a bit too, putting a little of her weight against Barrak's shoulder.

'It wasn't always so easy you know. We haven't always had the upper hand against the Narbool. For centuries people lived on the coastal fringe, all around the ruined city and the harbour and small villages north and south. But it wasn't safe, it wasn't secure from incursions by the Narbool. Life was precarious. Even before that, when people first started to regain their humanity and emerge from the fog of the dark times, communities started to form. Back then, attempts were made to secure the coast from the Narbool – you'll see the old border wall when we get to Scarborough. But it was never really completed and the Narbool still attacked at will.

'Eventually a warrior caste arose, first of all around the harbour, and then up and down the coast. They protected the people. Just poor bloody peasants they were, trying to scrape a living out of the dirt. The local warlords grew in strength and eventually the Narbool were driven out into the hinterland, then, in time, back beyond the dividing range and into the western plains.'

Striker folded his piece of rag and laid it next to his jar of oil, then picked up the jar and carefully screwed on the lid. 'Anyway, a kind of hierarchy of warlords developed over time, with each one staking a claim to a piece of territory and making sure it was protected. Problem was that protection came at a price. Maintaining an army of warriors to fight the Narbool was expensive. Taxes had to be raised from the local people. In some ways life got even harder. Some of the warlords were unscrupulous and their taxes crippled the ordinary people. So, they were safe from the Narbool, but sometimes it must have seemed as if they'd swapped one evil for another.' Striker shrugged and gave a sympathetic snort.

'The Sabu-gen, as these warlords became known, made the law in each

372

of their local districts and the warriors in their employ became highly skilled in combat. Warrior status was passed down from father to son and training started in childhood. Over time, Sabu swordsmiths refined their work until the Sabu sword became the perfect weapon it is today.' Striker gently eased his sword back into its scabbard and found a place for it in the shadows. A hush seemed to have settled over the old stone hut.

'Time passed. Centuries. An almost religious dedication to the warrior's training and code evolved. It became known as the Way of the Blade. Sabu warriors were also skilled in the arts and spiritual pursuits and their highest ideal was supposed to be protection of their people. But many of the warlords became corrupt and greedy. Their Sabu warriors became brutal and the code was forgotten. Dissent and disobedience was put down cruelly. A Sabu warrior literally had the power of life and death over his master's subjects.'

Striker shifted his position in the sand. All eyes were on him.

'Then about eighty years ago it all began to change. That's when the movement that would lead to the Guild of Historians began, that would be about right, wouldn't it, Professor?'

Truman Clay had gravitated to the conversation and was sitting in the shadows nearby. Barrak heard him murmur his agreement. Seamlessly Clay took over the telling and Striker fell silent and relaxed against his backpack, no doubt relieved to pass the baton to the professor.

'Yes, yes. True enough. But really, you'd have to go back at least another hundred years, to the birth of industrialisation. I suppose I should say rebirth.' Professor Clay nodded to himself and peered over the top of his glasses at Barrak and Jasmyn.

'That was *really* the seeding of a new order, which would eventually see the downfall of the Sabu-gen. Yep, it can all be traced back to Uriah Taske and his vision of a new and better society through technological advancement, mechanisation, modernisation.

'You see, for centuries, nothing much had changed. The people tilled the land and fished the waters and the Sabu gathered taxes and kept order.

'Taske envisioned a modern world where industry would provide a better standard of living for all, not to mention fabulous wealth for himself.' Clay gave a small grunt of derision. 'In so doing, he challenged *all* the old superstitions about the evils of technology, and somehow he got away with it. It was the right time I suppose, *and* his dominant personality and uncompromising vision – he was a force of nature, was Taske.'

'The Sabu-gen allowed it, because at first, the changes were only minor – some small factories, not much more than fancy forges or blacksmiths – and it provided them with another source of taxes. As Taske's industrial empire grew, and it did, very damn quickly, there was not much the Sabu could do, they were already addicted to the tax revenue. It was much more lucrative than taxing the poor peasants.

'A century later we had roads, power, mechanised vehicles, electronic communication, all manner of technology, and the Taske family's industrial empire and wealth had grown to such an extent that it made the Sabu-gen very, very nervous. But what could they do? It was an economic alliance that benefited them both.'

'So it was this Taske who came up with the modern weapons too?' asked Barrak.

'Yes and no.' Clay's reply was annoyingly cryptic.

'I'm not sure I understand,' Jasmyn interjected. 'What about the historians? This guild, where does that come in?'

'Yes, well, exactly Jasmyn. That's the thing, let me explain,' said Clay solicitously. 'It started as an idea really, a philosophical movement, about eighty years ago, just as Axel said. The idea was that for society to really improve and grow, we didn't just need modernisation and industry, we really needed to understand what had happened to the ancients, what were the circumstances that led to the Fall.

'You see, before Taske, people had been living around the ruins for so long they no longer really even *saw* them. They were just part of the landscape. Anything useful had been stripped long ago, back in the dark times. People had lived for such a long time like animals, barely human, so really, all memory of what had happened had been lost.

'History *itself* had been lost, and with that we had lost part of our identity, our sense of humanity.' The professor was giving his dissertation plenty of drama, as though he might be trying to engage young students in a lecture theatre.

'It was Taske's grandson, who was my mother's father incidentally, who came up with the original idea. He wrote a book – not that many could read back then. It was called *The Meaning of History*. The idea was revolutionary and it sparked off a philosophical movement amongst the educated people of the time, the wealthy industrialists and even some of the Sabu. They began to call themselves the Guild of Historians. The Guild was tolerated and even encouraged by some of the more enlightened Sabu-gen.

'Because, you see, the Guild wasn't seen as political, just as Taske Industries was seen as being outside politics, too.' Clay explained this as if fielding a question from a student. 'Political movements were not tolerated and had been brutally quashed in the past, right throughout the long rule of the Sabu-gen. Nonetheless, the Guild grew quickly. People were captivated by the idea and they took a great interest in the work being done and the discoveries being made.

'Basically it was an idea whose time had come.' Clay nodded to himself.

'Over a period of twenty years or so, many excavations and delvings were done in the Harbour region and surrounding areas. A lot of very interesting stuff was being uncovered. Much was being learned about ancient times.

'Then, about fifty years ago, give or take, there was a major discovery. This one was different, this was big. A bunker, in the surrounding hills. It was all underground and, more importantly, it was all well above sea level. And it was untouched, everything intact.

'So many artefacts!' Clay's eyes widened in the weak lamplight.

'One of the things they found there was a cache of weapons, an armoury. Buried. Sealed. Oiled. They were in almost perfect condition. Some still worked. It was like a treasure trove. No one had ever seen anything like it. These weapons dated back to before the Fall, before the Great Death, maybe even as far back as the Inundation itself.'

Barrak and Jasmyn sat stock still. Barrak's feeling of being a schoolboy caught without his homework was stronger than ever.

'The Guild kept the discovery of the weapons secret. But of course the weapons found their way into the hands of Taske Industries. By then, it was the great grandson, Coen Taske, in charge and he decided to study the weapons, also in secret, with a view to developing the technology and industrial processes to recreate them. It was a bold and very dangerous move, and had the potential to change everything.'

Clay paused for dramatic effect and looked around at Barrak and Jasmyn and the rest of his audience as if he were relating a scary fairytale to a group of enthralled children.

'The technology was beyond anything they'd seen. Even the machinery to make the weapons had to be engineered from scratch. And it had to be done in secret. It took many years.'

'Why in secret?' Barrak interjected.

'Well, by this time the Sabu-lords *were* beginning to see the combination of the Guild and Taske's industrial complex as a real threat to their power. You see they never expected the Guild to grab the interest of the common people the way it did. It seemed to inspire people, gave them hope. They hung on every announcement of each new discovery by the Guild. And as the influence and power of the Guild grew, factions within it began to talk in secret about the corruption and brutality of the warlords, and the need to somehow curtail their power. Some of these same guild members were also high up in the Taske organisation, including Coen himself. The discovery of the weapons was seen as the one, maybe the only, opportunity to deal with the warlords.'

'So the rationale for the weapons wasn't just to fight the Narbool, but also to sort things out closer to home?' Barrak asked.

'Exactly. These were dangerous times. As it turned out the weapons development *was* kept secret from the Sabu lords. And when the time was right, the Guild proposed the concept of a regional homeland Protectorate, controlled centrally by the Guild.

'Of course the warlords wouldn't have a bar of it. Scoffed at it.

Couldn't believe it was even being proposed. They made threats and refused to meet with the Guild. The Guild's head of security was assassinated.'

'Then what happened?' Jasmyn chimed in as Clay paused to catch his breath.

'There was a … um, demonstration, you might say.' Clay's voice had lost its lustre and he looked past them all for a moment. A last pale flash from the receding storm briefly lit up a nearby window like an old canvas hung against the dark stone wall.

'The new Protectorate went after the strongest of the city warlords.' Clay paused again. He looked glum.

'It was short and bloody.

'After that, the Sabu lords relinquished power to the Protectorate. Some were tried and executed for their crimes against the people. Most of the warriors joined the new Protectorate, at least most of the young ones did. That was all almost forty years ago.'

The professor sighed as if he or his dissertation was running out of steam. Striker took the opportunity to heft himself up to his feet and started to pick his way amongst the reclining bodies, making for the door. Clearly he considered the lesson over. After a few moments Barrak followed him, telling himself he needed to stretch his legs, but in truth, the more he heard from these easterners, the more his head swam with questions.

Outside the rain had stopped and the sky was clearing from the east. A gibbous moon was ensnared in the ghostly web of the old ruined dish and from all around a riotous chorus of frogs celebrated the new damp. Barrak located the commander by the red glow of his cigar against a tumbled-down wall where he'd found a comfortable perch, and Striker didn't seem at all surprised to see Barrak join him there.

'So what did you think of your history lesson, Councillor?'

'Well, I think I've still got more questions than answers.'

'Like what?'

'I dunno. Like, can these ex-Sabu warriors be trusted in your ranks?'

Striker blew out a big cloud of smoke and it hung in the still air like a thought bubble. 'All that was a long time ago. A whole generation has passed. We're a professional army with a training academy. The youngsters do two years of hard slog to qualify.'

'But the Way of the Blade, as you call it, that still persists?'

'Yes, in its purest form, I like to think.' Striker took a thoughtful drag on his cigar and then examined the glowing tip. The two remained silent for a while before Striker spoke again.

'Of course there were a few rogue Sabu operating on the fringes of civilisation, ones who never really did sign up to the new accord. Some of them are still around and I must admit they do present a challenge from time to time.' He looked at Barrak, trying to gauge his reaction, but Barrak remained silent.

'You might get a chance to meet one of them in two days, when we get to Scarborough.'

'Oh?'

'His name's Xenos Flynn. Calls himself the mayor. Scarborough's an old wall town, kind of an outpost. Used to mark the border between the civilised world and the badlands, Narbool territory. It still does really.

'Flynn's third generation. His grandfather was the local warlord back in the day, one of those who never really surrendered to the new Protectorate. And the place is just too remote for the Protectorate to enforce its jurisdiction … so …' Striker took another puff.

'Sounds awkward,' Barrak ventured.

Striker chuckled and blew more smoke. 'Can get a little tense sometimes. But we usually work something out.'

Barrak nodded and so did Striker and there was no more talk for a few moments, until Striker said, 'So, how about *your* story then, Barrak?'

'What do you mean?'

'Well, I think we've established that the earth isn't flat and the moon isn't made of cheese.'

Barrak felt himself tense up; Striker seemed to be gearing up for more of his misconceived humour about the supposedly backward nature of Eyrean culture. He stayed silent, glaring at Striker.

'So, how long are you gonna stick to this fairytale about you and Jasmyn looking for your lost cousin?'

'What?' Barrak bridled.

'Maybe it's time you told me what you're really doing here.' He took a last furtive suck of smoke before casting aside the spent cigar and putting a foot to it. Barrak was silent, so Striker stepped past him and, as he did, Barrak saw the moon had escaped the lofty metal maze and was sailing free in a gap between the scudding clouds.

Over his shoulder, Striker said, 'Any time, Councillor, whenever you're ready, we'll have a little talk.'

CHAPTER 26

THE SMELL OF WOOD smoke reached them an hour before they came upon Scarborough from the north. Cresting a hill devoid of trees and dotted with grazing sheep, they came upon the town suddenly, crammed between a slow, wide river bend and the forested foothills of a nearby range.

A wispy canopy of smoke hung over the town's roofs, which formed a riotous medley of tiles and thatch and tin and slate in a patchwork of elevations and profiles. The hectic clutter of buildings seemed at risk of tumbling into the river, but for a stout stone wall holding it all in place like a great granite band. The wide, imposing grey wall was maybe two or three storeys tall at its highest, with parapets and walkways along its top. Barrak was reminded of the preserved remnants of the old city walls back in Tamouer. The impressive barrier stretched away to the east and west along the southern bank of the river, well beyond the outskirts of the town, appearing to diminish in size and condition further from the town.

What was little more than a set of faint wheel ruts at the crest of the hill improved to a decent dirt road as they descended towards the river, which was as substantial as any they'd seen in their travels and formed a significant natural barrier. A solid old timber bridge spanned it where it ran straightest. Across the bridge, the stone walls were at their most imposing on either side of massive timber gates, guarding the entrance to the town.

As they approached they could see the fortifications were

incorporated into a complex of substantial stone buildings stretching perhaps thirty or forty yards either side of the gates and some way back into the town.

The complex was two and three storeys high with low-pitched tiled roofs, interlaced with external walkways and stairs connecting the elements of the stronghold. The northern façade had large windows which seemed out of place in the rustic structure and Barrak guessed they might have been retrofitted. And angled towards them on top of the red tiles, where the pitched roofs broke the line of the terraced parapets, was an impressive array of solar panels reflecting the late afternoon sun back at them, as they made their way down the hill towards the crossing.

Xenos Flynn stood quite still beside his throne-sized office chair, his diminutive frame cast in silhouette as the low sun struck the large picture window obliquely, enriching one corner of his well-furnished office with a golden mantle.

Titus Chen was the captain of Flynn's garrison militia, a ragtag army of mercenaries and Sabu traditionalists who, under Chen's uncompromising command, were charged with defending the sovereignty of Scarborough against all comers. He sat on the other side of Flynn's giant cedar desk, reclining in his favourite old swivel chair, his left foot resting on his right knee as he swung from side to side.

Looking past Flynn, he too could see the visitors advancing in single file down the hill towards the river, their long shadows stretched like skinny phantoms half way across the adjacent paddock. The other thing he noticed, to his mild amusement, was that Flynn was already wearing his sword and had also donned his tunic, the traditional embroidered fighting robe that, in the past, Sabu warriors passed down from father to son.

'Can you see who it is?' Chen asked casually.

Flynn nodded slowly. 'Striker.' There was a hint of annoyance in his voice and he let go a short sigh. 'Again,' he added through clenched teeth.

Flynn gazed at the line of approaching figures, paying careful attention to two in the middle of the group. Something about them seemed out of place – not diggers, not military. A tall man with sandy hair and a dark-haired woman. Flynn was intrigued.

'Better put out the welcome mat, I suppose.' Flynn turned from the window and faced his captain. Chen slapped his knees and pushed himself up out of his comfy chair with a grunt and turned to go.

'Titus.'

Chen paused.

'Maybe even give the Guild people and Striker some of the good rooms. Will you see to it? Have a word to Sanjay.'

'All right then.' Chen didn't try too hard to hide his surprise at Flynn's uncommon show of hospitality.

'Provided there's plenty of room, of course. And Titus …'

Chen raised a brow to his commander.

'Keep them on a short leash. And tell that arrogant bastard he can come and pay his respects at his earliest damn convenience.'

It was Barrak who inadvertently helped to defuse the stand-off at the bridge, if indeed it was a standoff. He did it by collapsing in a heap, gasping for air like a fish out of water and clutching at his chest. And he did that because, for all he or his body knew, he was having a full-blown heart attack.

It had begun as they reached the bottom of the hill and approached the bridge under the shade of a large willow that dipped its branches into the water just to the right of the bridge where thick swathes of rushes grew along the banks and out into the shallows.

Their approach scared a flock of waterfowl who rose up squawking from the rushes and flapped and splashed across the glassy green water. *Was it this that had startled him?* Or was it the clanking and grinding of the giant gates opening across the river and the troops spilling out and onto the bridge, the crunching of their boots resonating through the timbers of the old bridge as they double-timed across it?

Barrak's chest tightened as though it were being squeezed by iron and his heart knocked in his chest and seemed to press up into his throat.

The troops reached their side of the bridge and fanned out. There seemed a lot of them, but there were perhaps only twenty in reality. Barrak saw boots and leggings, swords swaying in belted scabbards, brown tunics with dark beading and some kind of insignia at the collars, and disturbingly, weapons not unlike the ones Striker's men carried, held at the ready or diagonally across chests.

Barrak couldn't breathe and felt strangely compelled to blow out air in short bursts, as if that might restart his lungs. His bounding heart had migrated right up into his throat and seemed to be blocking it.

Behind the line of troops, the walled town looked higher, darker and more threatening than it had before. Around him, Striker's men were fanning out along their side of the road facing Scarborough's troops. He saw guns and swords being fingered tentatively. The tension between the opposing troops was palpable.

The bridge was clear of troops but for one who strode alone down the centre of it with a sense of purpose. His black embroidered tunic seemed to mark him as a different rank and he carried no weapon but a sword, which resembled Striker's. He stopped at the end of the bridge and looked slowly up and down the line of Striker's men, his manner imperious, glaring at them as if they had committed some dire offence. Striker's men were clearly nervous, alert and twitchy, as though expecting a fight.

Gunfire flashed across Barrak's mind's eye, suddenly, violently, as if he had been plunged back into the midst of the firefight with the Narbool. He flinched and gasped but no one seemed to notice. He knew no such thing was happening at the bridge and he tried to shake off the premonition. He closed his eyes. But it came at him again, flashing bursts of fire, Narbool cut to pieces, screaming and the cacophony of battle.

The dark-uniformed commander had begun to speak, and Barrak tried to concentrate on what was being said. He could hear and understand but everything seemed to be at a great distance. He was trapped between two realities and the violence in his head continued unabated.

He knew it wasn't real, and yet it was real enough in his staggering mind. Amongst it all, Bishop's shocking visage joined the parade and he saw the flash of his blaster and then Nimbarra's severed head held high in Battle's gory grip. Barrak huffed and puffed and grabbed at his collar. He forced his attention back to external events, back to the road.

'Xenos Flynn, Mayor of Scarborough, welcomes the men and women of the Guild to take refuge on their journey.' Titus Chen pronounced this with considerable solemnity.

'Mighty civilised of you, Chen.' Striker had come forward to confront the captain and extended his hand.

They shook.

'What are you up to this time, Axel, you wily bastard? Flynn's just about having kittens up there, seeing you here again so soon.'

Smiles broke out between the two men and the tension between the opposing troops melted away.

Barrak tried desperately to attach himself to reality. The flashes of violence seemed to be abating but the tightness in his chest had become a searing pain and he was breathing as if at the end of a sprint. Jasmyn was beside him now, her hand on his arm. 'Are you all right Barrak? You've gone as white as a sheet.'

Everyone else was focused on the exchange between the two leaders.

'You know he wants me to take your weapons off you, while you're here,' Chen continued matter-of-factly.

'We both know that isn't going to happen, Titus.'

Chen shrugged and grunted.

'Well, you must've done something right, he's giving you the good rooms … in the hotel.'

Attention finally turned to Barrak as he went down on one knee, clutching his chest. Jasmyn was down beside him looking up at Striker and Chen, silently imploring them to help.

'Help this man,' Chen's order was crisp and imperative. 'Get him inside.'

A couple of Chen's troopers were already at Barrak's side, helping him to his feet, and Jasmyn hovered around them, a frown of concern on her brow.

'Take him to the infirmary.'

Barrak leaned against the stone parapet and looked down at the river below. The sun had not long set and pearly yellows and pale, bright blues in the western sky were mirrored in the water. The boughs of eucalypts growing outside the wall reached up towards the parapet and some of the tallest extended above to shade the walkway, almost as though the path were through a garden and not along the top of a wall, some thirty feet up. Evening birdsong from a dozen different species added to the effect and Barrak was impressed by, and grateful for, the tranquillity, which was in stark contrast to his anxiety attack of just one hour before.

That's what the so-called doctor had diagnosed, a bespectacled and white-haired old coot with a bent back and yellow fingers and teeth who, Captain Chen had insisted, was Mayor Flynn's own private physician.

'Seen it many times before,' he'd said, 'in soldiers and others exposed to battle and other forms of violent upset.' This after listening carefully to Barrak's chest and taking his pulses and pronouncing his heart as sound as that of an ox.

Post-battle anxiety he'd called it and given him a herbal concoction which Barrak could not easily identify by taste alone. When Barrak suggested to the doctor that perhaps aconite was best indicated for anxiety and shock, the old charlatan had patted him patronisingly on the shoulder and smiled. It was clear to Barrak then that the old fellow had no clue and had never even heard of aconite. 'Plenty of rest and try to relax,' was his advice and Barrak agreed with that part of the prescription at least and intended to follow it.

Jasmyn's relief that Barrak wasn't dying changed to unbridled excitement when they were shown the rooms they'd been allocated in Flynn's hotel, which seemed to take up a good part of the rambling complex contained behind the town's wall.

'Blessed quest, Barrak, a bed!' she'd cried and proceeded to bounce up and down on the thing like a child before pancaking flat on her back in the middle of it. She sat up on the edge of the bed and looked at Barrak with a sparkle in her eyes, hinting at the kind of joyful exuberance that had been lost to her for so long.

'It's so big,' she said, sweeping her hands across the bed linen. 'And look at this, sheets! And pillows! By Orlan, I never thought I'd be so glad to see a real bed again.'

Jasmyn's excitement morphed into a warm and infectious smile and as she looked at Barrak, her eyes widened with inspiration. 'We should celebrate,' she said conspiratorially. 'They say this place has a bar and a restaurant.' Then with an *ooohh* she jumped up and rushed to the other side of the room and flung open a door. 'Gods abide! It's a bathroom!'

Barrak had agreed to meet her later and left her to make good use of her new-found amenities while he located his own room. It was indeed impressive the way the old stone fortress had been refitted with the makings of a modern hotel. Certainly it wasn't a patch on Tamouer's top-end accommodation, nothing like it in fact, and really quite quaint, but following the privation they'd endured in recent months, it was luxurious, and Barrak understood Jasmyn's excitement. He himself was grateful and content to shave and wash off a hundred miles of grime.

He watched his face gradually transform in the small bathroom mirror, as he carefully scraped away his wild-man beard. It did him good. In the end, when a clean-shaven and entirely more couth Barrak stared out at him from behind the glass, he felt his anxiety recede a notch. It was almost as if the simple act of changing his appearance had allowed him to regain some small measure of control over his world and he felt better prepared to face whatever was to come. Perhaps this was the calming effect of encroaching civilisation.

With that in mind he'd gone out of the stairwell onto the external walkway and along the wall. *Some cool evening air and enjoy the sunset. Relax. Breathe.* The proximity of the river below was soothing and after walking a short distance along the fortifications he put his back to the parapet, near an overhanging canopy of eucalypt and took in the view out across the town. Some houses had little rooftop gardens and balconies and between the roofs of terracotta and slate were narrow streets in a deranged grid. Voices of the townspeople carried up from the street canyons and he glimpsed a cart of some sort, grinding and squeaking along the cobbles, and there appeared to be an animal like an ox or donkey pulling it. Away to the south-west, the roofs gave way to an open area lined with more eucalypts and with a couple of tall, steepled structures poking above the foliage. A town square perhaps.

'So, what do you think of Scarborough?' The professor surprised him, presumably having come out of one of the nearby stairwells with the same intent as Barrak.

Barrak said he was impressed and so he was. 'Not bad for an old walled town. What did the commander call it? An outpost?'

'Better than you expected then, Councillor?'

'Definitely. Jasmyn is pretty chuffed.'

'Chuffed?'

'Pleased,' Barrak clarified. After their time living with the Dzahn and learning their dialect, adjusting to the easterners' accent and unfamiliar pronunciation and words had been relatively easy. But occasionally he was still reminded of how different it was from his natural Eyrean. Some of the younger troopers could still barely understand him and Jasmyn, especially if they spoke quickly to each other.

'That was a nasty turn you had, Barrak,' Clay said, nodding toward the bridge below. 'The two of you have been through a lot, haven't you?'

Barrak nodded slowly. 'That's a fact.'

They stood for a moment, both leaning against the parapet and taking in the view to the west where the burnished brightness of the day had retreated to the distant hills.

'So what *did* you discover out there?' Barrak asked, nodding towards the western sky.

Clay assessed him with a critical eye, as though weighing up just how much he could tell; he didn't answer right away. Eventually he said quietly, 'We found a whole city out there.' The professor looked out to the west as though he could see his lost city from the parapet, then he continued in a strangely hushed tone. 'A whole city, landlocked, and so never inundated. Abandoned long ago. Immense. All kinds of infrastructure. We're finding some of it still intact, as we start to excavate.

'It's buried?' Barrak asked.

'Overgrown. Some of it buried over time.' The professor looked pointedly at Barrak. 'We think it was abandoned soon after the Fall, maybe around the time of the Great Death.'

Barrak spun around to face the professor, suddenly irritated by his own ignorance of terms he'd heard bandied around several times, as if they were common knowledge. 'What the quest is this *Fall* you keep talking about, and the *Great Death?* What do you mean by all that?' He surprised himself by blurting this out in quite an irritable tone.

The professor pushed his glasses up his nose and considered him. 'Back where you come from, Barrak, what do *your* historians say about the time before? Before your Orlan led his people to the Eyrean Sea and established the settlement, the city … what is it called again, I'm sorry, the name escapes me for the moment.'

'You mean Tamouer?'

'Yes, yes, Tamouer. What of the time before that? What does your average Eyrean know about the circumstances that led to Orlan's flight? I mean why … why would a group of people, there were twelve families weren't there, why would they leave everything they knew and travel so far into the wilderness?'

'You mean the twelve clans?' Barrak eyed the professor with no small amount of suspicion, wondering whether he, like Striker, was given to derisive humour about his homeland and its people.

'They fled the Chaos,' Barrak said simply. 'After the Flood. After the great flood there came famine and disease, chaos and pestilence.

'Desolation.' Barrak said the word as if it held an explanation in and of itself and it hung in the air for a moment. The professor said nothing, so Barrak continued, looking away into the distance as he spoke. 'The

388

cities of the iniquitous were destroyed. It was the wrath of the gods, the sky god, Ouranus, and Neptune, the god of the sea and the great earth goddess. They punished humanity for its wickedness. People had lost their respect … their respect for the gods and for the earth … and for each other. People had become greedy and evil and so they were punished. Great suffering was imposed by the gods. Their cities were destroyed. People lost everything. And then they turned against each other. Murder and mayhem. Lawlessness. A person could be killed just for a scrap of food. Brother against brother, father against son. Humanity was lost. Depravity and corruption were all that remained.

'Chaos.' Barrak blinked and saw the professor looking at him oddly. He shook his head slightly and blinked again. *How strange.* The professor's question had transported him back through the years, to primary school and the old story of the Punishment of the Gods. He'd practically recited it, just as he'd learned it all those years ago, along with every other Eyrean schoolchild.

The professor was nodding slowly, an odd, gentle smile on his face. 'Yes, yes,' he said in a hushed voice. 'So old Orlan leads his followers, the twelve clans, into the wilderness to escape the Chaos, all those centuries ago, all the way to the Eyrean Sea, and there, he declares the outside world out of bounds, and the rest of it is, well, history.'

Clay had slipped into his lecturer's voice again.

'Some in the Guild have taken a keen interest in Eyrean culture over the years. There's been some quite good research, but without access to actual Eyrean historical records … well, there's still so much we don't know. And so far, from our own research, there's nothing that places Orlan here in the east, before his flight west. We haven't identified him in *our* historical record. Not that that means much; the records from that period are so patchy.

'And how did he know to go all the way west, to find the Eyrean Sea? How did he know … or *did* he even know, that the sea level rise decades before had opened a great inland salt lake to the southern ocean, creating the inland sea that exists there today? And did he know that the inland sea would change the very climate in the surrounding area, turning what had always been desert into arable land, with a decent rainfall, fit for crops and livestock?

'And for all these hundreds of years your people remained isolated by distance and by design, while the eastern lands descended into a primitive dark age of chaos and suffering. It's incredible, really.' The professor blew a silent whistle of air and looked at Barrak, who felt he was being examined like a zoo specimen.

'Yes, but what about this *Fall* and the *Great Death*?' Barrak asked tetchily.

'We're talking about the *same thing* Barrak. Mind you, even after all these years we are still piecing together the timeline. But what *we* refer to as the Fall, is the whole damned catastrophe: overpopulation, climate instability, cataclysmic sea-level rise, we know when *that* happened … That's your *flood*. Cities inundated. Millions displaced. Then, an overwhelming influx of refugees from all around the globe. Result? Tens of millions homeless, starvation and disease, total economic and civil disintegration. No government, no monetary system, no rule of law – all gone.' Clay counted these off on his fingers.

'Civil unrest would've quickly become a fight for survival – survival of the fittest – or most ruthless and best armed.'

The two men looked at each other for a brief moment, searching each other's eyes wordlessly. 'As you said, Councillor, the wrath of the gods.' Clay stroked his chin. 'In a way, I think that's exactly what it was.'

'And the Great Death?' Barrak asked. 'Do you mean that many people died in the famine and the fighting?'

'No, no, that was something different. That came later, we think,' Clay's voice quavered slightly, 'decades later perhaps, we're not really sure.

'The poor sods living at that time, trying to survive, they must've thought things couldn't get any worse. Who knows what kind of conditions must have existed then – there are virtually no records.

'It was probably a virus. It was very quick, we think. There are precious few actual accounts. It seems like it literally dissolved the body's mucous membranes – a painful and ugly death. As a physician I'm sure you can imagine, Barrak: short, very short incubation period, probably only a day or two, and unbelievable mortality rate, worse than anything in medical history, we think greater than ninety per cent.'

Barrak was silenced by the gravity of what he was hearing.

'What we do know is that at every dig site we uncover bones, huge mass graves, and elsewhere single graves or in small groups – everywhere. Bones, like geological strata. Layers of human suffering. It's a sobering thing, Barrak, seeing one of these sites, and it makes you wonder, it really does.' Clay's voice trailed off and he shook his head slightly and looked down at his boots. The two men fell silent and the incongruously cheerful twitter of evening birdsong filled the air around them.

A few moments passed before Barrak asked the professor, 'What happened next?'

'Next? No one really knows. There are no records. For the few who survived the Great Death it must have been primeval, primitive, bare survival. We can only speculate. It was probably the start of the ascendency of the Nar-bool, and on the coast, perhaps the emergence of those who would, in time, become the Sabu warriors.' The professor eyed Barrak kindly. 'I wonder if your Orlan saw it all coming? When did he round up his followers and go west, I wonder? Was it just after the inundation of the coastal cities? Or during the decades of chaos that followed; or was he fleeing the Great Death?'

Barrak shook his head and took a long look at his own boots, searching his memory of the Quest Diaries for some point of convergence that could help make sense of what he was hearing.

'He was a visionary really, wasn't he? A true prophet. He knew what was coming and he knew it was going to be final; he knew there was no going back. The faith and the vision he must have had.' Clay was looking out into the gloaming with his eyes wide, the flat of his hand pushed up against his cheek. 'And the audacity!' he added as if inspiration had stuck. 'No sooner has the new settlement been established, than Orlan declares it *year zero*. Puts a line under it. We can start again! We can start from scratch and do it our way, Orlan's way. Amazing, really.'

It was Barrak's turn to look at Clay as though he were a curious specimen.

'Wait a minute, what do you mean year zero?'

Truman Clay examined Barrak critically.

'Oh well, your calendar in Eyre, I mean you know, the year, according to the Eyrean calendar is what, seven hundred and something?'

Barrak stared imperiously at the historian and said slowly and deliberately, 'It's seven hundred and eight.'

Clay let out a short sigh. 'Yes, of course, but you know that's not really the, um …' Clay paused as if trying to solve a puzzle in his head. 'Look, this might come as a shock to you, Barrak …'

'You see, we like to think, that is, we estimate from our research, that the year … according to the ancients, *their* year really, would be,' he looked uncertainly at Barrak. 'It's 2884. Here in the east, it's the year 2884. It was calculated by the first historians, eighty odd years ago, and it was made official back in 2850. That's when we officially adopted the old calendar.' Clay said all this quickly, and then he paused and raised a qualifying figure. 'It's all just relative though, I suppose, isn't it?'

Barrak looked evenly at Clay, observing the historian carefully. The professor seemed nervous under his gaze.

Barrak was utterly still. His mind shaped a single thought, rising up like a bubble to the surface of his awareness.

Preposterous.

He drew a breath to give voice to this idea but didn't get the chance because Clay's assistant, Teah, was suddenly beside them. 'You two better get downstairs. They're serving dinner. You'll miss out if you keep on gas-bagging up here.'

CHAPTER 27

THE SMELL OF THE food made Barrak's stomach gurgle and the effect of it on his senses was so intense it almost made him swoon. It was hard for him to tell if he was ravenously hungry or nauseous. After so long with so little to eat he was sure his stomach had shrunk and he counselled himself to be careful as he found his place, which Striker had kept for him.

Flynn had insisted on supplying a meal for the travelling cohort and Striker made no bones about his suspicions, maintaining that the gesture was out of character for the mayor, who was normally both frugal and mercenary.

A buffet had been laid out on trestle tables and behind one of them a young man in an apron and floppy white hat stood ready to carve slices from joints of meat. There were trays of roasted vegetables, bowls of some sort of mash, and dishes of rice and beans flavoured with herbs, freshly baked flatbreads and a salad of fresh vegetables and spinach, finished with an unusual and piquant dressing. It was basic food but tasty and nutritious, substantial fare for hungry troops.

Barrak took a small portion of meat and vegetables and ate slowly and carefully. But once his body woke up to the availability of nourishment, he was at war with himself: his shrunken stomach felt full to bursting after just a few bites, but the rest of his emaciated physiology demanded he consume more. He nibbled at small pieces of the tender, fatty meat, which was either goat or lamb, knowing the proteins and fats would help to switch off his hunger. And he tried to concentrate on what Striker was saying about the town and Flynn and the surprising level of hospitality, but he was distracted by his own thoughts, as he tried to make sense of the conversation he'd just had with Clay up on the wall. He was also distracted by Jasmyn, who had found herself a place with Hesta and Teah and a few of the young troopers. They'd already eaten and were getting relaxed and a bit rowdy, with two or three bottles of wine already accounted for.

Striker was running his plan past Clay, sounding him out on the idea of laying over in Scarborough for an extra night to allow their teams some much-needed rest and recuperation. They talked about the new dig site in the western plains and what had been discovered, and while he listened to them, Barrak imagined the layers of human bones Clay had told him about. When they mentioned their harbour city, Barrak tried to imagine the ancient eastern city laid to ruin by the chaos of the Fall.

A yelp of familiar laughter took his attention back to the table across the way. The whole group was on its feet and Jasmyn was in the midst of the them with a glass held high in one hand while her other arm swept through a wide arc in some kind of grandiose gesture that elicited another round of shrieks and hoots.

Jasmyn holding court. She clearly had the young troopers and diggers in her thrall as their small group gravitated towards the bar adjacent to the dining area.

Watching Jasmyn and her new friends making merry, his mind was elsewhere. Numbers were sequencing through his head, like a deranged desk calendar flitting wildly through the years as his mind struggled to reconcile seven hundred and eight with twenty-eight hundred and whatever-the-hell it was the professor had claimed was the year.

'Barrak, what do you say? Agreed?' Clay and Striker were both looking at him. Clearly he'd missed part of the conversation.

But his inattention was forgotten as the three of them craned their necks towards the bar, where a group had entered from the lobby: a phalanx of five with one dapper man at the front dressed in an embroidered tunic, his tailored trousers decorated with a gold stripe down the side seam. He looked around slowly, taking in the scene with a proprietary air. Something about his stance and his profile reminded Barrak uncannily of Meldrick.

He and his companions were quite close to Jasmyn and her new friends, who'd occupied a cluster of barstools at the end of the bar. There were shot glasses lined up along the bar, and Barrak suspected some sort of drinking game.

'Uh-oh, here's Flynn,' said Striker. 'This should be interesting.'

'Welcome to our humble town,' said Flynn loudly, embracing the room with his arms out and palms up. His head swivelled to take in both rooms and his eye lit briefly on Striker. The hubbub in the room gradually subsided.

'It is a rare pleasure to offer our meagre hospitality to the esteemed members of the Guild.' There was a hint of a smirk about his generous smile as he turned himself slowly from left to right before lowering his arms. Most eyes were on Flynn and a hush had descended over the room. But Jasmyn, with her back to the mayor, had not yet noticed him. She held a small glass at eye level as though examining it. 'Jupiter's orb!' she exclaimed – a traditional Eyrean toast – and then giggled. When she looked to her companions for encouragement, she realised their attention was elsewhere. She swivelled on her stool, with a slight wobble, to see what the fuss was about.

Flynn took a couple of steps towards her. 'But, what have we here?' he demanded with exaggerated curiosity. 'A new face, it seems. How delightful!' His four body guards moved up too and stared stonily at the troopers flanking Jasmyn on their bar stools.

Jasmyn stifled a nervous laugh, put down her glass and quickly straightened on her stool, exuding an air of demure indifference. She said nothing, but gave Flynn a cool and reserved smile. Flynn looked her up and down brazenly, his chest puffed out. The banal smile on his lips was negated by his vacant, distant eyes.

Barrak tensed and began to stand up. A cautioning hand from Striker told him to take it slowly and all three of them casually got up from their table and began to make their way towards the bar.

'Commander! Axel, old friend. How nice.' Flynn switched his

attention to Striker as the three men approached. Barrak saw that this was much to Jasmyn's relief.

'I trust you have supped well on the scanty provisions we've been able to offer.' Flynn's manner was curiously hard to define, he fairly oozed obsequious geniality, laced with subtle venom.

'Yes. We thank you, Mayor Flynn. Not scanty but generous, and delicious, and greatly appreciated after so long in the bush.' Striker was po-faced, formal.

'Yes, I'm sure,' said Flynn curtly. 'Well, it's been, what, about five weeks since you came through here on your way out? Where *have* you been, Commander?' Flynn's smirk indicated that his question was rhetorical, playful.

'You know I can't divulge that, Xenos.' Striker smiled, but his eyes were serious.

'Quite.' Flynn switched to stiff and haughty, to match Striker's demeanour.

'But it seems you *have* found some new friends, Commander.' Flynn gave Barrak a hard stare and a fake smile and then swivelled around to peer rudely at Jasmyn again, before turning his attention to Striker with a raised brow.

'And now, I'm not sure, but if my ears don't deceive me,' Flynn put a finger to his ear, 'I *do* believe I've detected the most intriguing of *accents.*'

Striker was stoic and silent, Flynn feigning breathless excitement. The tension between the two men was palpable.

'So fascinating and wonderful to have visitors from far-off exotic lands grace our dull little town. I can't wait to hear all about it.' Flynn was rubbing his hands together in anticipation. 'Perhaps you could all join me for supper later. But wait ...' Flynn engineered an exaggerated dramatic pause, 'Axel, where are your manners? You've not yet introduced me to your new friends.'

Striker closed his eyes for a moment and sighed. Meanwhile Flynn twirled an index finger at him as though beckoning a servant. 'Would you mind, Commander?'

'Xenos, this is Barrak Brethrenhope. Barrak, meet Mayor Xenos

Flynn, ruler of Scarborough and all who sail in her.' Flynn leaned forward and shook Barrak's hand, giving Striker a sideways scowl in acknowledgement of his sarcasm.

'And this is Jasmyn Mooney. Jasmyn, meet Mayor Xenos Flynn.'

Jasmyn gingerly raised a hand as Flynn approached. To her chagrin he grabbed it and took it to his lips. Jasmyn snatched it back with a lot less delicacy and tact than she might normally have managed.

'So, shall we say 10 o'clock? I'll arrange a supper in one of the private lounges – some light refreshments? Something sweet? Some strudel perhaps?'

Barrak noticed Jasmyn wipe the back of her hand on her borrowed dungarees, muttering something under her breath. Flynn ignored this and went on: 'I must say I'm very excited to hear all about it … some grand adventure in the wilds of … er, where did you say your friends came from Axel? Oh, but I don't think you did say, did you?'

'Xenos, we rescued these people from the Narbool. They're from the western plains. Farming people. They're lucky to have survived. They've been through a terrible time. I really don't think they're up to much socialising.'

'Nonsense!' Flynn swung to face Striker and flopped a hand in Jasmyn's direction. 'Miss Mooney has already been socialising. She seems quite good at it. And Axel, all I'm suggesting is a quiet little supper and a nice chat.'

It was dawning on Barrak that some kind of agenda was playing out. Flynn seemed uncommonly interested in him and Jasmyn, and his interest clearly made Striker uncomfortable, to the extent that he was prepared to lie about where they were from. He flashed Jasmyn a questioning look and she frowned and gave him her nonplussed look in return.

'Striker's right, Xenos.' A new voice, low and resonant, entered the discussion. It belonged to Titus Chen, the captain of Flynn's guard. He emerged from the shadows into the glow of the bar lights, with an air of concern tinged with ennui.

'I had to take this man to see your physician this afternoon. He is not at all well. The doctor has ordered rest and that's probably what they both need. Nourishment and rest, that's all, and no more wine, in such a weakened state.' Chen looked pointedly at Jasmyn and tipped his head ever so slightly towards the exit.

Striker caught Barrak's eye and made a similar gesture and his eyes said that now was the time for him and Jasmyn to leave.

Barrak reached out a hand towards Jasmyn. She slid off her barstool and took his hand in a way that was strangely compliant for her, and as they moved towards the exit it occurred to Barrak how strange it was that Chen, ostensibly Flynn's subordinate, seemed to have some kind of innate authority and that even Flynn seemed ready to acquiesce to his opinion.

They left behind the sound of a heated exchange between Flynn and Chen, which sounded like Flynn saving face and Striker attempting some diplomacy between the two, but the gist of it was lost as they retreated down the hallway towards the stairs.

Jasmyn sat on the edge of the bed and wrestled off one of her boots and let it drop to the floor. With a puff of exasperation she flopped on her back, raising the other leg up and pointing it at Barrak. 'Help me with this one will you Barrak?'

As he wrangled her boot off she shared her impressions of Flynn and Chen and the town and what the diggers and young soldiers had been talking about at dinner. Barrak wanted to tell her about Professor Clay and what he'd told him up on the wall, but she was distracted and kept flitting from one topic to another without really listening to him. She was clearly more than a little tipsy.

Barrak let her take the conversation on whatever convoluted path she chose. Passing on the revelations about Clay's bizarre calendar could wait until tomorrow.

Once they had her other boot off she bounded off the bed and wriggled out of her dungarees. She kicked them across the room and stood beside the bed clothed only in underwear and a white cotton undershirt, borrowed from one of the Guild women. It was long and reached almost to her knees and hung loose on Jasmyn's slight frame. It was the cleanest item of clothing either one of them had seen for a long time and contrasted with her slender legs, tanned from their months spent with the Dzahn. Barrak was a little shocked to see how thin she had become. Perhaps Jasmyn read his thoughts because she turned to examine herself in a narrow three-quarter-length mirror on the wardrobe door.

'Look at me, Barrak.' She rotated slightly from side to side while eyeing her own reflection. 'I'm so thin.' She pouted and put both hands to her breasts and then smoothed them down the cotton shirt, following the contours of her body, down her belly and over her hips.

'I've been on the 100-day lost-in-the-wilderness diet,' she said dreamily and wriggled her hips, making the hem of the shirt creep midway up her thighs. Her hands re-traced their route back to her breasts and she turned to face Barrak.

'Look at my breasts, Barrak, they're so small now. Her voice was girlish and a little mournful as she looked down at her chest and cupped her breasts in her hands, pushing them together under her shirt.

Barrak felt a stirring in his crotch that took him by surprise and shocked him. Jasmyn had flirted with him before, but this was different. There was something about her manner, tipsy and provocative, the fluid motion of her breasts under her own touch and the dreamy look in her eyes that had got under his guard.

Barrak felt as if he'd taken a step backwards, but in reality he hadn't moved.

He noticed a bright patch of moonlight spilling across the bed from the window. The weak electric light gave everything else a soft, syrupy look. Something drew his attention to the bedside table, which was bare but for the bedside lamp, and he looked at the open empty wardrobe, then back at Jasmyn in the plain white shirt-come-nightdress with her crumpled pants lying on the floor. *She has nothing. We both have nothing. Nothing but each other.*

Jasmyn was on one leg, trying to balance as she snatched off one of the socks and flung it away. She lost her balance and took three quick steps to re-gain it, bringing her face to face with Barrak. She put a hand on his shoulder for balance as she raised her other leg and removed the remaining sock, holding it between her index finger and thumb for a moment before letting it fall. She smiled cheekily and pressed herself against him.

'Are you going to tuck me in Barrak?'

Barrak's mind told him to back away. But a deeper instinct had him stand firm, rooted to the spot, as Jasmyn pushed a little harder against him. An old mantra was running through his head, *She's just a child, Enoch's daughter, practically his god-daughter, too young for you!* But it had lost its power, and in his head, a counter-argument overran it: *She's a grown woman, beautiful, sensual, Jasmyn, my angel.*

He felt the contour of her hip slide across his thigh as she turned and pushed against him. Meanwhile her hand wandered languidly from his shoulder to the back of his neck, and as she slid across him, Barrak felt first the flat smoothness of her belly and then the soft firmness of her pubis pressing against him. Her lips brushed his ear.

'Time for bed, Barrak,' she cooed softly.

She pushed harder against him, her legs enveloping his thigh. Any moment now she would feel for herself the strength of his desire for her.

Suddenly they were entwined.

Jasmyn's free hand was at his hip and sliding down. Barrak's cupped her breast gently, then a little more firmly, feeling her erect nipple pressing through the soft fabric. She sighed, her whole body shuddered, and her sigh became a soft groan. Barrak's other arm came around behind her and he swept her up and carried her to the bed. As he laid her down he remembered doing the same thing, seemingly so long ago, at the hotel in Tamouer, back when he could not admit his love for Jasmyn, not even to himself.

The memory fanned his desire for her now, made it somehow more urgent, overpowering.

'Barrak,' Jasmyn said in a throaty whisper, 'I've waited so long for you.' Her mouth was slightly open, waiting for his kiss, her eyes soft and dark, the pupils dilated in the dim light.

As he leaned over her, she sighed again and her scent was all around him, carrying him away to a heady place where there were no restraints, just the final blissful consummation of his love for her.

But something made him hesitate, then it hit Barrak like a slap, his inner voice, faint at first but insistent, repeating the same thing over and again. And the inner voice was Persephone's voice, which he hadn't heard for years, not since his unravelling.

Barrak, what are you doing? She's drunk!

He recoiled slightly and Jasmyn's eyes shot open.

'What's wrong?'

'Jasmyn, we can't. I can't. It's not right.'

Jasmyn's hand, lying on the pillow beside her tousled hair, formed a fist and she brought it down and gently pounded the bed at her side. 'No. No. No. Yes! Yes, Barrak. It *is* right. What could possibly be wrong?'

'You've had too much to drink. You might regret this.'

She gave a sigh of exasperation and arched her neck, looking up at the bedhead before growling out her irritation. She raised herself on her elbow and fixed Barrak with a determined stare.

'Do you think I don't know my own mind just because I've had a few drinks?' Her eyes were suddenly clear and penetrating. Barrak went down on his knees and looked deeply into her eyes. Suddenly he wasn't as sure of himself, but his mind was made up and he knew the moment had passed.

'It just wouldn't be right Jasmyn, not like this. Not tonight.'

'Orlan's blessed bollocks!' She fell back into her pillow and closed her eyes. He noticed her breathing gradually slow and after a few moments he wondered whether she would fall asleep. As he watched her he knew he loved her absolutely, unconditionally.

By and by a tear welled up and rolled down her cheek. She blinked it away and wiped her cheek before rolling over and looking into Barrak's eyes. She searched his face and he reached out and took her hand in his. Their noses were almost touching.

'Do you love me Barrak?'

'You know I do Jasmyn. I always have.'

She frowned and her eyes narrowed slightly.

'And do you *want* me Barrak ? Or am I too skinny for you, now that you've dragged me through the wilderness and half-starved me?'

'More than you could possibly imagine. But I want you with a clear head, with no reservations, no doubts.'

She looked at him for a long time. Her sapphire-blue eyes were a familiar landscape to him, one in which he could happily wander for the rest of his years. She seemed to be looking deep within him, cataloguing his soul and energising his spirit. Barrak was open to her scrutiny and could have gazed at her forever, now that the truth had finally been spoken between them.

She blinked twice and her eyes seemed to take on a new clarity. 'Barrak, don't you go back into your man cave after this, because when I'm sober, I'm going to want this even more than I do right now. You know we were made for each other don't you?' She held him in her steady, open gaze. 'We *should* be together ... Now get out!' This in a playfully assertive tone. 'I need to get some beauty sleep.'

He began to stand up and withdraw his hand but she squeezed it hard and drew him back down to her. 'One more thing, Barrak.' She looked up at him and her eyes sparkled. 'I love you too.'

She drew him closer and they kissed, briefly, deliciously, her lips and tongue exploring for a moment before withdrawing. She loosened her grip on his hand and Barrak straightened up, but she pulled him back down again and brought his hand to her lips and kissed his fingertips, then slipped her lips over the tip of his middle finger and sucked it gently for a moment.

'I'm right here, Barrak, if you change your mind,' she murmured dreamily before finally releasing him and falling back into the deep comfort of her pillow.

She snuggled further into her pillow with a strangely satisfied grin as Barrak tucked the blanket under her chin before backing away, watching her as he reached for the door. By the time he opened it and glanced back at her, she seemed to be already asleep.

CHAPTER 28

BARRAK MADE HIS WAY to one of the external stairwells and out onto the rooftop parapet walk. He needed some air. The memory of her kiss was on his lips and her smell still wafted deliciously though his senses. He could still feel the passion trembling through her as she'd pressed her body to his.

Gods! What had just happened?

Jasmyn. His mentor's daughter. Jasmyn, a child still, when he was first elected to council. Jasmyn, whom he had been charged to protect. How had this happened? It *had* happened quickly. *Was it the wine, was it just that she was tipsy? Would she even remember? Yes of course she would, she wasn't that drunk.*

Orlan's breath! What had he done?

He paced like a penitent along the cobbled walkway with his head down and one hand atop the stone balustrade to guide him. He was muttering to himself.

He didn't notice the moon, even though he was bathed in its light. Not until he came to a junction, a square terrace where one flight of stairs descended to the hotel and another curved up to an old watchtower, did he look up.

The moon was huge, like a lantern hung from the branches of the tall gums.

A full moon – not yet cast up into the void of night to shed its cold, white midnight light – but still kissed with tones of its earthly conjunction, a warm rich tint which gave its cratered countenance an almost human guise, like a smile not quite expressed. The soft brilliance touched Barrak and made him draw breath as though there was sustenance to be had from the luminous orb.

As he stood motionless under the moon, his mind fell silent and he noticed the only sound was an orchestra of night insects, practising a score that they had almost perfected. It occurred to him that he was absorbing the strangely potent light from the moon, not just through his eyes but through his body, as though he were transparent or made of moon-stuff himself.

The colour of the sky around the moon was indescribable, seemingly charcoal and blue and pink and yellow all at once in a single hue, a new colour unable to be conveyed by human word or thought – a *moon sky*.

A warm glow kindled inside him and grew until he was overwhelmed by a sense of wellbeing and contentment that was hard to recognise at first. It confused him and delighted him at the same time. He could not remember when he'd felt so good. He wondered if the supernatural moon had done this to him, but he knew it was Jasmyn, Jasmyn in his heart. And all at once his doubts were gone, gone so absolutely that it seemed ludicrous to have doubted at all.

He found himself smiling in a way he hadn't smiled for a long time, a smile of deep inner calm and contentment. He looked around at the bright stone walls and thought himself silly, perched on this wall in the night, fretting like a teenager, then he laughed at himself, laughed out loud and spun around as if looking for someone with whom to share the joke.

The deep black of the shadows around the tower and the stairs contrasted with the brightness of moon on stone, and for a moment he thought he saw something or sensed it, sensed someone else on the parapet with him, in the shadows.

'Who's there?' he asked the moonstruck walls. And he laughed again, nervously this time, at his own foolishness.

No one.

His laugh seemed to be echoed by his inner voice and Barrak

fancied that it was Enoch's rich, good-natured chuckle he was hearing, his laugh and his bright, wise old eyes suddenly fresh in his mind. And it seemed for good measure he'd conjured up a blessing from Enoch as Barrak's inner voice now spoke to him with an inflection that could only be Enoch's.

My dear boy, what did you think I meant when I asked you to look after her? You should be together. How better to take care of her, Barrak? After all, you know you were always like a son to me.

Under the intoxicating light Barrak could almost believe his old friend was there, lurking in the moon shadow, haunting the stone ramparts as if his restless spirit had mistaken them for the walls of Orlan's old keep.

Thank you, Barrak whispered to the stones.

No, thank you, Barrak. He gasped. It was Persephone in his head now, her gentle voice seamlessly taking over the inner dialogue from Enoch.

Thank you, Barrak, for being a good husband and a good father. I'm sorry we left you too soon. But it breaks my heart to see you all alone.

Barrak looked accusingly at the moon, sure now of its part in some celestial mischief that was playing with his mind.

You and Jasmyn were meant to be. Look at you. Two lost souls. You're meant to be together.

Barrak noticed he'd stopped breathing. He took a deep breath of cool evening air and put a hand on the balustrade to steady himself. A tear rolled down his cheek.

'Pers,' he whispered, but she was gone. His mind was quiet again. There was just the moon and the crickets. It really had been them, he was sure. His own inner dialogue, but their words. A message of grace. He wiped the tear from his cheek. He felt good. Calm. Sure of himself.

But it wasn't going to last.

When Striker's hand clasped his shoulder it seemed to come out of nowhere. Barrak jumped so high he was lucky he didn't go over the wall.

'Jesus, Barrak, why so jumpy?' Striker recoiled slightly and examined him carefully with a look of genuine concern. 'Are you feeling any better?'

'Yeah, much, until just now, when I nearly jumped out of my skin.'

'Yes, well sorry. I've been looking for you. We need to talk.'

As Striker and Barrak came through the lobby all was quiet, even though it was still quite early. In the bar a good portion of Striker's men and the Guild people were scattered about, quietly enjoying a rare night off duty. The lights were low and the conversation muted. Striker led the way to the far end of the bar, nodding and smiling the odd greeting to his people as he passed. A card game was going on at one of the tables in the lounge area, but the others were unoccupied. Striker chose a low table in the farthest corner, a good distance from the card players, and they settled on two old cracked leather lounges.

He raised a hand towards the bar and wagged a beckoning finger then reached out and dimmed the table lamp. Not for the first time Barrak was surprised and impressed that the place seemed to have ample electric power, even at night.

Striker turned his attention to Barrak and frowned. 'So, Barrak, what do you think?'

'What do I think about what?'

'Everything.' Striker said flatly. 'Being lost, being rescued, coming east. Us ... this place.' Striker waved an arm vaguely towards the lobby.

'I don't really know what to think ...' Barrak was interrupted by the barman who appeared from the shadows and placed two paper napkins on the table.

Striker pointed at Barrak and tipped his head. 'Whisky? They make something almost drinkable here.'

Barrak nodded and showed the barman a small gap between his thumb and index finger. 'Do you have any ice?' With a smile and a nod the barman was gone and Striker was scrutinising him again. His steady gaze made Barrak nervous and he shifted in his seat.

'I'll tell you what I think. I think you and Jasmyn are a long, long way out of your comfort zone. Am I right?'

'D'you think so?' Barrak didn't mean to sound so flippant, but there was something about Striker's manner that he found abrasive and almost galling. A flash of irritation lit Striker's eye and Barrak could see by the dim lamplight that he'd not yet bothered to shave, neither his face nor head, which seemed odd, given the amenities of the place.

'What are you *doing* here, Councillor?'

'I've told you already, we were lost.'

'No!' Striker cut him off and held up a finger for emphasis. 'No. I do *not* want to hear that story again. Look Barrak, we're not fools. We know what's been going on in Eyre. You people might have no interest in events outside your borders but the rest of us are not so insular. We, the Guild that is, we've been taking a keen interest in the Eyrean situation for some time. Before the Guild, not so much, but in recent times we've had reason to ... investigate.'

'How?' Barrak demanded. 'Our borders are closed and always have been. Sealed.'

'Really?' Striker held his eye for a moment. 'Then how did you and Jasmyn get out?'

Barrak leaned back into his couch with a troubled frown and smoothed his hand over his newly shaven chin. He stared at Striker, trying to gauge him. That last question implied he knew a lot more about the circumstances of their leaving Eyre than he possibly *could* know. Surely he was bluffing. Before Barrak could answer, the drinks arrived and the two men observed a truce to acknowledge the barman and see him off.

Striker leaned forward and rotated his glass on its napkin, but didn't pick it up. 'Look Barrak, the frog doesn't just jump out of the well for no reason.'

'What do you mean?'

'A physician and member of the High Council plus a young woman who's obviously Eyrean aristocracy, fleeing Eyre, not just to the border zones, but past the outer boundaries and all the way east? Leaving the Eyrean Sea? Fuck me, that just doesn't happen. You know it. I know it. Not without something big, something very bloody unusual making it happen.'

407

Striker leaned forward and picked up his drink and held it up towards Barrak. 'Honour,' he said.

'Health,' said Barrak and they both took a sip without breaking eye contact.

'So what happened, Barrak? Was it that power-hungry security chief, what's his name, Meldrick? Did you fall foul of him? Or did you or your girlfriend, or maybe both of you, get mixed up with that rebel movement of yours – is *that* what happened?'

Barrak heard a chorus of muted shouts and murmurs go around the card players at the other table and it occurred to him that he was engaged in a similar game with Striker. He was less sure Striker was bluffing now. It seemed he did know something about the situation in Eyre. Or maybe he was still just fishing?

Suddenly it seemed clear to Barrak there was little point in resisting. Striker pretty much held all the cards and it was obviously time for Barrak to lay his down. Whether they liked it or not, he and Jasmyn had thrown their lot in with Striker. Barrak was pretty sure that Professor Clay was a good and compassionate man and even Striker, though he could be abrasive, was clearly a man of principle.

So maybe it was time to trust in the fates, and strange though it seemed, the fates had cast him and Jasmyn in the role of emissaries from Gitan the rebel leader, sent to make contact with the easterners, the same easterners who had, strangely, incredibly, sent Elias back to Eyre on some kind of information-gathering mission. And it was that intention, that action by Elias, however ill-advised or noble it might have been, that had led to the boy's arrest, and sadly, probably his demise.

Barrak shook his head slightly and gazed away past Striker along the length of the bar. He was thinking about the convoluted and harrowing path that had taken him from that peaceful, mundane morning when Elias's mother had burst into his kitchen, right up to this point in time, sitting opposite Striker. Striker was looking at him expectantly but without impatience, perhaps sensing Barrak was arranging his thoughts, preparing to unburden himself.

It was likely that Striker and his Protectorate and the Guild were the easterners with whom Elias had made contact, so in a sense he was duty bound to confide in Striker, to honour Elias's memory, to do right by Gitan, assuming he still persisted in his fight against the tyrant Meldrick, and to give himself and Jasmyn the best chance of a life beyond Eyre.

He took a sip from his drink and placed it on its napkin and eased himself back into his lounge with a heavy sigh.

'There was this kid by the name of Elias,' he began.

He saw Striker's face relax as he too eased himself back into his seat and took a small sip of liquor. Barrak told him the whole story, starting with the disappearance of Elias and ending with Gitan the rebel leader and his revelation that Elias had been all the way east and had come back to Eyre to gather information.

Striker listened carefully without interruption and only at the end of Barrak's synopsis did he ask a few specific questions, mainly about Elias.

'So you weren't able to find out anything about what had happened to this Elias before you left?'

'Total stone wall,' Barrak told him. 'I fronted Meldrick directly with it and that irritated him no end. I *knew* they had him, Meldrick's response virtually confirmed it. By his own orders, I would reckon. And he knew I knew too, but he denied everything, of course.'

'And how long ago, exactly, was it that his mother came to your house to tell you Elias had been taken?'

'Exactly? Well, let's see, that must've been around mid-September, seven hundred and seven, and what is it now? January ... January, two thousand eight hundred and ... something-or-other.' Barrak looked at his fingers and feigned some confusion then continued, wide eyed, 'Must be the best part of two thousand years then.' He took a quick swig from his drink as if to swallow his own words, suddenly feeling a little awkward about his outburst of sarcasm.

Striker snorted and shook his head slightly. 'Well it *is* January – the tenth, I believe.'

Barrak looked at him sheepishly and shrugged. 'Yeah, well, very close to four months then.'

'And this Gitan, the rebel leader, what was his attitude to Elias? I mean, he fronts up out of the blue, asking Gitan to help him do a little spying – that's what you're telling me isn't it? Elias was a spy, essentially. He'd travelled east, got himself mixed up with these easterners, that's us I suppose, and returned to Eyre to spy on his fellow countrymen on behalf of a foreign power.' Striker left this hanging, not quite question not quite statement.

Barrak shifted uncomfortably and hunched himself over his drink. 'Well, it wasn't exactly like that.'

'Please, tell me what it *was* like, exactly, Councillor.' He eyed Barrak intently. 'Because I'll tell you what we do with spies, we shoot them, no questions asked. So the thing is, I'm trying to get my head around this Gitan just accepting your friend Elias with open arms and then giving him some men to go help him do his spying, because, correct me if I'm wrong, that's what you said happened, isn't it?'

'Look, I don't really know. We only spent one night with Gitan and his people. It was confusing. All hell had broken loose in Eyre after Meldrick took over. Gitan's people were preparing to defend their camp. We were being hunted.' He looked belligerently at Striker, resenting his line of questioning. 'It seemed to me that Elias had given Gitan the impression that you people knew something about what was going on, about what Meldrick was up to, that you had an interest.' Barrak paused uncertainly. 'I'll tell you one thing I do remember Gitan saying.' Barrak looked away past Striker into the smoky darkness as if this particular memory could be found somewhere in the middle distance along the bar.

'And what was that Councillor?'

'*My enemy's enemy is my friend*, that's what he said.' Barrak's eyes locked onto Striker like a challenge, and he felt fire rising in his belly.

Striker said nothing for a few moments, but he had that same expression Barrak had seen about him before, a fierce intensity in his eyes combined incongruously with a hint of ironic humour, as though he was undecided whether to shoot you or tell you a joke.

'And so, Barrak, have you and Jasmyn finally decided which side of the fence you've come down on?'

Barrak frowned and tilted his head questioningly.

'I mean, the two of you. *Aristocrats*,' he gave the word a scornful inflexion. 'Well, you *are* both high-born members of the ruling class back in the good old Eyre of six months ago, no? I mean, I'm just wondering if you're really ready to give it all up and join forces with a bunch of grimy dirt-farming rebels.'

Barrak's frown deepened as Striker went on. 'I know, I know, Meldrick may have suspended your parliament, fitted you both up with crimes against his new order and declared you outlaws, and it would seem, and I am dreadfully sorry if it *is* true, had Jasmyn's father executed, but I'm just wondering whether part of you, Councillor, just a little part of you, is hoping the whole sorry business might just blow over, so you and Jasmyn can go back to Eyre and claim your legitimate birthright.'

Barrak glared at Striker with undisguised annoyance.

'Or do you agree with Gitan?'

'What?'

'That my enemy's enemy is my friend?' Striker reiterated.

'Of course I damn well agree!' Barrak's voice rose more than he intended and he sensed a hush come over the room. A cold fire was rising in him.

'Meldrick's a maniac. Mad for power. Willing to destroy anyone who gets in his way –willing to destroy Eyre.' The words burst out of him and he had both hands clasped around the tumbler or liquor, clamping it to his breast.

'Orlan's mercy, man, he sent his men to hunt us down. They cornered us!' Barrak's hands began to shake and some of the liquor spilled, but he ignored it. He felt his eyes glazing with moisture and there was a tremor in his voice as he went on. 'Gods abide, we killed a man and another was badly wounded. They would have killed us both.' Barrak brought his eyes back to Striker. 'So yes, I agree with Gitan. Of course I do. I only met him once but it was clear that he is a man of honour and Elias had a questing spirit and was brave and he paid dearly for it, so yes, by Orlan's bloody oath, I do agree, Commander!'

411

In the end there was more than a hint of defiance in his tone. Striker nodded and smiled and drained his drink, depositing the empty on the table, then he slapped his thigh and said, 'Good!'

He got up and came over to Barrak's side of the table and stuck out his hand. It took Barrak a moment to realise that, as far as Striker was concerned, their meeting was over and he was meaning to shake Barrak's hand in some kind of gesture of completion or complicity. He gave Striker his hand and Striker gave it one short sharp pump.

'Well done, Councillor, you've passed muster ... for now. Excuse the interrogation, I'm not much good at it anyway. There'll be plenty more of that when we get you back – they'll probably put you through the wringer properly.' Striker was talking fast, leaving no gaps for Barrak to enter the conversation. 'We need to get you back there as soon as possible; they're gonna want to talk to you both, in detail about all of this, especially what you know about this Elias.'

'So you *know* Elias?'

'Look Barrak, I don't know that name, specifically. And what I do know, I'm not even supposed to know and I can't talk about. Like I said, our intelligence people will debrief you and Jasmyn in quite some detail. Maybe then they'll be able to tell you more.

'For now, we need to get going. On the strength of what you've told me, I'm bringing our departure forward to first light tomorrow. I'm not gonna be popular, and neither are you. So your best bet right now is to make the most of a real bed and get some sleep.'

Suddenly Striker was on the move, with Barrak trailing him. He moved through the bar making an announcement as he went. 'Darko, everyone, change of plan. We move out at first light tomorrow. Spread the word and try to get some rest.'

With that, Striker was out the door and into the lobby, leaving groans and grumbles of discontent in his wake and a bewildered Barrak, wondering what had just happened.

CHAPTER 29

JASMYN SAT ON A mossy ledge, just off the track where it widened to form a small rocky plateau. Before her, the tangle of rainforest foliage had opened up like a massive window to finally reveal the landscape below. A pale blue sky was threaded with high cirrus and below lay a patchwork of green and brown, invaded by ridged fingers of grey-green forest. In the distance were great swathes of virgin woodland where the air hung blue over the jagged hills. Between sky and earth was an impossibly broad expanse of bright blue ocean, extending to the misty cloud banks of an implausibly distant horizon, and away to the north and south the white-flecked line of the coast snaked and twisted as far as the eye could see.

This was it. The endless ocean.

It was just as Elias had told Gitan. And now, as she stood atop the great mountain range that had featured in Elias's stories of the east, the grandeur and the scale of the mountains and the vista laid out below took her breath away. But she wondered, if she and Barrak had known at the outset what it would take to get here, would they have ever even attempted it.

The afternoon heat mingled with the cool forest air and carried the smell of the sea, faint and yet unmistakable and somehow different from the smell of the Eyrean Sea. Far below and miniscule in the distance was a break in the line of the coast where the surrounding land had a different colour and texture to it. A faint pall of tainted mist hanging over the spot told her this was the easterners' Harbour City

413

and her gut tightened a little at the thought of it. She realised the vastness of the ocean scared her a little too.

The company had spread itself about the clearing. Some were sitting on packs or rocks, some prone on the ground, glad of a chance to rest after the long morning's march, which had taken them up hill and down dale, with each successive ridge line higher than the last and the air gradually becoming cooler and the vegetation changing to what Hesta called rainforest, made dense and exotic by frequent rains carried on moist air swept up from the ocean.

At one point they had ascended into a cold fog of low cloud hanging over the summit of a high pass, and she'd felt disoriented and a little daunted as the forest was enveloped by the ghostly mist. In the valleys between the ridges they found a calm, dimly lit tranquillity where the air was cool and still and the only sounds, apart from their own trudging footfalls, were haunting, unfamiliar birdcalls and the constant trickling of water.

The track they'd followed was mainly well defined, and sometimes there were bridges across the creeks and streams running through the deepest valleys. These reminded Jasmyn of the fallen tree bridge back in the Dzahn village. But these crossings were even more organic, composed of fallen trunks and boulders with sod and moss and branches and vines for hand holds; it was hard to believe at times that they were constructed at all, seeming instead to have sprung from the forest itself.

The filtered light in the dells gave it all an other-worldly atmosphere. Giant tree ferns lined the track like guardians, their great arching umbrellas glowing green in the subdued light. Above the ferns were tangles of deep foliage and vines, so thick in places they seemed to press down on the plodding file of humans. Elsewhere, great shafts of air and light opened up beside the towering straight trunks of mountain ash giants, the kings of the rainforest, reaching tall and straight towards the flickering sunshine far above.

So now, finally, they were within sight of their destination and that seemed reason enough to stop and rest. On the opposite edge of the clearing was a crouching clutch of figures, Striker and Darko Mars, and Barrak was there too, looking on as Jasper Flint, squatting next to a piece of equipment they called a radio, attempted to contact the city below.

Barrak must have felt her eyes on him for he looked up and smiled at her. Smiling back at him she remembered fondly how Barrak had woken her that same morning, before it was even light, with a kiss. It was as if he had been with her all night, even though she knew he hadn't. He'd smiled and kissed her again and waited for her to get her bearings and remember where she was and what had occurred the night before. She reached up and touched his cheek, as if she'd only just noticed that he'd shaved his wild-man beard, and then she took his face in both her hands and kissed him gently again and smoothed her hands along his jawline before Barrak reluctantly broke the spell and told her they had to leave before dawn.

All through that long morning as they trudged through the forest Jasmyn had felt a lightness of spirit and a rare contentment. The horrors of past months had somehow been eclipsed and part of her felt like a teenager again, thrilling to the excitement of new love. But at the same time, whenever she looked at him or when Barrak took her arm or whispered something in her ear, it gave her another less familiar and altogether more comfortable feeling, almost as if she had come home; it made her feel older, in a good way.

She felt strangely free. Her life was starting all over, and there was excitement too, which fed into and became part of her anticipation of their intimacy. At other times it was more like anxious expectancy, as she wondered about this eastern city and what sort of life awaited them there. But she knew it would be all right, because he was with her; she knew for sure that he loved her, just as she had always secretly loved him.

By some unspoken agreement they behaved as if nothing much had changed between them and Jasmyn walked at times with Hesta and Teah and the young troopers she had befriended, while Barrak spent some time in conversation with Clay and Striker. But they couldn't stay clear of each other for long, and besides, Barrak was anxious to tell her all about his amazing conversation with Clay the previous night, and about Striker interrogating him. Jasmyn had squeaked incredulously when he told her about the easterners' calendar year and pulled on his arm and had him repeat it twice, shaking her head and saying, 'That's insane,' over and over.

Jasmyn had been lost in her daydream for a moment or two, long enough for Barrak to leave the others and come to her. Suddenly he was by her side with a hand brushing her thigh as he sat down beside her. She reached up and ruffled the hair at the back of his neck and then brought her hand around his jaw, lingering to feel the fine sandpaper of his re-emerging stubble. She looked into his eyes with longing and saw in his eyes the effect it had on him. His gaze softened and became intense all at once, reaching into her. He took her hand and Jasmyn came easily to her feet and they went blithely along the track a short way until they came across an opening, a side track.

Barrak led her along the track a little way and she didn't resist, though they'd been warned not to leave the main track. *It was OK, they wouldn't go far and no one in the company was moving anytime soon.*

She felt like a naughty schoolgirl and held tight to Barrak's hand as the jungle flashed by, giant tree ferns, laurels and myrtle thickets in behind. The track widened into a small glade. There was the sound of splashing water somewhere. A waterfall. Barrak whirled her around and it felt like dancing.

They found themselves under the curving fronds of a large tree fern. The rough bark pressing into Jasmyn's back heightened her senses deliciously as Barrak pressed urgently against her. He still held her one hand firmly in his and the other went around her waist, pulling her in to him as they kissed, gently at first, both of them quivering with the exquisite tension of restraint. Jasmyn savoured the sensation of his lips, tenderly exploring hers as if she were a delicacy, and Barrak's scent excited her as it mingled with the earthy richness of the forest. Barrak groaned softly and Jasmyn caught her breath and caressed his neck with her free hand as she raised one leg and clamped her knee against his hip as if to draw him into her.

Suddenly, they lost all restraint and kissed as though they would devour each other, the force of their love finally given full rein, uniting them under one skin, with one breath. In all her days with all her loves Jasmyn had never felt a passion so precipitous, so powerful and so intoxicating.

She let it take her. An explosion of energy erupted in her heart and descended like the flaming trails of fireworks down into her loins. She whimpered as the heat of it engulfed her sacral centre with a pulsating animal urgency and she pressed herself even harder against Barrak. Feeling the urgency of his desire for her made her gasp and then Barrak's lips broke free of hers and he let out a cry as though from a pain he could no longer endure. 'Jasmyn!' he breathed. 'Gods, Jasmyn!' His lips went to her neck and he kissed her gently below her ear and then downward, kissing and nibbling at the exquisitely sensitive skin of her throat. Jasmyn let out a purring groan and caressed his head and neck with one hand while her other hand moved down his back to his buttocks. She squeezed him firmly and pulled him in against her. She was sure he could feel the heat of her desire for him, and all at once it seemed ludicrous and galling that they were fully clothed. Barrak murmured an affirmation as though he had read her thoughts, and began to peel back her shirt, his lips traversing her collarbone towards her breast.

A shadow fell over them.

They both caught their breath in the same instant. A figure was beside them, standing on the track, right next to their tree-fern bower. The figure stood very still and stared straight ahead. He didn't glance at them at all but his tense demeanour told them he knew they were there.

'Don't move,' the figure said calmly, quietly. 'Keep very, very still.'

It was Darko Mars.

They obeyed his instruction and as Darko moved forward slowly and carefully, Barrak and Jasmyn resembled a sculptor's homage to passion frozen amongst the flora. They quickly disentangled themselves and sheepishly peered out from behind the fronds as Mars walked towards a small clear area bordered by mossy boulders just short of an inky brown pool near the base of the falling water. They saw that he was unarmed and his movements were slow and deliberate with his arms before him.

A voice, indistinct and strange. It didn't sound like Mars' voice at all, and it took some time for them to realise it *was* him talking. But to whom? They strained to hear but they could not catch the words. There was more than one voice now, a conversation of some sort in an unfathomable dialect. Darko Mars appeared to be talking to the forest.

Straining to see past him into the forest Barrak perceived a flicker of shadowy movement and a voice seemed to be raised in anger. Shadows coalesced and a tall tawny figure emerged from the forest. With long matted ropes of brown hair and clad in earthy tones he seemed to be part of the forest one moment and human the next. Then, all around Darko Mars the forest appeared to quiver and shift, like a conjurer's grand illusion as other figures emerged from the undergrowth. Branches and trunks became arms and legs. Vines and shadows resolved into implements and weapons such as spears, held long and straight beside the lean, sylph-like figures, all similarly clad in colours of the forest. Darko was facing a semi-circle of forest people.

The tall man flapped a hand at Mars as though shooing away an annoying pest and his voice went up a note in pitch. This new phrase had an urgent tone and he repeated it for emphasis as he waved an imperious hand. Darko Mars' head was slightly bowed and he spoke evenly and calmly in return. The others remained silent. Now the tall stranger stretched out a slender arm and pointed at Barrak and Jasmyn. Jasmyn squeezed Barrak's arm hard and Barrak felt the panic rise as the tall forest-dweller seemed to look right through him. The words rolled out of him like murmuring thunder in a much deeper tone now, as he instructed Darko Mars on the error of his ways and again repeated a key part of his dissertation several times for emphasis.

His tone was imperative and demanding.

Darko nodded and said some appeasing words and began to back away from the forest folk. The tall one gave him one last dismissive jab of rebuke then glanced at his companions and shook his head. As Darko backed away, he continued to murmur a stream of advice, as if he were quietly chiding a recalcitrant child.

But then the glade fell silent again and the people were gone, vanished back into the forest in the blink of an eye. Mars straightened up and turned to face Barrak and Jasmyn. He said not a single word to them as he approached, no doubt content that his incandescent glare would express all he had to say on the matter. And as he came past where they stood under the tree fern, he still didn't speak or even make a gesture, just stared at them, one then the other, with an inflammatory look of offence. He kept right on walking as Barrak and Jasmyn quickly fell in behind him and scrambled to catch up as he strode back up the track towards the clearing.

As they came back onto the wide switchback on the main track it was clear that the company was almost ready to move.

Striker and Mars had a brief conversation with their eyes and Striker looked past his lieutenant at the two of them as they followed sheepishly behind, dropping back a bit now that they were on safe ground. It was a long time since anyone had made Barrak feel like a schoolboy hauled up before the headmaster, but Striker managed it with an expression that hovered somewhere between disappointment and astonishment. He approached Barrak and gave Jasmyn an awkward, puzzled look, but no words came. Then, quite calmly, he told them to get ready to move.

'We've made contact with Protectorate headquarters and they're sending some transport to meet us down in the valley. We'll be in the city by nightfall.'

Striker once again opened his mouth as though to add something, but again came up blank. He raised a hand as if to chop the air then blew out a sigh and put his hand to his forehead instead and massaged his temple.

'You know,' he pointed a finger at the sky and paused as if composing himself. He blew out another breath through gritted teeth. 'You know, *if* I say to stay on the main track, it's not a suggestion. It's ...' He shook his head and put both of his hands up as if conceding a debate.

But then he became intense all over again and came up closer to Barrak and squared his chin at him. 'The Fareem *own* this forest. They *allow* us to pass through it, but they have their rules.' He looked from Barrak to Jasmyn and back again, seemingly disgusted by their expressionless faces.

Striker held his thumb and forefinger up depicting something small. 'One little dart thingy,' he looked at Darko for help with the language and Mars obliged with an unfamiliar word. Striker jabbed his index finger into his own neck and made a noise like air escaping from a jar. Jasmyn flinched, disturbed by Striker's intensity. He looked at her sternly. 'The toxin affects the nerves.' Then he switched his attention to Barrak. 'Two minutes.' He showed Barrak two fingers. 'Total paralysis.'

It seemed Striker would leave it at that and he started to turn away. 'Ant food,' he shrilled cryptically, turning back to face them again. 'Paralysed. Still alive mind you, still breathing, while the forest consumes you. Not a pleasant end.' With that, the matter was closed and Striker turned to Darko Mars and said loudly, 'Let's get moving, before we start to lose the light.'

The truck was rigged for moving troops: bench seats running along each side, rock hard suspension and a metal scaffold that could be covered over in bad weather. The thing chugged and pinged and belched more smoke than Bishop's desert vehicle and its top speed didn't seem to be much better than walking pace.

The small hamlet where the trucks had found them was comprised of no more than a tavern and an all-purpose store on the flats where the track, descending from the hills, widened to form a road of sorts. Further along, where a rickety old timber bridge crossed a river, they passed a mill built from rough-hewn stone with a glorious old timber waterwheel slowly turning under the gushing stream that fell from a granite ledge.

Nearby was a small farmhouse contrived of stone and thatch with a thin trail of white smoke ascending from its chimney and a clutch of seven cows gathered by a ramshackle shed nearby, ready for milking.

As they continued east, all signs of the rainforest receded and the flat lands became a collage of cultivated paddocks and grazing land. Farmhouses were a more frequent feature along the road now, some quite elaborate with two storeys and multiple outbuildings, and others so meagre they looked barely habitable.

Once their two-truck convoy was stopped by a farmer moving a flock of sheep. Truman Clay stood up and pointed out an excavation to Barrak and Jasmyn, explaining that it was one of their current dig sites. Out in the middle of a sheep paddock was a seemingly huge cube of scaffolding standing in the middle of a wide area of levelled ground. It seemed like the whole gently sloping side of a small hill had been removed to reveal the lower levels of a large structure that stood some five or six storeys high. Even from a distance and largely obscured by scaffolding it was obvious the massive thing was crumbling and decayed, and its very presence in the middle of rural pastureland seemed eerily out of place.

An hour further on, farmland abruptly gave way to ragged cottages lining the road as they entered a small village. They got stuck in traffic, with a slow moving oxcart ahead of them and a motorised farm truck with goats in the back trying to pass them on the narrow road going in the other direction. Children and dogs came out and ran along beside the truck, the dogs barking, the children singing out and villagers looking up from their mundane tasks to watch them go by. They passed shops with open fronts and merchandise hanging from hooks or displayed on the roadside, and dingy-looking eating houses with tables and chairs set out in front and the village dogs vying for scraps around the patrons' feet.

The village centre was at the crossroad of the western highway and the main north–south road, explained Professor Clay. Straight ahead lay the heart of Harbour City. To the south was the main coast road and the southern coastal villages and to the north was the inlet crossing which gave the only access to the north shore of the harbour and the coastal villages beyond that.

Dusk was falling as they left the village behind and went straight on. The landscape changed again and had the feel of a semi-rural wasteland. There were patches of bushland here and there and other more open areas, seemingly disused and with strange irregular hillocks overgrown with thick vegetation. Occasional farms were interspersed with industrial endeavours, minor factories of unknown purpose, tin sheds with yards strewn with what looked like truck parts and other less identifiable mechanical innards.

They went past what looked like a quarry of sorts and everywhere lining the roadway were workshops. Some were deserted for the day and others seemed still busy even in the dimming light, with yellow orbs of lamplight blinking in their dark recesses.

Further along and away to the side of the road an elevated structure caught the last rays of the sinking sun. It seemed quite a long way off the road, which would make it a substantial size. It was like a bridge to nowhere, standing in the landscape. Its sloping ramp-like structure ran at a low angle with the end closest to the ground suspended just above another of the now-familiar overgrown hillocks. The other end finished abruptly at some height, its precipitous edge overhung with dangling vines. All along its sloping top were bushes and even a couple of substantial trees. The elevated slab was supported by pylons evenly graduated in height but so overgrown with vines and foliage that they looked more like the massive bases of the tree trunks they'd seen in the rainforest. It was clearly something man-made and yet it had been all but claimed by the land, giving it the appearance of something sprung from the earth.

When Barrak and Jasmyn turned with the same questioning look to Clay, he smiled his now familiar, sympathetic smile and said simply, 'Ruins.'

As the twilight deepened they entered the outskirts of the city itself and before long they were surrounded by a chaotic sea of humanity, hemmed in by traffic on the narrow road. Vehicles of all kinds vied for position and tooted their horns incessantly as though it would make a difference to the flow. There were trucks like theirs, bicycles, motorised scooters and more of the ox-drawn carts. Jasmyn nudged Barrak and pointed to a scooter that had a family of five somehow clinging to it and they saw a two-wheeled cart with a passenger reclining in it like a lord being pulled along by a bony man.

There seemed no rhyme or reason to the streets as they inched along what was presumably still the main road, which twisted and turned through the riotous sprawl. They were hemmed in by brightly lit, open shopfronts with ramshackle apartments piled on top, garlanded with strings of laundry. Throngs of people coursed along the hopscotch slabs of pavement, dressed in a garish, grimy potpourri of colours. The noise was unceasing.

Now they passed roadside bars with red lanterns hanging from canopies, repair shops with surly youths smoking and gawking, grocery stores, brothels, cafes and haberdashers all bundled together. It was almost too much for the senses as they rumbled past in the lumbering truck, pressing through the traffic according to the one apparent road rule, the biggest and loudest-tooting vehicle gets right of way.

After months in the wilderness the rank smell of massed humanity was overpowering.

Cooking smells drifted from the ubiquitous food vendors, whose mobile grills periodically erupted with great balls of orange flame and smoke, lighting up the street like an incendiary sideshow; the funky reek of human waste in the open gutters and the queer heady smell of fuel exhaust combined with the food smells almost made Barrak retch at times.

Then all at once the truck would round a bend and plunge into darkness, broken only by the yellow beam of the truck's headlights, which would sometimes show a lonely hooded figure trudging along the verge or dogs dashing across the road. These areas were like small pockets of wasteland within the city, inexplicably deserted. They had passed through several of them already where the only signs of life were dark dilapidated humpies and lean-tos cobbled together from found materials and scattered along the roadside wherever there was a flat piece of ground. The eerie contrast to the bustling streets made

Barrak's skin prickle and Jasmyn slid up close to him as they passed through yet another of these spooky precincts. Squinting in the dim light Barrak made out great amorphous mounds, not unlike the odd-looking hillocks they'd seen outside the city, rising up on either side of the road.

As the headlights swept an arc across the waste ground he caught a glimpse of long straight spires, like metal struts, rising up from the top of a hillock and reaching out into the blackness, beyond the orb of the truck's feeble beam.

Leaving behind the last of these waste zones, they entered what appeared to be the central part of the city. It was sited on hilly ground and the truck strained at times to climb the steep streets, which were lined with what appeared to be much more liveable apartments. As they progressed further they began to see individual houses, small and large, some surrounded by high walls with shards of glass fixed along their tops and large gates for vehicles to enter from the street.

There were fewer people in the streets and the shops and eateries had glass fronts and good electric lighting. They went past a rudimentary hospital and what looked like a large temple, and there were taverns offering accommodation and large dour multistorey buildings that Barrak assumed were offices or civic buildings. And yet even in between these more salubrious areas, there were still a few small dark regions of abandonment, where the uneven ground yielded no buildings at all.

Finally, their truck, and the one behind carrying Striker and his men, ground to a halt at the crest of a long incline, beside a wide residential terrace that ended with a sweeping bend devoid of houses on its outer curve, where the land fell away beyond a bright yellow guard rail.

They were at quite an elevation, a lookout of sorts. Barrak smelled the salt and could feel moist, cool air rising from the dark waters below. Laid out beneath them was a brightly lit boulevard running in an elegant, wide curve along the edge of the darkness, which defined the waters of the harbour. Directly below, occupying a small round peninsula, was a compound of grand old buildings with harbour

424

frontages and a large circular driveway behind them. Something about the architectural style of the complex was vaguely familiar and yet at the same time intriguingly exotic. Barrak was put in mind of some of the most elaborate of the grand old mansions overlooking Lillian Bay back in Tamouer, but these were grander still in some ways and with a hint of sophisticated artistry, obviously quite old, finely crafted and clearly built to last.

Away to the left were docks, with a series of long piers extending out into the dark of the harbour, with shadowy ships only barely visible by the dim lights of the marina.

Striker was out of his truck and walked along to where Barrak and Jasmyn were still in theirs, leaning on the side rail to take in the view. 'That's Protectorate headquarters,' he said blandly, pointing at the circle of old buildings directly below. 'Also known as *the palace*, because that's what it was once.'

Striker stood silent for a few moments and stared at the scene below; Barrak and Jasmyn, looking over his head, did the same. The buildings all around the compound were brightly illuminated, with a light in almost every window. And there was considerable activity in the compound and on the surrounding roads, with vehicles and people coming and going.

'Something's not right, Doc,' he said thoughtfully to the professor who was standing in the back of the truck, observing the scene. 'Way too much activity for this late in the day.'

Truman Clay leaned over Barrak and Jasmyn and looked up and down the harbour-side quay then back at the Protectorate compound below.

'Doesn't feel right, does it? What did they say on the radio?'

'Not much on an open channel, but they sounded a bit antsy,' Striker replied gruffly. 'C'mon, let's get down there.'

As Striker returned to his truck, engines gunned and gears grated.

Barrak felt a damp breeze swirl over the escarpment as he stared out past the busy bright quay-side compound. The oily blackness of the alien harbour stretched away to a distant shore, barely visible in the starlight and the faint glow to the east, of the moon not yet risen. The breeze made him shiver and he put his arm around Jasmyn and she snuggled into him.

Spread out in random clusters across the murky blackness was a multitude of red lights, like navigation lights but too numerous for that purpose, and he wondered what they could be. He thought he could see strange shapes protruding out of the inky waters as well. Jasmyn slid up even closer to him on the bench seat and they both stared across the dark harbour with its strange red lights, before the truck jolted and swung out onto the downward incline of the wide terrace.

CHAPTER 30

Axel Striker strode across the wide circular driveway with such a sense of purpose he seemed to drag the rest of them in his wake. Barrak found himself and Jasmyn hurrying along flanked by Jasper Flint and Hugo Lynx, almost as if they were guarding them. Striker stopped abruptly in the centre of the courtyard next to a large bronze statue, this mainly to avoid a careening vehicle, to which he offered a petulant gesture as it zoomed past.

He glanced back at the rest of them. 'That's Chen,' he said when he saw Barrak looking up at the bronze figure mounted on a rearing horse and slashing at the heavens with a dull sword. 'Lord Chen the Beneficent, as he liked to call himself.'

Barrak paused to examine the dynamic warrior, frozen in the midst of battle, mottled with green oxides and eerily lit from below. But Striker was on the move again, striding for the main entrance and yelling over his shoulder at Barrak. 'More like Lord Chen the soul-crushing tyrant! The dynasty he founded ruled the harbour region for 260 years. Produced the best and worst of Sabu rulership over the years. His grandson built this place, the vicious bastard; it was his palace.' Striker flung his arms up as they approached twin archways which served as an entrance and skipped up the steps, striding into the foyer of the grand old sandstone building. A vehicle skidded to a halt almost at Barrak's heel as he took the steps two at a time. In the foyer, people were rushing in all directions and he and Jasmyn had to duck and weave to avoid collisions as they tried to keep up with Striker.

'Striker! Striker! Christ!' A uniformed man had bailed up the commander and they were already in animated conversation when the rest of them caught up.

'Where the hell have you been? She's been asking for you. Jesus!'

'Yeah, never mind. Western plains. We got delayed. What's all the commotion? What's going on?'

'We don't know. Hell about to break loose or something. No one really knows.'

'What's *happened*?' Striker's intensity was such that Barrak almost expected him to grab the officer by his lapels and shake him.

'So far just radio traffic, like before, only more of it, *much* more, and different. They think something's *about* to happen ... maybe soon.'

'Christ!' Striker looked from the officer to his men and back, alarm in his eyes. 'Where is she?'

'You better go to her. She's been asking for you.' The officer was probably not much younger than Striker. There was a hint of alarm in his eyes and he backed away from Striker slightly.

'Where?' Striker demanded a second time, the intensity in his voice matched only by his piercing glare.

'Up in control, in the chamber. They've been at it all day, her and the chiefs.' The young officer went on, but Striker had already turned his back and surged away towards the ornate marble stairs at the rear of the foyer, which started straight and wide before splitting and curving left and right to the mezzanine above. He zigzagged through a throng of uniforms coming down the stairs and yelled over his shoulder, 'Come on!'

Fable Striker bit her lip. Her heart felt like a stone in her chest. A frayed and anxious facsimile of herself stared bleakly back at her from the other side of the big window, a disembodied spectre hovering in the night, like a care-worn fairy godmother above the glimmering red lights of the harbour ruins.

Around her the whole bright room was reflected against the blackness outside. Four of the five chiefs were there, hanging around the conference table, tense and expectant. Marx and his signals people were crowded around the radio receivers, each with a weather eye for the chattering telex nearby. Maps were plastered all over two blackboards and more maps spread out over the smooth beech conference table, together with empty cups and plates, hats and coats.

The control room, or chamber as it was known, having once been the Sabu lord's official audience chamber, had been a hive of frantic activity most of the day with dozens of the Protectorate's senior people hurrying in and out. Now it was down to her and her most senior officers: Moses Marx, head of communications; Carson Wade, in charge of regional security; Zeus St John, head of intelligence; and Lance Sax, the chief of army.

As director of the Protectorate, Fable Striker knew that this might be the greatest challenge she would ever face. She had forged a career in the Protectorate by balancing diplomacy and consensus leadership with staunchly decisive command decisions, and she had a razor-sharp instinct for knowing just what measure of each was required in any given situation. It had got her to the very top of the organisation, but this night, she felt uncertainty and doubt seeping into her marrow and it galled her that she had allowed such alien emotions to impinge on her professional domain.

A further pang of guilty regret stabbed at her heart as she thought of Axel and wished for the umpteenth time that he was here with her. Not that he could add much to their understanding of the current situation. His expertise lay elsewhere. Much to his mother's chagrin, he was more at home in the farthest flung reaches of the wilderness, hunting Narbool and protecting indefensible dig sites. But he had his father's knack of feeling out any situation; he was intuitive like that and she trusted his nous. And there was something about his presence in a room, just like his father's, that produced a sense of quiet optimism and confidence, as if a solution could be found to any problem.

He should've been back days ago.

'So, for all we know, it could be a full-scale bloody *invasion*.' As she turned around to face the room her tone was professional and efficient, if a little clipped. 'And as far as we *know* it could be imminent, any damn tick of the clock.' Her words hung tense in the air. The chiefs gave her their full attention.

'We have no idea who they are, or what the bloody hell they want. The radio communications have been ramping up for the last week or so, reaching fever pitch in the last two days. Those that are not coded are in a language we're still struggling to understand.' She threw a sideways glance at Marx, her signals chief, and he nodded almost imperceptibly.

'Although we're now quite sure they *are* from the same source as the messages we've been monitoring off and on for months now, between the interior and somewhere off our coast, correct?'

Marx nodded but remained silent, as did the others. They knew this was how she liked to think: out loud, recapping, defining the parameters.

'And we still don't know how they're doing that, communicating over such long distances without repeaters, bouncing the damn signals off the sky I think you said, didn't you Moses?'

Moses Marx opened his palms to show he had nothing.

'But we're reasonably sure about *who* they've been communicating with – it's the internal security forces of the Eyrean community, in the interior, yes?'

Marx and St John nodded their concurrence. 'It's the only plausible explanation,' St John offered. 'They're the only people out there who have any kind of technology beyond bows and bloody arrows. It has to be the Eyreans.'

'Different now, of course,' Marx chipped in. 'Especially these last ten days. All military command chatter amongst themselves and a lot more code.'

'No question it's ominous,' offered St John.

Suddenly she switched her attention to Carson Wade, her regional security chief. 'And plans *are* in place to evacuate the city, but it's under wraps, to avoid panic? Contingency only, last resort.' Wade's steady eye told her he had the situation in hand, but there was a hint of apprehension in his expression too.

'And these latest sightings, up and down the coast, these foreign vessels – huge damn things. We don't know how many, but multiple sightings now, mainly by deep-water fishing vessels; this is the most worrying development of all.' She addressed this last comment to no one in particular and looked past her chiefs towards the double glass doors that led to the mezzanine.

And there, all of a sudden, standing in the open doorway was her son, Axel, looking dusty and unkempt and smiling a casual, nonchalant smile as though he had just been on an errand across town rather than six weeks in the western plains. She hardly noticed the man and woman flanking him as her heart swelled with pride and relief and tears welled unexpectedly in her eyes. She took a deep breath to quell the emotion and straightened herself, making her mouth taut, but she couldn't keep the smile from her eyes.

'Glad you could join us, Commander Striker. We were beginning to worry.'

Zeus St John stood with his hands behind his back and stared past his reflection into the darkness, considering the totality of Barrak's account of himself.

Barrak had his elbows on his knees and his head in his hands, staring at the cold half cup of coffee on the glass-topped table in front of him. It was a pretty nice place for an interrogation, at least that was what he had thought at the outset, and he suspected it might even be St John's own office. But now it was beginning to feel like a cell.

For several hours St John and one of his officers had double-teamed him, going over and over the same ground, asking the same questions in half a dozen different ways then asking him seemingly unrelated questions, which turned out to be just the same questions again, but in disguise. They were trying to find holes in his story, trying to ascertain whether Barrak had some dark hidden agenda in the service of the Protectorate's enemies.

It was just him and St John now, the intelligence chief's lesser functionary having left at some point and never come back, possibly due to exhaustion or exasperation, or perhaps his shift was over. Barrak had long since become heartily sick of it, showing his disenchantment in ways none too subtle.

Now he just wanted to sleep.

'Let's go over this one last time, nice and simple.' St John turned to face Barrak. He had his kindly mentor's face on, but he looked tired and perhaps even a little disappointed. 'You yourself hadn't seen Elias, hadn't sighted him, hugged him, kissed him, hammered nails in with him, not since he worked for you two and a half years ago, right?

'Good. OK. Not hide nor hair of him, not until September last year, when his mother comes busting down your door, telling you he's been rounded up by our friend Meldrick. OK. So.' St John paused and scrutinised Barrak. Barrak returned his stare silently, still with his chin in his hands.

'And even then you still don't actually see Elias or talk to him, just his mother. And she tells you nothing of what, if anything, Elias has told her about his weird and wonderful travels, all the way to the east coast, all the way to … us.' He put a curious inflexion on the word *us* and gave Barrak a strange searching look.

'Nothing about what he'd been up to since he came back home, nothing about some information gathering he may or may not have been doing, nothing about places he'd been to, people he'd met with, since finding his way back into Eyre?'

Barrak sat back in the couch and looked frankly at the security chief, blowing out a big exasperated blast of air and opening his palms. He knew St John didn't expect an answer. They'd been over it all a dozen times.

'She just asks for your help to find him. Wants you to use your contacts to try and find out what's happened to him, which you do. You go to the city and ask around, but get nowhere before the shit starts hitting the fan.'

St John looked sympathetically at the dishevelled Eyrean slouched on his office couch. Much of the session conducted by himself and his debrief specialist had concentrated on recent events in Eyre, the civil unrest, political manoeuvrings, the rebel movement, and finally, the military takeover by Meldrick just before their flight.

In just a few short hours Barrak had provided him with intelligence gold, a first-hand account of just what had been happening inside the closed society of Eyre, and from a source connected at the very highest levels to the political elite. Normally he would have been delighted. Then again, normally they would've put both of them up in a nice hotel and spent a week or more carefully dissecting their stories individually and together and detailing every last element, with analysts, Eyrean specialists, historical boffins, the lot. Special project status, supplementary funding, all the trimmings.

Normally he wouldn't be grilling a source at three in the morning on his office couch.

But things were far from normal and given the current state of alert and the possibility of some kind of ill-defined catastrophe being more or less imminent, his appetite for normal intelligence was a little dulled. What he wanted to know above all, was the nature and the purpose of the radio communications they'd been intercepting between Eyre and somewhere off their own coast for almost a year now. *Who was talking to whom and about what?* His section had made frustratingly little progress since the first communications were heard almost ten months previously and they were annoyingly sporadic, sometimes months apart. And it had taken some time to deduce where the inland transmissions were even coming from. At first Eyre seemed unlikely, because the supposedly insular and eccentric Eyrean culture spurned the use of all forms of electronic communication.

At least his Eyrean guest had put that one to bed, confirming that Eyre's internal security force had turned its back on the old prohibitions on both electronic communication and fire-burst weapons. *Jesus! Had they developed these things themselves, in Eyre?* It seemed unlikely, which left the unsettling alternative that they may have been *given* the technology.

Finding out just what was going on between the Eyreans and the emerging threat off their own coast had become St John's highest

433

priority. Strange. Twelve months previously he wouldn't have given a tinker's curse for information about Eyre. The remote enclave had always seemed a bizarre and arcane backwater cut off from the real world and only of any concern to the special interest unit within the bureau.

How things change.

Now it was *his* obsession. It was why he had sent Elias back in there, to find out more information.

Elias had been his project. He'd found him, or at least identified him as a potential asset, when he'd turned up unexpectedly in their midst, arrested in a bar brawl and handed over to *his* people when the city police realised he was Eyrean. And he'd overseen his interrogation and later, his training too. Elias was special, he'd known it from his first sit-in. He was an altruist, an adventurer, a pathological romantic, in other words he was just like St John, and they had recognised each other as kin instantly.

Striker, when he came across the Eyreans in the wilderness, would've known nothing about Elias, and even Striker senior knew only of the operation itself, but not his operative's name. It had been strictly need to know within the intelligence bureau and the only one outside the bureau who knew was Marx. So when young Striker had suddenly appeared in the chamber with the Eyreans in tow and explained what the Eyrean had told him, even mentioned Elias by name, he and Marx had both pounced on Barrak and Jasmyn like starving men eyeing their first hot meal in a month.

That initial surge of excitement made St John's growing disappointment harder to bear as he finally had to admit to himself that the Eyrean had no real intelligence about Elias. Barrak had crossed paths with him before Elias ever travelled to the East and later they had inadvertently picked up some second-hand information about him before their own flight east, but it was not particularly illuminating. St John felt an uncommon sense of deflation and a deeper sense of gloom, which the old agent-runner in him recognised all too well. It was a dreadful thing to lose a source. It produced a multifaceted kind of despair, mingled with other things like guilt, regret, anger and denial.

As he looked at Barrak sitting on his couch, he could see the Eyrean's face change. Perhaps he recognised the slew of emotion in his interrogator's eyes. St John cleared his throat.

'So then, all you know apart from that, is what the rebel leader told you.'

Barrak nodded, his fingers pressed together against his lips.

'Gitan took him in, gave him succour, helped him on his way when he first returned to Eyre. They had a meeting of minds, they identified a common purpose and Gitan *knew* what Elias was there to do.' St John was again staring out of his office window, as though he could see the scene in distant Eyre playing out on the dark harbour.

'So he sent some of his men with Elias, to help him.' He gave this a questioning inflexion as though it still puzzled him in some way. 'And they were never seen again, not Gitan's men anyway. But we know Elias made it back to his mother's home before he was arrested in mid-September.'

Barrak nodded absently but didn't respond. The two men shared a poignant silence in the eerie quiet of the pre-dawn palace. St John's mind's eye, projecting out over the dark waters, showed him images of Elias languishing in a forgotten cell, or worse, his broken body discarded in an unmarked grave.

Finally Barrak broke the silence. 'Can I see Jasmyn now?'

St John turned with a heavy sigh and smiled wearily at Barrak. 'Of course. Wait here, I'll find out where she is.'

Fable Striker watched her son as he spoke to her and in the dim lamplight the lines of worry and weather on his face melted away and she saw again the young boy with insatiable curiosity, energy to burn and a naïve sense of social justice. She had an uncommon urge to reach out and draw him to her bosom. She could almost feel his compact body snuggling into her and his small arms around her neck, the way he used to hug her in the years following his father's death. It cost her something to push aside that urge and she nodded and said *aha* as she put down her empty mug and leaned on the kitchen bench, drinking in the sight of him and wishing to god he would not leave again to go into the badlands.

Axel finished his brief summary of his mission to the new dig site, got up and turned away from his mother, casting a critical eye around the apartment. He never got used to it. A small part of the original Sabu lord's private quarters within the old palace had been preserved and modernised for the use of the incumbent director. Axel thought it seemed more like a salesman's display unit than a home, with its polished timber and modern furnishings, plate glass, chrome, and harbour views. He looked disdainfully through the big sliding balcony doors and tried to make out the harbour spires in the darkness.

'Anyway, none of that's really important now,' he said quietly. 'What's your assessment of this current situation? What d'you think is really going on?'

'I'll tell you one thing I can't tell the chiefs, Axel, I'm scared, really bloody scared.'

Axel turned from the balcony glass and looked at his mother, a little alarmed by the quaver in her voice and the uncertainty in her normally calm eyes. She came around from behind the bench and approached him, touching him lightly on the arm. Axel gave her what he hoped was a reassuring smile, despite his own disquiet.

'We should've seen this coming, but we didn't. It seemed like an oddity in the beginning, when we first picked up radio signals between Eyre and somewhere out in the middle of the bloody ocean.' She turned towards the glass and gestured vaguely towards the blackness beyond.

'Why would someone *out there* want to be talking to the Eyreans?' she asked rhetorically. 'We had to find that out. St John came up with the Eyrean émigré, this young chap. He had him trained and sent him back to Eyre as an operative, a spy, I suppose you could say. That was months ago.' Mother and son stood side by side and peered into the darkness beyond the balcony.

'How strange you should arrive when you did and with a couple of

Eyreans in tow, and even stranger that they seem to know this young fellow.'

'Maybe Zeus will get something useful from them,' Axel suggested, looking at his mother's stern profile.

'I hope so. But I fear it may be too little too late.' She returned Axel's gaze and smiled gently. 'I'm afraid we were too slow to appreciate the threat.'

There was a moment of silence between them before she went on. 'Do you see the irony, now that our fate seems to be linked somehow to the Eyreans? *I've* always dismissed the Eyreans as irrelevant, isolationist, inward-looking. Denialists. But maybe we have more in common with *them* than we like to admit.'

Axel gave his mother a questioning look but didn't speak.

'I mean, look at what we now know that we didn't know a generation ago, two generations ago. Through the work of the Guild we know an awful lot, not only about our own history, but the history of the wider world, too. And yet we've considered ourselves separate, isolated from the rest of the world, by virtue of our geographical location. I think we've been complacent. I think perhaps we've had our heads in the sand, a bit like the Eyreans.'

Her son objected: 'There's been a lot going on since the formation of the Guild and the Protectorate and the overthrow of the Sabu dynasties. We've all been part of a momentous time in our own history, your generation and mine. There hasn't really been a lot of time to consider the wider world.'

Fable Striker looked kindly at her son, appreciating his support. 'Nonetheless, we can't unknow what history has taught us, what's been uncovered by the Guild. We know that 800 years ago there *was* a global civilisation, and back then, we were part of it. We know that overpopulation and the greed and corruption of the fossil-fuel barons ruined the earth's climate and created untenable inequalities. Climate change, rising sea levels, starvation, unrest, it all led to global destabilisation and eventually, revolution, even right here, in Australia.

'And we know something of the brutality of the crack-down of the neo-conservative political movement in cahoots with the corporations.

'The world was split in two by a great global popular uprising.

'And we know the world continued to fall apart as sea levels continued to rise and the climate ran amok. Food resources depleted, millions displaced. When war finally came between the two great powers, it spelled the end of global civilisation. A catastrophic global war. That put an end to it all, to history itself.

'The Fall,' said Alex quietly, as he sat on the back of the sofa watching his mother gaze sightlessly at the black glass.

'After that, well, of course some of the young historians have their theories about what led to the Great Death, what could have caused a global pandemic following the war. We thought we'd been spared but eventually it arrived on our shores too, and decimated *our* population. Some believe the disease was caused by weapons used in the final conflict, a disease created by humanity as a weapon, which then became uncontrollable. But no one really knows and perhaps no one ever will. All we really know is the world descended into darkness and it has taken us this long to re-emerge.'

Fable glanced at her son and noted his concerned and sympathetic expression, half smile, half frown.

'I know, I know, you've heard it all before,' she said defensively, 'I sound just like your father, I know. All I'm really saying is there *is* still a wider world out there. And we have no knowledge of it. We don't know how the rest of humanity, out there, has reinvented itself after the Fall. We just don't know. But I fear we may have been complacent and naïve not to consider that question. And I'm afraid we're just about to find out.'

'Is that what you think this is?'

'I don't see what else it can be.'

'How bad do you think it could be?

'That's the problem, we just don't know what we're dealing with. We haven't been able to decipher their code at all. But the signals people are quite sure the pattern of the transmissions suggests a military build-up of some sort. Our own patrol boats can't seem to locate any of these vessels, but several fishing boats have reported sightings. Their descriptions sound like warships of some sort. One report claimed that some kind of flying machine was seen rising up from the deck of one of them. And we've started to receive sightings of intruders in the coastal regions to the north and south of the city, reports of strange troops in armour and another report of a flying machine, this time over land.'

'So an attack of some sort could be imminent.' Axel looked intently at his mother.

'It's very likely.'

Axel was stunned that all this had happened during his short absence. 'So what contingency plans are in place?'

'Evacuation of the civilian population into the hinterland. We've already doubled defences in the harbour, around the heads and on the southern approaches to Bondi Island. Mobilisation of the civilian militia. If necessary, relocation of our headquarters to the new academy out in Monkswood.'

'No.' Axel pushed away from the back of the sofa and stood up. 'No! Surely we must stand and fight. We can't abandon the harbour. We can't run. We must fight them! We'll push them back into the ocean. Damn them!'

Axel's passion brought a warm but sad sympathetic smile to her face and the strangeness of her expression stopped him in his tracks; he tilted his head slightly to the side, perplexed.

'There's something else I need to tell you, Axel.' Her face was pained.

Axel frowned.

'One of these incursions – there was an attack. A patrol was attacked.'

'When? Where?' Axel's eyes grew intense at his mother's troubled frown. 'Who? Who was it?'

Fable bit her lip. 'It was Quaid's unit.'

'Quaid.' He nodded and his face brightened, his eyes no less intense. 'What happened? What did he say? Where is he?' He glanced

439

around as if his old friend and mentor, commander of the only stealth unit that could match it with his own, might be lurking somewhere in his mother's living room.

'There were no survivors.' Her heart ached as she saw her son's face fall. 'No, there was one survivor. It seems they purposely left one of the men alive long enough to carry a message.' His mother's voice had taken on the clipped, professional tone that he knew was her defence against intense emotion, in times of stress. He had a strange, fleeting recollection of her telling him his father was not coming home in the same matter-of-fact tone.

'Message?' Axel was aghast.

'"Tell your people what you've seen. Tell them to flee." That was all.' Fable sighed heavily. Axel's aggrieved, questioning look begged her to elaborate.

'Our medical people had never seen such wounds,' she said, her voice becoming even more distant and detached. 'I spoke to the boy myself, before he died. He said they were giants, bigger than our people. or maybe it was the amour – they had on heavy body armour. Our weapons were largely ineffective. Theirs were … horrific.' She blinked and tossed her head, as though to avoid a mental image.

'He said they didn't have a chance, and yet, he said there were only six or eight of *them*.' His mother's voice trailed off as though she'd lost her lines. Axel sat down heavily on the sofa back and his mind seemed to be blank and racing at the same time.

He felt his mother's hand on his shoulder.

CHAPTER 31

JASMYN WOKE WITH A START. She had become used to the strange, dream-like mental processes of finding herself as she woke in yet another unfamiliar place. It took her a few moments this time, the heavily curtained windows allowing just a faint wash of grey light into the small blandly furnished bedroom.

It was dawn, or was it later? *Another bed. Gods, she would become spoiled.* Then she remembered. *Damn*! She'd been trying to stay awake, waiting for Barrak.

Barrak was still being interrogated when Teah had taken her out into the chilly night and along the harbour-side esplanade to the Guild of Historians, just a short walk from the palace. There was guest accommodation on the third floor and Teah had shown her through the impressive foyer and up two flights and down a hallway flanked by offices on one side and what looked like a library on the other, to the accommodation wing, tucked away at the back of the building.

She flung off the covers and found her shoes and coat. *Where was Barrak? Why hadn't he come and found her?* She retraced her route from the night before and quickly found herself back in the lobby of the Guild headquarters. She stopped on the landing before the last flight of stairs, distracted by the grandeur of the great vestibule below.

Teah had given her a tour the night before. When they'd stepped from the chill damp of the small hours into the vaulted foyer, Jasmyn had been quite taken aback. In the eerie darkness, it had been like a tomb filled with ancient wonders, a maze of strange artefacts made mysterious by the dim night lights. The Guild lobby was essentially a museum, Teah had explained to her and she'd found the main switch and lit up the whole lot for Jasmyn to peruse in the hushed solitude of night.

How different it looked now in the muted grey dawn light. Even her dreams had been infiltrated by vivid, aberrant images of some of the exhibits she'd seen the night before, and as she looked down from the landing, she retraced in her mind some of what Teah had shown her.

There was a lot to take in.

The landing where she stood gave access to a mezzanine level, crammed with exhibits. Below her, on the expansive tiled floor, exhibits were arranged all around the perimeter of the building, and down through the centre of the gallery was another assemblage of artefacts, alternating with the structural pillars of the building and staggered and spaced for patrons to wander through.

As she made her way down she was startled by the echoing clip-clop of heels on tile as an early Guild member hurried from the front entrance to the main stairs, oblivious to Jasmyn's presence.

She felt like a burglar.

On the ground floor, the first rays of morning sun lit up the tall windows along the harbour side of the building and the scattered sunlight illuminated a mural on the western wall, a graphic time line colour coded to link up to key exhibits. She moved along the mural, progressing through time from Ancient Civilisations, The Age of Empires and The Industrial Revolution, to The Fossil Fuel Age, The Digital Age and the cryptically titled Age of Carbon Denialism. She paused where the time line ended with a disturbingly cataclysmic graphic montage, simply labelled The Fall. The images and the words conjured up fascinating and perplexing ideas and the related exhibits were even more interesting and puzzling.

None was more perplexing than the Digital Age display, which progressed through its own time line. Jasmyn had been particularly fascinated by a glass case containing an oddly shaped box with a mottled and cracked glass front, marked, *Ancient Computer*. Other cases contained things that looked like blackboards and slim briefcases all with the same worn and scuffed surfaces that looked like old, smoked glass. The accompanying text made no sense to her at all and contained so many words that were foreign to her, she gave up even trying to read them. Another display had what looked like an ordinary pair of sun glasses with a small square gadget attached to the side, and next to that, a graphic depiction of a human head with strange markings like an architect's renderings and a placard of explanatory text titled, *Digital-Brain Interface Technology*. She didn't understand at all, but nonetheless something about it made her flesh creep.

There was a whole area devoted to the history of energy production, which made a lot more sense to her, and she recognised milestones similar to Eyrean progress, with the development of solar array technology, tidal power generation, and solar towers. Here she paused again to look at the unbelievably horrific pictures that purported to be of a whole city laid to waste. She'd seen this the night before. The pictures seemed to be taken from a great height and were mind-boggling. But it was the caption on one of the accompanying explanatory texts that really defied belief and Jasmyn took a moment to look at the display again, trying to understand how it could possibly be true. *Catastrophe at Fusion Reactor Research Facility, 320,000 Dead.*

She moved on.

Jasmyn knew very well that she was working her way back to one exhibit in particular, one that had played on her mind the most and intruded on her dreams. She wanted to see it again, to check that it was real, that she hadn't just dreamt it.

Suddenly there it was. It was part of an exhibit that had appealed to Jasmyn right away, because there were images of the planets and the stars and other astronomical phenomena. Saturn's rings, Jupiter and its moons, and our moon … extraordinary images of the moon.

It was just a glass case containing what looked like a carefully preserved document, an ancient book or journal. Arranged around it were other related documents and pictures, but it was the central object that had captured Jasmyn's imagination. The cover was a photograph, very old and clearly the subject of some careful restoration. The image itself was beguiling and intriguing and confronting, all at the same time. And the four-word caption under the image was mind-blowing and hard to believe. Yet somehow it sparked in Jasmyn a deep-seated intuitive knowing that told her it *was* genuine. She stood there for some time, staring at the picture just as she had the night before, unsure whether to be excited or deeply disturbed by it, and she shook her head gently and breathed a heavy sigh that ended in a shudder of incredulity.

Barrak flung away the coarse woollen military-issue blanket that was prickling at his chin and swung his legs off the couch. The last thing he remembered was being interrogated by St John. He was still in his office, on his couch. It was dawn. *Gods be damned*, he'd fallen asleep and someone had thrown a blanket over him.

He found his way into the foyer and its cold white marble echoed like a mausoleum under his hurried footsteps. It was deserted but for a pair of bleary-eyed young troopers guarding the entrance, both of whom scanned him with intense curiosity as he hurried past, but neither was sufficiently moved to stop or question him.

Outside in the courtyard two Protectorate officers locked in earnest conversation gave him a curious but cursory glance as he rushed past. He took a tree-lined path skirting the northern wing of the palace, and this led him to the harbour.

The harbour-side promenade would lead him to the Historians Guild, which was where he'd been told they would be accommodated, and presumably therefore, where he would find Jasmyn.

The cool air off the water hit him like a slap and he stopped and put a hand to the cast-iron balustrade that guarded an eight-foot drop to the water below. The harbour had a murky emerald translucence under a heavily overcast sky.

As the water surged and sucked against the sea wall, Barrak heard the unmistakable *whoosh and whir* of tidal turbines. When he looked back along the curved sea wall, the subsiding swell revealed several large round inlet openings, covered with protective mesh grills. This explained the ready supply of night-time power in the city – the historians had harnessed the power of the surging waters of the harbour.

Taking in the wider view across the harbour, he saw a forest of spires, some twisted and broken, some with a regular grid-like structure. Some were tall and thin, reaching perhaps a hundred feet or more into the sky, others small and squat, sometimes barely breaking the surface. It took Barrak some time to process what he was looking at. When the realisation finally struck, it filled him with a sense of awe and dismay. These were the corroded, ruined skeletons of ancient buildings, submerged in the sea.

Suddenly the old myths of the punishment of the gods and the inundation took on a shocking new clarity. This had really happened. This sudden knowing hit him like a punch and sent his mind and senses reeling. It was at once horrifying and deeply fascinating.

He scarcely believed that buildings could ever have been as high as some of the ruined spires. He thought about the multitude of red lights he's seen over the dark waters the night before and realised that they *were* navigation warning lights, marking the position of the ruins.

Further out, clear water marked where he imagined the original harbour had been, and beyond that, along the opposite shoreline, he could see even more submerged ruins guarding the distant shore.

Looking back he could see more ruins on the hills beyond the palace, just like the ones he'd glimpsed in the headlights of the truck the previous night, but now they were stark and clear in the grey dawn light. Now it was clear to him. The ruins were everywhere, not just out in the harbour. The weird, irregular hillocks out in the countryside, the dark, deserted precincts of the city, with their looming mounds of unoccupied ground, these were all the remains of ancient buildings – huge buildings – some perhaps once stood as tall as the towering skeletal remains out in the water. Most were now just massive piles of rubble so old and decayed and so long overgrown, they were part of the landscape, waste ground probably too unstable to build on.

Turning full circle, it dawned on him that the scale of the ancient city must have been immense. It would have dwarfed Tamouer.

A flotilla of clouds to the east was lit golden by a hidden sun, in contrast to the grey sky looming above him. Between the clouds the amputated foot of a massive rainbow escaped the glowering sky and painted the foothills and ruins on the distant shore with an ironically cheery spectrum of colour.

As his progress along the promenade opened up a wider view of the harbour, something caught his eye. He increased his pace a little just to open up a better view of it.

Gods, it was a bridge!

He stopped and put both hands on the balustrade. *It was an immense bridge!*

At first glance it resembled the bridge across the Clare River near the university, back in Tamouer. It had a similar 'through-arch' design, but on an entirely different scale. This bridge seemed to span half the harbour.

But neither end was joined to the land. Instead it stood stoic and marooned in the middle of the sea, its long graceful arches encasing a zigzag lattice of girders and curving up to a prodigious height at its zenith. He guessed the bridge's highest point would rival some of the tallest ruins. Vertical columns extended down from the arch to what was left of the deck, the ancient roadway that Barrak imagined once thronged with vehicles and people. But now, standing just above sea level, much of the deck was ruined or missing, claimed by the ocean.

At both ends stood the tops of what must have once been massive twin pylons of stone which, even from some distance, appeared to be crumbing with age. Beyond the pylons there was no sign of the roadway that had once joined it to the land. In the ancient city, this incredible bridge must have spanned the entire harbour as it was then, before the inundation. Now it was just an island of ruin, forlorn and abandoned in the dark waters of the harbour.

Barrak's sense of awe and fascination gave way to an overwhelming sadness as he thought of the great civilisation that had once been and now lay in ruins. A sense of loss and grief welled up in him, which he knew and recognised only too well, but this was different, it was a grief that didn't belong to him. It came from another place, from outside himself, and yet from the deepest part of him.

He held the rail as if he were steadying himself at sea and the morning chill assailed him.

His hands felt frozen to the balustrade and a dark sense of foreboding stirred in him. Memories etched in the rusted, twisted, yawing ruins, memories of death and destruction, memories of the unimaginable loss of an entire people, coalesced within him and he knew the memories were part of him, part of who he was, somehow embedded in him, the trauma of it reverberating through him, down through his own ancestral line, through his own great great grandmothers and their grandmothers and all those who had come before him, linking him to the ancient harbour dwellers whose lives had been torn apart by calamity.

And bit by bit his grief turned to anger and then rage and revulsion and he pushed himself away from the balustrade and looked up at the glowering heavens. 'Gods,' he muttered at the sky. 'Why?'

All at once the anger and outrage seemed to collapse in on itself and fall away and Barrak found himself sitting on the cold cobbles staring at his hands.

He felt bereft, like a small boy separated from his mother, when all is lost and everything has become alien and threatening.

This made him think of Jasmyn. He found he had a terrible longing to be with her and feel the comfort of her arms around him and to share with her this revelation of the ancient city.

He got up and turned away from the bleak vista and continued walking, at first with the stiff hesitancy of a man woken from slumber and then with a stumbling urgency. He was almost there. The bluestone edifice of the Guild of Historians was before him and he made for the paved courtyard at the front of the complex.

The old building offered him a choice of entries and he opted for a revolving door of glass and polished brass instead of the large double doors by its side, which in any case appeared to be steadfastly shut. The whirling cylinder hissed and sighed before disgorging him into the vaulted foyer of the Guild. To his right was a wide staircase. At its foot was a sign on a metal stand with a pointing finger painted on it and the word *Reception*. The rest of the huge vestibule was devoted to some kind of gallery. As Barrak's eyes adjusted to the dimness of the room, lit only by the meagre morning light brightening the eastern windows, he realised it was a museum of sorts.

Guarding the entrance a statue drew his attention and he moved towards it. Its form was familiar to him. He approached it, touched it and moved around it, examining it with interest. It was much the same as the strange monument he'd stumbled upon, out in the western desert. The ornate pedestal was similar and the marble soldier with his upturned weapon and repentant stance was almost identical, expect in this case he stood in his rightful place atop the pedestal.

He had all but forgotten about the statue in the wilderness, how inexplicable and out of place it had been, the strangeness of it. It made this seem stranger still, finding its twin here. *What could it mean? What did they memorialise?*

'Barrak!' Jasmyn's voice echoed through the chamber and he spun around and spotted her at the far end of the gallery, beckoning to him. She was looking at one of the exhibits in a glass case, and even as he approached, her attention was fixed on it, until she looked up and smiled and reached out and took his hand, drawing him in. 'Look,' she said breathlessly.

The main item inside the case was a restored photographic book cover, very old. They both stared at it for what seemed a long time.

After the shock of seeing the ruined city in daylight, Barrak would've thought nothing else could faze him. But this took his breath away. 'Orlan's blood!' he whispered.

Jasmyn turned and looked into Barrak's eyes with an expression of utter bewilderment. 'Do you think it can be real?'

The picture was of a man, or presumably it was a man, a man in a bulky white suit and a massive helmet, as wide as his shoulders. The entire front of the oversize helmet seemed to be made of some kind of dark reflective glass, which made the figure seem faceless as he stared into the camera. He stood awkwardly, legs apart, as if trying to balance in his cumbersome suit with a huge backpack riding up behind his head and tubes snaking under his arm and knobs on his chest.

He looked like he was prepared for deep-sea diving, but there was no water evident. In fact he stood in the foreground of a barren, hostile landscape that looked like it hadn't seen water in a very long time. The scene was lit harshly from the side, the left side of the man's suit flaring bright white and throwing an ominous black shadow across the grey dirt. All about him were large boot prints, presumably his own, which looked like they'd been pressed into grey talcum powder. Behind him the flat landscape was chilling in its bleakness, every shade of grey with the low sun highlighting small dips and craters and random stones and boulders strewn here and there. Grey emptiness to the horizon.

Beyond that, the sky was black.

The stark monotone of the photograph was relieved by splashes of colour that drew the viewer's attention. One was just a large coloured patch on the shoulder of the suit, red stripes around a blue and white grid. Another was the reflection in the large curved visor of the man's helmet. In the reflection was another small white figure, possibly the photographer, and next to him loomed a large alien-looking tripod that looked disturbingly like a giant, golden insect, lit up by the bright sun.

Strangest of all was a thick-sliced gibbous moon, sailing in the black sky above and to the left of the man's helmet. Strange, because on closer inspection of the picture, ancient and reconstituted as it may have been, it was apparent that this was not the moon. Perhaps it was doing what a moon does, rising or setting, but this 'moon' was not silvery grey as one expects. In fact all the silver and grey was in the landscape below. The celestial body soaring above the strangely suited man clearly had swirls of white and blue covering its surface and even a hint of reddish-brown. The only conclusion, and a conclusion supported by the plain yellowing text captioned across the bottom of the photograph, was that this was *the earth,* rising in the black sky.

The matter-of-fact caption on the picture read: *MAN ON THE MOON.*

Jasmyn whispered the four words as if it was a secret and looked searchingly at Barrak.

Nonplussed, Barrak cast around himself, as if noticing for the first time the extent of the museum. There were exhibits and artefacts everywhere. He wondered how many of them had the capacity to shake his world view and shock him as much as this one. He didn't like to think. His mind was still reeling from the spectacle outside.

'Do you think it's real? It can't be true, can it?' Jasmyn was all frowning incredulity laced with wonder.

'Gods, I don't know Jasmyn.'

She looked at him strangely, imploringly, as if she needed reassurance, but Barrak couldn't offer her any.

'Nothing would surprise me after what I've seen outside,' he said softly.

'What do you mean?'

'The city, the harbour, in the daylight. It's incredible. You haven't been outside yet, have you?'

'No. Why? What is it?'

'It's … it's just incredible. The old stories, the myths. They're all true.'

The faraway look in Barrak's eyes worried Jasmyn and she frowned at him questioningly. She was a little disturbed by his demeanour and surprised that he wasn't more taken with her discovery in the museum. Seeing her discomfort, Barrak smiled reassuringly and took her hand in his.

'Come on, you'll have to see this for yourself.'

Even as they turned to go, they heard footsteps, hurried footsteps growing louder and echoing through the gallery. Seemingly from nowhere, Jasper Flint came skidding to a halt in front of them. As he caught his breath, he looked from Jasmyn to Barrak and then at the Man in the Moon exhibit and then back at Barrak.

He looked uneasy. 'They want to see you, back at the palace, as quick as you can.'

They met in a small conference room adjacent to the control room. Striker was there when Jasper first brought them in, and gave them both a wry, if somewhat weary smile. But soon, Zeus St John and the director herself came hurrying in.

Fable Striker closed the door behind her and cleared her throat before perusing Barrak and Jasmyn with candid curiosity, then she peered over the top of her reading glasses at her son, Axel.

'Let's get on with it then,' she said, skirting the chair at the head of the table and sitting herself instead on the other side, facing the internal office window to give herself a clear view of the frantic activity out in the chamber.

'Well now, hasn't been much of a welcome for you two, has it? We've got a bit of a flap on, as you can see, so, apologies. Anyway.' Fable looked at her intelligence chief, St John, and frowned slightly.

'Anyway, it seems we may need your help.'

St John drew a breath and the director gave him a barely perceptible nod as he took up the argument.

'Well, you now know your friend Elias was in our employ. He was a gift to us really, coming to us as he did, not long after we first started to monitor the radio transmissions between Eyre and these ... *outsiders*.' St John seemed to struggle to find the right word to describe the threat facing them.

'I want you to know that he took on the task willingly. There was no coercion on our part, nothing of the sort, not at all. He was willing and he was determined. He may have been just an adventurous kid at heart but he was an idealist and he was smart too. He trusted his gut, and he trusted me.'

St John paused meaningfully and glanced at Barrak and then at Jasmyn, holding her eye for a moment or two with a look of solemn regret in his. Fable Striker shifted in her seat as her eyes followed the activity in the control room outside before lighting on St John with a look of mild impatience.

St John forged on regardless.

'He had a social conscience and was appalled by the injustices within Eyrean society, and he had a deep distrust of your Meldrick's military establishment. It makes you wonder, it's almost as though he had a sense of what was to come.' He paused again and stared at a watercolour depicting the harbour ruins, hanging on the end wall of the conference room. He seemed oblivious to the director's increasingly impatient glare.

'He had plenty of sympathy for your rebel movement of course, if not their methods, but in the end, for reasons best known only to Elias himself, he decided to vote with his feet and set out on his own personal quest to find answers, to find out what the world was like outside the boundaries of Eyre. I think that made our Elias an unusual and possibly unique Eyrean.' St John shot a querying glance at Barrak and Barrak gave him a slight nod in return.

'I'd be happier if you'd stop referring to Elias in the past tense,' Jasmyn interjected mildly.

'Of course, yes, we all hope Elias has managed to extricate himself from Meldrick's clutches and gone to ground, no one more than me.' St John smiled sympathetically at Jasmyn. 'But we have to be realistic, too. Whatever *has* happened, Elias was not able to return east with whatever information he was able to gather. And with the current apparent escalation of the threat from outside, it's more important than ever that we find some answers.'

St John's demeanour became more intense.

'Last year, long before all of this started happening,' he swept a hand towards the control room, 'we began to intercept radio traffic between these outside forces and someone in Eyre, almost certainly Meldrick's security people. And it's gone on intermittently up until the current day. We still don't know why. But given the dire situation right now, it's more important than ever that we find out.'

As St John paused again and surveyed his listeners, a wave of heightened activity and agitation passed though the control room outside and Fable Striker followed it with anxious eyes and then, unable to contain her impatience any longer, she put her hands on the table and stood up.

'We want you to go back,' she interrupted. Her tone was abrupt and imperative.

There was a moment of shocked silence, which only served to accentuate the increasingly frantic activity outside in the control room. Fable Striker began to talk quickly in a clipped tone as if she were being timed.

'We have to find out why these people are communicating with the security forces inside Eyre. Back then, it was appropriate to send in an operative, and this boy, Elias, seemed perfect for the job. We had time on our hands then and Commander St John was able to train him and equip him for the task. Now we face a very different situation and we have little choice, in fact it would seem our only choice is to send one of our stealth units into Eyre. Commander Striker's unit is the most experienced, travelling in the western desert regions, and we want you to go with him.' Fable Striker paused and eyed Barrak and Jasmyn closely, registering the shock on their faces.

'Councillor, you and Ms Mooney have recently come that way and have some experience of the regions beyond the western desert, and once you reach the boundaries of Eyre, your knowledge of the border zones will be vital in getting you and Commander Striker's team into Eyre undetected.

Jasmyn and Barrak shared a look of disbelief as the director went on, her tone softening slightly at the look of horror on Jasmyn's face. 'Axel's unit is the best there is. He will get you safely back to Eyre, and after that, well, frankly, after that you may just have to wing it. Together, you'll find a way to get the information we need, to find out what the hell is going on, and just what connection there is between Meldrick and these …' Fable Striker was momentarily lost for words, '… these foreigners.'

Barrak implored Axel Striker with his eyes, begging for some kind of response, some indication that his mother's plan was inadvisable, but all he got was a raised brow and a shrug. Jasmyn took up the cause, shaking her head as though waking from a dream.

'No. No, no, it's not possible,' she said quietly. 'We can't go back.

We'll be arrested right away, maybe worse!' She looked to Barrak for support, then to Fable, but the commander's face was stern, implacable. 'We'll never make it in any case. It's ludicrous. We nearly died getting here!' Jasmyn's voice rose and she was up out of her chair, rebellious outrage suddenly welling up in her. 'We can't!'

'Please sit down Miss Mooney!' Fable Striker's request carried the weight of command and she stared Jasmyn back down into her chair before stealing a glance out into the control room where the excitement appeared to have reached a new level.

'Chen's mercy!' It was unclear whether she was addressing herself to Jasmyn or the unfolding calamity in the control room.

'You can be excused, Ms Mooney, for not grasping the full gravity of the situation we are facing here, because frankly none of us knows just what the hell *is* happening right now, but I have a bad feeling, a very bad feeling, that things are about to get out of hand. We may soon be facing a fight for our very survival. So I'm afraid I really am going to have to insist that you do exactly what you are told.' She surveyed Jasmyn coolly then gave her a taut smile.

'You won't be leaving straight away. You will be given time to rest and Commander Striker's unit will need time to equip itself and draw supplies. I expect you should be planning to leave in about what, two, three days?' She looked enquiringly at Axel and he tapped two fingers discretely on the table.

'How long to get to Eyre, do you think, Commander?'

'Through most of the western desert and beyond that, as far as we know, there are no roads, so we'll be on foot most of the way. Depending on the availability of some transport coming out of Scarborough and possibly something on the outskirts of the Eyrean border zone – two weeks, maybe two and a half.'

Striker got no further as the door flew open to reveal one of Marx's communication team, breathless and red faced.

'Christ,' said Fable Striker.

'You better come, Ma'am,' the young lieutenant said gravely.

The Protectorate's supreme commander held her breath and stood stone still at the shoulder of the radio operator, staring at the dimly lit console and straining to discern voices from the hiss and crackle of interference.

'You say there was a report of an attack? What position? Were there any details?'

'It was like two transmissions at once. One from Bondi Island, the other, I don't know, maybe the south passage.' The young signals tech was intent as he hunched over his equipment, almost oblivious to the proximity of the Protectorate's highest ranking officer hovering behind him.

'It was all broken up, too much interference. Wait.' He worked the controls with both hands, gently turning one knob while sliding a lever, as though coaxing a performance from a sensitive and arcane musical instrument. 'Wait, I think that's it!'

With a high-pitched hum and a final hiss and crack the channel cleared and a disembodied voice addressed them as clearly as if it were coming from the signals tech working at the next console, the panic and strain in the voice made all too apparent by the new clarity of the transmission.

'Christ, can anyone hear me? We're under attack. Fuck! No! Jimmy. JIMMY!' The transmission was distorted with background noise and the voice of the young operator cracked with emotion and fear as he screamed across the airwaves.

'This is control receiving. Please identify your unit and report.'

'Christ! Oh god! Yes. Forty-three. Unit forty-three. Commander Vail's unit. We need help, we're in trouble. Oh god, help us!' There was shouting in the background and then a loud volley of weapons fire nearby and scuffling that sounded like the radio being moved.

'Get Vail,' Fable Striker said firmly, gesturing toward the console.

'Forty-three, forty-three, put Commander Vail on, please.'

'Vail's dead!' The desperate voice rattled from the speaker in a distorted howl. 'They're all dead!' There was a short pause with more shouting in the distance. 'Oh shit, they're coming, they're coming!'

More scuffling was followed by a sustained volley, accompanied by screaming and grunting and expletives. It was clear to all those listening that this was the sound of the radio operator firing his weapon, then: 'Oh Christ! Oh no! My god, what *is* that!?

'No. No! Please.'

The suddenness with which the transmission ended made them all flinch and then the radio gave them no more, just a monotone hiss of unbroken static.

Fable Striker turned slowly to her son Axel who was flanked on one side by Barrak and Jasmyn and on the other by Jasper Flint. Her face was a stern mask, struggling to contain a melange of emotions – fury and fear, indignation and determination. But there was also a look of alarm in her steely grey eyes.

'We have to get our people out of here.' She stated it plainly, with a hint of something like sadness.

'Yes,' Axel said simply.

'All right. Sound the alarms. Evacuate the harbour precinct.'

CHAPTER 32

ZOLA STORM HIT THE pavement of the palace courtyard before the transport had fully come to a halt and barely even felt the impact despite fifty pounds of combat gear. Maybe it was the adrenalin – it was coursing through her like a torrent. It gave her a heightened sense of awareness and imbued the scene before her with a vivid immediacy; colours were brighter, sounds sharper and the throng of people swirling around her were more vibrant, more alive than in normal life.

She was more alive.

She watched her troops descend from the truck and crunch out into formation beside it and she felt what could only be described as intense love for them.

Love and pride.

It made her heart ache.

Her heart was racing. And there was fear churning through her too, but it was a fear that manifested itself more as exhilaration and determination, a searing sense of purpose – to protect her family, protect her homeland, protect her squad.

She took in and catalogued the scene with unusual clarity and speed, as if the chaos unfolding under the bright morning sun was nothing out of the ordinary. Towering over the east wing of the palace, a thick menacing pillar of black smoke rose from the direction of the island. A distant crack of thunder from a non-existent storm stopped the milling crowd for a moment as if it held a message for them all, then they continued their preparations with even greater urgency.

The courtyard was a confusion of comings and goings; a steady stream of Protectorate personnel were pouring down the stairs of the palace and being loaded onto transports like the one that had just deposited her squad. Lines of historians were filing from the promenade into the courtyard and being loaded onto a bus, and more troops were arriving to defend the palace.

A garish orange light blinked above the palace entrance and a siren wailed over the raucous hubbub of fleeing souls.

Protectorate headquarters was being evacuated along with the rest of the city and Zola wondered how it would go for them on roads already clogged. On the way in she had experienced an almost surreal sense of pride and purpose as they had zoomed past the all but stationary outbound traffic, wind in their faces, heading for the fray, heading for the palace, to defend it. She knew her squad had felt it too, pride, anticipation, and gut-churning trepidation, the heady cocktail of pre-combat consciousness.

Even as she surveyed the disorder all around her she spoke evenly to her squad, issuing orders, calming them with her steady resolve and the familiar routines from years of training. And so she was more than a little surprised when a hand fastened itself on her upper arm, urging her to turn.

'Zola, Zola! What the hell are you doing here?'

'Axel! Christ, I thought you were still up country. Hell, it's good to see you!'

Striker had the young unit commander by both shoulders, holding her at arm's length for a moment as if to see her better, and then the two of them embraced like bears, with much pounding of backs.

Barrak was intrigued, standing a few yards away, where he'd stopped when Striker had suddenly changed direction. *Who was this woman*, this squad leader, a good inch or two taller than Striker, broad-shouldered and lean, with chiselled, attractive features, shaved head and a buoyant, easy laugh?

'But why are you here? You shouldn't *be* here. A full evacuation has been ordered; Protectorate forces are falling back to the new academy.' Striker's voice was muted but intense and the two had moved away from Zola's troops, still formed up in their ranks, their sergeant ministering to them. Striker was clearly at pains to avoid any appearance of questioning Zola in front of her squad. Barrak moved closer to better hear the conversation.

'I suppose Sax didn't get the memo. We've been ordered to defend the palace, dig in, hold our ground at all costs.'

'Shit!' Striker hissed, struggling to keep his voice low. Sax was from Sabu stock, a hawk, and a steely-eyed military man. And he was putting lives at risk unnecessarily … and one of them was Zola's.

'It's too dangerous! No one should be here.' Striker cast around him, a look close to panic in his eyes as he struggled with the dilemma. 'It's too risky. Sax doesn't know what he's up against … Protectorate forces are to regroup at the academy, that's what's been decided.'

The imposing young woman squared her shoulders and gave Striker a cautioning look. Striker knew what it meant; Zola had her orders and she would follow them to the letter; nothing would sway her from that now. Barrak thought he'd never seen Striker look so worried.

'Zola, just promise me one thing. If it gets too hot, get your squad out, get them out before it's too late.' Striker dropped his hand onto Zola's shoulder for emphasis. 'Promise me.'

Zola nodded and the two clasped each other's forearms fervently in the informal Protectorate greeting. As they separated, they gave each other the formal salute, hand like a blade diagonally against the chest before sweeping forward.

As Striker turned and strode back towards Barrak and Jasmyn, he caught them both flat-footed and agog. The young squad leader's attention was already back with her men as she and her sergeant prepared them for the coming fight and Striker just swept right past the two gawking Eyreans. 'Well, come on,' he yelled over the clamour in the courtyard, and Barrak thought he detected a hard edge of irritability and angst that hadn't been there before. 'Let's get the fuck out of here!'

※

Jasmyn's head lolled in her hands as the truck bumped along the rough road. Even this lesser byway was clogged with fleeing civilians, most of them on foot. They parted like a human river as the transport chugged along and then they shuffled back together in its wake, faces haggard with desperation and fear as they stared up at the passengers in the back of the open truck.

Jasmyn could hardly bear to meet their eyes. She slumped forward with her head in her hands and her elbows on her knees. When she did look up, she caught the eye of a young girl standing on the verge, watching the truck pass. The girl stared directly at Jasmyn as though she knew her, and indeed, as Jasmyn returned her gaze, recognition seemed to pass between them. Jasmyn could have been looking at herself at age twelve or thirteen, the dark hair, the deep blue eyes, even the posture was familiar in some way, as she stood with her hip slightly rotated in support of the grimy red-faced infant boy she held in her arms.

Jasmyn felt a lump rising in her chest and a sigh escaped her throat as the girl gave her a flimsy, sad smile and hoisted the boy higher on her skinny hip. Her big eyes held not so much fear as sorrow and Jasmyn found she couldn't avert her gaze. They watched each other as the truck laboured past and the girl gradually receded into the human throng. Still Jasmyn kept her in sight, picking out the blue and yellow in her floral dress until finally that too was indistinguishable amongst the river of people.

Only then did she notice she was biting her lip and her vision was blurred with tears, but she refused to cry.

After she finally lost sight of the girl her gaze floated up and took in the view of the now distant harbour. It was mid-morning and the pillars of black smoke had multiplied to four. Like the minions of a grievous underworld, the grim billows rose up into an otherwise pristine sky. Tilted by a soft breeze, the highest pillar touched the morning sun, colouring it a smoky rouge and casting an ominous copper wash over the crowded landscape below. A murmur of fear and awe infected the crowd and some craned their necks to look up at the muted sun, as if it held some portent of what was to come.

If Jasmyn allowed herself to think at all, her mind swarmed with imponderable questions and scenarios. To dare to think was to risk plunging headlong into madness. *How on earth could this be happening?*

Was it not just twenty-four hours since she and Barrak had bumped along a different road, entering the easterners' city for the first time? Infuriatingly, this was like a distant memory to her now, and she jealously coveted the buoyant, almost joyful feeling she had experienced the day before. The flavour of it all but eluded her now, the sense that her life was about to finally start making sense again, that she and Barrak could start a new life, together. After all the trauma and privation of their odyssey in the wilderness, after the shock of being banished from their homeland, it had looked very much like this harbour city would offer them a safe haven, a new home.

How could it have all gone so wrong, so quickly? To have this first faint glimmer of hope snuffed out so suddenly, so cruelly, was almost too much to bear. Silently she cursed the gods. She had known her trials and tribulations were coming for some years, it was her trade to know such things, but she could never have dreamed in a thousand years that her challenges would be so great.

Havoc.

When Neptune, the god of ocean and spirit, opposes Pluto, the dark lord of the underworld, one expects havoc, chaos, confusion and loss of those things we hold most dear. *But hadn't she lost enough?*

She'd already lost her family, her home, her security. *Wasn't that enough?* Maybe it was she who was cursed. Maybe this would only end for her with the loss of everything. *Was that what Saturn demanded of her ... that grim teller of karmic debt, must she* die *to appease him?*

Jasmyn's head dropped back into her hands and she tried to deaden her thoughts and emotions, which had become overwhelming. Barrak must have sensed her angst and reached over and started to rub her back and shoulder gently. Suddenly she craved his touch and the comfort of his affection; she slid along the

461

bench seat and snuggled in to him. He put both his arms around her and she buried her face in the warmth of his fleece-lined jacket and pressed her cheek against his chest. The smell of him calmed her and she wondered whether there was still a chance for them to escape these troubles, to find a place to start over, together. Maybe somewhere like Scarborough; she could imagine them together there. It surprised Jasmyn how much his touch soothed her, even in extremis, and she snuggled closer.

Gradually, though, as she clung to Barrak, another worrying thought intruded ... this idea that they should accompany Striker back to Eyre. It seemed a bizarre plan and the thought of it filled her with an odd mix of dread tinged with curiosity and longing.

What would it be like to return to Eyre? Was it even possible?

Surely that idea no longer mattered, now that the city was actually under attack. Jasmyn squeezed Barrak's arm and looked up at him and he gave her a reassuring smile and kissed her on the forehead.

'We're going to be all right, aren't we Barrak?' Jasmyn asked solemnly, quietly.

'Yeah, we'll be OK.'

'Don't you ever leave me.' Jasmyn pressed her cheek against his biceps.

Barrak kissed the top of her head gently. 'I never will. I promise,' he said earnestly.

At that moment, the truck's occupants looked up in unison to a distant rumble, emanating like popping thunder from the harbour precinct. This one seemed louder and all eyes strained to see a sign to match the noise. In the distance, a small dark mushroom blossomed from somewhere east of the palace and even as it billowed and reached up into the sky, another thunder crack followed.

Zola Storm felt the earth tremble under her feet and watched, alert and tense, as a cloud of black smoke swelled into the sky beyond the Guild's headquarters and museum complex, barely a mile east of their position. Yuri Baker, her trusted squad sergeant, gave her a guarded sidelong look of unease and she replied with the faintest nod of acknowledgement.

'Settle them down, Yuri. We need them to stay cool,' she said quietly.

Yuri addressed the squad calmly, projecting his voice down the ranks as he walked the line, giving them his time-worn platitudes from endless drills. 'Check your weapons. Nice and easy now, you know the drill. Mark your targets.' Yuri's voice was soothing, fatherly. 'Talk to each other. Remember your training, this is what we do. Let's keep it tight.'

Zola lowered her field glasses as Yuri returned and she gave him a deadpan look of concern which she knew only he could read. They really didn't know what to expect – some kind of landing craft ... the rumoured flying machines ... armoured troops with advanced weaponry? No one really knew. She looked to the east along the promenade. Her squad had the south-west corner of the palace. There was another holding the north-east corner and another two squads were dug in around the Guild. Beyond that, along the Beach Road and the South Passage, she wasn't sure. Thick smoke obscured the area. She could hear the intermittent crackle of small-arms fire drifting in on the breeze and maybe even the faint sound of screams, but it could easily have been gulls.

'What *is* that?' Yuri demanded, pointing out into the harbour, directly off their position.

'What?' Zola swung her glasses to where Yuri's was pointing.

'There, something in the water ... Jesus Christ! What is that?' Yuri's tone was aghast, shocked.

Zola's binoculars filled with a dark shape and she dropped them to her chest. 'Christ! What the fuck ...?'

It was like a submerged ship raising itself from the depths. It wasn't that large, but it was close, maybe only two hundred yards offshore. As it broke the surface it made an unholy sound, like a trumpet or claxon, but ten times louder, and at such a low frequency it shook the pavement under her feet, sending a tremble through her gut. As the thing settled on the surface, dozens of waterfalls cascaded down its grey metal sides and the sound it made began to change in pitch. Hatches were opening all along its side, revealing round apertures, and the upper panels of the thing opened up like the petals of a great dark flower to reveal a smaller, sleek vehicular unit on top of the ship. As the low-pitched sound of the ship subsided, the smaller machine made a loud whining noise, gradually rising in pitch, and as they watched in dread, the thing began to rise up into the air, unaided.

Distracted by the astounding sight of the flying machine, Zola realised a moment too late that the apertures along the sides of the ship were weapon ports.

'Take cover!' she screamed. As she dropped to her knees and looked along the line, most of the squad were already taking cover behind the stone balustrade and the sandbag fortifications, all but one … one of her new recruits. He was just a kid. Frozen in fear he stood stock still for a moment too long, staring at the infernal contraption out in the harbour and its ungodly flying progeny.

'GET DOWN!' Her words were practically ripped from the air in front of her gaping mouth and slammed into the stone walls of the palace, together with shards of stone and dust. The sound of it was deafening, and in ghastly slow motion, she saw the boy's head vanish in a burst of smoke and debris and his limp, headless torso crumple to the ground.

Stone and sandbags exploded all around her and she pressed herself low in the corner of the promenade wall. Through the smoke and dust she watched a line of white wounds the size of dinner plates appear like a sudden cancer along the stone wall of the palace. She was deafened by the mindless cacophony of shattering rock and the air was filled with rock dust and sand and cordite; she could taste it. She stole a glance along the wall towards her fallen recruit but he was lost in a fog of smoke and dust.

A moment of stillness. Over the ringing in her ears all she could hear was a ghastly screaming like nothing she had ever heard, coming from further along the wall. One of her boys. Wounded. It was desperate and primal, a guttural shrieking full of fear and horror. Then the maelstrom started again and more rock and stone disintegrated around her.

Zola pressed into the wall and waited for the next pause. When it came she stole a glance over the wall to get a target and went back down, then back up with her weapon and let go a volley of fire in the direction of the enemy vessel. Between the vessel and the shore were small landing craft like motorised dinghies, with a handful of soldiers in each. She spent the last of her magazine on the nearest of these and then dived forward along the wall and crawled frantically through the debris, to vacate her firing position.

Sure enough, the section of wall she had just used for cover exploded into dust and vicious shards and Zola flattened herself against the ground. Her hand fell in a pool of viscous liquid and she gasped and recoiled as she discerned the crumpled form of her decapitated recruit.

Christ! Where was Yuri? What was going on down the line? She became aware that the screaming had stopped and was shamed by her sense of relief that she no longer had to hear it. A glimmer of hope came to her as a volley of shots rang out along the line and the raucous, manic voice of one of her men carried over the din. 'Get some of this you fu-ahhhgh—' Return fire silenced his zeal and her heart sank.

Zola was on her back, soaked in blood she could only assume was not hers, and above her, through the clearing smoke, she saw and heard it, more like felt it, the buffeting downdraft and jabbering stutter of its motor, the flying thing. It was above her and firing along the wall, firing at her men from above. She slammed home a new magazine where she lay and emptied the entire contents at the flying machine. To her surprise and dour satisfaction it banked and wheeled away like a bird of prey and was gone behind the palace.

The firing had stopped and there was a moment of sustained quiet.

Voices.

Yuri emerged from the clearing smoke covered in dust and blood, with a handful of men following him, all crouching low.

'Leave me Duncan and Varty with the 50 cal; we'll lay down

a suppressing fire. You take the rest and secure an exit. Find us a vehicle, we're getting the hell out of here!' She talked loud, assuming his hearing was as full of ringing as hers. Even as she yelled in Yuri's ear she kept a weather eye on the promenade. A break in the haze of smoke and dust showed her two dinghies nudging up to the sea wall below them, not more than thirty yards along, and she heard the clang of hooks against the iron balustrade.

The remains of her squad followed their sergeant and crept like dusted ghosts past the south-west corner of the palace. While Varty busied himself setting the heavy-calibre gun behind a double stand of sandbags, Zola clamped a hand on Duncan's shoulder. 'Come on Will, let's not give these fuckers a chance to get set. Follow me.'

Not far along, a swirl of smoke cleared their view enough to see two enemy soldiers right in front of them, one still climbing over the balustrade, one already standing checking his weapon. Zola took the nearest to her, the one clambering in panic now on the balustrade and nailed him with three short bursts of fire.

The first two bursts just seemed to glance off his body armour and he hung on grimly to the rail. With the final burst she crept her aim the merest fraction left and a round penetrated his armour from the side, under his arm. The soldier shuddered wildly for an instant and fell away out of sight. In that moment she knew she'd found a weakness.

The other soldier was trying to raise his weapon against a hail of Duncan's fire smashing into his armour. *Christ, what was this stuff?* The LK80 rifle fire should easily penetrate ordinary metal armour. Another moment and the hulking brute in his impenetrable armour would have his weapon trained on Duncan. Zola slid forward and to the left to open up the angle; going down on her knees she rolled onto her backside. Bracing herself against the wall, she opened fire, aiming for the same vulnerable point in the armhole, just as the enemy soldier raised his weapon.

It worked again. The brute jerked and grunted out a spray of blood, then fell heavily to his knees and crumpled forward over his weapon, his helmet clattering to the stone pavement. The air still rang with the echo of their gunfire and a shroud of smoke hung over them even as the last of their spent shells pinged against the pavement. She pushed off the wall and kicked the fallen enemy's weapon away from him and then winced slightly through gritted teeth as she put two rounds in his head, to be sure.

'Good work, Will.' She clapped Duncan on the shoulder and they exchanged a look of frazzled relief, but just for a moment.

The smoke along the promenade swirled and spiralled to the buffeting downdraft of the flying machine. It was back, with its shuddering wing beats and menacing guns. And on the ground, through the parting haze, a whole phalanx of the armoured troops appeared, advancing from further along the promenade in combat formation.

'Back!' Zola urged Duncan with a push in the direction of their sandbag fortifications, and as she ran beside him, she unloaded the remains of her magazine at the advancing troops, her weapon extended unsteadily behind, in one hand. As they tumbled over the bags, Varty's 50 cal was already hammering away, raining shells and spewing smoke in the surreal, deafened silence of battle. Duncan, on his back, looked shocked and scared and Zola grabbed him and shook him and checked he was intact. 'Are you all right?' she screamed at him. He gritted his teeth in answer and swung his weapon up onto the bag wall and joined Varty's barrage.

Zola slapped home a clip and rolled on her back once again, to take on the flying thing. All the while she was yelling, trying to make herself heard over the din. 'There's a weakness in their armour, around the armhole! Aim for the armhole!' But it was too late. Duncan slammed backwards into the pavement beside her, a fountain of blood spewing from a gaping wound at his neck. She tried to help him, tried to hold him as he writhed and squirmed, tried to stem the flow. *But with what?*

'Ammo! Ammo!' Varty was screaming at her over his shoulder. She wrenched open the ammunition box at her elbow with a desperate grunt and hauled a belt up onto his knee. By the time she looked back, Duncan was dead.

She helped Varty load the gun but he didn't get off a shot before his helmet left his head, along with the contents of his skull, and he too crumpled and settled against his dead comrade on the blood-slicked pavement.

Zola wrenched the heavy machine gun off its mount and flattened herself behind the bags. The deadly flying machine was over her, going past their position and banking steeply to return for another attack. With strength she didn't know she had, she raised the heavy gun and trained it on the offensive bird as it slowed and banked. The exertion and desperation of it had her bellowing and grunting like an angry bull, and when she opened fire the gun bucked wildly in her grip and hot shells rained on her face.

Somehow she held it steady and adjusted her line until she saw the heavy calibre rounds smacking into the armoured skin of the deadly bird; the thing even seemed to shudder a little with the impacts. But its armour held, even against the massive insult of the 50 calibre weapon. Then she got lucky. A round hit something vital on the mechanical bird and she saw smoke, first a puff of white and then a trail of thick black smoke spewing from its belly. Its engine coughed and it lurched and dropped before steadying itself and wheeling away in a slow arc, clearly struggling to maintain its height, before vanishing behind the palace walls.

Zola heaved the massive gun back up onto the sandbag wall. No time for the mount. She stood up behind it and squeezed the trigger. The muzzle-bursts percussed her eardrums and the rhythmic kick of the recoil wrenched her shoulders, but she squeezed the trigger all the harder. She was barely even aware that she was bellowing and screaming as if to compete with the noise of the gun.

But there was no fear in her. No anger. No conscious thought at all, just pure will and primal instinct.

Survival instinct.

The advancing enemy scattered in surprise as the heavy gun started up again and found what cover they could before returning fire. Zola didn't budge, she just yelled all the louder and clamped down harder on the trigger, her face a mask of pure animal aggression. A sandbag exploded beside her face, a bullet zinged off her gun and burnt her ear, but she paid no heed, she was now one with her weapon.

The enemy were too numerous to count – more than a dozen – they didn't even register with her. A calm objective part of her mind picked out targets, *enemy soldier, firing from partial cover of a buttress in the stone wall*. The power of her weapon exploded stone and ripped away his weapon and his arm. A glimmer of grim satisfaction was her only conscious thought, *their armour is no match for the heavy gun*. She sprayed fire down the promenade and found another target.

But something distracted her, something flew past her head and bounced off the back wall of sandbags.

It got her attention.

It seemed important, even in the midst of everything. It clattered to the pavement in the corner, out of reach, and a red pin-light winked at her when she glanced at it. She didn't know what it was, but she knew it wanted to kill her. Instinct was still in charge and she pushed away from the gun, took one step on the gore-mired pavement and then vaulted for the top of the rear wall of sandbags.

Blackness followed and there was nothing else – nothing save the vague, dream-like impression that somehow she had learned to fly.

Barrak strained to see what was going on in the distance. The harbour already seemed a long way off and was heavily shrouded in smoke haze. Earlier, they'd seen two of the flying things hovering and swooping down around the harbour precinct, looking like a couple of buzzing flies from that distance.

Later, once they'd left the outskirts of the city and were making their way up into the low hills of the rural hinterland, they'd seen one of them come closer and land down in the valley near a road, still clogged with refugees. There'd been some kind of commotion, and they'd thought they heard the crackle of weapons fire. *What the hell were they doing, shooting at civilians?* Darko Mars had stood up in the back of the truck, bristling with rage, trying to see what was going on.

Now, as they reached the top of a rise and came onto some relatively flat, high ground, the brash, bright buildings of the new academy came briefly into view, set amongst stately stands of eucalypt, before the denser forest of the foothills began.

Barrak wondered if they would be safe.

Jasmyn squeezed his arm as if reading his thoughts and he wondered when, if ever, they could expect to regain some elusive normalcy in their lives. Or would the world continue to lurch and crumble all around them as it whirled past like an ever-worsening train wreck?

He could feel the tremulous ogre of his panic-state stalking him from within, with particularly fierce intent, since the sudden attack and their flight from the palace. But he was learning to recognise its feral sign and he set himself to deny it traction. After all, it was just feelings, feelings and thoughts; it wasn't real. *He* was the ruler of his own inner landscape.

Denying the lurking panic allowed his anger to rise. He felt a slow rage welling up in him at the thought of these aggressive interlopers shattering his new world, a world that had looked like it might finally provide him and Jasmyn with a refuge. It felt like the last straw. The belligerence of the invading brutes made him seethe and transported him all the way back to Eyre and Meldrick's machinations, which had led to his expulsion from his own home. He observed his anger and let it settle and cool, and as he looked around at Striker's men, sharing the transport with him, he conjured an image of Meldrick and his CSF troops facing Striker's men with their modern weaponry and fierce warrior mentality.

He blinked away the image just as a gasp erupted from the passengers and all heads turned to see one of the flying things swoop up from the dead ground beyond the crest of the hill they'd just ascended.

It hovered like an angry wasp, as if eyeing them before tilting its nose forward and advancing. Alarm ran through the group and Darko was on his feet thumping a hand on the cabin roof. The truck wavered then surged, picking up speed. 'Everyone get down!' Darko yelled as he took hold of the heavy calibre gun mounted behind the cabin and swung its barrel towards the menacing bird.

Barrak rolled onto the floor of the truck and tried to cover Jasmyn with his body. But he couldn't help craning his neck to look up with morbid fascination at the flying machine. Up close it looked a lot more substantial and threatening than it had at a distance. He had never imagined anything like it, with its skin of sinister dark-grey panels angled strangely to each other, the shiny brown bubble of reflective glass at the front, perhaps housing its occupant, and an underside bristling with weapons like stingers. It seemed to be held aloft by some kind of whirling mechanism encased in a metal ring above it. If anything it resembled a mechanical dragon fly.

Smoke and flame blossomed from the front of it and the truck's side panels were shredded like tin foil as its vicious projectiles slammed home and shattered the cabin's rear window. The truck swerved and the air above their heads was riven by deafening percussive shocks as Darko opened fire. Barrak squinted up at the wispy trail of Darko's fire, hunting the whirling machine against the blue sky. It peeled away from the line and Barrak lost sight of it, his ears ringing from the hammering of Darko's heavy gun and he winced and Jasmyn moaned as they bounced and jostled, with the others all prone on the hard metal floor.

Then the thing rose up like a dark banshee, right in front of the speeding truck. Fire erupted again. The truck swerved and Darko wheeled around and opened fire once more. Great plumes of dirt rose up beside them and showered the occupants with grit. Barrak chanced to look up in time to see a fiery rose blossom beneath the hovering gunship and a plume of smoke ejected sideways. He thought for a moment that Darko had found his mark.

But it wasn't so. The thing had launched a more serious projectile.

The front wheels of the truck dug into the verge of the road as it lurched to evade the incoming rocket. Barrak ducked back down and clenched himself around Jasmyn. A torrent of dirt rained down on them and heat, as from an open furnace, seared his back. The front of the truck rose up as if it would take flight and there was a roar and the shriek of metal. Barrak clutched Jasmyn to him, trying to envelop her. The truck rose and yawed, they were weightless for a moment, and then gravity fell like a hammer and Barrak was falling and spinning into an ocean of darkness.

CHAPTER 33

ZOLA OPENED ONE EYE. The other was glued shut, seemingly fused to the pavement. Her heart lurched as if it had only just remembered how to beat and she sucked in a ragged breath. She knew exactly where she was, and yet she had no idea where she was, where in time, *when* she was.

Where she was, was lying right next to a turbine access hatch, *Property of Tidel Co., Authorised Access Only.* Her outstretched arm lay across its edge. She recognised it well, she knew how to open it, she could read the inscription. But beyond the hatch her vision was blurred. She blinked. Memories flooded back to her, but they were old memories, memories she sensed were not much use to her now. She tried to push them away, struggled to grasp her present, but it eluded her. She was remembering her job, as a technician for the energy company, and it was remarkable the clarity with which she remembered: turbine maintenance protocols, the maze of tunnels under where she lay right now, the safety protocols.

Was that it? Had she been in an accident?

She closed her eyes and opened them again, but the context still eluded her. This was her job, this had been her job, once. *When?*

Before.

Before what?

A shot rang out, shattering the hazy tranquillity of the promenade, and a jolt of electricity zinged through Zola's body.

Before the Protectorate. She was a soldier!

She tensed up to move and winced at the pain, pain she could not even place in any one limb or part of her body. Pain all over. Gingerly, she turned her head to look in the direction of the shot, and focused with some difficulty; a figure not twenty yards away, in fatigues and body armour, his weapon angled nonchalantly down, was pointing at a prone figure in Protectorate uniform, one of her squad. More armoured figures loomed a little way off, along the promenade. Another shot rang out.

Panic. Anger.

Her memory of recent events came rushing back. She tensed again and winced.

She looked around for a weapon, eyes darting, but hardly daring to move for fear of attracting attention to herself. She blinked again to clear the muck from her eyes and then she saw him, just a few yards beyond the turbine hatch, lying on his side, hard up against what was left of the stone balustrade; the top half of it was blown clean away.

It was Yuri; she could only tell because of the insignia on his sleeve. He'd sustained a gunshot wound to his head but somehow he was still alive. His face was swollen, misshapen, bloodied and black. One eye seemed to be open. Zola couldn't tell if he was conscious but his bloodied claw-like hand seemed to be reaching out to her. A red froth of bubbles dribbled from the corner of his mouth.

Yuri. No!

Her heart seemed to lurch into her throat and block her breath, and waves of intense emotion swamped her – sadness, fear, anger, coalescing like ocean swells doubling up on themselves.

If this was Yuri, then there was little hope for the rest of the squad.

The uniformed figure approached and stopped beside Yuri. Zola held her breath and watched through narrowed eyes, keeping still, feigning lifelessness. Fear gripped her. She could see his boots and she noted curiously how similar they were to her own Protectorate issue. She was fascinated to see one of the enemy close up, the strangely patterned fatigues, the body armour, his face obscured by a dark grey helmet and reflective amber visor.

474

Her mind was clear now, sharp. Fear always gave her that kind of clarity. She watched the soldier poke Yuri with the muzzle of his weapon.

He would shoot Yuri, then he would shoot her.

She could see the calm blue water of the harbour through the gap in the broken balustrade. A swell was building. Her mind gave her a clear picture of the generating plant she knew was directly below them, the inlet, the wave-capture apparatus, the turbines, everything. It was as if her turbine-scrubbing days were only yesterday. She was lying right on top of the turbine hatch, so she knew that she and Yuri and the enemy soldier were all lined up perfectly with the inlet opening below, in the harbour.

And so, she had a plan. It wasn't a detailed plan, it may not have been a particularly good plan, but it was all she had. And as she watched the lines of swell lift and peak as they approached the shore, it seemed that nature herself concurred with her plan. The only question was whether or not her body could carry it out.

Something felt broken inside her.

There was a puff of smoke from the enemy muzzle and a single loud crack. It was as if Yuri's departing soul infused her with a burst of sublime strength. A bright flash of memory brought an image of a starter's pistol on some sunlit oval of her youth and in that instant she *was* that lithe, student athlete again. She pushed herself up and sprang forward in a single motion. Two, three, four long strides and she was on him. He swung around in panic, raising his weapon, but Zola blocked it with her left arm, and smashed her right forearm into his chin.

There was a massive expulsion of air from them both and the world tipped sideways as the soldier's knees buckled against the broken balustrade. As the dark water rushed towards them Zola's arms locked around her victim's neck.

The impact with the water stunned her and robbed her of breath. She lost her grip on him. Then, he was all over her, grabbing at her, forcing her under. Exertion and the sudden cold of the ocean sapped her strength. She flailed an elbow where she thought his head should be and found something hard. His grip loosened.

Zola broke the surface and sucked in a greedy breath. They were at the opening of the inlet chamber. The protective grate was gone, no doubt blown away in the barrage of shelling.

She felt herself being lifted up by the first of the swells. But he had her by the leg, clinging to her. She kicked fiercely and struggled to keep her head above water as the wave swept her up and along, towards the inlet chamber and the sluice.

She'd seen for herself what happened to sea creatures sucked through the pressure hatch and down into the turbines.

Zola gouged at the water and kicked desperately to free herself. As the wave surged she knew the pressure doors would open at any moment and they would be sucked down the sluice into the turbine tunnels, down into the spinning blades of the giant turbines below.

They would be minced like cheap meat.

The wave peaked and she sensed the doors open. She was devoid of energy, helpless against the gathering current sweeping them towards certain death.

Just yards from the sucking vortex now, five yards, three yards, one.

Zola's hand smacked against the cold steel of the access ladder. Blind instinct had guided her to the ladder, protruding from the rocky wall, just before the doors. She had used it many times in her technician days.

She lurched and made a grab for a higher rung. Her grip failed and she slipped down the ladder, making a desperate, breathless grab for the bottom rung. Frantically she shoved her arm through the ladder and locked the bottom rung in the crook of her elbow, just as the wave crested and she was submerged.

She could feel her enemy clinging desperately to her ankles as the water all around them was sucked down into the depths of the generator tunnels.

Zola broke the surface and sucked a huge lungful of air.

Her adversary was clawing at her legs. He grabbed her belt and hauled himself up, trying to climb her body. This freed one leg and she kicked viciously at his face and head.

Somehow he absorbed the blows.

As she kicked and squirmed, Zola watched the approach of the next wave.

Her biceps sang with pain as she clung to the ladder. His full weight was on her, dragging her down. A wave loomed at the opening of the inlet and the water began to rise. She kicked wildly to dislodge him, gasping and grunting with the effort, but he wouldn't budge.

He lunged upwards, dragging down on her belt and reaching up with his other hand. His helmet was gone. All she could see was red-rimmed eyes, wide with panic, pock-marked skin and an ugly, avid grimace. The rising water took some of his weight and aided his upward lunge.

In a moment of desperate, blind instinct Zola slammed her head forward, smashing her forehead into the bridge of his nose as he rose to meet her. There was a sickening crunch and the merest groan of protest from the soldier. His grip loosened and he fell away. As the wave peaked, Zola tightened her grip on the ladder and went under once more.

The pressure doors opened.

As she broke the surface and shook the water from her eyes, she saw her adversary's feet rise out of the water as though he were completing a dive, and then he was gone, down the sluice to the turbines.

As the water receded Zola was overwhelmed by a sudden weariness. She shivered with the cold. Such was her lethargy and weakness, she doubted her strength to climb the ladder, or even to keep a grip on the bottom rung. This thought alarmed her enough to spur her on and when a small surge raised the water level, she used it to buoy herself up and reach for a higher rung. Once she had her feet under her, she gathered her strength to climb. Even so, it took a mighty effort to ascend the fifteen rungs to the top.

With each step, there was a searing pain in her chest and back, which took her breath away and jammed her mind with confusion.

The ladder gave access to a ledge, hewn from the rock, which formed a catwalk around the top of the wave chamber. The catwalk in turn gave access to service tunnels that led into the heart of the subterranean generating plant. She slumped against the safety rail and concentrated on steadying her breathing to ease the pain in her chest. A violent shivering assailed her and when it passed she vomited unexpectedly down her front. She watched, grimly detached, as the syrupy chyme pooled on the rock ledge and slid over the edge into the shimmering grotto.

Gradually Zola became aware that her left thigh was aching and throbbing from the exertion. It felt like a torn hamstring. She slid onto her side in order to explore her thigh with her good hand. There was a hole in her trousers. She winced and flinched when her probing finger found the corresponding hole in her thigh, a bullet wound, or shrapnel perhaps.

She woke with a start, slumped against the rock wall of the catwalk with her chin on her chest; she had no idea of time.

Had she slept for a minute, an hour?

It was still light, although the angle of the sun on the half-moon of ocean visible through the entrance of the cave suggested late afternoon. The water was a deep emerald green, and reflected light from its rippled surface danced on the walls of the chamber. This, and the ocean sounds echoing through the chamber, gave the dim grotto a serene ambiance. No wonder she had fallen asleep. She cursed herself for her carelessness and shook her head to try to clear it. She felt drowsy still. *Don't sleep, don't pass out, don't die!*

On closer inspection she noticed the dark waters of the chamber were marked by a long streak of sullied ocean where it met the bright green water at the cave opening. *Would her enemy's blood give away her position?* She doubted the enemy soldiers above had seen what happened, and besides, the only obvious way into the chamber and the turbine complex was through the hatches on the promenade, and they needed a special tool to open them.

Zola knew the tunnel complex extended for miles along the harbour, connecting with older tunnels below the palace and the Guild, also with tunnels from other tidal generators along the harbour and finally with the power station itself, at the western neck of the harbour. She knew the layout of the tunnels well. *If she worked her way west she might get beyond the enemy's lines before they extended their reach past the harbour precinct.*

But she must hurry.

She tried to stand up but the pain in her chest forced her back to her knees with a gasp. She gritted her teeth and struggled to her feet, albeit bent over like a dowager. Her thigh had stiffened up and the first step was agony, the second a little worse.

It would loosen up in time.

She staggered into the nearest service tunnel like an ogre in search of her cave and the grunting noises she made as she went would have done nothing to dispel the illusion.

Jasmyn shook Barrak gently and whispered to him. 'Please, wake up.'

He appeared to be unhurt.

Jasmyn's hip and side felt numb and tingling, like a bruise not yet erupted. They had both ended up in the long grass beside the road, surprisingly far from the up-turned truck, which was listing sideways across the roadside ditch, one of its front wheels still spinning lazily. Craning her neck to look back at the truck she could see one of Striker's men trapped under the side of the truck. He wasn't moving either and he looked like he'd been broken by the truck. She shuddered and returned her attention to Barrak.

He was breathing as if in a deep sleep.

'Barrak, please!' There was a desperate quaver in her whispered plea.

She began to hear noises, groans and muffled voices that seemed to be coming from the ditch or below the upturned tray of the truck, but other than that, there was no sign of Striker or his men. Besides, her attention was focused on the enemy soldiers gathered around the flying machine, which had landed in the field not more than two hundred yards away. She looked across Barrak's chest, using him for cover, as she watched the soldiers gather around the grounded flying thing. Some of them seemed intent on examining something on the side of the machine, maybe checking for damage. Another one, seemingly in command, had begun to bark urgent orders and point towards the truck.

Jasmyn thought he was pointing right at her.

Cold fingers of fear probed her heart.

She watched breathlessly as five of the soldiers formed a line and began walking towards her, weapons at the ready as they carefully scanned the ground in front of them. She hugged the ground beside Barrak, trying to make herself small, and put a hand across his chest and shook him gently, hardly daring to make any movement. Her lips went to his ear and she whispered frantically, 'Please, please, *please!*'

Panic rose in her and she glanced feverishly towards the ruined truck. Still no sign of the others. By the time she looked back, the troopers had covered almost half the ground between their machine and where she and Barrak lay. She had a sudden urge to run but she was frozen. The air around her seemed too thin to breathe and her hands began to tremble as she grasped Barrak's jacket. Her heart thumped and bounded as if it were ready to run off without her and her voice all but deserted her, leaving her with little more than a mousy squeak.

'Bar-*rak.*'

Slowly coming to his senses, Barrak experienced what they call tunnel vision. All he could see was Jasmyn at the centre, Jasmyn wriggling and kicking and receding from him with unknown hands grabbing at her, pulling her away. All else was a hazy dark cloud. At first there was no sound, but then all at once there was Jasmyn's piercing scream, spearing through him like a lance, *'Barraaaak!'*

He came awake with a jolt and sat up, gasping for air in one great ragged inhalation. His vision cleared and with full consciousness there came a searing pain in his temple and behind his eyes, as if the daylight were too much for him. But he ignored this because his pained vision was filled with the woeful sight of Jasmyn being dragged away by two soldiers, two soldiers in bulky combat vests and strangely patterned fatigues, anonymous, alien-looking fighters with amber-visored helmets and weapons slung at their sides to better hustle Jasmyn along as she struggled ferociously against them.

They looked like they were twice her size.

Barrak lurched forward to get to his feet, but only got as far as a low crouch before a swinging boot caught him square in the chest, sending him sprawling. He rolled and got to his knees, but he went no further, finding the cold dark muzzle of a weapon pushed against his forehead. A third soldier stared down at him with inhuman detachment, his face hidden behind the shiny gold mask of his helmet.

'No, no! Leave me!' Jasmyn shrieked and swung a kick at the shin of one of her captors, causing him to grunt and stumble. The soldier responded with a savage backhand. Jasmyn reeled away and staggered, the other soldier pushing her angrily back into line and yelling abuse at her in an unfamiliar tongue. She gasped and sobbed and stumbled again before righting herself.

Barrak's eyes focused on the barrel of the weapon and his face twisted into a snarl. *He would not let them take her.* With explosive suddenness he slapped the barrel away and sprang at his captor, screaming in mindless rage. But the soldier was too quick and side-stepped his lunging attack, swinging the butt of his weapon around and connecting forcefully with the angle of his shoulder blade.

Barrak hit the ground, stunned, on hands and knees. Before he could gather his wits a boot caught him in the midriff with such force it nearly lifted him off the ground and sent him sprawling towards the road. In the corner of his eye he had time to glimpse the up-turned truck lying across the roadside ditch, before another kick sent him sprawling again. Clearly he had angered this soldier, who seemed intent now on kicking him into submission. Barrak heard another shriek from Jasmyn, before a third kick found his hip as he balled himself up for protection.

'That's enough!' he thought he heard a voice say, or words to that effect. A hand fastened onto his collar and urged him to stand. The man held Barrak's collar with an authoritative grip, keeping him at arm's length. In his other hand was a weapon which seemed too large and heavy for one hand. He pressed its muzzle hard against Barrak's temple and spoke in a foreign tongue to the other soldier, in a tone that clearly marked him as commander. Barrak tried to get a glance at this new assailant, this commander, but he wouldn't let Barrak turn towards him.

'Move,' he seemed to say, and pushed Barrak towards the road. As Barrak turned to face the road and the crashed truck, he realised that Striker and his men had also been captured.

Striker and four of his squad were on their knees, lined up along the top of the ditch, their heads bowed and bloodied, showing varying degrees of shock and trauma from the crash. One of the enemy soldiers stood a few feet back, nervously training his weapon on their backs while another knelt down behind them, tying their hands with short, shiny, black cords. He'd done Hugo Lynx and was moving on to the next man.

Jasmyn's scream reached him again and Barrak flinched.

It was enough to unnerve the commander with the gun at his head and he pushed Barrak forward towards the ditch then planted the sole of his boot in the middle of his back and propelled him forcefully over the edge. Barrak catapulted into the dirt bank opposite with a thud and lay there winded for a moment before he managed to roll over and put his back against the embankment, grunting at the exertion and the sharp pain that seemed to be coming from his previously broken ribs.

He looked up at the commander of the invaders. Something about him reminded Barrak of Bishop, something about his skin and the dark shadow thrown by his helmet. Behind him in the distance he could see the top of the flying machine, but Jasmyn and her captors were lost somewhere in the middle ground. The foreign leader seemed to take great offence at Barrak looking in his direction and started yelling aggressively at him and pointing his weapon directly at Barrak's head.

Barrak lowered his gaze and winced, half expecting to feel his skull shattered by a bullet. When that didn't happen he looked up awkwardly at Striker who was kneeling on the opposite bank. Striker met his gaze with a hooded stare, stern and steely and tinged with a hint of alarm plus a fair serve of simmering rage. Barrak tried to remember the names of the other two soldiers between Hugo and Jasper Flint, but they weren't members of Striker's regular squad.

The foreign commander was yelling orders excitedly at his men. Barrak saw the one standing back move up and put the muzzle of his weapon close to Jasper's head. A sickening quiver passed through Barrak's gut as he realised why they had Striker and his men kneeling along the edge of the ditch: they were going to execute them, and him too.

Barrak looked at Striker with panic in his eyes. Simultaneously, a strangely calm part of his mind was crunching numbers. *Where were the rest of the men who'd been in the truck? He'd seen one man trapped under the truck, probably dead. But weren't there others? Where was Darko?*

Striker's eyes widened into a stern, cautioning look, almost as if he knew what Barrak was thinking. Barrak mouthed Darko's name at him anyway and Striker's eyes grew even more intense and one eyebrow twitched slightly before something that almost resembled Striker's paradoxical battle smile passed ever so briefly across his grim face.

The commander was yelling again and Barrak couldn't tell if he was issuing murderous orders to his men or demanding something of Barrak. He pointed his weapon at Striker and then at Barrak as if he couldn't decide whom to shoot first. Abruptly he seemed to decide and issued one last firm order to his men and took a couple of steps towards Striker, levelling the weapon at his head. The soldier tying the captives' hands hadn't even finished the job, but he stood up and stepped back and trained his weapon on them too.

Orlan's mercy, this was it!

In an instant, Barrak knew what he had to do. There really was nothing to lose – they were all going to die. He gathered his strength into his thighs and braced himself to push off the embankment and lunge at the commander, focusing all his attention on his outstretched hand, holding the vicious grey weapon at Striker's head. As his muscles tensed to launch himself, another desperate, disconsolate shriek of protest from Jasmyn served to validate his plan and spur him into action.

But then something changed.

It was as if a sudden gust of wind had snatched away the commander's combat helmet. One side of his face seemed to grimace and flatten itself, as if recoiling from an intolerably loud noise. But the only immediate sound was like the slicing of a butcher's cleaver or the rupturing of cartilage on the sporting arena. By the time the deep resounding crack of the shot reached them, the commander's opposite temple had already ballooned out in an aerosol of blood and brain, which seemed to hang in the hot afternoon air, even as the insidious captain crumpled and slid into the ditch, dead at Barrak's feet.

There was a moment of perfect indecision as the two remaining soldiers looked in horror at their fallen leader and then wheeled around with their weapons, searching for the source of the threat, out in the long grass of the open field.

They both flinched and ducked their heads involuntarily as the next chapter in their undoing erupted before their eyes. A cracking blast assailed the ears of captives and captors alike as a bright yellow fireball billowed up into the sky where the enemy's grounded flying machine had been. The sound of the blast gave way to the screeching of metal and a whooshing noise as the giant metal ring that normally crowned the flying thing spun and skidded like an errant child's toy, across the paddock and slammed into a nearby stand of tea-tree.

Before they realised the error of their distraction, another shot rang out and one of the two remaining soldiers was on his knees, both hands clutching hopelessly at his throat as an unstoppable torrent of blood flooded down his forearms, draining the life from him in just a few moments. Striker had taken the other one's feet from under him and wrestled him into the ditch where Hugo, with his hands still bound, was strangling him with his legs while Striker and the others tried to restrain his flailing limbs.

Jasper Flint found a knife in the soldier's belt and finished the job by slipping the blade with surgical precision between the soldier's ribs and leaning on it until the tip found his heart and stopped the struggle.

Barrak found himself standing up in the ditch, his mouth agape, surveying the carnage that was suddenly all around him. Striker, down in the mud, was hefting the third dead soldier off him while Jasper used his blade to cut the bonds restraining Hugo and the other two.

Striker looked up at him with fierce eyes and a stern set to his mouth, but then his trademark bastard grin flickered across his otherwise dour visage. 'Darko,' he said simply, with more than a hint of deep satisfaction and pride.

Yes, thought Barrak, it was Darko. Then he came to his senses. 'Gods! Jasmyn!'

He threw himself at the opposite embankment and scrambled up it, scanning the field beyond for Jasmyn and her captors.

There she was. She was on her knees, just short of the burning aircraft, the two soldiers standing either side of her looking around in bewilderment and shock. Tongues of flame licked from the blown-out apertures of the ruined thing's cabin and thick black smoke billowed up into the still blue sky. Even as he watched, another explosion wracked the blazing hulk and a vivid orange bubble of flame pushed up into the bourgeoning pall of smoke. All three figures flinched and Jasmyn took it as her cue to run, taking off from her crouched position like a sprinter. Maybe she'd seen Barrak. Maybe it was just opportunistic instinct. But she didn't get far before the nearest of her tormentors tackled her to the ground. She let out a mighty shriek as the soldier picked her up and flung her back at the feet of his companion.

Barrak bellowed her name as he scrambled up the embankment. He heard Striker shout, 'Wait!' but ignored him.

Then he saw Darko.

Even as he started his run to Jasmyn, he saw Darko running towards him. He had his combat helmet on and his face was blackened with dirt or blood. He seemed to be weighed down by the heavy sniper rifle, or the heavy going through the mud and long grass, or maybe both. He raised an arm at Barrak as he ran, waving him back.

485

'No! Barrak, get back!'

Barrak paused. He didn't understand. *They had Jasmyn.* He raised his arm and pointed at Jasmyn and shouted her name at the running Darko. Barrak started running again, but he hadn't yet noticed something that Darko may have already seen.

There was a second flying machine.

Perhaps it had come to rescue the occupants of the damaged bird. Probably they had issued a distress call before Darko had worked his destructive magic on the grounded aircraft.

Barrak only caught sight of it as the thing wheeled around, a mile behind Darko, maybe only a hundred feet off the ground. It straightened up and its nose dipped with hostile intent.

Barrak stopped dead. Darko was charging headlong towards him. 'Get back!'

The raucous chattering of the aircraft's wing beats all but drowned out Darko's words. Barrak saw telltale flashes of flame erupting from the front of the lethal bird and small plumes of dirt and grass erupted from the field behind Darko, as if a malicious and relentless entity was chasing him towards Barrak. The repetitive report of the craft's guns added to the raucous din of the thing's whirling blades. Barrak was rooted to the spot in fear and shock as Darko rushed towards him.

Darko was nearly upon him when the line of destruction caught up with him and he flung his arms wide, his rifle spearing past Barrak into the long grass. Barrak instinctively reached out to catch him and braced himself for the impact as Darko shuddered and jerked. His knees seemed to give way and Barrak sank down slightly and caught him under the arms as Darko slammed into him. They sprawled onto the mud and grass and rolled for a moment like boisterous lovers in a meadow.

The sound of the jabbering rotors changed key as the deadly bird flashed past overhead and Barrak laid Darko's head gently on a mound of soft grass.

Darko coughed bright red blood.

He looked up at Barrak with clear, urgent eyes and reached up and grasped a handful of Barrak's jacket. He tried to speak, but the words caught in his throat and brought on another spasm of coughing and more blood. Barrak cupped a hand behind his head and lifted him to ease his breathing, but he could see there was nothing he could do. Ragged exit wounds had torn open his chest and abdomen and he was soaked through with blood and reeking mangled guts. Further down, an ivory shard of bone protruded from a ghastly wound in his thigh. Darko's grip tightened on Barrak's jacket and he groaned. His eyes grew wider, more intent.

Suddenly Striker was there. His hands were all over Darko, pressing into his wounds trying to stem the flow. 'Jesus, Darko.' Striker glanced up at Barrak. He was already slicked with blood like a slaughterman, panic and desperation in his eyes. 'Help me, Barrak.'

Barrak didn't know what to say. He felt the world had slowed down as he watched Darko and Striker, bathed in the brave fighter's blood. It was as if he were viewing the dreadful scene from a distance and it seemed like they were slipping away from him.

'Christ,' Striker cried, 'hold on Darko,' he pleaded. He twisted his head around toward the men back at the truck and shouted. 'Get me a medipack!'

Barrak got to his knees and then slowly to his feet. His limbs felt sluggish. He was terribly tired but there was something he had to do. *Jasmyn. Jasmyn still needed him.*

He heard Striker pleading with Darko. 'No, no, Darko, not like this. Jesus. Hold on.'

'Medipack!'

He saw her there, across the field, flanked by two men. They were moving towards the second aircraft. It had landed in the field, not far from the one that was still burning. Their heads were bowed. Jasmyn looked around once at Barrak and he thought he heard her voice, but he didn't catch any words. He heard Striker cursing and sobbing and slapping the ground and he knew that Darko had died. He wanted to run to Jasmyn but his legs felt like jelly.

Then he saw Striker looking at him with a strange expression on his face and mouthing words at him. Barrak didn't really understand but he

487

followed Striker's gaze down to his own abdomen and saw he too was covered in blood. It might have been Darko's blood but it wasn't, he could see it welling from a hole in his side.

Then he was back on his knees again and some of the other men were around him, attending to him. He laid his head on the grass and it felt soft like a pillow. Across the way he saw Jasmyn climbing into the strange contraption. He couldn't remember what was happening. *Where was she going? Was it a holiday?*

Someone rolled him onto his back and he smiled up at the sky. It was the bluest sky he thought he'd ever seen. There was a loud mechanical noise far away and voices all around him, but they seemed to belong in another place too. A dark shape wheeled across the blue expanse above him, and its spinning blades clattered across his fading mind and told him that Jasmyn was leaving in her miraculous flying conveyance. He tried to raise a hand to wave her off but he was just too tired. A small frown crossed his brow before a sudden, powerful urge to sleep swept him away.